ISBN: 9781468198058

The right of Fusty Luggs to be identified as the author of this work has been asserted in accordance with the Designs and Patents and Patents Act 1988

Copyright © 2013 Fusty Luggs

All rights reserved.

The Blanket Hornpipe Reviews

'A Masterpiece of Theatre and Sex' MK ALEXANDER

'A fun romp through Edwardian Portsmouth' THE STRAND

'Thoroughly enjoyable' CORNHILL MAGAZINE

'Dolly and Joseph, I shall miss their com'pany' BLACKWOOD'S EDINBURGH MAGAZINE

'Well researched, the first of a trilogy, I look forward to reading the next two' THE ART JOURNAL

'Shades of Grey meets the Carry On Team. Upstairs Downstairs, Downtown Abbey, with Fanny Hill. What more could one want...' THE GRAPHIC

'I tittered ... thank goodness it's in a plain cover!' THE ARGOSY

'My only criticism, it's too short' WESTMINSTER REVIEW

'Portsea, Devil's Acre, a slum area of Landport. Hope Street, Chance Street, Squeeze Gut Alley, Charlotte Street. These existed ... I hope the people did.' LONDON SOCIETY

The Blanket Hornpipe

By Fusty Luggs

Chapter 1

She was just a Dockyard daughter,
Living there by the Dockyard gate.
For her father was a docker,
And this song's about her fate.

He hoped she wouldn't cry. He could cope with her anger, not her tears. He gave her ten shillings. -*Bloody hell, nearly a week's wage.* They'd go hungry this week, and may be the next.

***

"You've got a job. You'll start this Monday."

May looked at him open-mouthed, "Stay overnight?"

"Yes, and every other ruddy night."

May knew she was to get work, the summer days were busy though; running errands, helping with the wash, she liked being the woman of the house. Although she knew it had to change, she hadn't expected to go away, leave home. She'd imagined work in the Dockyard, the stay factory or a shop-girl, may be even, if she was lucky, work as a florist. Local though. "What sort of job?"

"You're to go and work for my old boss. He asked for you, special too. He needs some domestic help; you know, cleaning, washing, whatever he asks. And mind, you were lucky to get this job; it's all found plus six bob a week. That's bloody good."

"Where, dad?"

"Just up over the Hill; a tram ride away. You'll do as you're told. I don't want to hear any bad reports. So keep your nose clean and it'll be a good position. Now here," and he reached into his trouser pocket and laid a brown drawstring bag on the table. "Open it." Four big silver coins. May tipped them into her hand. They filled her palm. "Well?" He said.

"I ... thank you."

"Right now, that's half crowns, that is. What do they come to?"

"Ten-bob."

"That ten-bob is for you to kit yourself out; new dress, socks, and you know, your undergarments. Mind, the dress has to be dark, no pattern. Mr Spritely reckons he'll have a couple of aprons for yer; so no need buy those." With the speech over, he stood up rubbed some breadcrumbs from his beard, stretched, grabbed his cap, and was at the door…"And don't forget Glad and Lil; no hanging about. Once you're outfitted, get yourself back here. Right that's it, I'm off to work." The door slammed shut behind him.

May held the coins in her hand; the Queen in profile. She placed each coin carefully back in the pouch, drew the string, dumped it in her bag and walked to Charlotte Street.

"Give us a kiss." May ignored Walter and walked on. "May be she will and may be she won't …" Wally blew a long slow whistle.

***

A detached house, painted white with a short gravel drive led to the porch with a dark-blue door… May pulled the bell.

"Oh, my goodness! Side door, don't you know? Never the front." Mrs Proudley was rubbing her hands in a towel as she spoke; she pulled the door shut behind her. "Come on follow me…"

May followed the large figure as she turned a corner and was in time to see her vanish into what May must use as her official entrance.

"This is it. Come on, come on in. I'm Dolly, follow me, and you are?"

"I …"

"May is it, May Miller?" May nodded. Dolly put a cup before her on the wooden kitchen table. "There, sit." Dolly fetched over another cup. "You just make yourself comfortable and I'll get us a cup of tea." And she stooped over the range for the steaming kettle.

A jug and a teapot joined May's cup, followed by two plates and a larger plate that held slices of cake. Dolly lowered her broad hips into the chair.

"So you've come to join us have you?" May started to answer and Dolly said. "Well we're not a big household, so I'll dare say you'll cope. Not very big though, are you?" May's mouth moved but then Dolly asked, "How old are you?" May, now used to questions that needed no answer, stared into her cup reading the tea leaves trying to interpret their meaning.

"How old are you?"

May aroused from her foretelling said, "I'm ..."

"Well never mind I expect you're a bit shy... Ever been away from home before?"

"No ..."

A jingling bell on the wall interrupted. "That bell is the drawing room. See you can tell that by the writing over ... You can read can't you...?" Without waiting a reply, she left the room.

May looked around her; the kitchen was huge with a large range and a big kettle, refilled and coming to the boil it started to sing. Opposite was a vast ceramic sink with wooden drainers set under a small paned window. It was warm and clean; and smelt of recently baked bread.

"That was Mr Spritely. He wants to see you in half an hour," she said, then gulped down the last of her tea. "I'll show you where your room is, I'll dare say you'll want to freshen up." And with that, she was through another door and returned with a large pitcher she filled from the boiling kettle. "C'mon girl, follow me." May pushed her chair back, grabbed her bundle, and followed Dolly as they climbed two sets of stairs to the top of the house.

Two doors faced each other, Dolly said, "This one, get the door will you! Nowhere to put this down and we don't want to drop it do we?" Dolly placed the jug on the marble top washstand, took a step back conducted a spot inspection and content with what she saw said, "Right now, freshen up, then come back to the kitchen, and we'll go through to meet Mr Spritely. Might be a good idea to change your dress, you brought a dark dress did you?" And… she turned; her hips just clearing the door frame, and was gone.

May placed her bundle on the bed. She pulled out her 'new' cotton dress, navy-blue, a suitable colour. She folded her linen into separate piles and stowed the items away in a drawer under the wardrobe's mirror. She hung her coat and hat from a hook on the back of the door.

The items that remained to find their place were one brush, a comb, a toothbrush, and a Bible. The Bible she put in the drawer. The brushes and comb she placed on the washstand. Then she moved them and rearranged them into a fan shape.

May stared in stunned silence, a room, all to myself …

***

Mr Spritely stood with his backside to the fireplace, more out of habit than need because no fire was burning on this warm June evening. "May, May Miller," he said, as he pointed to a leather armchair. "Please be seated." "That's all, thank you Mrs Proudley." Mrs Proudley nodded and left the drawing room.

"So you're Ernest Miller's little girl?"

"Yes Sir."

"Good man, your father; good man."

"Yes Sir."

"Well you'll want to know about your duties. What's expected of you, and all that!" He picked up a piece of notepaper and perched himself on the arm of an opposing armchair. "This is a list my wife left, but she's away. Her job to hire the staff … needs must though. Eh?"

He placed a pair of glasses on his nose and began to recite the list of terms and details of conditions ...

"Six shillings per week, that's not bad is it?" he said, as if he couldn't believe the remuneration, just for a bit of a girl, to do some cleaning here and there.

"To live in, seen your room? Not bad is it?"

"Very nice, Sir."

"All food found. Mrs. Proudly, she'll show what's what in the kitchen, never go in there me self, without her say-so.

One whole Sunday off, every fourth week.

One-half Sunday every fourth week, fortnightly intervals.

Duties to include:

Cleaning.

Lighting fires, when asked.

Setting the range, at Mrs Proudley's direction.

Laundry.

Sewing.

Helping with all general household tasks, and answerable to Mrs Proudley and family members. How's that sound, not bad, not too bad at all, eh?"

"No Sir, I mean yes Sir."

"Mrs Proudley has some aprons for you, says here, also three caps." List read, he handed it to May who had to rise a little to grasp it. "You hang on to that, so we know what we're doing. Think that's all, anything else just ask Mrs Proudley." May nodded and rose from her chair, gave a little nod and closed the door behind her. In the hall May let out a huge sigh.

***

"There you are. Not so bad is he? Put a smile on your face anyway. Here are your aprons, arms out," she said, as she piled them onto May's outstretched arms. "And some caps, all freshly laundered; towels, soap, flannel ... "That your duties list from Mr Spritely?" she said, snatching it from May's hand.

"May, there's a cup of tea, just brewed, and a slice of Dundee cake," she said, as she set out the cups and plates on the kitchen table. The kitchen door banged open... "Boots!" yelled Mrs Proudley. "How many times do I have to tell you?" An elderly bearded man was hopping about on one leg at the kitchen door. "Not over that threshold Joseph! If I've told you once, I've told you a thousand times. May, take that stool over to him before he does himself a mischief."

May smiled at the old man as she placed the stool ... "Outside May, outside; outside the kitchen door. Mud, he trails mud! Tea is it Joe? I swear he smells it all the way from the shed. A piece of cake wouldn't go amiss either would it?"

"Ooh, that'd be nice. Now you're askin'." Joe came in, in his socked feet and sat himself down on the chair nearest the range. "Ooh that's better. Weight off me feet." Joe slurped his tea and bit into the Dundee slice. Then said, as the crumbs sprayed from his lips, "Going to introduce me then?"

"Joe, or Joseph, depending what particularly mood he's in, this is May. May, this is Joseph."

Joe smiled... His blue eyes twinkled and May realised he wasn't an old man at all ... A bit wrinkled, a little dishevelled. But not old, maybe the same age as her father.

"Nice to make your acquaintance May."

"Like wise, I'm sure," said May.

Joe smiled at Dolly and winked at May... "Reckon you're going to like it here then?"

"She's not here to like it, she's here to work," answered Mrs Proudley. Joseph pulled a, 'that's told us' face.

"I saw that Joe ..." Joe's face leapt into a surprised expression, this time unfeigned.

"Got eyes in the back of your head?"

"No! Joseph Bridger. But I now you and that face of yours..."

"Met everyone yet? That all right to ask is it Mrs Proudley? Only I don't want to go against the rules of don'ts and do's ... Number one being remove boots. Number two—"

"Don't slurp!" interjected Mrs Proudley...

"Well, I wasn't going to say that. It's an ever growing list, that's for sure."

"Quite!"

"Well, don't add anything else then..." as he took another bite, and the crumbs sprayed.

"Number three: eating with mouth full. Don't," said Dolly.

May smiled. And now they'd finished their conversation, she answered Joseph's question, "I've Met Mr Spritely and Mrs Proudley of course, and now you Joseph."

"A few introductions to be made still ... Mrs Spritely, I understand is coming home this Sunday."

"She is Joe. So I'd like some flowers for her room and some to set the dining table. And fresh fruit would be lovely."

"Righto! Can I finish me tea first? Got some lovely roses out; not in full bloom but by the weekend they'll be as fragrant as a young—"

"Joe!" snapped Mrs Proudley. Joe muttered into his tea. Pushed the plate away from him and placed his hands in the small of his back, and stretched. "Ooh, that's better." Stood up and rubbed his arse in front of the fire. "Gets in the bones see."

"It's June! When are you out in all weathers? You spend all day puffing on your pipe in the potting shed."

Joe strode to the door mumbling under his breath. Plonked himself down on the stool and tugged on his boots. He returned the stool to the fireside, a trail of dried mud ricocheted from his boots.

"JOE! Joe for goodness sake…I'm sure he does it deliberately…"

"I was just trying to help—"

"May could have done that…"

"Slave-driver you are… Slave-driver." And he went back to his shed and the comfort of his musty smelling, old and overstuffed armchair… He tapped out his pipe, refilled it with his favourite tobacco. "Bliss," he said, "bliss is knowing when life is good."

***

Henry had an idea, he had the best excuse to be outside May's door, for he kept his telescope at the top of the house their doors faced each other. He looked through the keyhole. She wasn't there of course; she was in the kitchen doing some women's work, cleaning, cooking, or washing.

He didn't expect to see her, but he saw nothing! Nothing at all, blank, black and blind. Henry tapped on the door, *-just to make sure!* After a moment's pause, he opened her door and entered. Her room faced north, a small window set into the eaves overlooked the garden; the room smelt of lavender. This side of the door, and there it was, the offending, escutcheon. *-Soon remedied!* Just have to undo that screw. He left her room and back to the Crow's-Nest, the room which housed his telescope. Dark clouds rolled in from the sea. Portsmouth sometimes hidden by rain, he was above, in the light, peering down on the gloom. But mostly he'd be the one shrouded in a blanket of rain, and sometimes through the breaks in the cloud he could see sunlight bathing Portsea Island.

In his desk, he knew he had a penknife. *-That'll sort it.* And there it was, and he did. May who didn't have a key to the lock on her door, now didn't have a cover for the keyhole. Henry content with his efforts, dosed off in his armchair with his telescope between his legs, he was awoken by her footfall in the hallway. He'd give her a minute then check his handiwork.

***

"So if you'd just run the bath for me…"

"I…"

"What's that?"

"Sir, I don't know how to; Mrs Proudley was going to…but..."

"Well come along and I'll show you." May gasped. She'd never seen anything…

"It's wonderful," she whispered. A big enamel tub with lion's paws stood beneath a huge copper.

"This is the boiler it heats the water, piping hot, too hot. So this tap here, is the cold. Now before we run the hot we put a couple of inches of cold in the bath. So no one ever gets scolded, again…"

May was not paying much attention to Mr Spritely, what was occupying her mind were her surroundings. So clean, the smell was fresh, nothing at all like the privy in Chandler Street, shared by all the neighbours and a public toilet especially on market days.

Mr Spritely noticed her distraction. "Like it do you?"

"I've never…seen anything ... so lovely. It smells of lavender and no stink at all even though your privy is here." -*Upstairs, blimey.*"

"Would you like ago on that privy?"

"Er, no Sir ... thank you Sir."

"Go on just a little flush, pull that handle there."

May obeyed her instruction; the handle releasing water which whooshed around the pan. Then the tinkling sound as the cistern refilled. "We're going to have to wait a few minutes for that to fill back up before we can start to run the bath," Mr Spritely said.

May went to the sink her hand lightly touching the moulded fragrant soap. She caught a glimpse of her reflection in the mirror and blushed, aware that Mr Spritely was watching her. May drew her hand away from the bar and looked down at her feet feeling a little awkward and self-conscious.

"Ah silence. No more gurgling we can now run the bath. Come here, and I'll show you what's what. Now you just stand there in front of me. Run the cold first, a couple of inches is sufficient. Now look in that little window, that is where we'll apply the match. Matches we keep here, on top of the geezer. Mm, you're a little too small, go and fetch that chair and you can stand on that."

May placed the chair in front of the boiler and lifted her skirt so as not to trip.

"Good," said Mr Spritely." -*Good indeed.* "Here, I'll help you down." And he twisted May to face him and with both arms, pulled her to him and slid her slowly down his body till her tiptoes touched the floor tiles.

"I'm down now Sir," she said. But he mustn't have heard her, because he was still holding her securely to his body.

"Sir!"

And at last, he released her. "Thank you sir." May was a little breathless, he'd squeezed her so tightly and her cheeks flushed hot. "Shall I put the chair back to where it was?"

"No don't think so, it'll be useful just there. Right you have the matches; now we have to concentrate. Don't want everything going off with a bang. See that little lever, push it up, and gently. Then strike your match and place the flame against that little nipple, there. Right, now look in the window see the little blue light you've just lit, and now we just turn this tap clockwise; releases the water, then you push this big lever here…"

There was an enormous boom, which set May jumping backwards, -*right sharpish* and bashing into Mr Spritely. He, gent that he was, grabbed her before she could topple over.

"Right that's that done then."

May straightened her cap and tucked up the escaped tendrils.

"Just have to wait now for the tub to fill, won't take long," he said. Mr Spritely sat on the chair and raised his foot. "Here, help me get out of these, they could do with a polish, you can do them after…."

Chapter 2

George Spritely walked along the hill from The George Inn. He was returning home from school, he was looking forward to a break from his studies. But then, after a week it became so ... boring. Fairview was away from town, the nearest village a mile distant. He'd like, just once, to stay with one of his friends, but then his mother insisted he came home, every term. But next year would be different, he mused.

The house was in front of him, he'd arrived. His feet crunched on the gravel drive. No one here to greet him, he heard his father's voice some way off. He went upstairs to stow the bag he'd carried with him; his trunk and cases would arrive later. He splashed water on his face, from the freshly filled basin. -*Someone's remembered I'm home today!* Mrs Proudley will have baked in his honour a Dundee fruitcake; something special for his return. Just as he got to the bend in the stairs he heard his father's door open, and looking over the banister rail he saw something that was to improve his summer holiday no end.

In the hall May let out a huge sigh.

"Tired already?" May turned on her heel trying to find the owner of the voice. "Here, up here.' Peering over the banister rail was a young man. He stood with a jacket slung casually over his shoulder.

"Hello," he said. The girl looked up and smiled.

"And who are you?"

"I'm the new girl."

He smiled as he said, "So you're our new maid?"

"Yes Sir."

"What do we call you?"

"May Sir, May Miller."

"May Miller! and may I say how very pretty you are."

"You may Sir."

And he laughed.

***

She fell for him the moment she saw him. Love at first sight? Possibly. But her heart did flutter when she saw him; that blond mop of unruly hair, that silly grin with the funny crooked eye tooth.

He's funny, warm, and kind. "Everyone loves him," Dolly said.

His mother insisted he came home; she could at least be bothered to show herself. George walked into the library.

"George!" said Henry, as he jumped up. Tossing the paper, he'd been trying to solve the crossword of, onto the table by his armchair. "How the devil are you? You're early; we weren't expecting you for another hour or so."

"Fine Pa, fine. A train arrived I got on it. Ma not here?"

"No she's gone off to see her sister; bit unwell, best not to enquire, we don't want all the details … Women's troubles probably! She's bred too much. That'll be the problem, hope she's not, well … expectant again. She'll be back later this afternoon."

"Well let's hope she quickly recovers," said George. *-Aunt Francis, always Aunt Francis.*

"I'll drink to that." And he pulled the bell by the fireside. "Walk from The George, did you? Nice day for it though, still …"

Several moments later Mrs Proudley appeared in the doorway. "Master Spritely! George. May said you were home. Well really, she just told me a young man had arrived I knew it had to be you. I've made a fruitcake, your favourite—"

"Dolly," interrupted Mr Spritely.

"Yes, Mr Spritely?" she said, her gaze remaining on George, a big smile on her large face. Her normally rosy cheeks flushed a bright red.

"I was thinking, George and I, we could do with a little snifter, by way of celebrating his return. Rum, George, or brandy?"

"Actually, I'd rather have a port, got quite used to it."

"That'll be a port and a rum then, Dolly."

Dolly turned to go, and with one hand about to turn the handle.

"Have a sweet sherry for yourself. Oh, and tell Joseph, George's home, no need to fetch out the cart."

"Thank you, thank you very much Sir," she said beaming.

***

George came into the kitchen; May sat at the table shelling peas. "I wondered if I could have a pot of tea."

"Mr Spritely! You should have rung."

"No … I wanted … Everyone's out."

"Kettle's on, it's always on the boil. I'll make a fresh brew."

"Would you mind if I sat … Took it here…"

"No, if that's what you'd prefer …" May said, as she warmed the pot.

George picked up the pods sitting on the table; he shelled a couple into the colander.

"Mr Spritely, you shouldn't be doing that."

George popped the peas into his mouth. "Isn't there enough?"

"No I meant … I thought you were going to shell them as a job."

"I am. You make the tea; I'll shuck some pods, fair exchange and all that."

May smiled. "Just while I'm doing this, then."

"Bring a cup for yourself too."

-Blimey.

May joined him at the table, and pulled the peas towards her. "Don't be greedy May! Leave some for me." They sat shelling peas and sipping tea in companionable silence. "Are you happy here May?"

"Oh yes, I like it here very much."

"I like coming home, but then, when I'm here ... I want to be away again. Too many ghosts I suppose."

"Ghosts?" May said.

"Oh, not real ghosts, if that's not an oxymoron! But memories ... Just a figure of speech..."

"Bad memories?"

"Just sad memories," he said, and he sipped his tea. "My mother had ... I had a brother and sister. Both dead ... They died when they were both young."

"I'm sorry."

"Nothing for you to be sorry about, it all happened many years ago."

"But still ... My mother lost two of her children ... My—"

"Silly isn't it the way we say lost, as if somehow they wandered off."

"I suppose." May finished her tea and concentrated on shelling peas.

"They were both younger than me. So I've been, I suppose, some would call it spoilt. Though sometimes I'd called it suffocated."

"Your Mother must have worried for you. Worried she'd lose you too."

"I expect so. I'd like not to bear the responsibility of her fears though..."

May felt sympathy for him but didn't know what to say; she began to clear the cups and saucers.

George said, "I'd better go," and as he got to the door he said, "Thank you for the tea and the pea shucking. I wondered if you'd come with me later, just for a walk? I could do with the company to be honest."

"Mr Spritely I'd like to go with you, but ... I have too much to do, but thank you, thank you for asking me."

George returned from his stroll, he'd needed a walk, take some air, stretch his legs. He presented May with a bunch of daisies he'd picked up from the graveyard, they were there and he was there, and he thought, May would like them.

He was on his own but his parents were due back, dinner was prepared.

"Your port, Mr Spritely."

"Why I come home? They're never here…"

***

May was going home tomorrow it was her day off. She was to give her father five shillings of her six-shilling weekly wage. She had amassed therefore; one sovereign and four bob. In the far corner, at the front of her wardrobe she stowed her little leather drawstring bag. Tomorrow morning she would remove one pound in shillings, wrap it in her hanky so it'd be safe before she handed it to her dad.

Mrs Proudley gave May her instructions on how to start the dinner preparations. "Most of the work's done, so you've just got to heat it … Oh yes custard, he'll want custard! Apple Charlotte this evening… Can you make custard? And don't forget they eat at seven, most evenings. Well he's on his own this evening so it'll be up to him, but aim for that time…" I think that's all. You'll be OK won't you?"

"I—"

"Good, good…" And with that, Mrs Proudley turned on her heel and was out the door. It was 3 'o'clock and Mrs Proudley's half day off.

***

From his bedroom window, George saw Mr Bridger and his son crossing the lawn, pushing a wheelbarrow towards the potting shed. May, had picked a bunch of pale yellow roses and was heading towards the side door. George watched her, black hair escaping in loose tendrils from under her cap.

He felt a stirring in his underpants. He lay on his bed and unbuttoned his fly and his hand pushed through his pant's slit; he held himself. He stood hard and firm. He rubbed himself slowly. He thought of May. May with yellow flowers, and he pinched himself. May undressed, and his fingers clenched. May in a transparent negligee, and his hand strummed. May naked, his hand gripped. May wet, fingers pull. May bending over, squeeze. May straddling his face, tug. May with her leg's spread, thrust. He couldn't help himself because he had to … he had to … have her. She was going to be his. Yes! George burst, erupting over his hand and into his pants. He lay there on his bed holding his sticky manhood and he smiled. There was nothing quite like coming to a decision!

***

Commercial Road, unusually quiet, the tobacconist was open. She'd have liked to have been here on a weekday, would've have liked to spend money in Charlotte Street market. Some ribbons for Lil, some pencils for Glad, and a ball for Freddie.

The tram halted. And there they were. Three little expectant faces looking up to her. May waved … "Those toffee creams look good enough to eat …"

"Oh, yes please," said Gladys.

"And Master Miller, liquorice or a sherbet dab?"

"Dab, dab, d-a-b." And he played with the sound as if he were sucking the letters to anticipate the taste of this special treat.

"Lillian, what would you like?" Lil stared at all the jars arrayed in the window. There was this yellow thing, some boiled wotsits. Goodness knows what all these sweetmeats were! But then she knew; she'd heard her choice spoken; they were lady-like confection.

"Parma violets"

"Ooh, 'ark at you, Parma violets, eh? Follow me your ladyship, while I enquire as to the availability of said violets of Parma." And she held out her arm to Lil who in turn grabbed Glad who was holding Fred to her hip. And in they went to explore the exotic inside of the tobacconists…

"And ten Senior Service please."

***

At home in Hope Street, with her family sitting around the table, May watched as Gert stirred the soup.

Her father said, "That smells good."

Chunks of cut bread sat on a board at the table's centre. Glad looked up and smiled at Gertie as she ladled the soup into her bowl. Glad leaned forward and sniffed, "Ooh lovely."

And just as she was going to plunge her spoon into the liquid, May said, "Wait." Everyone turned to her.

And her father frowned. "Wait until everyone is served. Wait until it's cold?" her father asked.

"Father should have been served first."

"Glad was nearest," Gert said helpfully. "As it comes, first served."

May thought, *-What the hell has it got to do with you?* When all were eating and slurping, May asked for the salt.

"She'll be wanting a serviette next," her father said.

"Napkin."

Her father banged his spoon onto the table. "Napkin? We don't have them either. You becoming a snob, May? Too good for us, are you?"

"I just wanted the salt."

"Here you are May." Gert placed the jar in front of May. "You tasted it first, that's good manners isn't it?"

"Yes," agreed May. *-As if you'd know.*

May pushed a severed carrot round the cream coloured slop. So looking forward to coming home, and she scowled as the carrot refused to enter the spoon's rim. Lil rose to clear the bowls. And asked Gert, Whether she should warm the milk for the custard!

***

George asked Mrs Proudley for a picnic basket, "Not much in it, just a few sandwiches." -*First part of plan: remove John the lad, get him out of the way, run an errand for me.*

George was waiting at the tram stop, and held out his arm for May to take as she stepped down from the tram. "Let me take those," and he took the bundle that contained her clothes and with her arm through his, they walked together, on this fine day, towards Fairview House.

"John couldn't make it." George said, as they walked. "So I volunteered." And he grinned, showing his crooked eye-tooth. May smiled, she pretended that she was walking out with her young man, she was a lady, and this gentleman by her side, her fiancé.

"That's very kind of you, but I could have managed."

"I don't think my father would appreciate you walking these lanes … unaccompanied. Besides, I was going out anyway and you're no trouble, are you? I enjoy walking."

At a kissing gate he held out his arm to her again, and dropping over her bundle he lifted May by her waist on to the plank. And over they went, into a flower meadow. "I, think we should have a little refreshment." And sitting down he unfurled a blanket from his bag and spread the tartan wool over the ground. "Here we are."

"I shouldn't … I should be getting back."

"You should? Why, the tram was late, wasn't it?"

"No …"

"It was! I can vouch for that. Stay here May, and enjoy the remainder of the afternoon."

May sat down and watched the swallows' flight.

"They'll be going home soon."

"Home?" and she rested her elbows on her knees.

"Africa."

George handed her a glass, and filled it with cider poured from a stoneware bottle wrapped in straw. Cool. May enjoyed sitting here watching the swallows dart, fattening themselves for the long flight home -*to Africa.*

"Here, some of Mrs P's famous cake."

"Thank you."

George lay back, his arms crossed behind his head, "Just to enjoy this sunshine! Here, lay next to me."

May lay down, she made out a face in a little cloud as it wandered across the sky. There was the sweet scent of honeysuckle on the breeze. May quivered when George accidentally brushed her hand as he shifted his position.

-*Stop being silly!*

But when he took her hand to his lips and kissed her fingers a charge ran through her body, she'd never felt anything like it before.

"Come on May, I'd better take you back, before I lose control of myself. And forget I am gentleman." And there was a mingling of disappointment. For May had felt relaxed for the first time, in the longest time. "Oh you could never not be that, a gentleman." May said, confidently. She collected the glasses and brushed the cake crumbs from her lap. George held his hand to her and pulled her to her feet. He stood looking down on her face, and stayed in that position for some while. And May looked up at him for what seemed an eternity. He lent down to her and kissed her on her cheek.

"Sorry May, I shouldn't have done that."

"It's ok...I..."

George kissed her again this time on her mouth, and tasted the apple on her lips. Her lips met his and she kissed him. And they stood for a while as lovers and anyone passing by would have smiled at this young couple in the field of grass and flowers.

"Come May, let's go back to the house or we'll have some explaining to do."

No words passed between them until they reached Fairview, and he said, "Thank you May, for the loveliest afternoon." And he left her standing at the gate, she watched him as he entered the house through the front door and she made her way to the side entrance.

And she thought, -*He loves me, and I love him.*

George bit into a peach and the juice trickled down his chin. *–Lovely.*

Chapter 3

The next morning George went into Dolly's kitchen and said, "Dolly."

"Yes George, what can I do for you?"

-Not a lot. "I was hoping we had some writing paper, I can't find any."

"There's some in the desk. I'll fetch it for you," she said, as she wiped her hands dry.

"I'm sorry I couldn't see it." *-And you won't either.* He'd take it back to school with him. They walked together to the library to explore the desk.

"And envelopes, thought I'd write to a few chums."

Dolly rummaged, shuffled, and raked, churning over the drawer's contents. "Funny! I could have sworn there was some here. I'll jot it down on my list for things to buy."

"I was hoping to write this afternoon. Don't suppose someone would go on the errand? May perhaps?"

"I'll tell her, she'll enjoy the walk anyway."

And with that, he left Dolly's company, and went through to the drawing room. From this vantage point, he would see when May left; *-and there she goes.* It'll take her half an hour at best. He started to finish Henry's crossword. After twenty minutes, George left the house en route to the Post office. He stopped; peering down the road, he saw her hat bobbing up and down like a bird hopping on top of the hedgerow; a funny, brown felt, monstrosity with some unknown specimen of wilted fabric flower stuck to its brim. It was now George untied his shoelace. May arrived, just as he started banging it against the fence.

"May!" he said, "Just let me get this back on and I'll walk along with you. Got something in my shoe."

"Oh, that's painful. All right now is it?" she asked, as George stamped his foot on the ground, in what he supposed was the correct motion of someone who had just removed a stone from their shoe.

"Here, give me that." And he took the basket from her.

Dolly had sent May off 'while she was about it' to buy other 'bits and bobs' whist she was at the shop. Now George was home 'a few extras wouldn't go amiss'. And so, with a laden basket May walked the mile there, and the mile back to Fairview; with George awaiting her return.

Further along, and nearing a small dip on the road, he paused and said, "Look!" And pointed to the prettiest blue butterfly, "That's an Adonis Blue; wish I had my net."

"Oh that would be a shame, it's so lovely."

"It'll be dead in a few weeks. Its prettiness would be forever, pinned in my collection; all beauty, like life, is transient."

George smiled, and handed her a flower that had been growing in the hedgerow. "For you, here, let me put it on your hat." George asked her about her family, and he said he thought he had some old toys that young Freddie might have. "No use to me any longer."

And May thought he was the most wonderful, and kind, and generous man she had ever known.

***

John and May sat on a bench in the garden. Behind them, the potting shed. Joseph's snores signalled he wasn't too busy to be eavesdropping. John covered May's hand with his, and kissed lightly her on her cheek. John wanted to ask her out wanted to make her his girl he wanted her. His hand brushed her knee. "May I ..." he hesitated.

"I better go, Dolly will be missing me." And she lent down and picked up the washing basket at her feet. John watched her go, watched her till she turned into the kitchen and was gone. He promised himself, -*Next time, next time, I will ask her.*

George watched them from the kitchen window; he'd rung the bell, no answer, he needed a drink. He stood by the sink. And there they were, sitting close, convivial, intimate. He watched as John leaned in close, his hand briefly touching May's knee. George had made his decision and, this John, this gardener, would not interfere with his plans.

***

He wondered whether May would take tea with him, at Jones' tea rooms. He would ask her, Sunday afternoon, after service. May wasn't sure she liked this vicar, or this church, it was all very ...white washed.

John asked what she would like. May looked at the menu. *–Asking not ordering, nice.*

"I know," said John. "What about a cream tea. It's clotted, all the way from Devon. The strawberry jam is made here, and some of those berries are grown by my dad."

May had never had a cream tea. And until he mentioned jam and strawberries thought it'd be a spoonful of cream dolloped into the teacup.

"Of course if you'd rather have something else?"

"No, that sounds lovely."

The waitress arrived, holding a notepad in one hand, a pencil attached by a piece of string to her belt, in the other. "What may I serve you?" she asked, and blushed as she smiled at John.

-She's moonin' at him, bloody baggage. Cheek. May wanted to kick her in the shin, tell her to bugger off. But she was too much of a lady to do such a thing.

"And to drink?"

"May, what'll you have?"

"I'm not sure..." *–Tea or ginger beer? Gran used to make it in a bucket with a root.*

"May?"

"Tea, please."

"One tea, one coffee, please." The waitress returned with four scones, a bowl of stand your spoon up in it cream, and a bowl of red jam.

"Ah, ha, you be a Cornish girl. You put the cream on the scone first." John slurped his coffee, "Sorry."

"Coffee, what's it like?"

"Never had it?" he said, as he handed her his cup. John watched her face, her lips pouting against his cup, the cup he'd drunk from. Lip to lips, and only that cup as go between.

May looked up and frowned, "It smells better than it tastes."

John smiled. She could say anything May, and it would be musical, a delicate chime. The blue of her eyes they changed colour ... Those dimples...

May licked cream from her lips.

-I'd do that. I'd love to do that; kiss those lips, spread cream all over body, lick it from her...

"Everything all right?" asked the waitress.

***

Outside May's door, on the floor, stood a box tied with a red ribbon pulled into a bow. A small box covered in oiled paper. May smiled as she pulled the ribbon's bow and the box opened to reveal, one chocolate. One chocolate decorated with a squiggle of a lighter chocolate. May sat on her bed and held the chocolate to her lips. Her tongue just touching its satin smooth circular shape, she sniffed. The fragrance was so delicious. She held it looking at its brown sensual form, and she held it tight; she'd never in her life before, tasted chocolate. She'd seen it, spied it through shop windows, contained in gorgeous boxes, decorated with ribbons; and the shapes, the square, the round, and the oblong. She held this round morsel for so long it melted onto her hand. She licked her fingers, tasting its smoothness for the first time.

In so short a time she had experienced much, this though, as her Gran would have said, 'was the icing on the cake.' And as she sucked, her mouth burst with the intensity of the flavour. And she bit, her mouth oozed with a cherry liquid, a pale red and pink confection. She wanted it to last, but she couldn't stop the chocolate. It was melting in her mouth...reducing in size...But even when the chocolate had disappeared from her mouth the taste lingered on... She wondered if a memory of a taste could remain.

***

George had tired of courtship. In truth, the inane conversations he'd had with her bored him, if one could called them conversations! He knew about her mother, who'd died recently! Her Gran or 'Nan' who'd passed away. The two siblings, who'd departed this life. Cause... -*Probably bored each other to death.* Then there were her living relatives, her church, and her priest -*Catholic for God's sake!*

It was time to up the stakes. He had enough of this oh, so gentle kissing. Though she was wearisome, she was a good-looking thing. He was certain of her willingness. He was convinced of it. In the library, he discovered her; he'd been touring the house, ascertaining the whereabouts of the residents. May had been dusting books, she was descending a stepladder, a feather duster held aloft. George said, "Hello there. Here, let me help you down."

"Thank you, kind Sir," said May, beautiful maiden and subject of a knight's quest. Although she wouldn't have believed, what his yearning mission was. George held out his hand to her. May made to step from the ladder and he caught her in his arms, holding her close she slipped to the ground, sliding down his body until her toes were on tip. And he kissed her, and she returned the kiss. But this time George held her tightly, taking May's breath away.

"Oh, May, what are you doing to me?"

"George. I ..."

And he held her close and rested his head on her shoulder. "May, you're driving me insane, I wish ... I, I want to marry you."

George stepped back to see the effect this statement had on the young maid's face. She'd flushed and looked down. May knew the truth of this. People said, there's but one thing a young gentleman wants from a maid, and it's not love, nor marriage. May knew that wasn't true, her grandmother disproved it; there was such a thing as love and marriage between the classes.

"Will you say yes, say you'll be mine?"

"George, I."

"Just say yes, please. Everything else can just go hang. I'll sort it, everyone loves me and they'll love you too May. We should be together, that's what I want. Am I what you want?" He stood away from her, watching her as she puzzled over this question, then she raised her eyes from her shoes and she said, "Yes George."

"May! You will?" And she believing she'd consented to her marriage repeated it.

"Yes George, I will."

George went down on one knee and said, "Thank you, thank you for making me the happiest man in all England, in this whole world." And he spun her round, and she was giddy with delight.

She kissed him with a passion and he embraced her, caressing her neck. And when his hand wandered to her breast, she did not push him away; because this is how engaged couples behaved. She saw them on her streets, couples who were to marry up back alleys. He, his hand up her skirt 'copping a feel', she, aching from need; a quick knee-trembler and lust spent.

And he held her close, her head clutched to his chest. And he wondered where and when he should have her. There were certain problems, but he would sort them. By next week, he would know her.

His lips touched hers again before leaving. When he was at the door, he turned and blew her a farewell kiss. May couldn't believe her fortune, how to explain this to her family? They'd share her delight, certainly. A spring wedding, there's so much to organise. Father Dolling, oh, surely she would have her wedding at St Agathas' ...

***

May's mother was well spoken, she read well and often. And with the meagre wage, her husband brought to the house she managed, with good taste and simplicity, to make a silk purse out of a pig's ear. She taught her children to read from the same books she learnt to read. Her mother, or so the story went, got into a 'trouble' with the lad who ran the stables. And so they'd run away together. Her family cut her out of their lives. The Isle of Wight to Portsea, and from one island to another a few miles apart but a thousand miles separate in class. This lady, with her few bits and bobs and books, who sold her jewellery to provide a roof over their heads; gave birth to her only surviving child, her daughter Lavinia, May's mother.

May hadn't spoken about her mother, not to anyone, to her sisters or her father. Hadn't spoken about the day her mother had jumped at the wall, elbows on top so she could see as well as speak to her neighbour. But she'd hit the wall hard and banged her chest. Later that afternoon she'd coughed blood. Her mother asked May to go and fetch brandy from the Eight Bells, but May wouldn't. That place was full of women of little reputation... Father Dolling said, I shouldn't ever go in. "Whores," her dad said.

But that didn't stop him spending part of his wages on those ragged women. She'd seen him with his arm around one, turning into a blind alley. She watched them as they shared a bottle of cheap beer. Taking a swig and passing the bottle over... The woman was still drinking from the bottle when her father lifted her skirt and spread her legs. And she saw how she continued drinking even as his thrusts were pushing harder and harder into her, the beer spilling on to his shoulder and dribbling from her mouth. When he'd finished she handed him back the bottle. He drained the last swig, wiped his mouth with the back of his shirtsleeve, and popped himself back into his trousers. She lowered her skirt, patted it down, and held out her hand…

"A shilling! Is that all?"

"Well it's the quickest earn you'll ever have."

"And who's fault that?" she asked.

"Take it or don't. It's all you're getting." She took the shilling and walked slowly away. Exaggerating the sway of her hips, as if her tatty covered, sagging arse was the most desired rump in Moors Square.

***

By coincidence, they bumped into each other more and more frequently. But when any other person was near, there was a formality. A brief nod, and George would say, "Yes May, if you please May." George was a charming, sensitive, warm man. Alone he could relax in her company, away from, 'it's not form', from the stuffy boundaries of class that engulfed them, she loved him, and she knew he loved her.

Every day for a week another chocolate in a tiny box appeared outside her door, wrapped with a different coloured ribbon. A whole box of chocolates she'd eaten. Her favourite was the caramel cream tied with bow of brown satin ribbon. She would never forget it, ever.

Seven ribbons, all of different colours. Of the red, lilac, brown, gold, lilac and pink her favourite though, was the forget-me-not blue. She tied it round the base of her brown felt hat and for good measure and because it looked so appealing and she had so many, she added a brown satin bow. Two ribbons, one hat! May believed it was the nicest hat any girl could possibly have.

Chapter 4

Dolly and Agnes were on the front garden, waiting for Dan and the donkey cart. Agnes carried a leather suitcase; Agnes was accompanying Dolly so far, until continuing her journey to Cosham and the destination, as always her sister's. The house wasn't empty though; Pa was here, John and old Joseph. George was standing at his bedroom window. He wore his dressing gown an emerald green quilted affair with a gilt G monogram on the breast pocket.

A wooden crate delivered earlier that morning was surrounded. Pa, Joe, and the dimwit son were standing around, and then dimwit strode off and came back with a crowbar.

Father waved up to his son, George threw on a few togs, just for decency's sake and headed out the front door. The object of their attention, a Ransome lawn mower.

"I've got some homework, an essay on Restoration England. Better get down to it at last."

They dragged the mower to the rear lawn. George could keep an eye on it, and them, from the library windows. Pa and Bridger senior, grinning like a garden gnome, gave advice from the sidelines. Bridger junior brandished a spanner. George had written two paragraphs on the warty Cromwell and was reading about Nell. May with oranges sprang into his mind. May with oranges, wearing a transparent silk negligee and stripy knee-length stockings, George rang the bell.

And as if by incantation May appeared, she smiled.

"Yes Sir?"

"Would you fetch some cider, thirsty work this writing."

"Of course, anything else?"

"Two glasses I think. Looks like they'll be busy for a while out there." And he nodded towards the garden. On

May's return he poured the refreshment, "Here May, have this." The afternoon air had grown heavy. "Thought they would've assembled that contraption by now."

"They took a break, retired to the potting shed."

"All three?"

"Yes, who knows what goes on in there?"

George couldn't care less, but thought it a shame he'd missed an opportunity. May went to the window to see what they were doing; they were fitting a chain to the side of the machine. May watched as the chain was off, put back on tightened, advice given, chain on again, spanner wielded and instructions read.

George came and stood behind her, he kissed the nape of her neck, smelling the lavender and musk of her body. "Oh May, what you do to me." And he threw his arms around her, gripping her to his chest. They stood so entwined looking through the window and the garden beyond. George moved his hand to her thighs and inched slowly the material of her skirt upwards.

"George they'll see us!"

And he twirled her around, moved her around and around, in a waltz. Until her legs hit the library table. He kissed her and May tingled at his touch. She kissed him and smiled up at him. So handsome a man. *-I'm so lucky.*

George pushed his weight against her, so May fell back and came to rest sprawled across the library table. His lips pressed on hers. May kissed him but this time with hesitation. His body was weighing her down. This is going too far, and she tried to stand. "Oh May my love, what you do to me no man should endure." And he kissed her again.

May bewitched by her allure returned his kisses. And George pushed his tongue in her mouth.

Oh, she tasted the cider on his lips and felt the crumbs of cake on his tongue. May felt both alarm and excitement, she had caught a good man he was beside himself in love with her. And she tried to raise herself from the table; she'd proved how much she loved him, she'd allowed him to touch her breast.

But George didn't rise, at least not from her body. She felt something hard and urgent knocking against her leg. She tried to speak but he smothered her mouth with his kisses. -*Such passion!* She never knew it could be like this. She was finding it harder to breathe. Her breath was shallow and she gasped for air as George removed his lips from hers. He gasped too, and as she stared into his beautiful brown eyes, framed so prettily with long thick lashes, just a flicker of something! Her senses told her it was a sneer, but as quick as that expression appeared, it vanished. And that lovely crooked smile returned and he buried his head against her neck.

Toying with the buttons, his hand thrust down the front of her blouse and he caressed her small firm breast. Tugging harder on the fabric he lowered his head and his lips touched her pinkness with his lips and he kissed her; long wet kisses.

"George please, I need to ..."

But George pressed his weight on her and after raising her skirt and her petticoats, unbuttoned his fly. May felt the rummaging, and thought, hoped, he would release her.

George took himself in hand, he was hard. Braced, he felt between her crotch less drawers, and placed his finger to her. He felt the little tendrils of curling soft hair.

"George."

He kissed her. He didn't want to hear her; he just wanted to fuck her. "Oh May," he said, as his arse lunged forward, thrusting himself on, and breaking into her. His mouth smothered her cry with a kiss, and his hand squeezed her breast. He was inside her and grinding down on her.

-*Bloody hurts. Stop George, it fucking hurts. You're killing me.* But none of this she could speak; not with his lips clamped onto hers like a limpet on the hull of a ship.

On he thrust, by God, thought George, you've a tight bloody fanny! He couldn't believe how wonderful this was. He'd had a few whores, could hardly feel a bloody thing, but this! His skin pushed so far back it was almost agony. He was being skinned. Of course, there was Sebastian, but that was different, different.

Another thrust, deeper, George finally pushed his way, all the way in, and another thrust and yes, so deep. He heard May moan from under him. He thrust now, harder, deeper, quicker. And then, then he burst, and he groaned. Dribble fell from his mouth onto her lips.

He stayed on her, but lay still, all lust spent. After:
-Bloody hours!
-A minute or two!

He looked at May "I love you so much," he said, and kissed her so tenderly. "Oh May. Thank you, my beautiful girl. Say you love me." He kissed her again lightly brushing her mouth with his lips. May looked up at him; she smiled and she kissed him. For this was her man, and this was how men were, and now she was a women, and she'd done what is only to be expected of a woman. And after all, they were to be married ...

***

May slid from the table clutching her skirt and rearranging her blouse. George handed her the now tepid cider, "Let's drink to us." And they chinked glasses, and he put his arm around her and said, "Oh May, what you did to me ... I can't believe what just happened!"

May couldn't believe it either, but knew it had because she hurt like, *-Bloody hell.* And she felt wet and sore and now something was tickling down her leg.

"George ... I."

"Shh, we won't mention it again, or to anyone, this will be our secret. We lost control of ourselves."

May gulped. The contraption constructed, the famous mower was to have its debut. Henry beckoned his son to come out and witness this first mowing. George unlocked the French windows and strolled over the paving towards the three smiling faces staring at this new contraption. May looked at the four happy faces standing around the mower. And George looked back at her and grinned.

***

With his eye to the keyhole, Henry could see May. She was going under the bed for the chamber pot. A piss in the daytime! Why doesn't she use the outside box? Poe's for when you're caught short in the night. But May wasn't taking a piss. No, she was filling the pot with water. -*Damn it.*

May knew what she'd done, what had happened…she didn't remember ever not knowing. Living in a tiny one up one down, well she'd seen her parents doing it from the earliest age… it was a fact of life.

May squatted over the pot, she raised her skirts. She was washing herself. If only she hadn't squatted there, in that corner. Opposite the door where his eye peeped, was a mirror on the wardrobe door. He could have, if it were possible, see himself looking at himself. May now stood; she raised her skirts and removed her drawers. It both excited and disappointed Henry, simultaneously. -*What on earth is she doing?* The drawers in her hand she dropped in the bowl on the washstand. Poured over the water she'd just washed herself in and scrubbed at the knickers. Wrung them out, and with fresh water, rinsed them, and hung them on the window clasp. Bloody funny behaviour! -*Women, strange creatures!* May tied up her hair and set her cap, Henry bolted for his door.

May closed her door and returned downstairs to her kitchen duties. Henry was bemused! But his main interest was. -*She's not put on any drawers! She's wandering the house, bare arsed.*

Henry left the Crow's-Nest and turned the handle to May's room. There were her drawers hanging from the window frame. Henry pulled open the wardrobe drawer; a chemise, horrendous stockings and no drawers. -*She can't have just one pair!* But May didn't just have one pair, she had three; all washed and drying, two on the washing line and this pair, on the window clasp.

***

Henry sat in the drawing room, drinking brandy and smoking his pipe. He'd rung the bell for May. He didn't know what else he wanted; or rather, he did, but didn't know how to ask. He knew she wasn't wearing any drawers; and with her here, in front of him, he couldn't get that idea from his head. "Build a fire May. I fancy a bit, of warmth."

May bent over the grate, and all Henry could see in his Mind's eye was her bare, white, firm, arse. And every time she moved … he felt feverish.

"Are you ok Mr Spritely? Not a chill is it? I could make you a lemon and honey cordial."

"No May, the brandy is enough, I thought a fire would be cheery, a little glow in the hearth."

"Goodnight Mr Spritely."

He took his brandy with him to the Crow's-Nest. - *Watch the boats…*

***

May had believed after the incident in the library he would afford her some respect, they had sealed their love. But now wherever May was, George was sure to turn up. He sniffed her out like a dog following a bitch on heat. But May wasn't in season. And his groping and kissing were relentless and rather than increasing May's love for him, every pass, touch, and grope she liked him less. His hand up her dress at the dining room table. -*No one saw, thank God!* His hand on her breast, his leaping out and suddenly grabbing her, she hated it. -Makes me jump out of my bloody skin! She dreaded turning a corner in case George was lurking, she felt like a hunted animal, and she supposed she was.

Why was he being like this? Is this how men are? She recalled her father with her mother; yes, there were the kisses and the cuddles, and the groans and the sounds of creaking bedsprings. But her mother gave herself to every caress and with love not fear. Is there something wrong with me? And May vowed, *-I will do better.*

George snatched her as she came out of the bedroom after laying up the fire, "Just in case there's a cold snap … best be prepared," Henry, warned.

She dropped the scuttle and coal dust fell in a cloud over the hall carpet. He pressed her against the wall, stealing kisses and telling her how much he wanted her. He told her how much pain he was in not being able to be with her, as he would have liked. He asked her, "You do love me May?" and May nodded, because she did, she was to be his wife.

***

May began the habit of listening at keyholes and peering round corners, if she heard the slightest rustle she'd turn on her heel; but she couldn't always avoid George. She did love him, she must. She'd heard some women disliked sex; perhaps she was one of them?

***

"Have you ever thought of marriage, Dolly?"

"No May, I've not had the chance."

"Would you like to have been?"

"Well, seems to me, all the women I know who got married, are living in poverty with umpteen brats. Lost all their teeth, and get a fist in their face on Saturday night and nine months later a new mouth to feed."

"Mm."

"I was never anyone's idea of a catch. Too big and plain, and I thank the Lord everyday for making me so."

"Have you never known a man then?"

"Known? Well of course there are men."

"I mean, known?"

"Ah right, in the biblical sense?"

"Er, yes I suppose."

Dolly sipped her tea and bit into a ginger biscuit; after a period of not speaking with a mouthful she said, "Well, I have as a matter of fact. Just the once mind, and that was enough, two minutes of agony, months of worry, and years of regret."

"Regret?"

"He was married; I feel the shame of it to this day. But that's enough of me. You'll want to marry, will you?"

"Oh yes, I want to be just like my mum, but with money! To a good man, like my father."

"You might like the women's role, some women do, I hear. Most don't, but it's their duty, as soon as men get you signed up to them, your body's no longer your own."

"S'pose not."

"Why all the interest anyway?"

"No reason ... I've been looking at some magazines Mrs Spritely has. Autumn brides, those gowns in velvet and satin ... they all look so beautiful."

"One day of pleasure, a lifetime of regret."

And they both laughed, Joseph walked into the kitchen and they yelled, "Boots."

Chapter 5

May at her washstand, sweaty from a long day. She soaked the flannel in the basin and squeezed the cloth dry. Lilac coloured soap with a fragrance of lavender; she loved its scent. May rubbed the bar against the cloth and scrubbed her neck. She stood in her cotton shift and petticoat. She raised her arm and the smell of her pits… "Oh dear," she said… then washed her other arm… The evening was hot although it was late summer; and the sweat trickled from the nape of her neck…

She removed the basin from its stand and placed it on the floor. Squatting over the bowl, she took the bar of foaming soap and rubbed her hands. She washed herself, the lavender fragrance mingling with her scent. She was just about to stand when she heard a click and her bedroom opened… "George!" She tried to grab the towel, but it was just too far from her grasp. He strode into her room pushing the door closed with the back of his heel.

"Don't get up on my account, May." And he smiled.

***

Mr Spritely had his eye to the keyhole, a view of May's world, which saw George in it. He supposed it was George one trousered buttock looking much like another.

George or John, either way he was up to some good … He smirked at his own wit. Then he saw him, George all right, young toad… So May's up for a bit, is she? Young flipperty gibbet. Mr Spritely moved his body, just to make himself more comfortable, and his knee knocked against her door. "Damn!" he muttered. May's running to this door…

-*My God!* Mr Spritely thought, I'm about to be exposed. The door flung open and his peeping Tomness uncovered for the world to see. But no, just as he thought that, George's arse covered the keyhole… Odd, dam odd, he thought… but then he heard George ask, "Like to see more?"

-Who's he talking to? Does he mean me? Henry tapped gently. A risk yes, but one worth taking, he hoped...

Mr Spritely watched...as he watched his excitement grew...especially in his trousers. *-Wanton hussy.* And he rubbed himself now fully exited his dressing gown...Gripping harder, he rubbed faster to the rhythm of the unfolding drama...When the action slowed so did Henry's hand...George so amorous... after his money is she...?

George's fingers were pinching her nipples, and they hardened under each nip. Nibbling her ear... Well bit strong that me boy, tearing her top like that. You'll have to pay for it. Still he's young, and see how she exposes herself. Her breasts, small and firm oh, and those pink pert nipples. Now her petticoat torn and discarded ... just her black stockings... Leave...those on ... And as if his son could hear him... He did...

May, naked, facing this door, bare except for a pair of black stockings.... Henry's hand slowed its thrust... just to gaze on her young loveliness... He wished the stockings were silk... these woollen ones... just not sheer... She was ripe, so pluckable, his hand quickened again.

May naked, with his George standing behind her holding her tight, May's eyes closed in the wantonness of lust. George took his hand and as she leaned against him, he parted her legs with his knee. Exposing her for the benefit of the eye at the keyhole...? Henry sped up his hand; beating a tattoo ... George lay May on her bed...

Well! And she just lay there ... not moving with her eyes closed ... Well for someone so young ... She's no virgin, lying there like that... George drew up her knees and pushed them so they fall apart... Henry now, saw her... Her pink nipples, her belly button, her dark curling hair and then ... She... Henry burst... groaning... he fell to his knees, to the floor. He splattered the linoleum and he stayed in that position while he gasped for his breath. When he was a little recovered, he returned his eye to the keyhole and saw George's buttocks thrusting up and down between May's thighs. He grabbed a handkerchief from his dressing gown's top pocket and wiped away the stains from outside her door...

Agnes heard noises coming from up above, footsteps? More footsteps and the sound of a door closing and opening; what on earth is going on? May moving about, or has she someone in her room? ... Agnes slammed her book shut and climbed the back stair. She'd turned into the hall where the girl slept and stopped... Henry! What on earth....?

Agnes couldn't believe her eyes... There, her husband, Henry Spritely, bending over with his eye to that girl's keyhole. She was about to call out when she saw what he was holding... And rubbing... Agnes sank down onto the top stair... captivated by this strange vision before her. She'd never seen it before. Never seen any man's maleness, apart from her son's of course, but that didn't count. Oh yes, she'd felt the sharp pain that first time, a couple of thrusts, and a grunt. She never imagined it looked like that. It was bigger than she'd thought. Although that first time she felt like a table leg had assaulted her; but after that, and especially the children she'd felt little at all. Then nothing for years... sharing the same house but leading different lives. She watched as he watched May. Watched her husband as his hand sped up and slowed down...stroked, then grabbed, and gripped ... hard!

***

"Morning May, sit you down and I'll make us a cup of tea before the family wakes up and wants their breakfast. Sit down May, making the place look untidy..." May sat at the kitchen table. She played with the cup set before her. Mrs Proudley turned from the range...

"May, you feeling alright you're looking a little off, where are those rosy cheeks?" And she poured the tea for them...

"One day I'd like to be a shop girl in a flower shop." May blurted out.

"Well now May, you've got to have a good accent for work like that. Speak well..."

"I don't speak well?"

"You're well, broad, as they say; a Hampshire accent but it suits you... Oh, and you have to be able to read and write..."

"I can read, and I can write."

"Not just your name and a few easy sentences, but letters; and be able to add up in your head. You been crying May? You're off home today. A whole day off, you should be happy... Not ill are you? I `pect you'll be looking forward to seeing your mother and all?"

"My mother's dead." said May.

"Oh May, I didn't know, I'm sorry... when did she pass away?"

"Last year..." She could no longer hold back the tears that had been forming, and they flowed down her cheeks.

"Oh May, come here now." And she drew May up in her big arms and held the little frame tight to her large comforting bosom.

"There, there now... Better to let it out. We all hold ourselves too tight in, and it does none of us any good...Come now." And she gently pushed May away from her, and looked deep into her eyes and with her hanky, released from her piny pocket, wiped away the tears from May's cheeks.

John burst whistling through the kitchen door, wiping his feet on the mat.

"If only I could train your father to do that."

"Any tea going Doll?" He asked.

"Just brewed."

"Everything all right?" he asked, looking at May's damp face.

"Everything's fine, just fine."

May blushed. Just a glimpse of him… -*Like he knows what I've done… Like…*

***

"We wondered, before you have your tea and there's buttered crumpets too, if you'd pick some flowers for the family's breakfast table."

"Okay, any particular sort?" said John.

"What do you think May?"

May's eyes narrowed. "I'd like roses please, yellow if there are any."

"You wish is my command, oh fair lady."

"There you are, you can start practising."

"Thank you Mrs Proudley." But May knew this was her last flower arrangement in this house because she was never coming back.

***

The family were in the dining room; they'd rung for service…

"Come on May, get a shift on …"

May grabbed the tray and paused … Dolly asked, "Yes May?"

"Nothing."

"Well, get a move on then. It'll be cold; the time you're taking."

May walked from the kitchen into the hall and paused… The door she needed to enter was just across the hallway, past the stairs, past the sideboard. May felt vulnerable she wasn't wearing her petticoat it was stained and torn. Nor her chemise, it too, needed repair. So here she stood, in her dress, stockings, and apron. Across this distance, George.

May stood outside the door…The hot water jug shook on the tray… She took a deep breath and pushed the door open with her foot. George had his back to her.

Mr Spritely wished May a good morning, a greeting echoed by Mrs Spritely, George kept his face turned away. She slowly approached the table...The jug wobbled on the tray, splashing drops of water and soaking the linen cloth.

May walked in a daze towards that blond bobbing head. The closer she advanced the larger the jug of water became, until it obliterated his skull. May placed the tray on the table, next to George. She held out the cup, the scolding hot water jug in her hand. His lap, his ugliness covered by a napkin. She wanted to turn that jug into his lap. Tip it over his head; bash his brains out with the salt ware pitcher. -Scold his bollocks off.

"May, don't you know, master George is not served first!" Agnes said. -*Lost the place I was reading now.*

"Too late for that," said Mr Spritely, and winked up at May. May flushed from her toes to her cheeks. Never had she felt so desolate and vulnerable, mixed with a desire to bash someone's brains out.

"I'll serve. May go and stand over there," Agnes said, pointing to a low cupboard. "Until we need you to serve breakfast." May stood. Here she watched the family slurp and sip. Mr Spritely took two sugars, and stirred his tea with great commotion making the tea lash the sides of the cup. -Bugger them. I could work the docks. I'd get paid for the privilege, and no housework! *Go back to learning though; that's what I want to do. Learn to read and write. Pick a book off the shelf and not allow the saying of the words to interrupt the story. Jeez, my nipples are sore.* The dress rubbed her, without the chemise to protect her. Her thighs hurt. Everything hurt.

-*I wonder if Dolly would allow me to use her needle and thread. I could sew up my garments on the tram. It takes half an hour. I might just finish it before we arrive at Commercial Road...*

"Are you in a trance May? Did you not hear George asking for a refill?"

"Yes, Mrs Spritely." And she stood over George's left shoulder and poured his tea, fresh and hot.

"Although, why you couldn't have done it yourself? George, you get lazier everyday."

George nodded his sweet crooked smile, and gave her his little, 'Oh silly me,' shrug; while his left hand travelled up May's skirt and rested on her buttock.

"Will that be all Sir?" May asked.

"For now. I wonder how long breakfast will be? I'm starving I could eat a nag." And he patted her bum.

Agnes said, "May go and check on Dolly. See if there hasn't been something untoward happened in the kitchen."

Agnes watched as she made a little bob before turning to leave the room. Such a pretty little thing, no wonder Henry is so obsessed. She wondered how long his keyhole peeping had been going on. Silly old goat, harmless though. Not as if he's forcing himself on the girl, and after all, she's not aware of it, or if she is, she's complicit. Satisfying herself on the merits of not raising the subject, she sipped her tea and continued reading The Lady's Realm …

Dolly arrived with breakfast. Dolly handed round the warm plates.

"Is May not to serve us?" asked Mr Spritely,

"Not today Sir, she's off home."

"Off home? Off home!" said Henry.

"It's her day off Sir; she needs to get off, to catch the tram."

"Day off! How's she getting to The George then? Walking there, on her own? George, chaperone her."

"John has volunteered his services," Dolly said.

"Ah, her knight gallant, eh!" sniffed George."

***

John waited for her on the gravel drive; holding a bicycle, his other arm he held out for her to take. "I am at your disposal." And they walked arm and arm through the iron gates; and into the lane that would lead them to The George Inn where the tram was due in twenty minutes. "Back tomorrow then May?"

"Yes," said May, almost inaudibly, she'd decided not to return, but it wasn't something she wished to discuss with John, now or ever. May smiled.

"I could pick you up tomorrow. What time does the tram arrive?"

"I, I ... don't know. I haven't got a timetable; I'll ask the conductor when I'm on."

"Good idea. I'll ask him and I'll be waiting for you."

"I..."

"Have you ever been on a bike?"

-*Been on a bike,* thought May. *-This is only the second one I've ever seen.*

"No, John! 'pect it's very difficult."

"Practise, that's all. First, you wobble. Then you ride and fall off; then you ride and don't fall off. Those are the stages of bicycle riding. Like a go?"

"Er, not really, these are my best clothes. Sunday clothes I'll be going to the service soon as I arrive."

"You do look lovely May, especially in that bonnet." And he picked periwinkles and dressed the flowers onto the side of her hat. "Perfect, a picture." He took May's chin in his hand and raised her face to him, and he, so gently placed the lightest kiss on her lips.

"John," she said. "Please I."

"May ... I thought you would like me to kiss you."

"I'm sorry, just such a surprise. I..."

And John wrapped his arm around her shoulder and escorted her to the tram stop.

***

They were waiting, Lil, Glad, and Fred. And although she waved, Lil wasn't smiling. "Dad's hurt his leg... and he's moved in with Gertie Mailer."

"What? Slow down."

"Father's left."

"Only temporary, Gert's looking after him. She reckoned it would be all a bit of a pinch if we all squashed into number 25. Anyway, he's in Nile Street, not to leave his bed. That's what the doctor said," Glad said.

"The doctor? How much did he cost?"

"Dunno, but dad's not in a good mood; and he says, as soon as you get here you've to go and see him."

"Let's go home first."

"But."

"Oh come on, he's not dying is he? You'd have said! A couple of minutes aren't going to hurt."

Her father had broken his leg; he'd fallen from the rigging of a hulk. He'd be laid up for, "Twelve weeks the doctor reckons," said her father. "So it's a piece of luck you're working ... least the rent'll be paid."

-Yes, it will, won't it! May's heart sank, she'd wanted not to return, never go back, never see Fairview or George again, ever! Now she had no choice, she'd have to return, there was no other income but hers...

"You listening to me May? You're such a ruddy dreamer. I was saying, Father Dolling has offered to help out, the doctor has agreed to take his fee when I'm mended, back at work."

"And I'll look in on the kids," said Gert. May smiled. *-Got what you want now, haven't you?*

"He'll be hobbling around in a couple of weeks; until then he has to stop here, in bed."

-Shut up, just shut up. "I'd better go. You'll be home next time I come then?"

"Between the two I reckon; that's what we think." Ernest looked at Gert, who nodded her
agreement.

***

In the garden May stacked away chairs into the summer house, and the door closed behind her. One push and he held her tight in his arms.

"Oh May, my darling, I missed you so much; stolen moments, and a thousand years of memories, we must be quick, saw old Joe just enter the green house." And he pushed her against the wooden slats of the house. His lips finding hers, he pushed his tongue hard into her mouth. He'd been eating cheese and onion sandwiches. His hand strayed up and under her skirt. His foot pushed between her feet opening her legs and exposing her drawer's open gusset to his probing fingers.

-Least it doesn't bloody hurt this time!

He raised and pressed his knee between her thighs. With the flick of five fly buttons, he exposed himself, raised her skirt, and rammed himself into her. One, two, three, four, five and then a final thrust, and that was that. May grabbed her hat and patted down her skirt before dashing along the path and the sanctuary of Dolly's kitchen.

"You're flushed."

"I walked too fast Dolly, after putting away all the chairs."

Well sit down there, take the weight off your feet, we won't be needed for a while yet. Kettle's boiled, so we'll have a brew."

"Thank you,"

"Something to eat?"

"I don't think so, no… thank you Dolly."

May sat in her room, this can't go on. I can't go on; not like this. May weighed up her limited choices.

She'd not have Lil, Glad and Fred, even her father, no, they would not go in the workhouse, -Not if I have anything to do with it.

Chapter 6

Preparations were underway for George's return to school. Next week was the last week in September and next year he finished school, forever. Dolly was airing his trunk. George packed and ready to go, he left tomorrow morning. In a moment of capture in the hallway leading to the breakfast room he said, "It's my last day May, I've so enjoyed myself this holiday." And he smiled. May didn't meet his gaze.

George kissed her, "I'll see you this evening."

May went to her room; the family had dined and she had a moment to herself. She stared with puzzlement at a box that sat on her bed. A tin soldier, a top, and a picture book … Freddie will be delighted, May smiled. She felt relief at George's coming absence. Just as she had that thought, George was in her room. She hadn't heard his knock.

"Do you think Fred will like those?" he asked, nodding at the box and the toys.

"He'll love them, so kind of you George."

And George smiled at his own kindness, "There's an old doll, a china thing with glass eyes, but Ma, well, she won't part with it. Would have been nice for your sisters, they're not going to be jealous?"

"Of Freddie? Oh no, they'll be pleased for him; if he's lucky he might be able to tear them away from Glad and get to play with them himself." And May smiled at the thought of chubby cheeked Freddie; she was looking forward to seeing his big eyes grow wide, when he, -*Cops a look at these!*

George kissed her, "You look so lovely, those dimples, that smile. Come May." And he patted the bed. George lay back. "Come here May, please May…"

"George please. I'd like you to leave, you've been drinking. I…"

"I can't leave," he snapped.

May had no idea what he was talking about. *–Just go. Please, just bloody go.*

"I don't think you want me to leave. Not really." And he patted the place next to him on the bed, again.

"No."

"May, I'm sorry, you're right; I have had too much to drink."

May exhaled a little of the breath she was holding.

"I'll leave then." And he turned to the door. But he rushed her, grabbing her in a tight embrace. "Be quiet May, that's a horrible noise. If you think anyone will come to rescue you … Out, all are out. Ma's visiting. Dolly has gone home. Joseph and his dimwit son are probably at The George by now." George offered her his hand, but she kicked out at him and her back reached the wall…

"I don't understand you May. Why are you making it so difficult for me, and for you? It's not as if you haven't done it before."

"I've told you, I want you to leave, I don't want you, and I never wanted you before … I …"

"What?" You enjoyed it May, why do women always pretend?"

May caught sight of herself in the wardrobe mirror … *-Christ.* Her hair shaken loose tumbled untidily in snakes of black tendrils. "Just like any street hooker, that's what I look like."

"What May, did you say something?"

"Like any old street hooker," she shouted. "That's how you're treating me." And then she said, "You want me like this? Then I'll be like it. A crown, that's what I'll have." She held out her hand. Strangely, this had the most peculiar effect on George.

"But!"

"Did you think we were lovers then George?" Past the point of care, she went on, "Or did you like the control, the power it gave you?"

"Don't."

"Or what? The power it gave you! Big, strapping George taking and overpowering women, make you feel like the little, big man did it? ... A crown. You want it, it's a crown."

"George fumbled in his pocket, I've only a shilling."

"A shilling! Do you know how much it costs to take the plug of a girl? Even on the streets it'll cost you five sovereigns?"

George wasn't sure what had happened here, he wasn't even sure he fancied her anymore, all mouth and sneers. No vulnerability, where had all her feminine charms gone? She looked like a Wagnerian, bloody Fury. George made his choice; or the content of his trousers did, which was retreating rapidly with every word she spat at him, made it for him. And he simply rose from her bed and left...

***

George did not appreciate being spoken to like that. *–In my own house, and by the maid! But if she wanted to play the whore ... Well, it may be fun.* He'd pay her, why not? It's only money. So on this, his last night he handed May a coin, and he slowly closed her fingers over a big silver crown...

***

If he were going to have her body then he'd bloody pay for it. *-What's spoiled is spoiled! – Fine!* Chances are I would have ended up selling meself on the streets anyway. This way, I can keep my family from that ruddy workhouse. *-Least I get something from it.* May wondered how she could have been so bloody stupid. But now it was time to make the best she could from this bad situation. *– Gullible, stupid, cow! Right now, May Miller, pull yourself together.*

And after giving herself that good talking she filled her head with new concerns...Would this make me a prostitute? And if it did, would that matter? She'd seen many a woman sell herself in the back alleys of Portsea just to feed their children. Which was nobler, not to sell yourself or let your children starve? Weren't all women who married, prostituting themselves, selling their bodies for a home, food on the table, while their husband's had the rights to their bodies?

***

Henry was relaxing in the Crow's-Nest with a good rum and a bad book. He'd heard May's door open, then close. -May. Henry looked through his keyhole. He was about to step across the passageway when George appeared, jacket-less and with his braces hanging loose at his hips. George tapped, didn't wait a response, and entered. Henry decided he'd leave them for five minutes before stepping across the hall and spying. But no sooner had Henry's hand reached his knob than her door opened and closed. Again!

"What on earth's going on?"

So a few minutes later after watching George leave, he decided to satiate his curiosity. With his eye to her keyhole, he saw May. May, sitting on her bed, unrolling her black stockings, May, unpinning her hair, it fell in thick waves down her chest. Henry watched on. May, removing her apron, now her blouse... Henry was a little preoccupied. He didn't hear George's return. George watched his Pa. And Henry watched May as she removed her petticoat. She wore a cotton chemise.

Henry felt most fortunate, she was inches away from him, he placed his hand on the door, pressing the wooden panel at her hips. She removed her chemise and as she reached up he saw the short black hairs between her thighs, and he gasped. Her white thighs and that black hair, such contrast! She took the nightgown from the hook on the door and replaced it with her chemise.

George smiled, at his father peeping. Say nothing, or say hello? And although they both knew Henry had been peeping, and Henry knew George knew he'd been spying, it went unsaid. -*Nothing, it was!* George padded half way down the stairs, paused, turned, and coughed.-*Damn!* Thought Henry, and scurried away.

A tap at her door and the handle turned, and George. He stood there, black suede slippers and an emerald velvet robe. May had loosed her hair, tendrils curling, tumbling over her shoulders.

May had dressed in the negligee George had bought for her, and stockings that he'd taken from his mother's drawer. The negligee was a sheer silk, low-necked affair that fell in a pool at her feet. "Come, stand here." And pointed to a spot in front of the bed. May wore stocking of white silk. "You look stunning." And George stepped across the room to kiss her.

Henry was back in position as soon as he heard that door close. George had the girl in an embrace. Now his boy tore off his robe, he was starkers! George naked as the day he was born. Except, he carried before him a huge erection, it was so full it was positively perpendicular. Henry could only remember when he had stood so firm. – *May's staring at it, she looks, almost surprised!*

George's hand pulled at the ribbon holding the robe around May's body, it floated to the floor, a puff of cloud. And there she stood, in her little heeled slippers and silk stockings. George, his son, standing before her, George took her hand and escorted her to the bed and he kissed her and May accepted those kisses. George pressed his weight on her. His lips brushed her breast and he kissed its pinkness and when he sucked, it stood erect for him. His hand uncovered her and she opened her thighs to him. George stood back, kneeling at the side of the bed and looked down on her. Henry looked too. George felt like an actor in his scripted play; he'd give his father something to remember. So he moved in such a position May was displayed for his father's delight and no doubt delectation.

***

George went to bed a contented and miss spent youth; he'd need to tap his Pa for funds tomorrow, that half sovereign was worth every penny, of course, but he'd need money at school. He needed to replace that coin. So over breakfast, and while John and Joseph were dragging his trunk and cases to the cart he said, "Don't suppose you'd give me an advance on my allowance? I know I shouldn't ask, but for some reason I'm a bit short."

"What on earth do you spend your money on George?" asked Agnes. "There's not much about here for you to spend your money on." Henry raised an eyebrow.

"I know Ma, I have bought a few essentials for school, and a few friends a drink."

"I'll get you something later after we've eaten. I'll send your pocket money as usual with our letters."

"Oh yes do. I owe old Hornsey a guinea."

"A guinea?"

"Henry, don't shout at George, we're at breakfast, not the races."

"Er."

"Sleep well, last night Pa?"

"No, something kept disturbing me."

"Is that why you're so bad tempered then, Henry?"

"Agnes, I'm not bad tempered." He felt in his pocket to see what change he had stowed there. "Don't s'pose two bob's any good to you?"

"Er, well it'll buy lunch…"

Just as George was leaving, his father slipped a rolled up five-pound note into his hand. George smiled, "Thank you pa." And Father and Son hugged. "Look after everything here for me, won't you?" and he winked.

"Of course, of course."

Dolly and Mrs Spritely stood on the step, each held a handkerchief, and both were dabbing their eyes. May joined them. Agnes stepped down and kissed her beautiful boy farewell, and slipped a guinea in his trouser pocket. George climbed on top of the cart and turned and waved as the cart with Dan, Joseph and George turned into the lane and the donkey's hooves faded to nothing.

Agnes wiped away a tear; Dolly blew her nose and Henry turned and ushered the three women back into the house; all used the front entrance on this special occasion.

***

"Do you see much of George?" said Agnes.

-*Oh, what's this about?* thought May. *Has she found out?*

"What do you think, isn't he the most fine-looking young man?"

"Oh yes, indeed."

May took her hair in her hand and swirled it into high chignon. "Oh, May that's lovely." And she handed her some pins. May so used to dressing her sisters' hair, and there it was. May stepped over, picked up a hand mirror, and held it so Agnes could see the back of her new style. Agnes patted the back of her head. "Delightful."

"It's you that are lovely." May picked up a hair slide decorated with marquisettes in the shape of a bow. "Maybe grow out the fringe." And she nodded towards the cover of The Lady magazine. Your hair is so thick it'd take the style, no need for you to place hair pads."

"It used to be lovely, grown dull, like me."

"Oh, no, that's not true."

"Streaked with grey."

"My mother used to colour her silver bits with strong tea. There's all sorts can be done."

"My sister gave me some cosmetics brought direct from Paris, so she said. I looked like a clown in the end, that or a wax doll. I've read of different applications but it's shopping for them...so embarrassing … just vanity. Some of the things I'd never heard of."

"Can get anything where I come from, comes off the boats. My mum used to use ash round her eyes."

"Ash?"

"From the fire... mixed with a little whiting, sometimes beeswax."

"Didn't that look rather peculiar?"

"Well, when she wore it people said how lovely she looked and when she didn't they asked if she was feeling peaky."

"Really?"

"Would you like to try?"

"Well...no, I don't think so..." *—Ash and tea! Ridiculous.*

***

Back at school Sebastian and George now shared a room rather than dorm, this, their last year at school. After the unpacking, and choosing of who was to sleep in which bed, George said, "That's it, I'm off to choir practise."

"You! What has the esteemed choirmaster, Mr Gregory, done to deserve the tuneless balladeer? Apart from siring an illustrious daughter?"

"Nothing."

"So it is, the lovely Susannah. She's turned every pupil's head. But she's turned her nose up every time. No chance."

"I Sebastian, will have her."

"I bet you, George, five guineas; by the last day, of our last term she'll be as intact as this glass."

"You're on. Sebastian, I shall hold you to that." And for dramatic effect, he grabbed and tossed that glass to the floor.

***

Sebastian lay on his bed. "Good grief George you're making it up."

"I kid you not."

"Susannah will take a lot more effort, not for her the price of a chocolate box and a few ribbons. Besides, Sir keeps a beady eye on her."

"Oh, but Sebastian, what a prize."

"You won't get there, George, not without marriage."

"She'll cost me much, but she's worth it."

"So, not like your little maid then?"

"There is nothing like May. She is a true delight, a woman who granted me much pleasure."

"And did you show her the delights."

"I think she'll look forward to seeing me again."

Sebastian threw a book at his head, but George ducked. "I must come and visit you one holiday George, sample the delights of the Hampshire downs."

"You're more than welcome, Christmas term, come then."

"Would, old chap, but family beckons on the festive season."

"I should come to you."

"No George, my widowed mother and sister are not fair game, and Charlotte will remain intacta until her wedding day."

George regaled Sebastian of all the doing and undoing of May, including his Pater standing erect outside the bedroom door.

"Oh my God, oh George I have to come, I really do."

"Sebastian, consider yourself invited." Sebastian and George used to be close. They knew each other in the Greek sense. But now they'd both moved on, although, sometimes the old times reared its head. Out of comfort or lust, they united again, giving in to those powerful emotions.

"For a box of chocolates, a few ribbons, and a box of your old toys you amused yourself!"

"Put like that, yes…"

They laughed.

"You'll introduce me to this treasure?"

"Oh no, she'll introduce you to me. You forget she is our maid."

Chapter 7

Now he was a Naval Captain,
Up from town upon a whim,
And she, a poor man's daughter,
Took a fancy unto him.

John Bridger sat on the wooden chair by the stove. The kettle began to whistle and May rose to pour the hot water into the teapot. John watched her. He loved to look at her. When she smiled, which she did infrequently, dimples appeared on her cheeks. The two wooden chairs faced each other either side of the hearth. May pulled a skillet out and slid on two slices of bread, hot buttered toast and tea.

"May," John said, as she sat waiting for the tea to brew and watching the bread turn from bread to toast, turned the slices. "Would you do something for me?"

-Oh right! Here we go, jump on, the pumping, leap off. May looked at him not quizzically, and waited.

"Would you untie your hair?"

May took the toast from the tray, buttered it, and handed John the plate. She put her hand to her hair, withdrew a clasp and a couple of pins, and shook down her hair. May bit on her toast, liquid butter trickled down her chin, and her lips shone with grease. John laughed.

"You can laugh John Bridger, look at the state of your face, all butter and crumbs, like you have a beard."

May smiled, her dimples indenting her cheeks. John sighed, and sipped his tea. He would sit here forever if he could, just to look at her. Today there was nobody in the house; Dolly was on an errand, Mrs Spritely to her sister somewhere in Southsea. Old Mr Spritely had taken himself off to the mess in Portsea. And the younger Mr Spritely had returned to his school at Winchester.

So John was content to look and stay a while, his chores, his jobs would wait. As May was clearing the cups and plates, running water into the sink, John came and stood behind her. His lips kissed the nape of her neck. She smiled, hesitantly John turned her to him, and he bent his face to her, his lips met hers, and he kissed her. Then his arms surrounded her in a protective embrace.

"May, I love you, I love you so much." And he sighed.

From his pocket, John withdrew a small package wrapped in yellow paper and tied up with a blue ribbon. "This is for you." May took the little box and pulled the ribbon and the package loosened showing inside a little box with seeds written on the side.

"Sorry, it was the only box I could find." Inside the seed box were silver drop earrings in the form of flying doves.

"Oh John, they are beautiful." And May smiled, again.

-Twice today, I've seen her smile.

John took the earring intending her to wear them. But as he took the earring and pushed back her hair, her ears weren't pierced.

"I'll pierce them when I'm back in Portsea. They're so beautiful, thank you."

"They are silver so your ears won't go green and drop off."

May held them to her ear to see how they would sit, John held her hair back.

"Gorgeous."

"The earrings or me?"

"Oh the earrings, skinny bean pole like you!" And she slapped him before aiming the wet dishcloth at him. John grabbed her and held her tight; May felt him harden against her body. "Oh May, I wish we were married."

May poised for the lunge and grope; but she waited in vain. John released her. He kissed her, and he thanked her for the tea and said, "I must get back to my work." And he left May standing at the sink, and she watched him walk across the lawn to the potting shed.

***

Mrs Spritely sat at her dressing table, brushing her hair. May brought hot milk. "Will that be all, Mrs Spritely?" "Call me Agnes May, at least when we're alone. Agnes handed May her hairbrush, "Would you mind?" she asked.

"Course not; would you like lanolin on the brush?"

"Oh yes, well why not!"

May brushed and brushed, and Mrs Spritely closed her eyes, "How's that?"

"You've not finished have you? So relaxing…"

"Just halfway through," May lied.

Agnes looked at May. "You are a pretty little thing, I expect all the boys are after you?"

"No Mrs Spritely, I'm not interested."

"But I've seen you walking out with John?"

"He's my friend." May had her fingers crossed behind her back.

"Mr Spritely has grown fond of you, do you know?"

"No, Mrs Spritely."

"Agnes, please call me Agnes."

"He's always kind to me." May didn't add, John had come courting. But to know May you had to know May; to ask the questions you had to have the answers. And May never volunteered, anything.

***

Henry decided to visit the mess in Portsea. The officer's mess stood off Unicorn Gate. A fine day, he had walked to The George Inn and waited for the tram where he alighted at Commercial Road.

Henry turned down into Charlotte Street. Thursday was market day; costers were selling fruit and veg. Hawkers trading old clothes, and new clothes. The street bustled with meat vendors, fish sellers, women selling wares, and women selling themselves. Everything and anything had a price. Street urchins, pedlars and scavengers, old bruised fruit picked up from the gutters made into pies or jams and sold on. He made his way past Pye Street and Chance Street. He stopped on the corner of Hope, hesitated, and then walked down the Street. He stood outside number thirty-one, the number of the house where he'd stood many times before. He'd never found her alone when he'd called. He would confirm Ernest was at work; but there was always someone with her, an aunt, a friend, or a neighbour.

She was beautiful, May's mother. May would never be as beautiful as her mother. but she was a handsome girl. Had he not had acquaintance with her mother he'd have thought no lovelier creature could have walked these crude streets. Just then, a couple of children came dashing along the street, dressed in cut-down sailor's trousers, and turned into coarse cotton dresses. Bare foot, they stopped for a moment and then gambled on and finally burst into Charlotte Street.

Henry was sure he saw the curtains twitch at the house. But then maybe, hoped he had, but that time was past. And for all his efforts, he'd never been with, or knew Lavinia. She was always Ernest's wife, and now after her death, would remain his forever.

***

"Ern, there's a bloke out here looking at this house, rent been paid has it?"

"May has, saw her do it meself. Probably someone using us as a cut through."

"Well, for someone doing that, he's stood looking at this house for long enough," Gert remarked.

"What's he look like?"

"Come see for yourself." Ernest hobbled to the window; the stranger had turned the corner on to Chandler Street and disappeared.

Henry stopped again, this time at the entrance to St Agathas'. At this hour of day, this day of the week it should be empty. He stepped out from the sunlight into the shade of the church, and walked slowly towards the altar decorated with white lace cloths. Each square edged with drawn needlework and measured just eight inches across, stitched together to form one whole. -*Probably so she could sew at home with the small squares on her lap.*

He touched the cotton …

"Beautiful workmanship isn't it?" a female voice said, behind him.

Henry turned and saw a middle-aged woman stuffing dahlias into a vase, a guise for a flower arrangement. "Lovely," answered Henry. And he walked up the aisle, past the artistry of the florist. She nodded and he doffed his hat. He turned right onto Chandler street and then across the main road into the base, and sanctuary. The sentry nodded then saluted. Henry returned his salute, and walked on. -*I need a drink.* And ordered a brandy.

Thursday, he would have expected a little more in the way of companionship. There was an old salt puffing on a pipe; he was already, two or more sheets to the wind. Henry gulped down the brandy and walked from the mess on to the base proper. He strolled past the old offices through the cobbled streets, and the large huts where the rope stretched on tenterhooks, and on towards the dry dock, where he asked after Ernest Miller, "Off mate."

"Off?"

"Broke his leg in a fall." And he pointed the end of his pipe at the mast of a hulk.

"I see."

Henry began to wish he'd never come. He could've had his own company at home. And the memories he'd opened, the unrequited love, for Henry it was love. Love unfulfilled on the part of Henry, it always was with the women he chose to love. He was beginning to sink into a maudlin mood. He decided he needed cheering up! So another drink. - *A rum, brandy always made me mawkish.* Then a visit to the old haunts. But now The Mess had come to life; an atmosphere of cigar smoke and profanities curdled the air.

"Henry! Henry over here mate. Let me introduce you, this is Chalkie."

***

May poured boiling water and salt in a pot, and dropped in a needle and the earrings. May took the pot and sat at the table looking in the mirror. She fished the needle out with a pair of tweezers; and with a cloth wrapped over the eye, held her lobe with one hand and in the other the needle. She pushed the needle through her ear lobe, until it stopped. It hadn't hurt, not that much! But now the point of the needle pushed so far through snagged on the skin as it neared its exit, and the back of her lobe stretched like canvas over a tent pole. May pinched the two sides of her ear lobe together and heard the sound of ripping as the back of her lobe's flesh tore. But she was through. Not too bad, and she wiped away a trickle of blood. Withdrawing the needle, she fished out a silver dove and pushed the point of the earring through her newly pierced ear.

One ear with dove earring! May looked into the mirror and admired the effect. May took a deep breath and repeated the piercing on her right lobe. Funnily enough, this didn't hurt half as much as the left lobe. The needle tried to puncture the back of her ear, the skin stretched tight. The more it stretched, the more she removed from the pain; as if the puncture was performed on someone else. No, not someone else, because then, May would have felt every stab sharply; and possibly fainted from the sight of blood. She felt not just relaxed, but contented, almost dreamy. The right earring set in its place. May pulled her hair to see the full effect of her surgery. She loved them, a present, her first present from her fiancé. That's it, fiancé. I am engaged to John Bridger; May Bridger that worked, Mrs May Bridger. She recalled his face, the black hair, and those blue eyes. They looked similar in many ways, they could almost be siblings.

***

Agnes met her sister at the Royal Pier hotel in Southsea. Cucumber sandwiches cut as thinly as tissue paper. Potted duck in little jars… Francis stood as soon as Agnes entered the tearoom; as did the gentleman seated next to her.

"Agnes, may I introduce you, Mr Baker, Sir William Baker, my sister Agnes." Francis bit her tongue, she wanted, and would by custom say, her elder sister, but she wasn't sure that she wouldn't have to endure some unstated criticism! A quizzical look, or a glimmer of surprise. She had no intention of subjecting herself to that!

Mr Baker clicked his fingers. A waiter immediately appeared.

"A fresh pot," he said, pointing to the teapot, "Unless of course you'd prefer something else. Coffee or chocolate?"

"I can't say chocolate in the afternoon, seems the right thing."

"Oh, Agnes! It's French; they even serve it at breakfast," said Francis.

"That may well be the case, but I prefer to waken in the morning before returning to my slumber. I shall save chocolate for my night time drink. Tea please."

***

Henry, paused opposite outside May's door, he wanted to peek. But fiddling in his waistcoat, he pulled out his key and stoically about turned 180 degrees and with the key fully inserted turned it in the lock and entered the Crows-Nest.

Henry's room faced south. With his eye to the telescope, he saw Portchester Castle to his right. And on this clear day, in the distance the dockyard and further, the Isle of Wight. Shortening his lens by twisting on the girth, he came to Cosham and beneath him the slopes of Portsdown Hill. At Easter, it would be covered with the sights and sounds of fair ground laughter. Every Easter since who knew when, it was so. Fairview House so named because it overlooked this old market. And it was this fair he came as a boy. Brought as a lad to shoot ducks, pin donkey's tails and eat toffee apples, until one day he broke a tooth…But that was months away.

Tethered ponies posted along the hill sheltered among the bushes and trees, so short, starved of nutrients as the value of the soil tumbled into the sea. But there! Walking, young Bridger, out with a young woman, no less, Henry could not make out this young filly, her face hidden by a big hat, decorated with flowers and a blue trailing ribbon. Until she looked up at the house and Henry said, "May!" She has Michaelmas daisies threaded through her hat. They walk side by side. But now his view is hidden by a shrubby bush -*There now. Ain't going to have her are you?* It filled Henry with both frustration and jealously.

If there were to be shenanigans, he would with his extended telescope like to bare witness. The thought of a common boy granted the delights he so wanted, and were, to be had for the price of *-or probably free, wouldn't do!* But as these ideas rushed through Henry's head, they both reappeared the other side of the bush as if nothing untoward had occurred. It hadn't, but Henry found that hard to believe, he knowing something or two about the world.

John and May reappeared from behind the shrub. And started to climb, John held out his hand to May. Henry saw May smile. -*Dimples!* Dimples in her cheeks; ain't seen them before. And he twisted his telescope to keep the focus on the lover as they neared Fairview. On the drive, gravel crunching under their feet, John whispered, "I love you." He reached down clumsily but lovingly and hidden from prying eyes under the brim of her hat, kissed May on her lips. And he said, "I love you May Miller."

And Henry said, "By Jove, she's not for you lad." He was relieved when May and John separated, she to the side door, and John, with hands stove firm in his trouser pockets to the potting shed. And sighed....

-I love you May. I love you May Miller. He said to himself, and breathed deeply the smell of peaty compost.

***

May looked so much like Lavinia. Henry's younger self revived. He was no longer the be-whiskered slightly portly, middle-aged naval officer. He was the younger man. Henry hungered for her, she reminded him of his younger, unmarried days. Now George was away... In the Crow's-Nest he peered through his telescope, Portchester Castle clouded in grey, the Isle of Wight vanished under the sea's haze.

Henry heard May's door open, and close. He sat with his telescope lowered to seated height and stared out at the horizon. But his mind was not on the sight that appeared through this lens. Henry knocked and May answered her door not with a, 'Come in,' but by opening the door a little and peering out.

"Mr Spritely, how can I help you?"

"I wondered if you'd like to well, have a look at Portsmouth, maybe see if we can find your home?"

May stood behind the telescope with her eye set to the lens.

"See anything?"

"Just grey."

"What about this?"

"Greyness."

Henry peered through the glass; he was staring at a cloud! He lowered the trajectory and aimed it at the sails of the tall ships bobbing on the water. Henry stood behind May. He could smell lavender and a slight tangy smell of sweat. He leaned in closer and kissed the nape of her neck, then not repelled, reached up and cupped her breasts in both his hands.

"May I have something to ask you?"

"Yes, Mr Spritely," said May, fascinated. She'd just sighted St Agathas', her family were just a minute's walk from there. She could almost reach out and touch them.

Henry walked away and stood with his back to the fireplace, embers glowed in the hearth.

"Wonderful," May said.

"It is. I spend many a pleasant hour viewing the harbour and the boats." Henry cleared his throat. "I expect you miss George, now he's back at school."

May hadn't given much thought to him. Apart from Dolly reminding her, by her talk of her golden boy. She was enjoying being in this house without being under attack at any moment.

"I would like to help you. I … I …"

"Yes Mr Spritely?" May turned her gaze from the telescope to Mr Spritely.

"Well, please call me Henry. Just in … only in private though, can't break ranks."

"Of course, Henry."

"I would like to know you. I would like to …"

May watched Henry as he stuttered, spluttered, and slurred. *-Fuck me.*

"You would like to?"

Henry pulled from his pocket a half sovereign. "Just once a week, I just need …"

And he held out the coin for May to take, or not. If she took it, she agreed, or if she didn't, then she didn't.

Chapter 8

Agnes wanted new reading matter something more suited to her newly awakened senses. How to start? Does one just go into the booksellers and ask for some romp? - *Suppose so, if you're a man…* How do I go about it?

***

Agnes rang the bell. She looked at the flower arrangement on the drawing room table and touched the petal of a rose between her fingers. May's hand no doubt, so talented. "Ah, May some tea please, Henry, would you like something, another cup perhaps, a fresh brew?"

"No, thank you my dear."

"May a fresh pot and one cup, and May …"

"Yes, Mrs Spritely."

"Bring it to my bedroom; I'll rest before dinner."

***

"Ah May. Place the tray here," Agnes said, as she pointed to her writing desk. "I have something to ask you." May waited. "I should like you to try and buy those items we discussed."

-What items? May, must have looked blank.

Agnes continued. "Something for my hair …" There was a silence for a while, just until Agnes found the right way to rephrase it. "I recall you said … you could get anything, from where you come from, off the boats, you say."

–Oh! Is this girl trying to make it as awkward as possible?

"Yes Agnes." May suddenly cottoned on. "Of course, henna for, and ... healthy skin preparations."

"Yes, that's it, health products; you think you'll be able to …obtain them? What about a book? Could you get that?"

"I can ask, but yes. Anyway if you write the name of the book, I'll pass it on."

Agnes relaxed. *-Not so difficult.* But Agnes didn't know any titles of the books she wanted.

"I'm almost certain ... but ... My next day off ...It's just..."

"Just?"

"It's my day off ..."

"You would like extra time?" Agnes snapped.

May tried to swallow her sigh but the frown was more difficult to mask. "My day off is Sunday, the market isn't held on Sunday." Agnes wondered, *-What on earth is this girl talking about.* And drew no correlation between her needs and a street market!

"Thursday is market day, that's when all the traders arrive." *–Jesus, what else do I need say?* Agnes was confused, a silence followed.

May said, "May I move my day off to Thursday? It'll allow me to buy the items we need."

"Oh yes, I suppose ...sort it with Dolly will you. I'll write the list while you brush my hair, you can take it with you..." List written, folded, and pushed into May's piny pocket for safekeeping.

***

John and May sat on the garden bench. It was Late October and the leaves were turning to red and gold. Some had already fallen and were dancing along the path spurred on by a light breeze. But it was warm. An Indian summer ...

"I'd like you May, to say you'll be my girl."

May gaped at him, "I ..."

"May, I love you, I want you to be my girl, and later my wife ... say yes, May."

May looked into those beautiful blue eyes which crinkled at the corners, always looked as if there was a smile ready to break on his face... Then he jumped from the bench and on his knee in front of her, he asked her, "Will you be my girl?"

May, blushed, how she loved this silly, young, lovely, boy-man. "Yes, I'd like to be your young lady.... But—" And with that he stood sharply up dragged her from the bench and whirled and swirled her around the garden.

"What shall we do to seal our bond?" And the summerhouse came into view and he held the door open with his foot and gently pulled her into the little room.

He drew her close in his arms and kissed her hair. Then he bent his head and kissed her lips, first gently and then firmly. Tasting the saltiness of her skin and the sweetness of her breath, "I love you May. I think I loved you the moment I first saw you." May returned his kiss, but hard and lustily … With the men she'd lain with, and their unwanted selfish lust, she so wanted him … To have a shared love… But it was his turn to pull away … He gave her a faintly quizzical look.

May reddened; of course he wouldn't want me, not if he knew… I'm probably his first love. I will know more about this than he will. But he must lead the way, and at his pace. And, that's what George did, wasn't it? He saw something he wanted, and he wanted it fast, there and then. And now here was John, he too saw something he wanted but he wanted to lead a slower dance… Both getting what they wanted … But then she thought. There is at big difference; I want him too. I want him now. Like I wanted George once?

"You've gone quiet May, sorry did I hurt, you? Your feelings?" "I've never felt anything like that before John…I, don't know what came over me…" This of course was true, or true in the greater part… Then she allowed John to kiss her again, she would never make that mistake again. He would make the time and the place; she would allow him to lead. …The sun was setting on a beautiful day.

***

May was fond of John, she loved him, she supposed. But she wasn't good enough for him. He would need, deserved someone better than she could ever be. He was dear and sweet, had the same silly loveliness his father has. *-I'm just a discarded old tart.* A young tart, but I have ambition. I was stupid, maybe. But he, George, horrible. Bloody wine that does it to him, but no, it wasn't the drink that first time in the library. She hadn't smelt it on his breath, but then she'd had a drink too …

"You day dreaming May?"

"I am John Bridger, I'm dreaming about hiring you as me gardener."

"Hire me? I won't want paying. You'll be me wife and I'll do it for love and duty."

"I was thinking about that, about marriage. …"

***

Mr Gregory looked up from the hymn stands when George walked into the cathedral. His face wore an expression of bemused surprise.

Susannah had a bubble of blonde hair and deep brown eyes; she had a retrousse nose and a pert air. She was a woman, a rose in bloom. *-This would take some work.* He needed a plan, but first he needed her to know him and enjoy his company. Knowing his voice was not a sound anyone would want to hear. He made himself useful in any number of ways. Song sheets handed out; candles placed. George performed these chores with sanguine good nature, especially when Susannah appeared.

When she acknowledged him, he'd nod briskly. Nothing, he supposed would intrigue this woman, the object of lust and love of hundreds of randy schoolboys, more than disinterest. He argued this would make him unique, stand him out from that crowd.

***

May thought she heard a click when she was in the hallway. Instead of turning to the stairs, she went left.

Henry witnessed this from his spy hole in the Crow's-Nest. The spare room next to May's held odd, unwanted items from the house. May could use anything from this room to furnish hers.

Henry watched as she dragged out a Persian rug; although it was a little threadbare in the middle, she liked the richness of its pattern. There followed a black papier-mâché table with mother of pearl decoration, a matching chair with a wobbly leg. But she found something else, two oak picture frames with wooden backboards. -*Perfect.* These she tucked under arm and took them to her room.

She held a print against the mount, checking for size. -*It'll do!* May removed the wooden backs of the two picture frames she had claimed from the storage room. In one, she placed a chromolithograph of Our Lady. Behind her print she laid a piece of cardboard, tacked in some spacing chocks made from folded card. It was here that May put her coins, lined them up on the backing cardboard and then covered them over with the wooden back board.-*Guard over them sacred mother, keep it safe.* Then she thought, -*Maybe Holy Mother wouldn't want to guard a whore's lucre!* But she hoped she would understand. The other was to be a present for her father, brighten up their room.

Chapter 9

May stared at the coin. It would add nicely to her savings, take her further towards her destiny. Henry held the coin out, willing her to take it. May stepped forward, lifted her palm and paused.

"Thank you Henry."

"Oh, May."

And he reached out and undid her apron string, and removed the white cap from her head. May reached up and undid the hairpins and her released hair tumbled down.

"Your skirts now." And May removed them.

Henry walked to his chair by the window and turned it so it faced into the room not out, at the view from the wrong end of the Grubb. May stood in her boots, stockings, and her chemise, it reached to just above her knees.

"Ah, silk stockings." And Henry sighed.

May reached down and took the chemise off, dropping it at her ankles and stepped from it. She stood before Henry in her drawers, her shoes, and stockings.

Henry sighed, "Come here."

And May stood before him, "Sit over me May." and May faced Henry, her legs straddling him as he sat in his chair.

His fingers between her crotch less drawers. And taking his finger, he massaged her inner thigh, brushing the back of his knuckle against her lip, teasing himself. Gently then, he slid his finger from outside to her inner lips opening her like a flower. His index finger pushed into her and his thumb pressed down on he, moving slowly. Henry bent forward and sucked her nipple.

Her skin glowed in this firelight and she smelled of lavender. A bead of sweat appeared on Henry's forehead, which May leaned forward and kissed away. May undid the old man's trouser fly and felt the hard, but not ramrod straight dick. She pulled it from its constraint, it stood just in front of her, and May moved forward and raised her bum off Henry's lap and touched the end of his dick to her. She moved her hips gently back and forth over him rubbing him against her lips. Clasping his cock in her hand, she squeezed the head. She pushed it against her and slid it along the edge of her lips. She paused, took him in her hand she sat over him, it banged against her and pushing forward she lowered herself over him. Henry gasped.

She bobbed up and down, like a little boat on the ocean. And Dear Henry, rolled with the waves, ripples of pleasure washed over him. Then May did something Henry found most extraordinary she, -*She's bloody squeezing my dick, with her fanny!*

Gasping, Henry was out of control for May had taken the high ground. He could only thrust if she shifted her weight from his lap. And Henry wanted it faster now. She was keeping him from … May lowered herself and squeezed, up and down.

Henry was set to fire, but he couldn't because she'd stopped. Finally, finally, she rose, he was on the crest of … And then she… stopped again. -*Why is she torturing me?* Henry grabbed her arse and hoisted her up, no sooner had he done that -and she just a slip of a thing! Lowered herself again. And the tide ebbed away.

And it was then that May raised herself up and dismounted him, like she was clambering off the rigging, and she knelt before his thighs. And pulled his cock. -*Not too bloody gently!* Towards her mouth, and she nibbled and sucked, tasting the saltiness of this dog. Henry could not stand any more. He came forward from his chair and pushed May back. He jumped on her, took himself in his hand, and between May's thighs, with one well-targeted thrust, rammed his dick home. He was a cannon rammed, ready for firing and with one final salvo, discharged.

May held Henry's head and kissed his forehead, he'd gotten up a sweat, the old man, and she cuddled him. He reminded her of a child; although he'd just fucked her. She didn't feel either brutalised or degraded, perhaps she should! But she felt a tenderness for him. One moment she didn't want sex and now she was doing it of her own free (at a price) will, but only to a purpose. And she kissed old Henry on his cheek. May had purpose, and that purpose was self-improvement.

This was the pattern they agreed. As good as his word, once a week, and depending on the coin in his pocket, if the coin were small then so were May's favours. But if the coin were half a sovereign, she would perform better and in this unspoken way, May trained Henry. The more you pay the more you get, simple. And as Wally said, that's what makes the world go round, capitalism.

***

"Walter, I have a list of things. I want you to get for me."

"What is it?"

"Stuff, you know ladies stuff."

"Can't you ask Gert?"

"Look, do you want to help or not?"

"What's it worth? Go on May, you raise yer skirt, and I'll think about it."

"I'll raise my bloody fist in a minute."

"Got to be worth at least that."

"A shilling, and that's too much, and you're not to tell a living soul, or I'll come for you, Wally."

"So, what is it yer want then?"

"It's on this list."

"Yer know I can't read…just bloomin' tell me."

"Ladies stuff, there's rouge, and rice powder, etc, etc."

"What's all this for then? You going on the streets?"

"Walter Rackett, I swear if you want this shilling you just better keep that buttoned." And she jabbed at his lips.

"Just bloody tell me, I'll remember."

"Well like I said."

"I know, rouge, and rice powder, blah, blah. What else?"

"A book, a book called e-ro-ti-c."

"Erotic!"

"Yep, that's what it says. I've never read it so…but can you get it?"

"Dunno, should think so … who wants it then?"

"None of your business, Wally."

May swung round, shoved her nose in the air, and walked back to her home.

***

Reverend Dolling knocked on the door at Hope Street. May reddened, "Father, please come in." "Thank you May… And Father Dolling led the way to the fireplace where last night's embers were grey ash in the hearth. He turned his back on the fire. "Just came to see how you're doing May? Your father is getting better. I understand."

"Yes Father, in a couple of months he'll be right to return to his work"

"And you May, how are you faring at your new occupation?"

"Very well, I believe they … the family are pleased with me…"

"Good, good; your father's old commander you're working for isn't it?"

"Yes Father. He's very kind."

"I just came to say May you're not to worry about your family while you're away. I look in, and there's Mrs Whittle, she's helping too, just until your father finds his, well, finds his feet again … We missed you at mass…"

"Sorry Father, I had…"

"Don't apologise," and he put his hand up as if he were brushing away a fly. I hope on your next day off you'll come to the service."

"Oh yes, dad'll be better and I won't have to…"

"Won't what, May?"

"I just had errands to run, for Mrs Spritely."

"Don't think do they? This your only time off….Oh well, why should they?" And he started to make for the door.

"Father would you like some tea?"

"No May, I must get off." And he placed his hat on his head… and without turning back said, "Next leave May…I'll expect to see you…11 o'clock…don't be late."

"Yes Father."

***

May poked the embers. The others had gone to bed … A rapping at the door… "Walter?"

"Come on, let me in."

"Shh, just keep it down, they're asleep…"

May jerked her head towards the table where Walter dumped down a bundle wrapped in a dirty cloth."

"That's everything."

May raised her eyebrows she hadn't expected such a large parcel… "And that's not a book…that erotic. That's a dirty book…" May looked at him.

"What do you mean it's not a book, it's a dirty book?"

"It's a book alright, but a book with… dirty bits in…It's a book…"

May began to think Walter was having a bit of a laugh at her expense, "Have you brought me the book or not?" asked May

"I've got a book that has Erotic written on the first page."

May was starting to get cross with Walter.

"The book called erotic, but it's not the erotic book it's an 'erotic' book." Wally smiled, pleased with himself, he'd quoted it exactly as was told to him. May opened the bundle and placed the contents on the tabletop. Brown paper parcels...Boxes and packages... And a book wrapped in paper with a string tied in a bow...

"Blimey there's pounds of the stuff; it's for painting a face not the bloody Guildhall."

"Well?" said Walter. Standing with his palm outstretched. May took a shilling from her purse and handed it to Wally. Wally bit into the coin and placed it in his jacket pocket.

He then stood aside as if to leave then made a sudden lunge at May.

"Get off Wally, for goodness' sake."

"Oh come on May. Just a little kiss, let me look at yer. Go on May... Just raise yer skirt, just a little..."

"Walter!"

"Please." And he grabbed her around her waist.

"Walter, let go, you bloody nitwit..."

Walter bowed and left...whistling as he made his way back home. Very pleased he'd managed to have a feel of May's breast, insensitive to the clip round his ear hole. Bloody stung now though!

And he rubbed it, get some feeling back.

***

Monday morning. The tram journey would take half an hour. May had all the decanted little packages in a canvas bag. The book wrapped in paper was on the top of all the other parcels ... May decided to take a peep at this book, what harm could she do? She pulled the string and the bow unfurled. A little book with blue cloth boards, entitled: The Adventures of Father Silas. Published by The Erotic Bibliography Library.

So this is what erotic means...A religious text. Father Dolling probably has this book too. May read on...And blinked. She couldn't believe what she was reading... This is a monk's initiation? It can't be so... - *Bloody hell.* One monk on another, and another...a chain of monks, a chain of fucking monks... In front of the altar...! E-ro-ti-ca, this is a word she would look up...Do I have the right book? Do I hand this to Mrs Spritely? May didn't know what to do... It was a dilemma she'd have to solve before she reached Fairview House.

I hand over the book. If it is what Agnes wants, then all will be well. And May twirled a tendril of her hair in her fingers. If it isn't, it will shock her, she'll think I'm an idiot, or a wanton, or both. She'll sack me... Glad, Lil and little Freddie will starve now me dad's not working.

I don't hand the book over! I lie, I say I couldn't get the book, but then, Mrs Spritely will of course expect to have her money returned...Which means ... I'll have to pay for the book, I'll have to replace the money... books aren't cheap...all my hard earned money ...

Pondering her position, she hadn't noticed the man leaning over her shoulder, reading the book that lay open on her lap. The monks anal fucking in full swing. May snapped the book closed. The man leered at her; his eyes roaming over her face, to her breasts, back at her face and he smirked. He suddenly stood up; May pulled back wondering what he would do.... She sighed as he made his way to the exit. He turned to her and winked... "Religious little thing are you? Good Catholic girl...?" he said, as he jumped from the tram.

May flushed, and concentrated on the very interesting cobbles outside the tram window, interlaced with mounds of moss and horse shit.

***

May intended to head for the library. Greetings exchanged; Dolly asked May, after she'd freshened up, to take Mrs Spritely a cup of tea and a bourbon biscuit. Mrs Spritely was taking an afternoon nap. May nipped up to her bedroom, placed the packages in her wardrobe; splashed water on her face, and tied on her apron as she ran down the stairs to the library. She knocked tentatively.

No answer. May closed the door behind her. Reference books were on the shelf to the left of the window. Enc-ylo-ped-dia. Thesaurus. Dic-tion-ary. May heaved the huge dictionary on to the table. B, C, D and E ... Er-o-tic; From the Greek net.pl of erotikus. Pl. amatory (see erotic) originally a bookseller's catalogue heading... Well, that's clear! -*As mud.* May flipped back to the A's. Amatory am-a-to-ry adj. Of, relating to or expression of love especially sexual... *Blimey!*

May took the list from her pocket turned the pages to E's and letter-by-letter compared. Well, that's that then. Who'd have thought ... Mrs Spritely...? Well I never! May wasn't sure why any woman would want to -have sexual carnage. As she followed the chain of words, ca-rnal, carnal knowledge, without the need of a coin or five, Bloody hell, it hurt and it was wrong... But if you're married, it's not wrong, it's sanctified.

Confident she'd acquired the knowledge she needed to hand the book to Mrs Spritely, she closed the dictionary and heaved it back on its shelf, and returned to the kitchen. "Perfect timing," said Dolly, as she draped a linen cloth on a tea tray. May placed the teacup and saucer, and plate, with three bourbon biscuits, onto the cloth. "No one has to tell you twice, do they? said Dolly, smiling. "Now, don't forget, knock and then enter. Gently call her name to wake her."

"You've already told me that," said May giggling.

Dolly tutted. She was growing fond of that girl ...very fond indeed, and she went over to hold the door open for May to pass.

***

Agnes lay on her day bed, her long hair loose, trailing over the cotton pillow like a red river. May opened the curtains, sunlight bathed Agnes' face and gently woke her from her slumber and a disturbing and an extraordinarily naughty dream. Agnes smiled and stretched, like a cat bathing in a pool of light. "Hello May, lovely, tea. Tea and bourbon biscuits!" she said, as May poured water into the pot. While she waited for it to brew, she helped Agnes sit up, plumped her pillow, and set it behind her back.

"Come and sit beside me May," and she patted a place on the bed. "Did you manage to find any of those articles?"

"Yes Agnes, they're in my room," she said, as she fished in her apron for the list. May had written alongside the list the cost of each item. She handed the paper to Mrs Spritely.

"How exciting… As soon as you've poured my tea, go and fetch them to me."

***

The packages lay scattered on the bed. "May, lock the door we don't want any disturbance!"

Mrs Spritely was turning over the packages trying to work out what they all contained. The book was back in its wrapper and tied up with a string bow. Agnes pulled it open. She read aloud, the title impressed in gold on the front cover: "The Adventures of Father Silas!" she said, frowning. May continued to open the packages…

Mrs Spritely read. Her eyebrow rose… She looked up. May wasn't looking at her, that's good. -*My goodness what are these monks doing? And on an altar.*

"Everything alright?" May asked, as she tidied away the last of the paper.

"Oh, yes May, just surprised…It's the book."

May went pale, so it was the wrong book. "Is it not what you wanted Agnes?"

"Why yes, and rather more. I'm pleased, it's just I had no idea there could ever be…well, such writings."

May stood in front of Mrs Spritely lost for words; she had no idea whether this was wrong or right. -*More than she wanted?*

"Come sit. Have you read this?"

Chapter 10

"Oh no. I just asked for the e-rot-ic book as you wrote it and I was given that...but you like it?"

"I'm not sure if like is the right word, intrigued I think, is the correct word." May frowned, she didn't know what 'intrigued' meant either. May made up her mind to educate herself, she would listen to this family and copy their voices and mannerisms; steal time in the library and borrow the books ... But not starting with the dictionary, - *it weighed a bloody ton...*

***

May mixed the henna with warm water from the jug and mixed it into a paste.

"What we'll do is a few streaks, just to cover the..."

"Grey," said Agnes, helpfully.

"Silver. You never know how it's going to turn out," said May. I've seen some women look brighter than a ginger tom-cat."

"Oh."

"Don't worry. I'll do a few tendrils so we'll know how your hair takes it. My mother did her hair with tea; she never washed it out, just left it on. I'll just wrap this towel round your shoulders. It's a bugger to get out! Sorry, difficult...hard to remove."

May pinned Agnes' hair into a topknot and pulled a few tendrils down and combed with henna paste. When she had finished she said, "Lean back," and she took a little brush and brushed it lightly over Mrs Spritely's eyebrows. Agnes glanced at herself in the mirror, looking at her profile this way then that. It looked like mud and it smelled, odd.

"May have you used henna before?"

"Well... Now we leave it on ..."

"How long for?"

"Well, that depends... how much colour we want, an hour at least. Meanwhile I'll go and fetch the other things

I need from the kitchen. And I can let Dolly know where I am at the same time."

"Dolly! She doesn't need to know."

"She'll be working on her own…. Making the dinner and —"

"All she needs to know is you're with me; that's the end of the matter. I don't want her knowing of this. Is that clear? The servants, thinking I'm a vain, silly woman."

"No, Mrs …I'll just say I have some work to do for you. That I'll be running a bath … so she doesn't get too nosey." May said, as she pulled a little of the paste away from her hair to check the colour.

"How does it look?"

"You're going to be the belle of the ball."

"That won't be difficult! Only Henry for dinner."

***

"I think that's ready, I'll run the bath for you now Mrs… Agnes."

"Very good," said Agnes, not sure it would be good, whether she'd been rash to trust this, girl. Oh well, it's done. And she slid the monk's story from under the cushion and read on…

May tested the water, adjusted the cold tap a little, and added lavender oil. The towels were warm. She'd never seen a bathroom such as this. That tin bath in front of the fire, the water shared with her father, her mother, then her, didn't count. Since her mother had died, she'd moved up the ranking, just after her father. Freddie was the last in the tub, and the last user of the water after the other four bodies; it wasn't so much getting clean as spreading the grime around…. "The bath is ready for you now Agnes."

"Thank you." Agnes rose to follow May, slipping the account of Silas' Adventures back under the cushion. In the bathroom, Agnes raised her arms; May removed her gown, folded, and placed it on the wicker chair. Agnes stepped into the warm lilac coloured water.

"Lovely."

"We're going to wash it off now, the henna, so, dunk."

"Dunk?!"

"Dunk, dunk your head."

Agnes dunked. Emerged spluttering, rivulets of stained water ran down her breasts and the water turned a rust red. "Don't worry about that," May said. May reached for the jug and filled it with fresh water from the basin to pour over Agnes' head. "Hold your breath." Agnes inhaled deeply. "Stand up now." May took the large pitcher and poured the water over Agnes' body removing the last of the henna's muddy streaks. May offered her the warm soft towel and Agnes stepped from the bath.

May turned back and looked at the state of the bathroom. *-Looks like bloody murder in here!* May followed Agnes through to the bedroom. Agnes sat in front of the dressing table's mirror and May removed the towel from Agnes' head.

"Well?"

"We'll wait till it's dry, then we'll see," May said. Agnes' hair hung in ringlets almost to her waist. May pulled the comb gently through the plentiful locks; teasing the tendrils with her fingers. The combing over, Agnes sat in her chair at the fireside, her head bent forward to dry her hair.

Agnes returned to the Monk's adventures: 'She was panting for breath; her arms lying down, and her bosom heaved with astonishing rapidity. My eyes ran over every part of her body with inconceivable expedition; nor was there a spot on which my ardent imagination did not fix a thousand burning kisses. I sucked her bubbles, her belly; but the most delicious place, from which my eyes, when once they found it, could not be removed, was ...

You understand me. How charming did that jewel appear to me! Oh what lovely colouring! Although covered with a white froth, it lost in my eyes nothing of its brilliancy. By the delight I felt, I recognized in it the very focus of pleasure. It was shaded with black and curly hair. Annette lay with her legs parted, and it seemed as if her lechery was in accord with my curiosity, in order to leave me nothing to desire.' May returned to the bathroom, and mopping!

May picked up the hand mirror from the dressing table. "See." Agnes took the mirror, and blinked. Turning her face this way, then that, Agnes didn't see a ginger cat, no, she saw ... looked closely again; her hair shiny, lustrous, red lights glinting in the glow from the fire; she saw her crowning glory. Her brows arched and defined, she had definition. She smiled at herself, then at May. "May, my hair it's lovely."

"It is the most beautiful hair I've ever seen."

"I never expected ... I do have beautiful hair."

***

The second time she met Sir William Baker it was an improved Agnes who greeted her host. "Agnes darling, you do look well," Francis said, as she kissed her on both cheeks. One eyebrow rose in puzzlement at this change in her sister. Mr Baker had a certain twinkle; the more his eyes shone the more Agnes glowed.

"Coffee?" said Francis. "Well, you've become more adventurous since I last saw you ... two weeks a go!" She added, presumably for dramatic effect.

"I shall join you Agnes, a pot of your best Arabica ... and a jug of cream," said Sir William Baker.

"Sir Baker is working on improving the lot of the Dockyard men," said Francis.

Agnes was impressed, not with the fight against poverty, of which she had little knowledge, and even less imagination to consider their plight; but Sir William's hand had come to rest on her knee. Agnes smiled and nodded wisely.

Francis looked at her sister. *-Something odd, something is different.* Francis would have said superior, but she was finding it as hard to be charitable as it was for Agnes to stop her eyelashes fluttering. She doesn't look like Agnes. The third meeting and Francis unfortunately couldn't witness the final stage in Agnes' metamorphosis. She wasn't invited.

***

Francis was not content with the change in her sister; she was not jealous. *-Of course not ... but, in two weeks, since I last saw her, she's dropped at least ten years and is now a coffee drinker! Something's afoot! I shall get to the bottom of it; that is a promise.*

***

The honourable Sir Baker, MP leaned back in his chair and rubbed his paunch. "I suggest, lovely ladies; on a day such as this, we take a stroll along the prom. Promenade along the Esplanade. Catch the sun's rays." The ladies rose as one. Mr Baker held out both his arms. "A beautiful lady on each arm, no man could ask for more!"

"Oh, Mr Baker, I must decline," said Francis. "I am recuperating, and I wouldn't want to risk ... my recovery."

"My dear Francis, how insensitive of—"

"Don't be silly, you're too much of a gentleman ... I need my sleep, just go, be gone and leave me to rest."

"Surely you won't disappoint me Agnes?" he asked, as he held out his arm to her.

"No, Mr Baker, I will not refuse you. I shall enjoy a stroll." And the two disappeared from the hotel lobby and down the marble steps ... Watched by an intrigued Francis. They passed the newly installed drinking fountain on Clarence Parade and headed, arm in arm across The Common towards Clarence Pier.

"Well this is a good starting point. We'll walk to South Parade Pier." Agnes rested her hand lightly on his left arm. A gentle breeze blew from the sea. He showed her the Isle of Wight, shining like a jewel in the green sea. He pointed to the sea forts and gave her a little of their history. Agnes loved walking with him. She felt proud of the attention he received and if just to prove her point a gentleman nodded to him, and raised his hat to her. It happened again, and again. A few auburn curls escaped from under her hat, tendrils she tried to push back, but finally gave in to their freedom seeking cause. Her cheeks blushed a soft pink from the bracing air. Not artifice! But she was glad it wasn't raining.

Mr Baker motioned to a bench, "Let's take a moment. I have something I'd like to ask you." As they sat facing the sea on the bench closest to the pier he said, "I want you to do something for me Agnes. I'm invited to a gathering; would you do me the honour of accompanying me? I do find these events tedious. But with you by my side, I feel well … I may enjoy it. Please say you will. I warn you though; it will be deadly dull." Agnes looked down at her feet. This shift in her position masked her face from Mr Baker's gaze; hidden by the extraordinary arrangement of flowers, fruit and parrot wings perched on her head.

Her fingers played with the ivory parasol handle. She turned her face to him; her eyes shaded by the size of her hat. She said, "You make it awkward for me to say, no. I'd love to, William, I'm sure it won't be dull. It will please me to escort you for the evening."

***

In two weeks, just two weeks. Agnes would be stepping out, staying away, from home…In a hotel. No harm done; just a little white lie. He, Henry never missed her while she was away, staying with her sister, or when she looked after her mother in the last few weeks of her life.

So at breakfast the following morning … "Francis wants me to escort her, to a soiree, in two weeks, a rather dull affair," she said. "She doesn't want to go alone, wants someone to talk with."

Henry without looking up from his paper said, "Yes dear." And that was that.

But Agnes continued, "I'll be staying overnight, back next day…" Henry muttered something, and continued reading. Agnes sighed. Probably hasn't heard me at all; just interrupted his reading about someone or other's misspent money and losses on the stock market.

***

Agnes draped a veil over her face. She'd had her cosmetics artfully applied by May. Agnes felt self-conscious, but also something else, she felt excitement. She wished May could have accompanied her. Wished evening were here, and candle, not daylight were playing on her face.

But she couldn't involve May, couldn't share her deceit with a servant! Even though, it was innocent. - *Nothing had happened, nothing could happen. –Stupid, feeling so guilty.*

***

Agnes had a room in the Royal Pier Hotel. A pearl clasp in her hair held silk roses surrounded by sprigs of gypsophila. She wore a satin midnight blue, silk dress; a pearl choker with a sapphire centre stone adorned her throat. Agnes admired herself in the mirror. Her mouth stroked from the little pot of paraffin and beeswax stained with bergamot, made her lips glisten in the candle light. Her hair shone with amber lights and cheeks, just blushed pink …

The porter knocked and informed Agnes a gentleman had arrived, and was waiting in reception for her. Agnes took a deep breath and left her room. Mr Baker was standing by a large tea palm. He watched as Agnes descended the stairs, coming closer at each tread. He smiled, Agnes nodded, and he removed his top hat and bowed.

They stood on a balcony overlooking the Solent, and although it was early autumn, the evening was clear and bright. William said, as he covered her hand with his on the balcony railing, "I enjoyed this evening and it's only because of the excellent company."

A quartet of musicians played and Agnes paused before she said, "A lovely evening, I'm sure it would be lovely regardless of the company." *-Good grief, I'm fishing for compliments, how vulgar.* And she glanced down, embarrassed at her lack of sophistication.

"No, because and only because of the lady who is by my side." He took her hand in his and lowered his lips to her hand and kissed her fingers. He pulled her to him, and she not resisting, kissed her lips. She neither returned his kiss nor turned away. Mr Baker repeated his kiss on those red lips, and then she did, she kissed him. Mr Baker knew it was going to be a splendid evening, indeed.

He escorted her through the throng and outside her room, he cupped her face in his hands and pulled her towards him. He kissed her, pushed his tongue into her mouth. Mr Baker the right honourable, wished her a good night. He bowed and returned to the soiree. He chatted amiable for half an hour. *-Should be a respectable enough period!* He took a brandy and walked to the balcony and watched the waves roll onto the shingle beach. He cut and lit a cigar. *-A pleasurable way to spend the interlude,* he thought.

"Mr Baker, William old chap, enjoying yourself, are you?"

"Councillor Michael." *-Good grief, the town's bore.*

"Mind if I keep you company?" He said. "Smashing night, what? I'd have thought you'd be with that rather lovely red head. Not with the wife then?"

"No, Mabel alas, couldn't be with me tonight. Too many soirées, rather fatigued by them."

"Not like us, eh? Our duty, to be both seen, and see," he said, accepting the proffered cigar. So instead of drawing breath he sucked on the end of a Havana.

He blew out a long puff and it formed a halo above his head.

"Saint Michael," he quipped."

William smiled encouragingly. *-How many times have I witnessed that jape?*

William sipped, then threw his head back and gulped. Michael asked about the lady on his arm. "Wasn't introduced see …!"

"That's because you were busy engaging every one with your conversation." Mr Michael ignored or was ignorant of the knock. *-There's a benefit to being a fool, a bloody thick skin.* "Well, Richard, off to my bed; I'll see you for breakfast, shall I?" And without waiting a reply, he left, nodding to his fellow guests as he strolled from the meeting room.

Chapter 11

Agnes sat at her dressing table. She combed her hair, released from its pins it cascaded down her back in ringlets. Her dress lay tossed over a chair. Her silk lace nightgown was loose at the neck revealing snow-white shoulders. Agnes looked at her reflection, her appearance pleased her. It seemed such along time since anyone had taken much of an interest in her, and indeed, she'd taken little interest in herself. But now ...

A light tap and a pause before the interconnecting door opened. William Baker filled the frame carrying two glasses set on a tray. "A nightcap," he said.

Agnes though surprised, nodded, "I hadn't realised ...."

"We don't want all our time together determined by gawpers and gossips..."

"We were ... That you were next door ... I"

William stepped forward and placed the tray on her dressing table handing her the brandy filled glass.

"Here, just a little nightcap." And he chinked her glass. He went down on bended knee. *-He can't propose. I'm married!*

"Agnes," he said, as he placed his head on her lap. "Let me stay for a moment." And she touched his head and stroked his hair.

William took her glass from her hand. "Kiss me," he said. Agnes made no move towards him; but Mr Baker turned towards her and kissed her. She did not respond, so he kissed her again, slowly, pushing his tongue between her lips, and Agnes did respond. She kissed him. Agnes decided! She knew what Sir William, wanted and she'd decided to give it to him. He nibbled her ear, he whispered, "Agnes, I need you."

***

Agnes smelt cigar smoke on his breath, and tasted the brandy on his lips. He kissed her neck and Agnes raised her head, and their lips met. He tugged at the silk ribbon on her gown and the neckline slipped just enough to reveal the red uppermost part of her breast. William lowered his mouth pushing away the cloth with his lips. He sucked her nipple. He sucked while his head lay across her chest, and she stroking his hair.

Agnes said, "Shh." Gently rocking William Baker as he lay in her lap, his lips nibbling so gently on her breast. He wanted to see more. He wanted her, but he wanted it all. He eased himself from her and looked at her with her nightdress hanging loose at her waist her breast exposed. He pulled off his jacket and threw it on the floor, there followed his tie and shoes. He offered her a sip of brandy from the glass the held. She sipped, wetting her lips. He knelt down before her and he opened her legs, pushing his face between her thighs.

William pushed his tongue gently as lightly as a butterfly's wing, kissing her soft white thigh. He heard her sigh. He licked, harder now... Agnes groaned, it was then he paused, raising his head he looked up at Agnes, her eyes were closed and her head thrown back.

He bent her legs up on the chair so her feet rested on the seat. And here she is, this beautiful woman exposed, and he wanted her. "My god, so beautiful. Oh Agnes ... so lovely. Agnes ..." He opened his fly and he took himself in his hand, kneeling in front of Agnes, he stove himself into her. But after just a few thrusts, he withdrew.

He placed his head against her inner thigh. She quivered beneath his questing fingers, and he stoked her hair, keeping his distance, before lightly brushing her lips, touching her with his tongue.

Agnes thrust her hips forward. -*This is torment,* she thought. She pushed for an end to this exquisite torture. She wanted him... but again he kissed her, and again he paused. Agnes moaned. And Mr Baker stopped... again.

"Please," she whispered.

Agnes' breath came faster and deeper, she was poised on the edge of a precipice … And he stopped.

Agnes cried out, "Please."

William pulled her from the chair and flung her gently but firmly to the floor. Tugging her nightgown to her waist, he drove himself into her.

Thrust after thrust. Agnes sighed. But Mr Baker withdrew, once more… Agnes trembled with frustration. - *He's driving me insane.* William took her in his mouth and he kissed her with his tongue, hard now and fast. Agnes shivered with sheer wonderfulness. He touched her with his thumb, his fingers hard and urgent… so hard. Agnes thought she wouldn't, couldn't bear it. Wave after wave, a thousand pleasurable sensations, rolled over her body. Agnes raised her hips and thrust upwards. And while Agnes was in the throes of abandonment, Mr Baker drove his cock hard into her; once, twice, three times, on, and on…

***

"Let me stay the night. Let me sleep in those white arms," he pleaded. He didn't wait for permission but jumped beneath the covers. "Agnes come." The clock on a nearby church struck two. Agnes shifted her position and William curled into her back. She felt his hardness, and whether he knew she was sleeping or not, he entered her and he thrust gently and comfortingly, in and out. He pushed himself further now, and as Agnes sighed he shuddered, and gave an involuntary groan …

He kissed her neck and whispered, "I must go. My dearest, my most lovely lady." He kissed her hand as he left her bed, gathering his clothes he said, "Parting, a sweet sorrow…" And the interconnecting door closed behind him. Agnes heard the key turn in the lock.

The following morning after the hotel maid had packed her cases, Agnes slipped down to reception to pay her bill. In the dining room William and a gentleman were in close conversation, or rather William was listening to

Mr Michael councillor, with rapt attention!

"Bill's paid Madam," said the desk clerk.

"Really?"

"Yes Madam, you're the guest of Sir Baker, Madam. Porter! The lady's baggage, if you please," he said, as he snapped his fingers. Agnes swept out of the Royal Pier Hotel and into a carriage that would drive her to the station. She glanced back through the rear window and saw William. He stood on the steps looking after her, and he continued to watch until she turned the corner onto Osborne Road.

Agnes had had the most wonderful night. Mr Baker was the most loving gentleman she'd ever known. -*Well, I've only known two, and one of those includes Henry, and he doesn't count.*

***

"Thursday, I'd like you to accompany me to Southsea, Palmerston Road."

"Yes Agnes." -*What the bloody hell does she want me for, in that part of town?* May had been there once, a fish out of water with her homemade dress and scuffed boots.

As if Agnes had read her thoughts she said, "Shopping. I'm going shopping and I'd like you to carry and make yourself useful." Agnes had thought of asking her sister, but she'd seen that inquisitive expression, she'd ask far too many questions. There was Dolly of course, but again, far too curious.

She could carry of course. Dolly could carry an ox if necessary. But in taste and artistry, she was a pumpkin. May had advantages, as both aide and adviser, but her main asset was her lack of curiosity; she hadn't been in her employ long enough to become ... familiar.

May wondered what she should wear for the excursion. She felt both excited and nervous. "You're uniform of course," answered Dolly. "You'll be working, it's not a day out for you, you know. Make it pristine… scrub up…"

***

Thursday morning came; Joseph took Agnes and May to the station, in the cart he'd hired from Dan Hawkins, at Cosham.

Handleys department store sat on the corner of Palmerston and Osbourne Road, huge windows displayed all manner of goods. May followed Agnes through one of the many doors held open by doormen wearing bottle green uniforms with gold braid trailing the seams on their trousers.

Agnes made her way to the fabric department via haberdashery. "Madam, may I help?" said a man, with his head held at such a tilt head! *-All I can see is the hair up his nose.* He swept forward, brushing May aside as he showed Madam the, "Velvet Madam, forest green; feel the richness of this fabric." May saw a blue, peacock blue, an iridescent heavy silk, its weft emerald, she took a sample to the window the sunlight made the colours shimmer.

"Lovely, of course," Monsieur said, determined to press his favoured fabric; snatching the swatch from May's hand. "So suitable though, green, for such colouring as yourself." And he smiled. -Sneered! At Agnes. May thought, *-Not so much forest as khaki; if you want to camouflage yourself; hide among the mother-in-laws-tongues, perfect.* This green velvet though, and May's fingers stroked the nap, this apple green is beautiful.

Agnes decided, because she couldn't decide, she'd leave it. Monsieur aware that he was about to lose a customer, agreed with May! "The fabric she held was beautiful and would suit Madame well." -God, am I never to be rid of this bolt of velvet? Been hanging around since last season's collection.

"For a dress Madam?" he asked. Agnes nodded. "Twelve yards then. And may I recommend an excellent seamstress, from Paris; Louise Le Merchand." He handed her a card: Madame Louise Le Merchand, Great Southsea Street, Paris Couturier.

"If you were to use Madame Le Merchand, I could have it sent directly to her. Please mention my name when you see her, for the best service." -*Otherwise, I won't get my commission.*

Agnes said, "And wrap the twelve yards of apple green velvet. I'll return for the bundles after I've visited other departments." And with that, she swept out with May trailing in her wake.

Hats! Hats on shelves and hats on stands, hats on women's heads. Tried on and taken off. Hats of straw and hats of velvet, hats made of felt. Parrot feathers, pheasant feathers, ostrich, peacock, and paradise, an aviary of birds trussed to each ensemble.

***

Agnes sat at a dressing table, May stood to her side. A lady shop assistant appeared. "I rather like the ivory silk," Agnes said, pointing to a hat on a stand. And after trying on twenty hats, she decided on the ivory silk, and a fruit cocktail construction. "No need for delivery, I'll take them with me."

May now stood in the underwear department; a manikin wore the newest steel bone corset. Agnes chose half a dozen silk stockings in various colours. Two silk petticoats trimmed with lace, and four pairs of drawers trimmed with satin ribbon. May prodded that corset, 'a la mode', May hummed, 'Only a bird in a gilded cage.' And twanged the corset's metal strap.

The haberdashery a dazzling array: ribbons, trims, lace, buckles, buttons, and bows lined the glass counter for Agnes' approval. And she did approve, she liked everything she saw. She'd never given Henry cause to complain about her expenditure, now she was making up for it, spoiling herself, a little, she deserved it. She didn't allow the thought of her lover receiving the benefit of these goods to intrude.

"After we collect our packages we should take a little refreshment." So after gathering all the bundles, parcels and packages, including two striped hatboxes, they headed to Osborne Road.

May who carried the bundles struggled to keep up. Agnes said, "Let me help you." And took a parcel containing lace trimmings. May was shown to a back room where other women, who served, received refreshment. At the front of the rooms on the first floor and overlooking the department store, Agnes was shown to her table.

From this lofty position, she could see all of Osborne Road. She enjoyed looking at the ladies, their hats. She decided she would see which one she liked the best. *-No! Or that…!* Then an idea came to her, she would buy May a new hat … and a gift for Henry.

***

May hated this room. The walls painted a gloss green over anaglypta wallpaper; a colour similar to that horrible fabric Monsieur wanted to foist on Agnes. The other women eyed her with curiosity. One put on her glasses so she could peer over the lenses. May studied much like any insect.

After an interminable time, gawped at by the women's league of old maids, at last, "Your mistress wants you." *-Curt!* May gathered the belongings and headed for the main dining room where she could help Agnes with her package. May carried two rolls of fabric, two hatboxes, three parcels and three bags hung on her arms from string and ribbon loops.

"Come May, I have something else to get." *-Blimey I've no more limbs spare, there's my head, s'pose she could stuff something on that.*

And that was exactly what Agnes intended to do. So off they strolled down Palmerston Road with May straggling some few yards behind bearing her burdens, with she hoped, great dignity.

"Come May."

"May I help you?" the assistant asked.

"I want something for the girl. May put down the packages. You are going to have a new hat."

"I … thank you."

"Now what would be suitable, I wonder? This little straw boater." May gaped. "Then we could dress it, well you could. But there's sure to be some bits and bobs left over from those trimmings. Try it on." And May did.

"Well look then, look in the mirror tell me whether you like it?"

May looked. *-Blimey, look at that.* A new hat and with some ribbons and fresh flowers … she could ring all sorts of changes. May cocked her head and smiled.

Agnes said to the assistant, "We'll take it." The box, tied, handed over, and shoved under May's spare arm. "5/6," said the assistant.

-5/6. Five bloody bob! That's nearly our rent for a week. I'd rather had the money! And she told herself she was being bloody ungrateful. And anyway, it is the best hat she'd ever owned, a new, new hat. She'd never owned anything that hadn't been worn, frequently out, by someone else. The shape of it altered. Clothes that fitted a woman in the 1880's cut down for a girl in the 90's. A child, then a baby the next beneficiaries. completing its life as a dishrag after service as a patchwork quilt.

They continued further, May paused to shuffle the packages into a more comfortable position, and looked up in time to see Agnes disappearing into a shop three doors along. May stopped and looked in a shop window. This tiny shop, its window with old panes of glass and painted a dark brown, can't have been more that twelve-foot across and that included the door. But what caught May's attention and fired her imagination was the paper notice pasted to the window; To Let, it said. Contact messrs: Fifty pounds per annum, payable in advance. *-Fifty pounds per annum? Fifty pounds! Wonder what an annum is?* She heard a low whistle then was surrounded and jostled by a young boy, his chum, and then another. "What you got there then?"

"Come on luv, give us a kiss."

"Making a bit! All for you is it?"

"How much'd charge then?"

Fortunately, Mrs Spritely came out of the shop just then. "I say!" Agnes cried. A passing gentlemen who had shown no interest in May's predicament, was all solicitations and good will when this lady appeared. - *Terrible circumstances, to have her maid accosted so.*

The boys ran off, and at some safe distance called back rude insults to the gentleman, and, "Sort you out next time, right good." May tried to pick up a bundle she'd dropped, but in doing so only managed to drop more. The gentleman sighed, stooped, and picked them up. May held out her arms for him to hang the bundles, much like a tree at Christmas.

The next stop was a tobacconist, in the window there were bowls of tobacco with exotic and fragrant names. There were silver lighters, gold cigarette boxes, and ivory cigarette holders. Agnes saw a cigar cutter in silver, perfect for William. Inside the shop she asked for two ounces of Golden Ambrosia tobacco, for Henry, after all he'd done for her!

On the train May said, "What does annum mean?

"Annum? Annum means a year or per year."

"Oh … right." May thought the shop could be bought for £50.

Agnes smiled gently and closed her eyes she'd had a tiring day.

Chapter 12

Mr Spritely had purloined, well, borrowed a rating's uniform while he was at The Dockyard visiting the mess. May, in the Crow's-Nest dressed as a matelot in that same sailor's uniform. Her hair was pulled up tight and secured under a naval cap. She wore bell-bottom trousers, a tight hip hugging tunic with a big square collar, the material was, -*Itchy as hell.* But then it always was. This was a sovereign day. May gulped. But she stood to attention and she saluted him as he strode past. But then May called him Henry and not Sir. Henry blew a whistle and yelled, "Time to come aboard." And he yanked down the rating's trousers to show the young matelot who was the officer, commissioned, and who was the deck scrubber. He took the cat in his hand and whisked it across May's white arse. She flinched and he did it again and again, ten lashings.

Then he rubbed salt and oil over the reddened cheeks and coming aboard charged headfirst up May's arse. The whole act finished with May dancing a hornpipe wearing just the sailor's cap. And another sovereign increased her collection.

She counted her stash, three pounds two shillings and sixpence, and a sore arse. What May needed him to do was have a sovereign experience every week. That way, in under a year she'd have the fifty quid she needed for her shop.

So every time he offered her just a half sovereign she lay as still as a barnacle. Henry moved about inside and May made groaning noises. But he never had a half sovereigns worth of cock sucking again. Henry handed her a sovereign and she sucked his dick. And so the bargain was struck.

And this was the pattern of their life until George came home, and he assumed his rights over May. With the brass neck not to leave May even a shilling. But

Henry was no help at all, he was happy to leave May in the hands of his son. *-What can be going through his head?* But what May hadn't realised was old Henry loved peeping just as much as he loved poking. So with his eye to May's keyhole and without a coin in his hand he got all the excitement he needed.

***

May was cleaning the library. She was perched atop the library steps with a feather duster in one hand and a copy of The Royal Natural History in the other. She was dusting the shelves from top to bottom, the title of a book impressed in gilt lettering, caught her eye and her imagination.

She intended to have just a peek; an hour later, engrossed her fingers tracing the coloured engravings; she'd reached the Gurnards section, such pretty colouring on such an odd-looking fish. May could read fairly well, but formed the words by joining up the sounds they made (platy-ce-phallus); she knew she was making excellent progress. She hadn't realised she was no longer alone, hadn't noticed the door opening, hadn't heard the tiptoed steps crossing the room.

George sat under the ladder. He was as absorbed in looking up her skirt, as May was lost in the strange names and illustrations she'd discovered in this book. Although they looked dusty and were musty, *-just a bit, they were also exciting and above all, beautiful.*

May swung her legs back and forth. She hadn't noticed her dress, where she'd plonked herself down, had ridden up slightly revealing the top of her boot. She was wearing woollen stockings knotted at the knee by a pearl button.

May flicked and then scratched at her knee. This meant her dress shifted even higher, and now a glimpse of her thigh was revealed. George groaned. "George," May said, as she jumped, the book fell to the floor as May attempted to straighten herself, and hopefully pull herself together. "I was just looking, such a lovely book."

"Just looking May? I've been here a good half hour; you were doing what you were doing for goodness knows how long before that."

"Sorry Sir." I've meant no harm."

"You may have meant no harm, you may have done no harm, but have you done any good? Eh? Show me." And his brown eyes slid down to May's breast, as he held out his hand.

"Sir?"

"Show me what you have there, the book. Show me the book."

May handed George the book; her eyes cast down, staring at her boots as if the stitching were a biblical text.

"Ah, the platycephallus interested in that, are you May? The phallus?"

May felt her face growing hot, wishing she could be anywhere else but here. How she hoped she'd never picked up that bloomin' book, she should have carried on dusting.

"So you read, May, do you?"

"Just a little Sir."

"I'll hear you then"

"Sir?"

"I'll hear you; read, read to me." George turned and chose at random a well-worn old book. *-Probably doesn't want me to spoil it,* May thought. George flicked though the tired, dog-eared pages. "This, read this to me." George moved over to the fireplace and settled back in the leather wingback chair, one leg hooked over the arm. May began.

"Can't hear you, May." May spoke louder. "No good, still can't hear you'll have to come here, stand there." And he pointed to a place on the rug with a downward dispatch of his thumb. May began to read. George closed his eyes and listened to the tale. His breaths came deeper and faster. May stumbled on a word but tried to work out the right way to say it. She broke each letter down, and formed the sounds on her parted lips.

May come here, sit there and he again gave the downward gesture with his thumb, this time to a point on the rug in front of his knees. May handed George the book and leaned forward showing him the word, she watched him as he spoke the word. "Fellatio, fellat-io. It's an Italian word."

"Italian? What does it mean?" And May began to follow the word with her finger and her mouth shaped the sounds. Fall-a-ti-o.

"It's a kiss, a secret kiss that can only be given to a man."

"I won't ever be given a fellatio then?"

"No May, you will never have it, but you may give it."

"How can I give something I never had in the first place?"

George thought about that for a second. His eyebrows pushed puzzled towards each other. He decided to ignore that stupid question; she was just a dim-witted girl, all be it a pretty one.

"Carry on May. Start from just before the fellatio part."

May started to rise to her feet, but a firm hand on her shoulder told her to stay. "Sit! Sit there May. I'll be on hand if you falter. I may help you to read properly. What do you say May? Would you like that? May, would you like it?"

"Yes Sir, I would like it."

With permission granted, George pushed May, who was kneeling at his feet, her face turned towards him, her body twisted awkwardly as he leapt from his seat and pinned her to the to the floor. May cried out in alarm and pain.

George brought the palm of his hand down onto her mouth … "Shh. This is what we agreed. I teach you reading, I get a something in return, and that's fair isn't it?" May lay under him unable to move, unable to make a sound, but able to feel that pain in her leg weighted and jammed under the chair. "Well May? George shifted his weight on to her twisted leg.

May nodded and tears filled her eyes.

"Sorry May, not hurting you am I?" He shifted his weight again this time relieving the pressure on her limb."

"Answer me May."

"No Sir".

"Now we fulfil our bargain. I'm going to help you with the word fellatio."

"Sir, I understand it. You've shown me the meaning."

"No May, I haven't, I'm going to show you the meaning, and you're going to show me you understand the meaning of the word, literally."

May went to speak, but George put his finger to his pouted lips and whispered, "Shh." He pulled May to a kneeling position in front of the chair. He nudged her aside as he climbed over her shoulder and settled himself on the seat with May between his opened thighs. George unbuttoned his trousers and slid his hand down and pulled out his up standing member.

May went to move, but George held her back, "Stay there, till I tell you to move. Carry on, read on." George stroked himself, staring at May, and he stroked... His breathing came faster. "May I want you now... now... before..." And he grabbed May's hair and jammed her head into his lap. "Kiss it." May pulled back. "Put your lips to it." He was urgent, he dived into his pocket, and pulled out a coin, she stared at it, a half crown! "Do it and you'll have this, don't and I will fuck you." She snatched the coin, and lowered her mouth to him. *-I could bite his bloody dick off. Sink me teeth in so far, his screams would echo like the cattle at slaughter in Moors Square.* But he'd left it a little too late and he spurted over her face, dripping from her chin and dribbling down her neck.

"Fellatio, can only be given to a man, understand? Well, do you understand?"

"Yes, Sir."

"Good, now serve my lunch, I'm hungry."

May clutched her coin and left his company.

***

May was due for her day off tomorrow. The first time she'll have seen her family since the festive season. She'd wrapped her presents in hand painted paper and tied with the ribbons she'd saved from her chocolate-box of delights. Glad and Lil would wear them in their hair. But the evening post brought a letter addressed to May.

Funny! Thought Dolly. "Looks like Mrs Spritely's handwriting. Why would she be writing to you?"

"I don't —"

"Better open it."

May was all ready reading the letter.

"Well?"

"Mrs Spritely, she wants me to visit her in Southsea, tomorrow!"

"Tomorrow, but ..." and for once Dolly was lost for words. "I expect you'll have a few hours off to see your family."

"I expect so." May looked at the small pile of gifts on the kitchen table and sighed.

"You'll take them with you; don't think you won't see your family 'cos you'll make it so."

***

The porter knocked on the door of room No 16.

"Who is it?"

"A Miss May Miller for you."

May went through to the hotel room.

"Oh May come in. Put your belongings over there." Agnes nodded to a dark mahogany table with blue chintz fabric covering its legs.

-Blimey even the table legs have trousers. Huge windows opened onto a balcony and beyond overlooked the shingle shore and the dark rolling sea.

"You do have a lot of luggage, May!"

"Mm, yes ... Some presents for my family, I haven't seen them since before Christmas."

"Very nice! Now May, the reason I sent for you."

May was agog at the opulence of this room. There was gold on picture frames, gold on the ceiling, gold braid, on the curtains, gold buttons on the porter's uniform and fresh white Christmas Roses—

"May, would you pay attention please!"

"Sorry ..."

"I'm attending an important event and I would like you to dress my hair and apply my make up. I also have this list which I expect you to fill." Agnes held up the note for May to take, "I want you to collect these items, run a few errands. Fresh flowers in my hair…"

"Yes Mrs Spritely." *-See formal. You're horrible, you. Cow.*

But Agnes appeared not to have noticed. "You can travel back with me tomorrow."

"Yes, Er, I wondered if I could go home this afternoon. Drop off my presents?"

"Oh no May, you'll have far too much to do. Tomorrow, tomorrow morning, then we'll catch the train from Portsmouth and Southsea station."

"Now, while you're running those errands I shan't waste any time, I shall take a bath."

"Yes Mrs Spritely."-*If that's not too taxing for you!*

"Will you stop doing that, it's Agnes ... when we're alone!" she said, as she placed two sovereigns in May's hand.

May read the list as she made her way down the stairs:

Book: Ordered and ready for collection.
Perfume: Yardley, Lily of the valley

Cigar: Cuban, six inches
Fresh flowers and ornaments for hair

***

May was out on her own, with money in her pocket. She carried a drawstring bag and she swung it to and fro, as she walked towards Palmerston Road on this, typical dull, grey, January day. May would buy the cigar first, which required her to pass the shop which she so coveted.

But! And now May's heart sank. It was no longer empty. It was filled with trimmings, braids and ribbons, buttons and feathers, of every colour and design. A middle-aged woman with a chest like a courting pigeon said, "How may I help you?" And sniffed.

-You don't think I'm going to buy anything do you? You think I'm on the nick. The woman's gaze followed May as she handled the merchandise.

"I'm just looking, for the moment." May picked up the silver ribbon, this would be perfect.

"That has real silver, threaded through it," advised the shop owner. May wasn't sure if it was advice or a warning.

"It's beautiful. I'll take a yard."

"A yard? That'll be half a sovereign!" The woman snatched the reel of silver threaded ribbon from May's hand, stretched it against her measuring stick, and snipped off an exact thirty-six inches.

Two ladies entered the shop. The proprietress smiled and asked them, "How may I help you."

"Oh please, carry on serving. We're just browsing."

The purchases wrapped, May consulted her list:

-My bloody day off. So she decided she would treat herself. She would take tea in The Queen's teashop. Not in the back room with the other servants, but as a customer.

"May I help you?"
"Yes, a table for one please."
"I'm not sure we have anything available."

May surveyed the empty room, bar two tables occupied by the window.

"I'll check with the Maitre De." The manager came forward.

"If Madame would like to follow me." He showed May to a table at the back of the room next to the staff door. He shook out a napkin and handed it to May and then waved out a card before placing it on the table. May took the gold edged menu card. The manager hovered.

"I'll have tea, cucumber sandwiches, and cakes please."

"As you like."

-I don't like, stuck-up prig. May wished she hadn't come. When she was served, she was presented with cucumber sandwiches, curling at the corners and tea stewed and tepid. And just four cakes on the cake stand. And not nice ones either. She felt like crying *-Getting above myself, but it doesn't stop them taking my money. – No pride.* Mrs Spritely received a tower of cakes to choose from, balanced on little paper doilies.

May gathered the cakes, all four of them into her hanky and into her bag. She'd give them to her family later, tomorrow. She left the payment on the table and walked out. *-Should have let a tip ... a dirty farthing.*

May checked the list, bookshop.

"May I help you?"

-I'm going to ask something else when I have a shop.

"I do have something to collect." And May read out the title and the author she required.

The man raised his eyebrows, "Not for you then?"

"No, not for me."

"Your employer?"

"Yes."

"Male, is he?"

-For fuck sake. "This is beautiful." As she picked up a book from a table:

"The Language of Flowers." "Those prints are the finest quality chromolithographs."

***

Agnes and May progressed Commercial Road. May had no intention of taking Mrs Spritely to her home. She would not have her family embarrassed. So reaching the end of Commercial Road and bypassing Charlotte Street. May led her to the church of St Agathas'. May prayed: - *Please Mary, let Father Dolling be attending, tending over his wayward flock.*

Chapter 13

But one day from down in Dartmouth,
There came a lad to catch her eye.
And when he smiled, she was in heaven,
But when he spoke, it was naught but lies.

St Agathas' was quiet. Agnes looked around her surprised, she'd never been in a Catholic church before, and perhaps she was expecting devils to prod her up the arse with pitchforks. But this church was modern with stunning architecture. Agnes played with the lace on the altar cloths. Just when May thought she'd better get a shift on, Father Dolling appeared. "May, May Miller is it? And how are you? Quite the young lady."

"Father Dolling, I'm fine, thank you. Let me introduce Mrs Spritely." As Father Dolling eyed the lady by Miss Miller's side.

"Ah, May's employer! And is this young lady doing you a good service?"

"Indeed she is, we're very pleased with her."

"These embroideries are sewn by May's mother, a fine woman, fine."

"So that's where May gets her talent."

Mr Dolling, who had an eye for money and a need for a benefactress for his new gymnasium, thanked God for his divine intervention. "May, I understand your brother and sisters are expecting you: yesterday! Why not run along and see them while I show Mrs Spritely the work we do here."

And May thanked Mr Dolling and the blessed virgin, and waited for Agnes to agree.

"Why of course May, I'm sure I shall be in the best of hands," *-Oh you are, and that hand will be in your pocket and you'll willingly yield up everything, without theft.* Agnes left in more buoyant a spirit and lighter of three hundred pounds, pledged to build a new gymnasium.

May shot through the front door and Lil and Glad looked up.

"May we thought you weren't coming."

"I haven't got long. I have to meet Mrs Spritely in an hour."

"But I thought it was yer day off. It's not fair."

"Not fair," echoed Freddie.

"Here let's be quick. See, I've brought all your Christmas presents. Where's mum's photo?"

"I'll get it; I think it's in the drawer."

"Here you are Freddie."

And he had three unopened packages laid out in front of him. Freddie couldn't take his eyes off them, and he touched one, just to make sure it was real, then another, then the last. He watched as both Lil and Glad got their presents. May opened the back of the wooden oak frame, popped Lavinia's photograph to the back of the gilt mount. Tacked the back on and restrung it. "There that's dad's present done."

"Oh May, that's lovely we should find a place for it," said Lil. "Here May, above dad's chair, by the fire."

And so May found a nail and bashed it in the wall with the heel of her boot.

A banging echoed. "Oi! We're trying to sleep in here. Bert's on nights, yer know."

"Sorry Ethel," and May pulled a face.

Glad opened her present, tied with a pale pink ribbon.

"Here, while you finish unwrapping it, I'll tie it in your hair." And she pulled her hair into a side parting with the bow lying to one side.

"Me now. May, do me." And May tied a bow into Lil's hair with a lilac satin ribbon. Freddie clapped his hands.

"Well come on, open them. I can't stay long. Oh, and before I forget, here." And spread out the squashed cakes. Freddie unwrapped a present, the biggest. "Here let me show you," and Glad grabbed the top from Freddie and pumped, and it hummed and whirled around the floor. Freddie shared the cakes between them.

"One of them is for dad. So make sure you leave him one for after his tea."

Freddie unwrapped present two, a toy tin soldier. He set it aside. Then a picture book, Freddie lined them up on the table, just touching them.

"You can play with them you know," said Glad. But he knew they were too precious, he'd have to be careful with them. Maybe get them out on special days, like when May came home.

Lil unwrapped hers, a small handkerchief with a letter L embroidered on the corner, scented with honeysuckle.

"Oh May, it's ... a lace border! And it smells, so lovely."

Glad came back to the table and took her present from its paper, The Girl's Annual. "Oh thank you. Look Lil."

"It's just like Christmas all over again," said Lil, and she pressed her nose into the handkerchief and sniffed. "Wally was asking after you, he wanted to talk to you, came yesterday."

"I don't suppose it was important. I've got to go, big cuddle."

And May waved her final farewell as she turned the corner onto Chandler Street and through the gate to St Agathas'. Three little faces poking out from the doorway waving her goodbye.

***

Agnes sat at her dressing table, May stood behind her brushing her hair. "I'm pleased with you May." Agnes relaxed, her eyes closed and her head tilted back.

"I'm going to the dressmaker. Madame Le Merchand, that's her card." She nodded towards a tray overflowing with hatpins, and the detritus of the beautification of Agnes and the scalloped edged card. May brushed.

"I've looked through some of the latest Parisian designs," and she nodded again to the dressing table this time at two well-thumbed magazines with pieces of notepaper between the pages,

-Probably acting as place markers. May thought.

Agnes didn't have an artistic or creative idea in her head. She knew what she liked when she saw it. She understood the result but not the means. May had an innate sense of artistry. Fortunately, for Agnes, May reared in Devil's Acre, her talents not rewarded as adequately, had she come from rarer stock.

Agnes was flicking through a magazine and showed May the couture she had short-listed. May agreed her selections were stunning. Agnes smiled, pleased May agreed with her choices. A frown quickly shadowed her brow. *-Why on earth am I wanting to please this little snipe?*

May said, "Of course, with the fabric, the velvet it's much heavier than the silk and it will hang differently. See how many folds and pleats it has. Imagine all that bunched around your waist." *-Look like a beached whale.*

Agnes turned the pages and referenced those models wearing only lighter autumn fabrics. "I have made a decision."

-That's good, thought May.

"I shall have a day dress and an evening dress, which fabric to use for which though?"

-A decision to make a decision, well it's a step forward. May's thoughts lost in finding something; her mother's voice came to her: A journey starts with the first step. Something like that, anyway. May stopped brushing, well over a hundred strokes! *She'll be bald if I carry on,*

as she tugged the tangled red hair from the brush and placed it in a bin at the side of the table.

Agnes held the magazine up. "I like the idea of green velvet evening dress, but then again the blue silk …."

"The blue under candle light would be stunning; would shimmer."

Decision taken …"The green velvet, trimmed with sable, a tea dress, perfect." and Agnes glanced up at May.

"Oh, beautiful."

"Belgium lace and green velvet ribbon trim. For the hat, bird of paradise feathers, gripped by a jade buckle." Agnes smiled at her choices and inserted a notepaper into the pages of the magazine. "Hand me a pencil." And she made a note addressed to her milliner. A hat of the same green velvet. *-Mm, maybe I should buy another yard or two for the hat...* Why not? I can make cushions or something with it, if it's too much.

The evening gown Agnes chose was a modest affair, her décolletage hidden with a high-necked blouse. "That is a good choice if you're ancient, but you have a good chest." *-Who knows for how much longer?* And pointed to a picture that Agnes had seen, but dismissed.

"Don't you think it's a bit well, risqué?"

"Risky! I don't think so! I saw Princess Maud wear something similar on the front page of the court rag, and she's ancient."

Agnes pulled aside her dressing gown and stared. She had to admit that she was wrinkle free. -It's true; none of us know how long we may keep ... our gifts? - *I'm bewitched, she thought. -Bedazzled by love.* And a momentary hesitation, I have time to think, and made another note-pad insert.

***

Agnes was staying away, attending to her sister's needs. Henry was sitting at the library table, a brown parcel tied with string sat before him. Henry fumbled in the drawer looking for some scissors, his search unrewarded he decided to open the parcel with his paper knife. After stabbing the package several times, Henry stabbed himself,

"Damnation."

***

May finished the beans and placed them in some salted water. Peeled potatoes and dropped them in with the beans. "Well that's all I can do for now," she said. And plopped herself down in the chair by the hearth; she'd just prodded the cushion into a comfortable position when the bell jangled on the wall: library, read the label above the bell.

"Oh bugger!" She checked her apron for grubby marks, patted down her hair, and went to answer the call. May stood outside the room drew one deep breath and tapped lightly on the door.

"Enter."

May on entering the room gave a little bob and awaited her instruction. Mr Spritely sat with his back toward her and seated at a table. He turned to look at May.

"May," he said, "I've cut my hand rather badly on this bloody paper knife."

"Oh Sir! I'll fetch some bandages… Salt water that'll kill the germs … I'll…"

"May! There is disinfectant in the bathroom. I'll come with you, we'll clean it, and then I'll take a bath. Trouble is…" and at that moment he swung round and revealed a large bandage, his hanky, on his right arm. I'm a bit incommoded; thought you could help out, don't want to get this bandage wet..."

"Yes Sir, of course."

***

May bent over to help her master remove his shoes. She took off his sock -*Blimey*, thought May. *His big toe nail, just like a horse's hoof!*

"Thank you May. Now if you'd just help ease me out of this jacket."

Mr Spritely eased himself back into the wooden chair and stretched; his neck resting on the chair-back. His beard pointed upwards like a hairy mountain peak. He fumbled with his collar studs.

"Ruddy hell!" He shouted.

"You can't do studs with just one hand; and with it being your right arm that's injured… I reckon it's near impossible."

"You're so very clever. So very clever and so very kind. Not embarrassing you am I?"

"No Sir, I'm just happy to be of service; in your service."

"Must say May, you look even more fetching with that blush upon your cheeks."

May could feel her face getting even hotter. *–He thinks I'm blushing.* It's bloomin' boiling in here, lobster ruddy pink. Mr Spritely lifted his arms so his shirt could be more easily removed. He sat still as if contemplating the bareness of his feet, mapping the network of veins on his toes. His chest naked, save for the tufts of wiry greying hairs.

He fumbled with the buttons on his fly.

"Let me help," May said.

Mr Spritely stood up and watched as May's fingers tugged at his buttons. He stepped out of his trousers and stood naked but for his woollen underpants. May stooped to gather the trousers from the floor; her head now on the same level as his growing interest. He wondered if she'd noticed the bulge in his pants. His hands went to the button on his under wear. He fumbled, but this time May did not offer to help…

May turned her back and busied herself collecting his clothes, which she folded and hung over her arm. Mr Spritely had managed with difficulty to remove his undergarment and climbed into the tub. May turned to him after she'd heard the splash... She had her hand on the doorknob...

"May, bring my dressing gown back with you."

He dunked his head under the water droplets of water sprinkled over his beard. He tried to lather the soap with his good hand but the soap leapt from his fingers and dived to the bottom of the tub...

"Your dressing gown, Sir".

"Place it on the hook there." He said, pointing at the door.

"Anything else, Sir?"

"Yes May. Yes there is. Had some bother with the soap. Can't control it with one hand. I hold the sponge in one hand and the soap in the same; it just doesn't do. Bloody bar's dived into the tub, Can't find it. May you're going to have to help me."

May didn't say anything nor did she move from her spot by the bathroom door. She stared at the paisley pattern on the gown trying to make sense of the swirls.

"Oh come May. No need to be shy."

"Your father said he'd told you to do as you're told. Is that right?"

"Yes Sir, he did... I..."

"Then if you would just help me, I can't do it alone, I've dropped the soap."

"Yes sir." May turned and stepped forward. May rolled up her sleeves just as she would have done at home. She'd scrubbed her father's back sometimes; the tub dragged in from the yard and set before the fire.

Mr Spritely found the soap, he handed it to her with the sponge. May rubbed on the sponge until a white lather burst from her fingers. May sponged his back and shoulders. Mr Spritely bowed his head allowing May to rub his neck.

"Dunk," she said.

This was how May was with her father or her baby brother. Mr Spritely the man who she'd known for a few months had disappeared cleansed into a lather of familiar action. Mr Spritely dunked his head and came up with such speed he sent a shower of water over the tub and soaking May's Pinafore and dress. He hummed a tune that was familiar ... She'd heard the boys on the market whistle it as they pushed their carts.

May lathered her sponge, first his chest. He straightened his arm for her to scrub. His hand rested on her breast. She reached across him, to reach his other arm. He left his hand touching her bodice. She lathered his arm taking care not to wet the bandage. -*I'm bloody soaked.*

That was when May noticed it. She didn't know why she hadn't before. Standing its head proud of the water. Mr Spritely watched her as she glanced at his erection. And with her gaze upon him, grew larger still. May held the coin tight in her palm. She'd stow it later. It was a crown night...

***

George diligently aided Mr Gregory. Apart from acknowledging her presence with a small nod, his eyes would remain steadfastly averted from Susannah; a gnat held more interest for him. And it should make her, if not cross, intrigued. -*If I know anything about women's nature.*

Late evening the choir had finished practise and left the Cathedral, Mr Gregory was working with his organ, it would take some time. Susannah did not want to wait, and besides there was someone who, if she coaxed, would not as a gentleman, refuse her.

"Master George?"

George was collecting hymnbooks, his eyes on the task he said, without raising his head, "Miss Gregory."

"My father, Master Gregory, intends to complete his work here. I'd rather ... I'd rather not remain, would you be kind enough to escort me to my home."

George looked up now and smiled, he turned his face and looked into those huge brown eyes. "I'd be delighted." George collected his coat and hat from the chancellery, while Susannah told her father George had kindly offered to escort her home. This now, was his opportunity. He offered his arm to Miss Gregory, who of course would not refuse. They were walking across the green and towards her home. George told her about the butterfly he'd seen, how he'd wished he'd had his net.

"Oh, what a shame it got away."

"I do have one in my collection although it seems such a waste. It'll be dead by now. All that beauty, wasted."

"My father has a collection of exotic butterflies."

"I should like to see them."

"Then Master Spritely, I shall invite you."

George smiled, "I would be honoured to accept." And he stood in front of her blocking her way and was chivalry itself when he kissed her hand.

"Saturday, come Saturday at 4 'o'clock."

"I look forward to it."

George stopped at the gate, and watched as she progressed to the front door. She turned and smiled at him. George smiled in return and turned back across the green allowing her to watch his retreat.

***

"Long time since I've been in here," Henry said, as he entered her room without knocking. Mr Spritely opened the wardrobe looked inside, closed the door. Pulled open the drawer below and peered in, then he looked under the bed.

May wished he'd leave. She didn't like him in her room, this is who she was, and there was no pretence here. She wanted to make herself presentable. Serve his dinner then service him, but not here, not in this room. It would soon be dinnertime and the fire would certainly be out by now. Mr Spritely grabbed her, his mouth on her lips pressing her to him. May couldn't breathe he was holding her so tightly she felt her lungs would burst.

"May you have to help me with this, say you will. Say you will, May. Kiss it better?" He asked.

Chapter 14

So the next day, just after the bell had rung for the dinnertime, he ran over to the Choirmasters lodge. The girl informed him Mr Gregory was not at home. And would he like to see Miss Gregory? George nodded and smiled at the young maid, and said, "I rather like what I'm seeing now." Emily flushed.

"But please, inform Miss Gregory…"

"Who shall I say?"

"George, George Spritely."

George waited in the hall; his bum on a hard mahogany hall chair, half an hour had passed. George was not happy; he didn't mind a ten-minute wait, decent interval say, no rush. But this was too long. He sat and tapped his hat on his knee. The drawing room door was open, so he pushed it further and went in, a piano. He decided he'd play a few bars… The music filled the house.

As he tinkled the ivories George, who had already decided he would have her and there was a bet riding on it, which meant it was serious. However, he would have her on his terms. And still she didn't arrive. So he rang the bell by the hearth and within a couple of trikes, the little maid arrived.

"Would you tell Miss Gregory, I cannot wait any longer. I'm due back, and am late all ready."

"Yes, of course Sir, anything else?"

"A kiss?"

"Oh."

And he stole a kiss from her lips, which left Emily quite breathless as she explained to Susannah panting that Mr Spritely had to leave."

***

It was a surprise for May when Henry came and placed in her hand a sovereign, a gold sovereign. *-What's he want from me; swinging from the chandeliers?* But no,

Henry didn't want that. Henry had, by his chair a jar of Brilliant. "Just raise up your skirt and bend over the desk May."

May wasn't sure she liked the sound of this but she liked the look of that coin. And if she were to receive one of these every week, -*why I could have me bloomin' flower shop in a year.* So May bent over Henry's desk, her chest resting on his ink blotter.

***

Henry tugged up her skirts and pulled the bow that held her drawers together, loosed them, so they hung awkwardly around her ankles. She made to step out from them but Henry said, "No! Stay there, I'll tell you when to move."

Henry, unbeknown to May, was reacting a scene from his life onboard HMS Cormorant. That young recruit, so undisciplined, but when Henry had gone on to chastise him, beating the young tyke on his bare arse with a cat's tail. Henry discovered he'd grown rather excited. But Henry, never took advantage of the young bugger. He was an officer, the men and the boys, their welfare, was his responsibility.

So May spread-eagled over the desk her arse in the air and Henry buttering up her buttocks reliving the missed opportunities he should have had with Lavinia. Whether that made him a good man, or a man who simply didn't seize the moment, he didn't know. Or at this instant, care. He was just about to shove his dick up both the tyke's arse and into Lavinia and rewrite history.

And here he was fucking May, who was both Lavinia and tyke. He stood over her firm arse in the air, rating her, May with the small tight arse of a boy. Two in one and Henry rewrote his regrets. And stuck his dick into May's arse and without a thank you! He pumped away until he reached the crest of his wave and May clung to her coin and gritted her teeth, as the old dick thrust painfully inside her.

Henry had ridden the surf, rode the waves crashed onto a shingle shore. He pushed himself tidily away, "Pick up your drawers. There now! Get dressed, straighten yourself, and don't make me do that again."

-*Didn't want you to do that in the first place.* But she held the coin tight, a good one for her collection.

May hadn't a clue sometimes what Henry was going on about. There were, it seemed two Henry's, the one who wanted just a two bob fuck, and then the weirdo bossy one clutching a whole sovereign bit, person. May preferred the two bob bloke but liked the sovereign better.

***

The following day George knocked, and the same procedure followed that had occurred the previous day. Except Miss Gregory appeared after an interval of five minutes of George's arrival.

It had become a habit for George to escort Miss Gregory home; and Mr Gregory was grateful to young George for the service. It meant he could stay longer in the cathedral, enjoying the ambiance. Being there, just for the sake of being there, which is where he wanted to be.

On this night with Susannah on his arm a cold wind blasted, leaves danced in the gutters, it suddenly rained. George tore off his Jacket and held it above Susannah's head. At her front door, she looked at George, his shirt soaked through, he was shivering.

"Oh George, you're drenched. Please come in, I'll find you something dry to wear. Emily, fetch some towels please."

He stood facing the hearth, his back to the room, wearing just his vest and trousers, his braces hanging loosely over his hips. Emily arrived carrying a tray, "Miss Gregory asked me to bring you this," and handed him a large brandy. Emily blushed as he took the glass from her, his fingers lingered over hers. He bent down and placed his lips on her cheek.

"Thank you," he said.

"Will that be all?"

"Ooh, now there's an offer."

Emily was speechless, but she wasn't dumb, she giggled.

"It's Emily isn't it?" And his mouth moved to her lips, and he kissed her.

She wasn't at all sure how she should react. He was a guest in her employer's home. A good slap around the chops was the only way to treat unwanted advances from the opposite sex. Yet, a guest is to be served with dignity and respect and their desires fulfilled and their requests obeyed. Besides how unwanted was his advance? Emily awaited further instruction. George took her continued presence as a compliant signal, so he touched her breast, and kissed her again.

"Please, sir!"

"Emily, would you like to come out with me one evening when you're free?" Just a walk perhaps, or take tea?

"I ... Oh no Sir, I couldn't," she giggled. -*Tea, me? Blimey.*

"Thank you Emily, that will be all." Susannah said,as she swept into the room, clutching one of her father's shirts and an overcoat. "These will see you home. You can collect your other clothes from Emily tomorrow. I'll see to it they're aired and ironed." George began to pull on the shirt, Susannah said, as she watched him, "They're going to be a tight fit, I think."

"Have some," he said, pointing to the glass of brandy on the table. George threw on the coat and made for the door but before his exit, he took the glass from her and gulped it down. "Thank you, just what the doctor ordered, that'll keep me warmed up." He took her in his arms and kissed her.

"George."

"I, I'm sorry, I shouldn't have." George wore his; I'm such a clumsy fool expression. "You've overwhelmed me."

"George …"

"May I kiss you?" And not waiting for an answer. How could a properly brought up young lady possibly agree to her desire? He kissed her again. They stood embracing in front of the fire. He took her chin in between his thumb and finger and looking down into her brown eyes, he said, "I love you, I don't know what spell you have me under, but I surrender myself. I am in your hands." George turned around at the door and paused to blow her a kiss.

Miss Susannah Gregory, smiled to herself.

***

Sunday morning and Henry was reading his paper, a cup of tea at his side. His hand swathed in a large white bandage.

"Good morning Henry." Agnes said, as she swept into the breakfast room. "Henry! Henry, what on earth have you done to your hand?"

"Cut it opening a ruddy parcel. Bloody paper knife slipped. Good morning Agnes," he said, in that order.

"Oh, my goodness… You cleaned it well I hope; did Dolly sort it for you?"

"Dolly? No, Dolly … yesterday was her day off, don't you know. Typical, there's an emergency and no one around to help."

"Oh come, it can't be as bad as all that."

"Don't it? Hurt like bloody hell."

"Henry, language please."

"Well, if it weren't for May being here God alone knows what would've happened."

"Not quite alone then; she helped you out?"

"Cleaned up the blood stains, such a mess! Scrubbed away the stains, there see." Henry said, pointing to a remarkably bright spot of carpet. "Sorted me out first, though ..." Agnes agreed that patch of carpet was particularly clean. -*I had better have her wash the rest of it,* thought Agnes, as she removed her hat.

***

John watched her. She was, he supposed and believed, the mostly beautiful woman he'd ever seen. Joseph told him to, 'Stop mooning,' and get on with his work. He loved her. He knew he loved her because his heart pounded and his balls throbbed whenever he saw her ... as soon as saw her. Hanging out the washing, beating the carpets.

-*I love you.* There, I've admitted it.

May understood she wasn't good enough for him. He was lovely; he'd make someone a wonderful husband and she recognised it couldn't be her. He was good, kind, and honest. -*And me? I'm not. He's John; he's good. I'm May; I'm not.* I'm not want he'd want, not if he found out.

Dear John, I love you. That's why I won't marry you. That's what she'd like to write. Yes, because it would lead to questions: But if you love me? He'd argue with her and ask her to explain herself, and of course, she wouldn't. The worst is, she wanted him to talk her round, and why that letter would remain, unwritten. And she placed the last peg on the sheet, walked from the washing line, and returned to the kitchen.

***

Agnes, bless her was out at a dressmaker's. Well, there's a thing. Oh well, the old girl had never been one to spend money on herself. So he shouldn't mind; waste of bloody funds though.

Henry was in the mood for a tupping. Unfortunately, Mrs Proudley was in the house. He could not relax into the mood. Or to advantage exploit his lust with May, not with the possibility of Dolly bursting through the door at any moment proffering a pile of toasted muffins. No it would not do, Agnes was due to return by 6 o'clock. His opportunity had just four hours to exercise itself. He pondered on the excuse he could use to rid the house of Dolly, send her on an errand. But for what? A bottle of rum from The George Inn would take half an hour to fetch, there and back, and besides, the house may have some in stock. No, Henry wanted the afternoon, a couple of hours ... But how to arrange it?

His head ached from the thought of it ... Just then he spied old ... so-and-so coming along the gravel drive. A mere ten minutes later Dolly solved his problem! She asked if she could take the afternoon off, there was sickness in her family. She promised she'd make up the time as soon as possible.

"No not at all," said Henry. "Please take all the time you need."

"Thank you, Mr Spritely." -*Such a kind man*, Dolly thought as she left the house. I'm so lucky; and she walked home briskly to see what had happened to her old cat, Ferdinand.

Henry in the library poured himself a rum. 2 o'clock, four hours, he sipped. He'd had lunch, and this was his afternoon stinker. Henry lit his pipe. He held a rum in one hand and his pipe in the other. His mind wandered. It wandered to May, just as his hands would, a little later. He gave his mind full reign, and his thoughts made his body react, he felt a stiffening in his Long-Johns. He threw the rum down in one gulp, and tapped out his pipe. He pulled the bell by the fireplace.

He knew the area where May hailed from. He'd visited her house, indeed met her mother. The area was a den of poverty, and prostitutes. Was he making May a prostitute? No, a mistress? Or was he helping out her family? Her father was a good man, and good grief, his wife! Lavinia, she was a bloody handsome woman, where May gets her looks from he supposed. But May had something else other than the guttersnipe she was, as her mother had, a presence. Something about them ... May knocked.

"Come in."

"Sir."

"May sit there in that chair," and he pointed to an identical winged chair opposite his own, the other side of the hearth.

"Happy here?" He asked, not interested in the answer, but it was an opening, and one that warned her that this was not a 'answering the bell' for tea and cakes appointment. "I'm going to write to your father," he said, without waiting to hear whether May was happy or not.

"Oh?"

"Oh, don't worry. I mean to tell him how pleased I am; indeed, we are, with you. That you have here a permanent position and that your trial is now over." May hadn't realised she was on trial, but thanked Mr Spritely very much.

***

George believed he had given, even someone like May, enough information, even she would understand! Sebastian had written the letter. *-No evidence in my handwriting, thank you!* So Sebastian took up his pen and wrote as George dictated.

He'd send a new boy by train to Portsmouth. The post office was directly opposite the station. He could hop off, post the letter, and have time to catch the same train on its return journey from the terminus at Portsmouth Harbour. With luck, he'll be back before anyone would miss the little blighter.

"All roads lead to George. Do you think she'll understand who sent it? What if she buys something ... tawdry?"

"We'll see, but perhaps you're right. I'll tell her to buy a brooch, simple, stylish. Mother trusts her taste implicitly."

"How do you want me to sign off?"

"Oh, I don't know … Respectfully yours?" And grinned

"Here you go, all yours, done." Sebastian threw his pen at him quickly followed by the letter.

Chapter 15

Dolly said, "Here's a letter for you! Portsmouth and Southsea postmark." She held a postcard, with a picture of Winchester Cathedral and two letters, one addressed to May.

"I spend most of my time in the Cathedral. You'll be pleased to know I'm not singing!" wrote George.

"It's from George, bless him."

"If you have a moment, would you send me a fruitcake? It'd make a great doorstop! Only joking, would be much appreciated. George."

"There's a letter too, for his parents, I recognise his hand." And she placed it on the breakfast tray. "Who's yours from? Family is it?"

May had torn open the letter, the only time her family were to contact her was if there were a family emergency! "Don't waste money on postage stamps," her father said. May didn't recognise the handwriting on this envelope, but then she'd never seen her father write, not even a note. Two coins tumbled from the package. Guineas! May covered them with her hand, as she read.

"Dear May, I do hope Fred enjoys his wooden soldier. I've enclosed two guineas. I'd like you to buy—"

"All right, is it?"

"Yes Dolly, no emergency... Thank goodness."

Dolly rattled the teacups. She was rather agitated at this lack of information. -*After all, I shared my postcard!*

"A brooch ..."

"Father, not had a relapse?"

"No, he's back at work now," said May, without looking up.

Curiosity was driving Dolly to wanting to tear that letter out of her hand. -*It was an educated hand that wrote on that envelope*, of that she was certain.

"I'd like you to use your contacts, and skills to choose something tasteful, refined but expensive in appearance. I trust you to choose well, I have it on excellent authority you have a great artistic sensibility." May was confounded. The letter continued, "Please send the piece to my Winchester address." May turned the letter over. -*No address!*

"Rest of the family all well, are they?"

"Yes Dolly, I'm sure I'd hear from them if there was an emergency."

The only person the letter could be from, was George, she guessed. Who knew about the wooden toy, but him? But why the different hand? And why no signature? Then it came to her, of course, he hasn't informed his parents, he doesn't want them to know. It suddenly made perfect sense. Well not perfect, she would've have liked to know who the brooch was for.

May knew now, it was from George; of course, she had his address. It was there, on the dresser, propped against a milk jug, with a photograph of Winchester Cathedral on the front. She'd copy the address from the postcard, as soon as she got the opportunity.

***

Emily was most impressed; George escorted her to a tearoom, The Brown Bun. They were served hot buttered crumpets and tea, followed by fruitcake. Emily wore her best hat. George was most interested in her family. "I've not got a father, I did have, of course but he's dead now. My sister, she's in service too; and my mother, well she takes in washing, and we help her out of course. Oh, I'm talking too much."

"No, I'm interested, please don't stop." George's crooked little fang showed now he smiled, so fetching a smile. He looked fascinated, he gazed into her eyes. They'd stayed a good hour, and George offered his arm as they slowly walked to the corner of the square. Here he reached down and taking her hand in his pressed her fingers to his lips and one by one, he kissed them.

Emily blushed.

"I have some tickets. I don't suppose you'd accompany me; a new act is coming to town."

"Oh, I would. I'd love to see a new act." -*Never seen an old one!* Emily agreed, they would meet again the following Saturday. Emily was beside herself with excitement. Such a gent, they say if a gentleman comes after a working girl he only wants her for one thing, but not George.

Saturday came and the evening went on, and on; but Emily seemed to enjoy it. George wasn't sure why or what he was doing, this escorting of Emily, for he had no feelings for her, but then of course, -*I must. I am seeing her again!*

As he walked her home, he said, "Emily I want you do to something for me, would you?"

"Well, rather depends."

"It's about Susannah, I like her, but not in the way she likes me. If you understand me?"

"Er, I … think so."

-*OK, so I'll spell it out for you.* "She's rather taken with me, and I like her. I have no wish to hurt her. I have a high regard for both Mr Gregory and Susannah. …"

George looked into Emily's eyes trying to recognise any degree of understanding. He didn't have a clue what he was talking about either. He had this bubbling up of an idea, but he wasn't yet sure how, or to what effect it could be used. So using the rule: when in doubt, change the subject, or lie, or both. He pulled Emily to him and kissed her. "It's you; it's you whom I love." And he smiled into those deep brown eyes.

It stunned Emily into silence!

"Don't you see? Susannah suspects my feelings for her aren't … well, how she'd like them. Of course, she suspects there is another who has stolen my affections, but she doesn't know it is you..."

-*Me? Blimey!*

***

She stood before him, while he sat. He was so placed his eyes were on a level with the triangle of dark hair that curled between her legs, such contrast, her hair so black, her skin so white. He gazed at her small firm breasts topped so prettily with pert pink nipples.

Henry sighed inwardly, his ball bag throbbed, but this moment he would savour. So May stood while Henry placed his hand on her thigh and slid it until he touched her lips, he slid his finger inside her and felt her dampness. He leaned in closer and he sniffed, inhaling her sweet musky fragrance. Then only then, as true connoisseur, he tasted. And he pushed his face to her thighs.

"Stand with your legs wider apart."

Order not request, he was a naval man, subordinates did as he said, when he said it. Obeying orders without question; ask, they hesitated, tell them, and they obeyed. Withdraw the doubt, no suggestion, not even a hint there is a choice.

May stood with her feet exactly one foot apart. And Henry put his face to her inner thighs, feeling the down under his tongue. He slid his tongue between her lips and he felt her judder. -*Christ his beard's itchy.*

"I think you've been naughty."

"No sir, I have not."

"I do!"

But he gave her the coin anyway or because of her naughtiness and May held it firm in her grasp.

"Thank you, Sir."

"That's what we say when our superior's offered us chastisement, thank you, so we may know our errors, and be thankful for the education."

May hadn't a clue what the old buffer was talking about but she knew what this coin meant; it meant another portion towards the purchase of her flower shop.

"May, bend over my lap. Like so," and he bent her over his knee as you would spank a naughty child. That's what Henry did, he spanked her. She hadn't been chastised enough for Henry, he raised her chemise, exposing her firm white buttocks. He spanked her again, until they blushed a warm rosy pink. May gulped.

"Please Sir."

"Enough is it?

"Yes Sir, I'm sorry." She had no idea not buying something could be so wrong! Spending money you didn't have could be punishable. But she was sorry for the pain she felt. But after she had cried out and the tears had stemmed, he smacked her again.

"There, there, now come here and I shall forgive you."

Henry lifted her and sat her again on his lap and held her dark head against his chest.

Her tears flowed but she didn't let go of that coin.

"I'm sorry, I did wrong."

"There all over now. Shh."

He held her close to his chest and held her tight, his hand which had so gently stroked her head, now played on her white supple thigh.

"Good girl." he said, as he stroked her thigh and every now and again, his finger would accidentally brush against her curling dark hair as he soothed her, and comforted her. He turned her face to him; and kissed her forehead as he held her in his arms. He wanted to fuck her, but he had time enough, he wanted to see her.

Henry had an idea, he needed, wanted, yearned to see more. He pushed her from his lap so she stood before him once more. "Lay down." And he pointed to the rug that lay between the chairs and in front of the hearth. May lay on the rug, naked apart from her black stockings, Henry considered her, never rush a good meal: savour; but oh, he wanted to dive in. He allowed his gaze to slowly crawl over her body. Her long black hair spread out like a halo around her head, tumbling onto the rug; small tufts of dark hair in her armpits. But there oh, that triangle of black curling hair that sat where he wished he were sitting, between those milky white thighs.

He ordered, "Open your legs." But she hesitated. - *Obviously not an order!* So he barked, "Open your legs." That's better; he was torturing himself, deliciously. He could of course, fuck her now; he could see a little bit more than just the triangle of hair. There, a glimpse of pink amongst the dark, so teasing, so tempting, almost irresistible, but Henry stoic, would endure.

"Bend your knees." May blinked, but she did as commanded. "Now flop them open." There was a fleeting reluctance, but she did it. She lay on the rug with her black stockinged feet towards him. And now with her in this position he could see her pink lips, he swore they were pouting for him.

And while she lay on the rug exposing herself, by the drilling orders of Mr Spritely, he unbuttoned his trousers and withdrew himself.

-I'm standing to attention like a sixteen-year-old cadet. "God Save the Queen." And he jumped onto May pushing himself onto her. His hand holding his staff he found that opening and he jammed himself into that … oh so, tight fit. He'd show her, what was what. The mature male … and he thrust two, three, four times and he burst.

Salivating… In his maleness he sniffed, the odour of spent male mixed with female secretions, nectar!

"Oh May, you naughty girl."

He lay on her for five-minutes,

-Wish you'd bloody get off me!

Basking in the after glow.

-Bloody heavy lump.

Henry finally removed himself from May's body and his member slunk back to its trousers.

"Thank you, May." He said, "That'll be all."

***

"Wally, where can I buy a brooch?"

"A brooch? Who wants a brooch?"

"It doesn't matter who wants what, I just want to know, who can get me one."

"Charlie, he'll have it. Or if he ain't got one, he'll get one."

"Where will I find, this Charlie?"

"You cannot be serious? You can't go."

"Why not? Where is, this Charlie?"

"May you won't get out of there in one piece, if you know what I mean. It's down The Hard, Half Moon Street."

"Oh."

"Got it now, have yer?"

"Well bring some back here, you fetch some, and I'll choose."

"What? Have you gone mad? Stroll Devil's Acre with a tray of jewellery!"

"Don't call it that."

"It's what it's called! And rightly bloody so."

"Father Dolling …"

"Dolling, Father Dolling. Will you shut up about, Father bloody Dolling."

A silence ensued. Both glared at each other. Then …

"Stroll through the town with a tray of jewellery like it's ruddy…" and here Walter struggled for the name of a jewellery shop, said, "Riddlers."

"Riddlers?" May giggled. "That's a pawn brokers."

"Look, May, I'll come with yer, but I'll do the talking, you choose and I'll pretend it's a present for you. An engagement, present."

"For me!" May giggled again.

"It's the best I can do, you think of something then."

And as she couldn't, she said, "That's a good idea, my fiancé."

"How much do you have?"

"Two guineas."

"Two guineas? Guineas?" he repeated, and blew a long low whistle. Guineas! Where'd you get that sort of money anyway?"

"I got it to buy the brooch, and I'm not telling you who, so don't ask me again."

Wally, used to clandestine behaviour said, "Won't say a word, more than me life's worth. Hope you're taking something off the top."

"No, I"

"Well you may not be, but I'll want something, bloomin' risky, this is."

"I know, I mean of course you'll get something. And take that silly grin off your face, Walter Rackett."

"Who's it for then?"

May didn't know. "An old Aunt, I think," said May, making it up. Because she hadn't a clue who it was for, and she wondered why she hadn't asked herself that question!

They arrive at Half Moon Street. Wally peered around, when he was certain he looked as furtive as possible, they ducked into Squeeze Gut Alley; at the end of which was a rust coloured door with flaking paint. Wally knocked.

"Yeah, who is it?"

"Walter."

They heard the sound of a bolt scraped back. A head appeared from behind the door. A jabbing nod of his head pointed to the end of a corridor. A feint glow from a smoky oil lamp came from the room ahead of them. A man sat in an over-stuffed armchair. An under-stuffed owl sat on a painted tree branch in a glass case above him, peering down with blind glass eyes.

"Well, what can I do yer for?"

"We'd like a brooch or something."

Charlie rummaged in his desk drawer to the left of his puffed up chair. "This is it, all I've got at the moment." He looked from Walter to May and narrowed his eyes as he studied her. "How much did you want to spend?"

"Fifteen bob."

"Fifteen? What d'ya want then, brass? Something that'll stain her finger green?" And he jabbed his pointed finger at May. He peered at May over the top of his prinznez. "Have a rummage though the box in that drawer. See if there's anything in there you fancy. We can negotiate, but 15/- that's pushing it."

May took out the pieces one by one; she glanced quickly at each item, and placed them in a growing pile.

"Ain't yer going to check their quality?"

"No, I haven't seen anything in here I like yet."

"Oh, ain't yer?"

***

May looking at H Samuel's window in Commercial Road; a padded tray with a collection of previously owned jewellery, on that tray sat a butterfly. A butterfly brooch of rose gold filigree, the delicate trace work wings lined with small diamonds and further, pearls and sapphires forming a pattern.

"That's what I'd buy, isn't it lovely? She wasn't asking Walter just stating her opinion.

"Ten guineas, bloody hell!"

"S'pose, I could show him, but to be honest the more I'm not in his company the better I like it. I'll let someone know, they can take a look, get an idea."

***

The Evening News reported a daring, daylight robbery perpetrated on H Samuel. The robber stole a tray of jewellery. The haul included rings, bracelets, and brooches. A man of distinguished appearance is wanted in connection with the robbery. Witness's described the villain as, well dressed, his speech slow and deliberate. He was dark haired, dark eyed and of average height and build, possibly be foreign. He was last seen, heading down Charlotte Street. Further down the page, a ruffian had stolen a suit of clothes hanging outside Rowes Department store.

***

May looked at the brooch she'd seen sitting in Samuel's window now sitting in a box in her hand.

"Isn't this the same one, I saw in Samuel's?"

"Looks the same, sort of, one butterfly brooch being much like another"

May frowned. *-Is it?*

Wally gave her half a crown.

-Not bad.

"Always May, take something off the top, that's good business."

May boarded the tram and waved goodbye to Walter. He jogged alongside her for a moment before turning a sharp left and with a wave disappeared among the milieu that was Charlotte Street.

***

Charlie took £1/15/00 for the brooch. He'd given Dodgy Dave, 10/- and Sam the Man, 5/-. This left Charlie with a grand profit of a quid, plus a tray of jewellery, a good day, no outlay, a small profit, and other stuff to flog. Charlie pulled open the drawer in his desk. "Yep, a good deal is when there's something in it for everyone."

"Apart from Samuel's Charlie, they lost their stuff!"

"No Dave, the shop didn't lose, insured yer see; and the insurance, they didn't lose either." Charlie closed the drawer on the jewellery he'd just deposited.

"How'd you work that out, then?"

"Well, without things being nicked, they'd be no business for them. They'd have no money, no business. Sometimes they have to pay a little bit out, but only so they can suck more in."

"We're an asset then? Necessary, or they don't have a business. We're almost a charity; doin' it for nothing an all."

"Exactly. You Dave, are a philanthropist, despite having no arse in your trousers."

Dave left Squeeze Gut Alley smiling. He wasn't a common criminal, no! He was a businessman, a philanthropist, ragged trousers an all.

***

Agnes went to Great Southsea Street, her first fitting. Madame had adjusted the dummy, pushed, and pulled at various wheels until the figure adapted to the exact bodily proportions of Mrs Spritely. Agnes was undressed and redressed in a green velvet tea gown. She turned and she had to confess, even in this unfinished state, it was gorgeous. Agnes twisted her body to view the back. In response to her reflection, she raised her chin, and she smiled; she liked what she saw.

Madame Louisa Le Merchand, was no more French than the poodle at Jones' teashop. Her accent dropped in and out of Hampshire to a strange discombobulated, strangulated, hopefully French sounding, accent. Which she believed made a convincing cover for the dropping of her aitches.

"'Ello, 'ow may I 'elp you?" It worked well, or so she thought. It wasn't her Frenchness though; that kept her clients coming back. She was just so good at what she did best, and what she did best was sewing. She turned matrons into maidens, ducks into swans and an attractive woman into a beauty. If the waist were small, it would be made, "'Ow you say? Smaller."

Mrs Spritely had a yard or so of fabric left over. Madame suggested either a small drawstring bag or a little bow for her hat. "Make eet match, no?" Madame was no milliner, as she explained, "I'm no 'at maker." However, with judicious use of a swatch of fabric, "Voila!" the 'at would match the dress and the ensemble be, "magnifique". The evening gown was still a bolt of fabric, but next week …

"I weel of course, 'aver it on theez modelle."

Mrs Spritely thanked her and as she was leaving, Madame said, "Eef you would let me 'ave a leetle something on account."

Agnes frowned, but withdrew from her bag, two crowns.

"Will that do? I didn't know."

-*No your sort never do, do you!* "Of course, perfect. I weel see you next week. Oui?"

Agnes passed by the clock tower. She'd decided to walk to Palmerston Road. She wasn't due to meet William until next week. And she was looking forward to it.

Chapter 16

George used a paper knife to open the package he'd collected from the bursar. *-Let's see what we have here.* George didn't care what it was, as long as Susannah liked it. He aimed to please her. George held it in his hand, it was more than he expected.

A blue butterfly brooch, much like the one he would have impaled and added to his collection on that day with May. *Clever. -I'd better watch out.* Perfect; hunted, netted, and pinned. Ephemeral beauty captured forever in this brooch *-Couldn't have chosen better if I'd bought it myself.* It wasn't until mid July George would have the opportunity to give his gift to the, oh, so lovely Susannah.

***

The last week of term loomed, the last term of the final academic year and the end of George's school life. George was leaving the next week for home. He had kept the little brooch for long enough and now it was to be his gift to her, his leaving, but remember me, present. Until today, there had been kisses and fumblings. But today… Miss Gregory had appeared at his door. She too bore a gift, a book on native British butterflies.

George smiled broadly at Susannah, "Won't you come in."

And Susannah stepped over the threshold and into a different world. George stood with his back to her adjusting his shirt buttons and as he was trying to tie his bow tie, he fumbled. "Sebastian always does this for me, where is a chap when you need him?"

***

"Here," she said, "let me."

She stood in front of him and began to adjust his tie. As she put this loop over that loop and tugged, his hand caught behind her back and forced her forward. He kissed her, and she returned that kiss. They kissed and kissed, until George touched her tongue with his tongue, and she wasn't at all sure she liked that! And she made to step back, but George held her.

"Oh, what you do to me. Please just hold me," he said.

Susannah was most impressed with this most handsome young man. And she kissed him to soothe him. He dropped his head to her shoulder and rested it there and held her in his arms.

"My dearest love. I have something for you, a leaving gift." And he handed her a little package tied with a gold satin ribbon.

"Oh George, what on earth, what can it be?"

"I shall miss you so much."

Susannah tore open the package the gold ribbon tossed to the floor. "Oh George it's exquisite." And she went to pin it to her chest.

"Here, allow me." And he pinned the butterfly brooch to her blouse, just above her breast, and George allowed his fingers to linger.

***

"There's a lovely view of the cathedral green from this window. Here, come see." And she came and stood by the window, looking out while George poured them both a glass of Port. "Cheers," he said, and they chinked glasses. George took her glass from her and stood it next to his on the little side table.

***

He took her in his arms and he kissed her, and she returned that kiss. And as he held her and kissed her, with his other hand he was inching up her skirts. He held a great roll of fabric in his hand when at last he had reached her knee and he felt the lace edging on her drawers, he let go of her dress and it remained supported on his arm; so shielding his hand from prying eyes but allowing him access to her under skirts. George felt the boned corset.

He held her tight to him as he ousted himself from his trousers.

"Touch me Susannah; I'll guide your hand, I'll show you what you've done to me." He led her hand to his dick and she tied to pull away! He searched with his free hand and found the split in her drawers and felt his way between the gap and touched tendrils of curling hair. Susannah stepped back, away from him! However, the only place she was going was her back pressed firmly against the wall. George thrust himself forward, the stickiness of him caught against her hair and tugged at her.

"No!" she screamed.

George covered her mouth with his lips. Then he whispered, "Shh, I won't hurt you," as he brushed an escaped tendril from her cheek.

He held out his hand to her and she took it, but instead of helping her, he assisted her to his bed. He pressed his mouth to her lips; and pushed her backwards, and George went with her on this slide. And Susannah who had never done a day's physical work in all her life, resisted him as far as she could. Yet, George didn't take his weight from her and onto his elbows, but let her take the full heaviness of him. When she tried to make a sound, he smothered her mouth with his kisses. His hand once more under her skirt, searched, and found the rent in those so accessible drawers.

His hand touched her and she groaned. George rubbed and tickled, he stroked, he fondled, and he flicked, but nothing! George was now at the, -*I don't give a fuck, stage.* And just wanted to fuck her. -*How long does this women need?* Why does everything she do, have to take so bloody long?

He lowered himself between her legs her skirts drawn up, covering the brooch with his body. And he pushed himself on and into her, inching his way. Susannah struggled beneath him but she was stuck on his end like any butterfly on a tray. He pushed forward, onwards and upwards. Inch-by-inch he gained ground. Then, with one last shove, he was at last, fully sheaved within Susannah. *-She's taken all of me, I knew she wanted me.* Though he was, as Sebastian had insisted on telling him, "No bigger than the average in length, but in girth, good God! Now you are a giant among men."

George licked the sweat that trickled down and across Susannah's neck. He bit her ear and as his excitement grew, he began to suck her neck. *-Explain that to your father.* And he continued his thrusting. Susannah lay still. *-No longer making a racket.* And his thrusts became bolder, and the springs in his bed banged a bloody percussion, in rhythmic time to his thrusting. And he went deeper, and he started to give himself up, yield himself to his sensation. So absorbed was he hadn't noticed the tears falling gently and so slowly from the lovely Susannah's eyes. Had he seen, he would of course licked them away! George lay panting on his prize; and she lay still and quiet beneath him.

Still joined, he whispered, "Oh Susannah what have we done? What will our parents say?"

Susannah thought that's what she heard; and then she knew she had when he repeated it. "What, what do you mean? Tell my father? We can't, you wouldn't?"

George breathed a sigh of relief. *-That's all right then.* "Susannah what we've just done, I can't believe we just did that."

"We can't tell anyone, you won't," said Susannah.

"I don't know, I don't know. Oh May, I … Oh, may I say, I love you?" George vowed then, never to use a woman's name in lust, ever again!

George helped her to her feet and he held her in a tight embrace. Susannah cried and he whispered, "Shh, I give you my word as a gentleman, I won't tell a soul of what we've just done. You're not to blame at all for this Susannah, I accept full responsibility." And he held her in his arms and kissed away her tears. George watched Susannah dash across the green covered square, it was raining hard the wind blew in gusts.

"I take it I lost the bet," Sebastian said, as he entered the room.

"Sebastian, a gentleman never tells." Sebastian joined George at the window and watched Susannah dash from their view.

***

The following day George called at the Lodge, Emily smiled widely.

"Who shall I say?"

And George took her chin in his hand and said, "You know very well." And whispered, "I love you."

But loudly he said, "Susannah please."

"I'll see if she's available. I'll let her know you are here."

George walked into the front room. *-No rush.*

After a short while, Emily reappeared. "I'm sorry but Miss Gregory is indisposed and can't see you."

George frowned, and whispered, "What! What's up with her, or is it just me she won't see?"

"I don't know, she's in a right funny mood. Hardly spoken to me ... or her father for that matter."

"Um, I see, I hoped we could have put all of that behind us. Dearest Emily, I don't want her to feel jealous, I like her. But I love you. She may say to you things that aren't true ... about me; I don't want you to believe her Emily. It will be just envy speaking. I had to ..." And here, George gulped and hesitated ... "I had to reject her advances, she came to our school house, as you know it's out of bounds ...."

And Emily stared into his beautiful dark eyes and said, "I wondered what was wrong with her, your room! Gosh."

Emily was flattered by the confidence into which George had taken her. And of course, his declarations of true love would cause Susannah hurt. Jealousy! Her rival for the affections of this gentleman was her servant! Only natural. -*Why, it was just like one of those stories, in what me mum calls, 'The Penny Dreadfuls'.* Emily was most impressed with herself.

Then George said loudly, "Tell Miss Gregory how disappointed I am. Of course I understand, I'll call again when she's not ... indisposed." And George opened the door and closed it again, but remained in the hall. He grabbed Emily by her arm and dragged her into the kitchen.

"Oh, Sir!"

"George, call me George."

"What'll Susannah say? I ..."

"She won't say anything, because she won't know, and you're not going to tell her, are you?"

"No George, I won't if you don't," and giggled.

George kicked the kitchen door closed with the back of his shoe.

"Come here, I need to whisper something."

And Emily rose on her tiptoes. He placed his lips to her neck and kissed her earlobe. And reaching for her lips he kissed her, biting gently on her upper lip.

"Oh, well I never," said Emily, as she attempted to pull away.

"Oh, I can't believe that."

"Oi, cheeky! If the Mistress, Miss Gregory, should come in!"

"Does she often come into the kitchen?" he asked, while he pulled at the buttons on her blouse.

"Well no, once she did."

"There now, safe!" he said, as he turned the key in the lock.

"But now if she tries to, and she finds the door locked ..."

"It stuck, that's all you need say. Or, how on earth did that happen?"

"But what if—"

"Shh, too many questions." And he silenced her with a kiss. George pulled her to him, bent his head, and covered the crown of her head with kisses. And he held her close. He swirled her round, her thighs pushed against the kitchen table. And George lifted her up and sat her down on the scrub top and came forward and placed himself between her legs.

***

"Oh my Emily, I love you so much. And his hand went up under skirts; and she pretended to resist, as all decent girls should. But she loved him, and he loved her and this was exciting; her life once so humdrum she was now the heroine of her readings. And those kisses tasted of honey. She should push away his exploring hand. She would, but ... not yet.

George had now pushed aside the closure on her bloomers. Emily felt his hand moving in places it shouldn't, but then ... so what, it felt so good. And George took his finger and gently stroked the hair that sprouted with abundance between her legs, and in so doing brushed against her lips, as lightly as a butterfly's touch.

George groaned, "Oh Emily," and he widened her knees and now his body stood between her open legs, her skirts drawn up, pooled over the wooden table. George undid his fly. Emily stared. "Hold me, hold me in your hand." Emily held it, took him in her hand. This bloody big thing somehow had remained unnoticed, buried in his trousers. Emily held it, warm, like velvet, smooth as satin.

"Move your hand along me, like this." and George covered her hand with his and moved it up and down. George groaned as he released her hand from his grip, and she continued to move her hand, her big brown eyes watching him with great curiosity.

"Cuddle me, hold me." And Emily held him close. And she felt this great smooth hardness pushing at her most private place. George pushed her down on to the table and raised her feet to its edge, he stepped back and threw up her skirts and they covered her face. And there was no one here! No one more than a cunt; a disheaded cunt, ready for fucking, and George slid his finger into the fleshy folds and the moisture he tasted from his finger.

Emily was glad her face was hidden. It hid not her embarrassment, she knew she shouldn't be doing this, it hid her lust; she thought nothing of exposing her most intimate parts. George stood between her thighs his hand on her knees. He eyed his target, took his dick in his hand, and stepped forward. He pressed against her, pushing forward, he was in no hurry; this girl so willing. And he pushed again.

"I'll try not to hurt you, I promise you." And he searched for her face under the crease of fabric. "I love you." And he kissed her. And she kissed him. George pressed his hips forwards and felt her body yield just a little to him. He pushed forward again, again. Emily murmured beneath him, but she clung to him and held him to her, her legs wrapped around his buttocks.

Emily hadn't known love before! This sensation rolling through her body was a ripple, like having your hair brushed or lulled into sleep. But no, so much more. - *Oh God*. Then his fingers, touching her, there; rubbing so fast and hard and he stopped his thrusting, and waited. And then -*Fucking hell*. Emily thought she was going to die of sheer pleasure. Her body trembled and George thrust into her again and she was panting. The sweat from him trickled onto her face and she licked away his saltiness.

If she could have just pulled him, pulled all of him, absorbed him into her body just then, she would. A birth in reverse. George thrusting now, harder, faster and deeper. Every thrust of his hips, she met with an upward thrust of hers. Her feet pinning him and pulling him back towards her. As if she were afraid he was going to leave, abandon her when she'd only just had him. So a tussle began, he withdrew a portion, to thrust again, but Emily pulled him back.

The kettle on the hob poured steam into the airless room. George was dripping water. The coals in the stove shifted, sending sparks shooting up the chimney. Emily was in love. It was then the bell on the wall rang. The finale, they groaned to the timbre of the bells.

"Oh Christ."

And Emily layback covered in sweat, flour stuck to her arse and in her hair. Broken eggshells covered George's hand, then the bell jangled once more.

"I'm going to have to go."

George sighed and withdrew himself, he held out his hand to her, so she could pull herself from the table. They attended to their dress. And Emily seized and tied on a new and clean piny. Just as she was opening the door he grabbed her, and kissed her, and said, "I love you. I wish you didn't have to go." He took from her hair a piece of broken shell.

Chapter 17

George knew then, he had achieved his goal but to what end? Even George didn't understand. George was trying to work out what had happened between him and Emily. It was the best fuck he'd had so far. He lay on his bed savouring every detail. And as he lay thinking about his dick bursting in Emily, he again become hard. He wanted to go back, recover the old ground. He wanted her here now. Sitting on his dick and ...

"What are you thinking about, as if I couldn't guess? Your blankets propped with a cock pole."

"I, Sebastian, am thinking about love."

"I think I noticed."

"Who's it this time?"

"It is Emily."

Sebastian sighed, "I thought you said love. Not lust."

"I can't get her out of my mind."

"Sex, it does that!"

"If she were here now ..."

"But she's not George, so I'll have to do." With that, he pulled the blankets from George. There stood George, pants open at the fly, his hand holding his dick. Sebastian took George's hand away and replaced it with his own. Sebastian glanced up at George who lay back, his head supported by his arm.

"Thinking of England?"

And Sebastian spoke no more, not for the next few minutes because his mouth was full of George. With his hand he stroked his shaft, with his lips he sucked. George pushed Sebastian away and rose to his knees. Both now knelt on the bed confronting each other. Sebastian took off his trousers. George's hardness met with his hardness. Sebastian leaned and reached for the oil on the washstand and placed it on the floor by his bed.

Sebastian pulled George to him, and pressed his lips to his mouth. George did not respond but sat kneeling, watching, and receiving. He nibbled George's ear and still no movement. Sebastian kissed his lips and took George's dick in his hand and he kissed him, jamming his tongue into his mouth. The taste of port, a sweet tangy smell of sweat just turning stale filled his nostrils.

Face to face, dick to dick. George's abraised face, turning a becoming, blush pink. Sebastian's hard and urgent fingers rubbed and oiled George. Sebastian turned George over, yanking at his long johns.

"Fucking fine arse George," he said, jabbing the firm buttock with his index finger. Sebastian's arm embraced George and found and held his slippery cock. Sebastian licked the nape of George's neck, and thrusted between George's legs. He dribbled oil onto his buttocks it trickled down, seeping into his cleavage.

George thought of Emily. That soft cunt opening like an orchid, the damp velvet, the fragrant peaty scent.

Sebastian hands slid up his shaft, squeezing the head between his thumb and finger. Her legs open, the delicate forms, so soft. The shaft tilted, oiled and primed. Sebastian thrust himself forward. George groaned, Sebastian felt George stiffen, harden in his hand. Her body enclosing him in a warm velvet embrace. Sucking him down. Pushing him up. Sebastian thrust and lay his head on George's shoulders, faster now, deeper now. George took the weight of Sebastian on his elbows. Sebastian plunging, diving, one hand on George's dick the other squeezing, holding his balls.

Behind him, he growled in his ear, a deep roar. Under him, she mewed like a kitten. He roared in George's ear, a hurricane. She whispered sweet nothings, a gentle breeze.

Sebastian pushed deeper and faster. George's dick, hard and firm.

Yielding, soft and moist.

A salty scent.

A musky fragrance.

He covered his body with his strength.
She wrapped his body with her softness.
Sebastian's hand quickened, one final urgent push.
George trickled through Sebastian's fingers.

They lay together in the late afternoon, back to stomach, Sebastian held George firmly, held him clenched against his stomach.

***

They pulled away from one another; they lay on their backs, side-by-side. Sebastian's dick hung on his left thigh and George's on his right. *-Like a couple of bookends.* But these would keep nothing up. A small spider spun a web above their heads.

"Which do you prefer George, cunt or cock?"

George sighed. "It's rather like asking do I prefer fruitcake or roast beef. I like beef and fruitcake, I like both, but at different times and in different ways. What about you?"

"I thought, I believed, like you did. But I know now, I prefer meat."

George chuckled.

"What? Oh for goodness sake." There followed a silence, broken by Sebastian. "I don't think I'm cut out for women."

"Have you had one?"

"Well yes … no."

George looked at his friend, and smiled. "You don't know?"

"It was this girl; I've known her for years. Then one day I met her, she was riding a bicycle …" George turned on to his side facing Sebastian his head supported by his hand. "Well?"

"She was wearing these trouser thingeys, no bloomers. She wore a tie at her neck; she looked almost boyish with her hair tied up tight under this boater. We walked together, and then well, you know how it is. But once she was on display and I was on top of her, I was just about to give it a good shove."

George rubbed his friend's shoulder. "Well I couldn't, I was as limp as a wet chamois; it was almost as soon as he saw where I was trying to shove him, he thought, bugger that."

"Or not."

"Exactly."

"So how did she respond? Not well, I suspect, women don't like it if you thwart their desires, they can't ask for it you see. They want it, probably more than we do, but the onus is on us…"

Sebastian thought about this for a moment, "Anyway as she couldn't see my condition I told her, I couldn't do it, out of respect for her."

"What did she say?"

"Well, nothing."

"Nothing?"

"No, she cried."

"Frustration … you haven't seen her since?"

"I did once at a party my mother gave."

"Awkward, was it?"

"I suppose you could say that."

George looked into Sebastian's eyes. Just then, someone rapped his knuckles on the door. "Who is it?" shouted George, preparing to leap from the bed and into his dressing gown.

"Jeffrey Sir, Jeffrey Walker."

"Bugger off."

"The bursar asked me to… I have a letter for you."

"Shove it under the door."

"Yes Sir."

After a minute … and no letter forthcoming, George bellowed, "What are you doing out there?"

"I … I need your signature."

"For God's sake, shove it under the ruddy door, I'll sign it."

"Oh for goodness sake," And Sebastian got his arse off the bed and flung the door open. "Give it here."

Jeffrey's gaze went from Sebastian's hand, his face, to his dick. Sebastian walked over to the desk, picked up a pen, and thrust them both at George, "Sign here." Jeffery's gaze followed Sebastian; he saw George and his dick. George was going to cover himself, but he liked watching Jeffrey as he stared on him, that look of surprise, precious. And the more Jeffrey stared, the more George liked it. Sebastian took the paper from him, "Down George!" Sebastian thrust the paper at Master Walker. "Here, I'm sorry, I don't have anything on me right now."

George chuckled, "We'll catch you next time."

Jeffery turned and dashed awayt.

"So what happened at the party?"

Sebastian stepped into his pants, as he buttoned them, he said, "Laughter, that's what happened. Amelia and her closest friend Constance, pointed, stared, they whispered; hands in front of their mouths, you know the sort of thing; they giggled. When I looked up at them, Constance dragged Amelia away to the veranda."

"Women! Mind though; it may have been you didn't fancy her. She was the only woman?"

"Well yes..."

"Right we'll try you out on someone else."

"No George I am decided. I shall be a confirmed bachelor."

"You're mother will have something to say about that. No Sebastian, you have to try it. Close your eyes and think of something else. Your mother will be wanting children, your inheritance would be placed unnecessarily at risk. Besides, a wife and child will be an excellent cover for you if you're determined to keep floating your barge up that particular canal."

"I do, it's nothing to do with choice, this is who I am. You can step one way or the other, I'm ... the other."

"Look we'll find someone. Someone's who's a bit well, not overly feminine. What you need is a small tight arse."
"I know."

***

Dolly held a wicker basket filled with the ginger fur ball, Ferdinand; the tomcat with a chewed tail and a dicky leg. Dolly nursed him back to rude health after a contretemps with mad Max. Ferdinand wasn't badly injured but his pride was seriously damaged. Ferdinand left out his tail from the safety of an upturned wheelbarrow. This misjudgement had allowed the teeth of that terrier to sink into that offensive extremity.

"Why's that dresser door moving?" asked Joe.

"That's Ferdinand, I'm keeping an eye on him."

"The doors closed, you can't see him."

"He's safe in there. It's only for a week till he's better."

Joe went to cupboard

"Don't!"

One ginger, fur covered, cannon ball, trailing a bandage from a bloody tail, shot from the dresser and scowled at his tormentors from beneath the sink.

"Well, that's that. How we supposed to get him out from there?"

"Bribery."

"If he gets out ... Agnes doesn't like cats."

Joe put a saucer of cream on the floor. Tapped out his pipe and sat on his chair. "He's not looking happy, Dolly."

"Well would you, if someone had sunk their teeth in your tail?"

"Well, I ... depends who that someone—"

"He's out!"

Cream lapped. That was it, the great big, grapefruit shaped head, banged against Joe's leg. "All right mate, I'll shove over." And so he did, and there they were. Joseph and Ferdinand, together; sharing the warmth of the fire. Dolly almost wept for joy; but told herself not to be so, -Ruddy stupid.

***

George on his return home to Fairview, wrote to Susannah. He wrote every week. In this next letter, he wrote:

Dear Susannah,

I feel I must write to your father, I am concerned I haven't heard from you. I ought to offer to your father an explanation something of what happened between us. I worry have befallen you. I am so vexed.
Please reply to me I am so desperately worried. I would give anything to rewrite our history.
Please forgive me if I've done anything to upset you. Do I deserve such removal from your heart?
Yours sincerely
George

The following morning the postman delivered a letter:

Dear George,

I should of course have replied to your letters. I'm trying to understand the meaning of that unfortunate occurrence. I should be grateful, it isn't necessary that my father should be so hurt. I rely on your discretion.

Yours truly
Miss Susannah Gregory

George set down to reply immediately, if he posted it now it would reach Susannah by the evening delivery.

Dearest Susannah,

Please do not reproach yourself. It is of course out of bounds for ladies to visit the boy's rooms. But I do not condemn you for it.
Yours sincerely
George

***

May went to the fire and took a piece of charred wood that had tumbled onto the hearth. She crushed it with the back of a spoon and added a drop of the lanolin. "Must remember this isn't the correct recipe, but it'll give you the idea of what I mean. Close your eyes." May gentle outlined her eyes using a nail stick, then brushed her brows. "There, what do you think?"

Agnes looked at herself and blinked twice. "Why May…you're a witch; I can't believe … my eyes look twice as big." May smiled, pleased with herself.

"I wouldn't have thought it possible … in so short a time too … such a transformation."

After May left, Agnes stood in front of her mirror; she didn't know how that girl had achieved it. *-I look at least ten years younger,* well, a lot more attractive anyway! She turned her head this way and that so she could view this new woman. Agnes allowed the satin dressing gown to fall from her shoulders and didn't stop it as it slid to the floor. Agnes stood in her corset and stockings and heeled slippers. She looked at herself *-Not bad, not unattractive, not for a mature woman who's borne three children.* Agnes was bending over to pick up her gown when the door banged open and George said, "Mother!" The door slammed behind him. He paused in the hall, took a few deep breaths as leaned against the hall wall.

***

George was trying to make sense of what he had just seen. Make sense of his mixed emotions; obviously embarrassment, and a little disgust, but something else too or so the tautness in trousers told him. He intended to rid himself of that particular ball ache and he knew just the slut to help him out of his predicament.

May returned in time to witness George disappearing up the backstairs, to the attic. *-I wonder what he's up to? There are three rooms off that passage, the storeroom, the Crows-Nest and my room. I'm not there and my money is hidden. So if it's my room enjoy, Georgie boy, have a rummage through my drawers, at least I'm not in them.*

May knocked and entered, "Your ... whatever's the matter?"

"Oh May, I'm so ashamed." Black smudges ran under her eyes.

-Oh blimey, don't look so good now, she thought. That's the trouble with paint, only a temporary fix.

"It was George. George! He came in....He saw me, standing naked. I've never been so mortified... I just don't know how I'm going to face him."

May bumped into people in assorted stages of undress and 'how's your father', everyday at home, and thought it not worth making, *-Such a bloody fuss about.*

"I don't think George has a clue about women yet. I'm his mother... Poor boy he must be so embarrassed." She wrung her hands into her gown and twisted it in a knot. "May, be a dear, and run a bath." May crossed the hall to the bathroom and slid the bolt ...

***

Tuesday morning a package arrived addressed to Mrs Agnes Spritely; a small parcel wrapped in brown paper and tied with string.

"Careful how you open that," said Henry.

Agnes weighed the parcel in her hand, she didn't recognise the hand.

"I'll use scissors, I'll open it later."

"Can't be too careful." And he returned his attention to the marriages section in The Times. Agnes placed her parcel next to her side plate; toyed with kedgeree on her plate.

"Excuse me Henry, I'm not hungry this morning." And took the package and rose from the table.

"Not sickening for something are you?"

"No couldn't be better." And she clutched the parcel to her chest.

"Good girl. Miss Norman-Watt is to marry Captain Andrew Hunnicutt. Well, that's not surprising."

-*Then why are you reading it out,* thought Agnes. But said, "Really, that's nice." And she left the breakfast room and headed for the library.

Sitting at the library table Agnes cut the string on her parcel, revealing a book of red leather boards and gilt lettering the title read. Ancient Manners, Pierre Louys. Inside on the end paper: Sweet love. We were one, two laurels with one root.

***

...And he wrote it on the back of a postcard with a butterfly printed on the front. Susannah didn't reply. So two days later he sent an invitation to a party his family were giving, not that they knew this yet. Again, no response, so George wrote to her father, and included the invitation. The next day he received a letter from Mr Gregory:

Dear George Spritely,

I'm pleased to hear from you George.
I do think Susannah is more upset than she allows herself to believe by your absence. She's far too quiet and spends much time alone in her room.
Surprisingly she doesn't want even to attend the Cathedral's services.
I believe your party would just do the trick. I shall insist she attends. She would never not, obey her father. In all ways, she is a good and obedient young lady.

I regret of course, that I will not be able to accept your kind invitation; I have rather too much to do before the school term restarts.
Don't worry George, when she sees you, I'm sure it will change her disposition.
Yours sincerely
Mr Cecil Gregory

***

Agnes walked around the table several times with May in tow, arranging and rearranging the name-place cards. "Sir William, will sit to my right, he is the most important guest; and to my left, Mr Robert Nash. Next to him Francis, and she'll be seated next to George; Susannah then Henry, Miss Underhill, Sebastian and Mrs Underhill." -*Poor Sebastian surrounded by Underhills, but he won't mind.* It's the best I can do. "We'll want centre pieces; Ivy and holly, sugared fruits ... This I will leave in your capable hands, May."

Henry was not overly impressed, and became quite vexed when he discovered whom she had invited. "You're seating me next to Miss Underhill? Why, the girl has teeth like protruding cannon on the decks of a man-of-war." His mood changed when he saw, on the night of the party, who was going to be seated to his right at table; a glimmer of a smile when he spied the glorious Susannah, he didn't know her, and it was generous of old Aggie to place the loveliest girl in the room beside him.

Chapter 18

May received the visitors, she wore a new piny, and a new dress, and cap. She took the guests through to the drawing room and announced each and everyone as they arrived.

George chatted with his chum Sebastian. "I don't reckon she's going to show, George." George didn't respond, but kept glancing, every time the door opened and a new guest arrived.

As Sir Baker was sticking two fingers on his forearm, and someone shouted: "Tom Thumb!" The door opened and Susannah floated into the room. She looked stunning, or as Sebastian noted, "Bloody ravishing." She wore a gown of cream silk with a choker of pearls around her honey coloured throat, and at her cleavage hovered a blue bejewelled butterfly.

May was aghast. She, not only was a cloud of perfume, puffed blond hair the epitome of elegance and fashion. *-Heads turned!* But she was wearing, *-That's my bloody brooch.*

-Ruddy late, always late. George rushed over to take her arm and introduce her to the other guests. Henry lowered his spectacles.

Emily stood by the door and May, who was curious, cross and worried; boiled together in the, *-Bloody brooch it was for her!* Stew; sidled over to Emily and asked, "Who is she?"

"That's Miss Susannah Gregory; she's the daughter of the choir master."

"Oh." May watched this woman glide around the room as if she were on casters. "They an item then?" She couldn't stop herself from asking.

"Oh, no! Miss Susannah hasn't been well, and Mr Gregory her father, insisted, insisted she get out of the house and enjoy herself. She didn't want to come."

"That's a beautiful brooch." May wished she could, - *Bloody shut up!* But she couldn't; she wanted to know about this, wanted to know about him, her, and that butterfly brooch. Curiosity had unleashed her tongue.

"First time I've seen her wear it, but isn't it gorgeous? She has lovely things. I think her father bought it for her, although she never said. And I never asked!"

"No …" -*Ooh, you never asked. But I'm a nosey cow, and I did.*

"He collects butterflies, has loads of them on tray in a big chest."

"Lepidopterist." - *That'll show you.*

"Eh?"

"That's what they're called; the people who collect butterflies."

"Oh … I."

Agnes summoned May. "Would you check for empty glasses and refill them. Circulate, more drinks and show that girl, what's her name?"

"Emi—"

"How to do it, get her to help you! Standing around chatting, we won't get anything done like that."

May said, "Yes Mrs Spritely." -*Blimey, one is right up 'emselves tonight.*

Sir William, was standing now in front of the roaring fire, warming his backside, and was joined by Henry. "Got some good-looking women in the house tonight, eh?"

"Indeed, Henry most impressive!"

***

The dinner at seven was ready, and Dolly was about to do, what she'd longed to do for a long time. She'd done it only once before … And that was to give the gong in the hall a big, bloody bash.

"What the ruddy hell?" Henry dabbed at the rum stains he'd splashed over his shirtfront when he'd jumped, - *out my bloody skin!* George picked up the cards Francis had thrown into the air. Francis was of a sensitive disposition and, complained she was about to faint.

Dolly, uncertain the gong was enough to convince them dinner was now on the table, came though and bellowed, "DINNER is served."

The guests, having recovered their composure formed an orderly line, and escorted or clutched their partners across the hall and into the dining room, and reviewed the seating arrangements. The room was beautifully decorated. Agnes was much congratulated. "The candles, perfect. Oh, and the centrepieces! The flowers, the fruits!"

And Agnes thanked the guests, "You're too kind," she said. Agnes had given much thought to the guest list. Henry of course, would be at the head of the table and she, opposite him. Agnes cleverly, had managed, which unfortunately meant an invite for the Underhills, an even number of males to females, and an equal amount of young to … not so young, people.

***

Joseph sat in the kitchen eating a starter, a smelt, Dolly bent over the stove. He was imagining her arse, unclothed. Those huge great mounds moonin' at him, and he chuckled.

"What you sniggering about Joseph Bridger?"

"I was just thinking, what a fine looking woman you are." *-Her arse is even bigger than I remember, that day many moons ago,* and he chuckled again.

"Joseph Bridger if you don't stop your sniggering I shall beat you with a wet flannel."

"Please."

Dolly shook her ladle at him showering her apron with carrot soup, (a la Crecy). "Now look what you've done."

"Didn't touch yer, not bloody near yer." Joseph was thinking! Joseph decided he'd served propriety long enough, it was two, or more years since Lizzie had passed over.

May watched the party at dinner, George leaned into Susannah, and Susannah moved away. Henry brushed her hand and she flinched! Emily explained about the household. Susannah was not a fast eater. Half an hour passed and she was still pushing at the soup with her spoon.

Henry couldn't take his eyes from her spoon. As if raising a spoon to her beautiful lips were just too exhausting, no sooner did she fill it, it'd tilt, and empty, and the process would begin again. Not allowing the physical effort of raising it to hers lips to interrupt the soup's tidal flow. After being mesmerised by her beauty, his appetite for food returned and his stomach gurgled. – *Fuck. For fuck's sake, put your ruddy spoon, down.*

Dolly made two appearances at the door. Agnes, after Dolly's third 'just checking.'-*My dinner is going to be ruined,* appearance. Agnes insisted Susannah's soup is cold, and Dolly, "Please clear the plates."

Menu
Carrot Soup a la Crecy
Fried Smelts with Dutch Sauce
Mutton cutlets with Soubise Sauce
Oyster Patties
Rump of Beef a la Jardinière
Boiled Chicken and Celery Sauce
Roast Hare Eggs a la Negle
Artichoke Buttons
Meringues a la Ring
Orange Jelly
Cabinet Pudding
Transparent Jelly Inlaid with Brandy Cherries

Henry replaced the napkin on his lap. He was looking forward to the cutlets and the onion, -*Ooh sorry, Soubise sauce.* Fortunately, Susannah was going to have the oysters. This, thought Henry with relief, was a good idea. -*She wouldn't tax herself overly, by chewing.*

***

Joseph was already sampling the roast beef, which he chewed while staring at the huge bare arse of Dolly Proudley. He decided he'd do without the roast hare and finish his meal with the orange pudding.

"That's a fine spread you have there, Dolly."

"You say one more word Joe and I swear, that'll be the last morsel you'll be able to eat with all your teeth." And she brandished the ladle at him. Joseph stood up and gathered the huge woman in his arms; he clung to her back like a barnacle on a boat while she stirred something white in a pot.

"Joseph, will you take your arms from me! I don't know what's come over you?"

Joseph did, he'd been alone too long, and here was Dolly with that huge arse thrusting itself about the stove. What man wouldn't be tempted? What he'd like to do would be throw her over the table and give her a dam good rogering.

"And you can stop all that nonsense as well." Dolly pushed him aside and started to lay another tray, ready for the third course.

Sebastian was trying to work out who was the most desirable person in the room. He decided it was George. He could fuck him now, right this minute. And willed him to drop his fork so he could crawl under the table and give him a good seeing to.

***

Dolly wheeled in the third course balanced precariously high on a trolley. May and Emily were set to serve. Emily was faster than a greyhound out of the traps. She managed to serve George every course, in the correct order! A different wine was served with each course, and conversations became louder and looser. George pushed his hand up Emily's skirt while she served him Jelly with brandy cherries. May watched this from the sanctuary of the sideboard and raised an eyebrow. After that helping, he clutched at Susannah's hand but she withdrew it and settled it in her lap.

Sir William plunged his spoon into cherry jelly, leaving his left hand to claim more interesting wares. It sat idly in his lap, but the devil made work for it. His fingers searched for Agnes' leg and while Mr Nash spoke on about developing The North End, William's busy fingers pulled up Agnes' skirt.

Henry was impressed with his wife. The two men either side of her were obviously talking business over her head and she kept a most serene expression. -*Like a Mona Lisa!* And Henry admitted to himself he was enjoying this evening and was, as an after thought - *Proud of my wife.* William found the lace edging of her drawers.

"Of course any help that you could grant us Sir William, in gaining approval ..."

William's hand tugged Agnes' hair, the tablecloth hiding the straying ingress.

"Of course a commission would be forthcoming."

And Sir William nodded, as his fingers stroked Agnes and he slipped his fingers, into her.

"The soil is a little boggy of course."

Henry withdrew his hand. Agnes sat with her skirt hem resting above her knees on her lap. From his lower jacket pocket, while his right hand fed jelly into his mouth, his left pulled a Cuban cigar.

"There are the allotments to deal with of course."

And returning his hand to Agnes, he rubbed the cigar against her cunt. Agnes apologised to Mr Robert Nash as she knocked her knee against him and sat forward a little on her seat. This allowed Sir William to push his cigar further, slipping it into Agnes. William smiled in agreement. Agnes nodded, wearing her beatific smile.

Sir William asked, "Sorry my dear, we're not boring you, are we?"

"No of curse not, I'm enjoying ... these developments."

And William plunged his cigar, right up to the label.

"Understand you're much in support of gaining wage increases for the dockyard men?"

William slowly withdrew and returned the Cuban to his pocket, "I am, the conditions they live and work under are deplorable."

"Course it has an effect, they receive more money, the costs go up, etc."

"Depends, on how the pie is sliced."

"Our maid's father, he works in the docks bawled Henry, from the other end of the table. "Doesn't he May?"

All eyes turned to May who nodded.

"Father's hurt, and May supported the family. Isn't that right May?"

May nodded again. -*Will you just leave me out of this!*

But wine and rum were freeing tongues. "Of course we helped out, gave her a little extra."

Agnes downed her pudding spoon. -*We did?* Henry had taken such a keen interest in the maid. But as Sir William guided her hand to feel how big his dick had become, all interest in May evaporated, and she nodded at the guests, smiling benignly.

George smirked. -*Oh, yes, helped her out. Of her drawers!* He thought of Emily, he'd given her nothing, apart from his dick. -*I've fucked, and been fucked by four people in this room!* With that, he allowed his hand to brush Susannah's knee, she flinched, he smiled at her, his best smile.

May watched these people at table. It was the first time she was aware of a distinction between them and us.

***

Henry was quite taken with Violet Underhill. Susannah may be a stunner, but -*By God, if she got any slower she'd be dead!* Violet smiled a toothy grin at Henry's quips. *-The canons in the gun ports ready for discharge!* But she did have the liveliest eyes that creased up at the corners and her nose crinkled when she chuckled. *-I would like to screw you, now.*

"Sorry. What did you say?"

"Anything I can do for you? More wine, perhaps?"

"Thank you." And she held up her glass, which Henry most generously filled.

As the party neared eleven, Agnes tapped her glass, "Ladies, have we finished?" She chose to ignore Susannah who was still fighting with a cherry, a battle she was more than likely to lose.

"Let's all withdraw and leave the men to their cigars." The ladies stood up as one, apart from Susannah who was already waiting impatiently for the door to open. "May, Emily, please serve the port and leave the brandy on the table and then the men on their own. Thank you, ladies." Maids instructed, Agnes withdrew from the dining room.

May and Emily gathered dirty plates from the table and trundled them out of the dining room leaving a clearing for the men to talk manly chat and think masculine thoughts.

"Come on down this end, no need to bellow." And the men exchanged seats so they could sit closer together. Sir William rose, but instead of reseating himself, stood with his arse to the fire.

And Henry asked, "Cigar William?"

"Thank you Henry, but I would prefer to smoke my own." While the others at the table cut the cigar's tips, lit and puffed, he withdrew a cigar from his jacket pocket.

"Special is it?"

"Cuban, rolled on a virgin's thigh." And Sir William closed his eyes and ran the cigar under his nose and sniffed.

"Ah, I can smell her now, ripe for the plucking." And they guffawed as one.

Henry lit a taper from the embers, and held it against Sir William's cigar.

Here, Henry try one, and he reached into his top pocket and withdrew a large cigar and handed it to Henry. Henry sniffed, and cut the tip, lit it, checked the glow, sucked and puffed out a large cloud of smoke.

George leaned back in his chair and stretched out his legs. Ties loosened as were their tongues.

"All a bit over you young lad's heads, eh? said Mr Nash. "Not plucked yet!"

Henry scoffed, "Like a hunter at the fox, he's bloodied all right."

Sebastian rolled his eyes.

"What about you, young fellow, are we all men together?" George looked at Sebastian and they both laughed.

"I have it on good authority that our Sebastian has, rampantly, been fucking."

And to that, they gave a toast.

"To the fucking fanny."

"The fanny."

And Sebastian raised and chinked his glass against George's.

***

"See I told you," said Emily, "she has no interest in him whatsoever."

"Mm." -*Emily could be right, it did seem as though George's advances weren't welcome.*

"If anyone should know, I should. I am their maid!"

At the close of the evening, Sir William had agreed to dropping off the Underhills. "No, no, no. I won't hear of you walking, in this weather!"

It would be a squeeze until Francis and the Underhills disembarked, but it was only half a mile along; then the onward journey to Southsea. Sebastian was sleeping with George. Susannah lodged in the Crow's-Nest and Emily had a 'zed' bed laid up in May's room.

***

Emily tossed and turned, the Zed bed creaked, and she was lying in a draft.

"May, I'm cold."

"Go and get another blanket then."

"It's a long way, I'll freeze. Could I get in with you?"

-No, bugger off.

"Please. Oh, go on."

"Oh … But don't fidget."

***

May, after hearing strange noises coming from her room, looked through the keyhole. Her mouth hung open, agape, so absorbed was she in the sight that met her eyes she didn't hear Henry approaching.

"What's that you're doing May, peering through to your own room?"

"Um Er."

Henry lowered his eye to the opening. What Henry could see was the iron bedposts and bedspread and on that spread was a pair of white buttocks with a spot; thrusting buttocks. And if he wasn't mistaken those buttocks belonged to, *-By George!* So who was that then, underneath him? Wearing those red stockings, with her legs wrapped round his hips? And her thrusting up and he pushing down. Henry looked away confused, glanced at May just to ensure he hadn't imagined her standing there. Henry was about to take another peek, when there was a sound from the Crow's-Nest. By jolly, he'd forgotten about Susannah.

Henry grabbed May and dragged her along and into the spare room. They listened as Susannah's door opened. They held their breath waiting for the door to shut and then footsteps, but they both started to giggle like naughty schoolchildren. But what with the giggling and the laughter, as if a dam burst, May shed a tear, and then wept.

"Now, then, what's all this?" And the tears flowed down May's cheeks. Henry took her in his arms and cuddled her.

May cried, she didn't know why she was crying, but she knew it felt good, as good as when she'd stuck those needles in her ear lobes. "I hate him," she blurted out between sobs.

"Now come on May, can't be all that bad, just a shock. I must say, I was bloody surprised." And he held her tight and stroked her hair. "Shh, there now."

At last, the sound of bedsprings rattling ceased. And Henry pushed May away, withdrew a handkerchief from his breast pocket, and handed it to her. May wiped away her tears and blew her nose.

***

George hearing a sound outside the door and hid in the wardrobe. Not that he was scared, but confrontation meant explanation, and would contradict the high opinion he held of himself. And explanation would rather spoil the view others held of him, and to which most people adhered. -*Apart from May!* She didn't like him. This dislike of course, had little to do with George. But jealousy is a hateful emotion and one which she sort to unburden herself by loading onto George's shoulders. But George did not accept it. -S*hould be bloody grateful.*

***

This was the last night of Emily sleeping in her bed, this night she hadn't even asked May whether she could join her. She was in bed already. Tucked up and staring at the ceiling. May undressed to her chemise.

"Budge over."

"Warmed it up for you."

"Certainly did."

Emily stared out the window, looking up at the stars, dreamily remembering George.

"George is your lover. It's George, isn't it?"

"Well … How do you know?"

"I saw you, in here. I saw you." -*On my bloody bed.*

"Peering through keyholes were you?"

"My bloody room, if you weren't making such a racket I'd have just come in."

Emily sniffed. "Look, I couldn't help it, he just turned up …"

"Didn't appear like you were resisting him from where we were standing."

"I … Didn't … We?"

"Mr Spritely, he saw you, and for all I know Susannah did too."-*So take that.*

"Susannah?"

May tossed over, turning her back against Emily, accidentally kicking her sharply in the shin with her heel as she did so.

***

Now the thing about upsetting people before they turn to sleep, is they don't, sleep. They toss and turn and fret, and in a bed, measuring just two feet six in width meant that neither had much sleep that night. Emily tossed. Every imaginable slight, insult, every happenstance, and upset came delivered not as a dream but in a waking state.

***

May took the handkerchief with the blue anchor and wiped away a tear. She'd offered it back to Henry, washed, starched and ironed but he had refused to accept it. Lack of sleep had caused May to return to her room after she'd served breakfast for a rest. 1 '0' clock and the knocking at her door roused May from her nap.

"May, It's Dolly."

"Come in."

Dolly had waited, respected her room, her privacy, unlike the Spritely's who though they would knock, would enter without pause.

"Oh dear, what's the matter?"

"I …"

"I'll send up something."

"I."

"You do look a bit peaky. We've got a stew, and dumplings with a hint of sage. Now you just rest, I'll bring your dinner up."

Dolly returned with a steaming bowl of beef stew with potatoes, dumplings and two hunks of bread. "I'll put it on this table. You've made it so nice in here, just stuff out of the spare room too, who'd have thought?" Dolly set the tray down "Well come on, before it gets cold."

"Thank you."

And Dolly left, slamming the door behind her.

Chapter 19

Well he courted her most cruelly,
Filled her head with hopes and dreams.
Told her she would be a lady,
But nothing was wot it had seemed.

May sat at her table she removed the handkerchief from her pocket. And as she'd see the guests do at dinner, she laid the napkin on her lap; not tucked into her collar or worse gone without. She picked up the spoon and practised eating.

May concentrated at pushing the soup away from her and leaving the bowl flat on the table. May wasn't sure it was etiquette to dunk chunks of bread in the bowl, she'd have to find out, but she did it anyway; because she didn't know, therefore she couldn't be faulted. And she wouldn't hold it against herself as an ignorant etiquette crime.

May could see her feet in the mirror but that was all. She wanted to know if she looked how the guests at the party behaved. So she dragged the table to the middle of the floor along with the chair. Rearranged the hanky, serviette … Napkin on her lap and watched herself pretend to eat the soup, which she'd already gulped down and wiped the bowl clean with the remaining crusty chunk. Push the spoon away from oneself. Don't slurp, and don't lift bowl to lips.

May looked and practised. She was a lady, lady what's her face, of Ponconby. She smiled at her reflection and pretended to pass the salt.

"Would you, Sir Prancelot like some water with your wine? Of course, I come here often. How do you do, my name is May, I'm your hostess." May giggled and nodded and raised her glass of water to herself reflected in the mirror. "Cheers me dear." May returned the table to its position and all semblance of normality resumed just as Dolly returned.

"How was it?"

"Very—"

"Joseph he's had seconds all ready, honestly where he puts it, I don't know." The door slammed shut as she made her way to the kitchen.

***

"Something's wrong," said Dolly, wringing her hands in her apron. "He's home, George."

"George?"

"A week or so early, looked a bit peaky, I thought, when I saw him, but then there was this horrible shouting and banging of doors. Well, I wanted to ask them if they'd like tea, but I daren't." Just then, another door slammed, followed by the sound of footsteps running up the stairs.

"Whatever can it mean?"

"Don't know, something to do with G— "

"He's not due leave 'til next week."

"Perhaps he's discharged."

"Discharged?"

May shrugged.

"George! Discharged?" Rather than soothing Dolly this unconsidered news sent her into anxiety. Fortunately for May, Joseph appeared.

"If you think you're treading mud all over this floor Joseph Bridger, you are mistaken, out!"

"Out?"

"Out."

"Ooh, I love it when you're feisty!" and he put his arms around her, but was repelled.

May rolled her eyes to heaven. The front bell rang, and May seizing her opportunity to be away from the tempest answered the door to the postman. A letter addressed to Mr H B Spritely.

"Who was it?"

"A letter for Mr Spritely—"

"I'll take it." And Dolly placed it on a tray and stormed out of the kitchen, curiosity overcoming her concerns.

Dear Sir,

A certain matter has been brought to my attention of such gravitas that I insist we meet.
I will be calling upon you tomorrow morning at 11.30.
Yours faithfully
Mr CJH Gregory

"Anything I can help you with? Trouble is it?"

Henry so absorbed in riding this storm hadn't realised Dolly was still in the room with him.

"That'll be all. Leave me."

"Yes …"

Dolly slammed into the kitchen, "I was dismissed, never in all my days … Such a … the way he spoke to me!"

"Must be serious, Mr Spritely, well he's never one to be rude."

Dolly considered this, while battering a roll of pastry into a pie dish. Silence reigned in the kitchen. May quietly sewed, accompanied by the rolling pin, pummelling the pastry. After five minutes, a hand appeared at the back door, a hand holding a bunch of white flowers, waving back and forth.

"Oh, get in here you daft beggar," Dolly said, and moved to warm the pot. Joseph had pre-emptively removed his boots; he'd give her no excuse to eject him from the kitchen. He took his place by the fireside. Bashed out his old tobacco and refilled his pipe. Joe turned his head to May, and with a sideways nod at Dolly wrinkled his nose. May answered with a shrug, and a grimace. And Joe replied with an understanding nod. Joe sighed.

"What's that sigh for?"

"She speaks!"

"May would you place those flowers in water for me, you can use that jug up there."

May did, and said, "These are lovely Joe."

"Roses, Christmas roses."

Joe took the pot to the table and poured the tea, three cups. "May, Dolly, tea's up."

"Thank you Joe."

They both looked to Dolly, "Thank you."

And they smiled as she weighed down on a groaning chair.

***

Mr Gregory stood with his back to the room, staring out of the window to the garden beyond.

"George will be down shortly."

Henry fiddled with a pen on his desk. Then moved over to the fireplace and leaned on the mantel. The silence in the room made both of them uncomfortable, but neither had the will to break it.

"Coffee, I think!"

"What's that?"

Henry rang the bell. When, after a second it wasn't answered, he pulled it again. "Coffee, unless you prefer tea?"

"Thank you, either will be fine."

Henry looked at the clock and checked it against his watch; he pushed the minute hand forward. May appeared.

"Coffee May, and tell George we're waiting for him."

"Yes, Mr Spritely."

"Well?" Dolly said, as May bumped into her in the hall.

"He wants coffee and he wants George, now."

"Right you make the coffee, I'll see to George." And Dolly's bottom vanished round the bend on the stairs!

George came into the library and stood by the desk. He coughed for good measure. Eventually his father said, "George you'll know of why Mr Gregory has come for this interview?"

"Er, yes ... I"

"Well, what have you to say to Mr Gregory?"

"I ..."

George didn't have anything to say, and fortunately, at that moment he didn't have to because May arrived with the coffee.

"Thank you May, just place it on the table, we'll serve ourselves. And May, we do not want to be disturbed."

"Yes, Mr Spritely."

"What's to be done?" Mr Spritely said, coffee overflowed into the saucer. "George, what will you do about this regrettable situation?"

Mr Gregory at that moment wanted to charge across the room, and throw a bloody good punch, right on that sod's nose. And he would have too, if he weren't a gentleman, and a guest and, standing only five foot six in height.

"Well, what have you to say?"

But before George could reply, Mr Gregory said, "He'll do the right thing by her. By Christ he will."

"Of course he will! Of course. We just need to decide what the right thing is."

"What the right thing is? Mr Spritely, What the right thing is?"

"Mr Gregory, call me Henry, please. I don't know what the girl would prefer..."

"Don't know what the girl would prefer!" he gasped.

-*Is he going to repeat everything I bloody say?*

"Well, we don't know her preference, but then how could we? This'll be our decision."

"Our decision? Our decision?"

-Bloody well is! Everything is going to be said twice, we'll be here all bloody day.

"May I suggest?" And without awaiting an answer, Henry blundered on.

"Father...."

"George let me finish. We'll give the girl fifty pounds."

"Fifty pounds?"

-Grief the man's a bloody parrot. "Yes, then it's up to her what she does with it."

"Does with it?"

Henry sighed.

"George what do you think? You're not thinking of supporting this girl with an allowance."

"Not supporting, not supporting." Mr Gregory had become red in the face, he couldn't believe his ears. storming over to the table, he banged his fist down. All three coffee-cups leapt from their saucers. "He'll marry her!"

"Marry her?" *-Christ I'm doing it now.* "He won't, I'll not have George marry beneath him."

"Beneath him? Beneath him, I'll have you know her mother was Lady Farquis, of Bath."

Henry blinked. "Her mother had an unmarried liaison, an adulterous?"

"What?"

"What? ... George!"

"I..."

Mr Gregory added, "George?"

"I ...! I will."

"What?"

"What!"

"I will marry her."

Henry couldn't believe his ears; "Do you want to ruin your life? She'll never be accepted."

"Not accepted!"

-Blimey, he's off again.

185

"My daughter, not accepted?"

"Your daughter?"

"Susannah, you do remember her, I suppose?" Henry had to sit down.

"Who did you think we were talking about?"

Henry blinked. "I don't …"

"George?"

"I've agreed, haven't I? I will marry her."

Mr Gregory picked up his cane, and with out so much as bye or leave, left. And Mr Gregory stormed out, as much as a little man can, out of that madhouse.

***

May and Dolly stood before Spritely.

"I've summoned you both here to inform you, that George is to be married."

"Oh, Henry, Mr Spritely, congratulations."

"Who will be the lucky lady?"

"Susannah, Susannah Gregory."

"Oh, she's so beautiful." -*Humph. A beautiful girl! All box, no chocolates.*

"When are … When is the ceremony? This happy event?"

"In two weeks."

"In two weeks?"

-*Good God, she's repeating me now,* "Am I making myself clear?"

May pursed her lips together and stared at a scratch on the floor.

"Perfectly, Mr Spritely!"

"Yes Mr Spritely," echoed May.

"Good, there is much to do. Dolly, we'll have a feast of course. Agnes will provide you a list of her wishes; menus, etc, all the necessities for such an occasion as this. May you will make the flower displays and decorations. You'll be supplied with ten pounds each. I will not go over this sum! Careful budgeting will be necessary." -*Careful budgeting, with ten whole pounds!*

***

"Well! Who'd have thought?" Dolly said, to herself, as she chopped carrots into slices on the block. "Marry."

At that moment, Joseph entered the kitchen. "I will," he said.

"What?"

"Marry you."

"This is serious."

"I pledge thee my troth, and all my worldly goods."

"George, It's George."

"Over my dead body."

"What?"

"I won't allow it; he's far too young for you."

"Joseph if you haven't anything sensible to say, stop talking! In fact, if you heed those rules, you'd be dumb."

Joseph grabbed her from behind, "Go on say you will." And he planted a great wet kiss on her neck.

"Will you be still?"

"Not until you say you'll wed me?" And he stood behind her pressing both his palms over her opulent breasts. "Ooh, you're all woman."

"Joseph behave, I don't know what's got into you. Don't know what's got into this entire house!"

"I love you Dolly, and I want you for me wife."

"Will you take your hands off me!"

Joseph did not remove his hands, they felt so comfortable, and he imagined his head sleeping on one of these warm, soft, white pillows. And that thought set his trousers tight, in a taut, tent pole position. "I'd like to tip you over this 'ere kitchen table and give you a good rodgering."

"You try it Joseph Bridger and I'll give you a good battering."

"Ooh, I love it when you talk dirty."

But Joseph had noticed that she hadn't shaken his hands away from her breasts. So he slid his finger inside the seam between the buttons. He found the top of her corset. He tried to thrust his finger but he got caught in its crushing grip. Mind, it did have a big job trying to constrain the wondrous flesh of Dolly.

"Say you'll be mine. Go on."

***

Dolly was getting very merry. The few guests that had come to celebrate the marriage of George Alexander Spritely, taking Miss Susannah Octavia Gregory, had left. George and Susannah were escorted on their honeymoon destination to Portsmouth harbour by Emily who was to travel with them; and Agnes and Henry who'd come to wave them off. Sebastian had gotten off one stop earlier; "You wouldn't mind old boy?" He'd decided he would have some fun in the sights and lights of Southsea.

Dolly brought the last of the food from the banquet to the kitchen. Some of the food would be reused through the week, but much of it would go to waste. The kitchen table was piled high, a mountain of food, well, ten pounds was a lot of money to feed such a small party, and Dolly had spent every penny.

"Here get that down yer."

"You trying to get me drunk, Joe?"

"The bubbles get right up yer nose."

"Well it'd only go flat, shame to waste it." As Dolly threw it down her throat, "I could get used to this."

"I'd drink it from your slipper."

The open champagne bottle finished, they started on the cider, brought in for the surrounding working folk.

"I prefer the champagne," hiccoughed Dolly.

"You, my goddess are a woman of discerning taste."

And Joseph popped a cork on a bottle of champagne. "Joseph!"

"You've worked hard this last week, you deserve it."

"But still …" The golden bubbles dancing before her eyes seduced her into silence, a rare thing!

"Put your feet up, on my lap." They sat in the two chairs opposing each other by the fireplace. Dolly placed her surprisingly dainty booted feet onto Joe's lap.

Joe undid the lacing and removed her boots.

"Oh, you daft bugger!" Dolly said, as Joe poured champagne into her boot and supped.

"Ambrosia, nectar of the gods."

"Well, if you think I'm doing that with your boots, you can think again."

Joe took her foot in his hand and rubbed the stockinged foot, massaging the overworked feet.

"Ooh that feels good, Joe."

"Give us the other one."

Dolly sipped Champagne with her feet up, and Joe rubbing her tootsies; she felt comfortable, relaxed. Joe lit his pipe with Dolly's small feet resting on his lap. His face hidden in a cloud of smoke.

"You, Dolly have the most beautiful feet. Cinderella wouldn't fit into your shoes."

Dolly smiled, -*S'pose I do have dainty feet.* And she looked at her feet resting on Joe's lap and turned them a little bit here, and pointed her toes. -*I do, never thought of it before.*

"Shame to keep them covered." And he tugged at the stocking's toe.

"You can't pull them off from there, just like that."

"I can't?"

"You have to undo the button."

"Where's that then?"

Dolly raised her skirt and showed the top of her stocking which finished just below her knee and twisted into a knot with a button in it.

"Oh," he said, "I see that now, would have been awkward." Joe's trousers tautened to impersonating a tent pole after catching sight of Dolly's drawers. He put his pipe on the hearth and reached over, "How's it work then?" His hand coming to rest on her knee.

"You just untwirl it, like this and undo the button and then they just come down."

"I'll try it on the other one, now you've done that one. Ah, bit fiddly."

"You get used to it."

"S'pose so," he said, and he removed her stocking and hung them over the arm of his chair. Joe rubbed her naked feet. "Prettiest toes I've ever seen," he said, as he raised her little foot to his mouth and sucked her big toe. He nibbled along all the way to the pinkie. Dolly sipped her champagne. Joe pressed his thumb into the instep of her foot. He straightened her leg and brought it to rest on his shoulder and then sucked and nibbled the left. Dolly's skirts had slid up, and Joe was happy to view her knees; and then as he moved her other leg to nibble the other footsie he caught a glimpse of lace.

So now, Joe had Dolly's feet on both his shoulders. - *Now comes the tricky bit, one false move. I'm doomed!* Dolly had closed her eyes. This didn't mean she wasn't alert, a sleeping giant. Joe massaged her ankle, this time her calf, and every so often, as he pushed upwards his fingers would brush her knee, and touch the lace edging on her drawers. Joe dragged his chair a little closer to Dolly.

"What are you doing?" Dolly asked, one eye open.

"Making myself comfortable, I'm at full stretch here."

Dolly closed her eye. Joe had moved his chair forward, he had her knees either side of him, he was now if he edged forward between her legs. Joe leaned forward. This time as he rubbed, he allowed his fingers to rove higher, under the lace; touching the soft, warm, flesh of her thigh, comfy as a pillow, soft as marsh mallow.

He brushed his fingers over the drawers and between her legs. These wonderful drawers with their open crotch. He found the slit in her drawers his finger rested. Dolly was not offering any resistance to his fondlings, so urged on. His hand poked through the split in her open crotch drawers. He touched her curly hair. But alas, that was as far as his curious probing fingers could go. Her wondrous thighs clamped shut the object of his desire by the protective arms of the welsh stick chair. Joe had to have her off that seat, but he was also aware that to disturb her reverie could change her mood.

"I fancy a nibble," hoping this would raise Dolly from the chair that bound her.

"I noticed."

"I meant one of them salmon sandwiches, they won't keep will they? Probably curling up all ready!"

"I don't know where you put it?"

-I know where I'd like to.

Dolly rose from the chair, it gave a creak of relief as her weight eased from its spindly legs.

No sooner had Dolly made it to the kitchen table than Joe came up behind her.

-Now ... or never.

Chapter 20

Never had a male approached a female with such trepidation bar the male spider to the black widow. He stood behind her as Dolly collected sandwiches and placed them on two plates. His arms reached round to her breast. He kissed her, the nape of her neck. She smelled of wine and cakes. The aroma of baking permeated her every pore. She stiffened under his embrace but she hadn't elbowed him aside. He rested his head on her shoulder his hand pulled up the hem of her skirt. He could see those big bloomers and giant arse constrained within. He wanted to peel them off like the rind of an orange, squeeze the juice from her …

"What do you think you're doing?"

-*OK, now. Show no fear!*

"I'm going to give you a good rodgering."

"How do I know it'll be good?"

-*Success.*

"You're about to find out."

And he raised her skirt, looked at that fine arse its mounds hidden by taut white cotton.

"You are a fine looking woman."

Dolly wouldn't own up to it but she enjoyed being an object of desire.

Joe slid his hand between her big white thighs, the crotchless drawers yielding to his probing fingers. He bent and put his face to her backside and kissed each soft mound. He untied the cotton ribbon and her drawers dropped like a mainsail. Joe stepped back to admire this view. Big white dimpled flesh. With his hand on her cheek, he asked her to, "Step out of these." And she raised one foot and then the other. Her drawers he tossed over the wooden chair.

And here was Dolly, barefoot and bare arsed, with her skirt up around her waist. He slid his finger between the crease of her cheeks. He didn't want to risk turning her around in case the sight of him brought her out of her daydream, and reminded her he was just an old, grubby, gardener. He slid his hand to her front touched the soft white thigh, stroked the curly hair spreading over and between her legs. He pushed his finger further and slid between her lips, and he felt the moisture of her under his finger. He pushed at her again and his finger sank into her. And she was a sight as he remembered her all those years ago, but bigger. *-For such a big woman she had the tiniest feet and the tightest of cunts.*

Joe unbuttoned his fly; his dick free, waved at Dolly's arse.

"Put your elbows on the table." *–Blimey, she's doing as I tell her. He stood between her thighs.* And with her arse raised and her cunt in view, Joe with one big thrust entered her flesh. Soft as marshmallow, warm as apple pie.

Dolly moved. "Stay, still girl," he said, like he was cooing to a big shire horse. But Dolly did as he urged, but as his thrusts grew so did her desire, pent up years, now expressed. She twisted sharply, throwing Joe off her back. She stood now with her back to the table looking at Joe. Joe with his trousers round his ankles and his dick dribbling as it nodded towards her cunt. And she didn't see a grubby old gardener, no. She saw her lover, her man.

Joe lunged for her. He touched her mouth and kissed her lips, tasting champagne. She had a scent, a mingling fragrance of baking; cakes and cinnamon buns. He pushed her back onto the table. Salmon sandwiches so carefully placed scattered. Joe climbed aboard. He found her cunt with the head of his dick and pushed forward, driving into her abundance. Dolly kicked up her heels and the fairy cakes flew.

Joe thrust and Dolly thrashed. The remains of the sliced ham hit the floor, followed by the cream jug. Joe pounded harder, a cacophony of crockery rattling on pine table legs, creaking beneath the pounding flesh. Joe sought her lips, and Dolly found Joe's mouth and kissed him, powerfully, ardently. Spoons, forks, and glasses crashed from the table. Joe felt himself coming and he pulled back. -*Think of celery seedlings, think of potato sets.*

Dolly heaved under him.

"Just wait my beauty he cooed, hold still there."

He withdrew from her. Dolly would get cross if only she could summon up the will. Joe drank from the champagne bottle, he took the mouthful and trickled it over her cunt; he sipped it from her, supping from those full lips. He would have stayed with his face buried amongst the folds, but he couldn't contain himself, she was open, moist, and he was as hard as he could possibly be. So he jumped on her and thrust into her, over and over, she wrapped her huge thighs over his back.

-*Can hardly move me arse!* In one big, last thrust, Joseph lay spent and exhausted in her vice like grip. "Christ woman, that was worth the wait!"

Joe rolled off her scattering the last of the vol au vents to the floor. He held out his arm to her, helping her from the wreckage of the kitchen table. He lowered her skirt and after pushing himself back into his trousers. -*Show a bit of decorum.* He went down on one knee. "Marry me!"

"I."

"Say you'll be mine.'"

"I-"

"Say you'll be …"

"I will."

"I love you Dolly."

"If you just shut up for a moment."

Joe paused …

"I WILL," Dolly bellowed.

***

Henry bought George a house. Not a big house. A semi detached affair further down the hill. Anything bigger, he'd have to work for it. The property was furnished with money from Mr Gregory. That was that. Their wedded life had begun....

Mr Gregory missed his daughter, and he missed his servant, Emily. -*By Christ, she was a fine fuck!* He'd now to go to the trouble of finding someone else, which would distract him from the life and work of the Cathedral. He had five women to interview. How should he choose the right one? How had he done it with Emily? It took a year before he could bed her. He didn't want to wait that long. He was a man after all, with a man's needs. Of course, there were always the girls of the theatre. They'd show you their wares for a shilling. But Mr Gregory's custom was paying servant's wages, -*All found!* A servant's wage plus the cost of the other, well, that was just too much.

He'd arranged to see the five women over the next two days, a short interview in the mornings leaving the afternoon free to consider more important, spiritual matters.

The first woman arrived at nine in the morning, the appointed time. She was pleasant enough and her references were good, he read them and he listened to her reasons for wanting this particular post. As she spoke, he wondered whether she'd open her legs and allow him to shove his dick up her cunt. Perhaps he should ask her? - *Will you throw a fuck in with the dusting and ironing?*

"So what do you think, Mr Gregory?"

"Mm ... Oh, ...Yes ... I do have some other women to see, but you're references seem much in order."

"Never given any cause for complaint!"

"And why did you leave your last establishment?"

"Oh, the goings on, you just wouldn't believe it. Well I'm not living under a roof such as that. Immorals, that's it, immorals."

"I see. Thank you, I'll let you know, leave your address on the hall table, you'll find a pen and paper." And as she left, Mr Gregory scored through her name.

The next woman seemed rather young, "Have you any experience?"

"No, I'd learn on the job, that's what me mum said."

"Ah, well you see, there's no one to train you here. It would just be you, with all the responsibility, and me. I wouldn't be able to. I wouldn't be able to afford the time. Indeed, I don't know how those things are done."

"Oh."

"But please tell your mother, I'm disappointed I cannot offer you the position. Make sure she knows; tell her, I'm very impressed with you."

"Thank you, Sir."

And Mr Gregory scored through her name. *-Pretty thing, shame she couldn't iron.*

Only three more ... At eleven, the third women rang his doorbell. Mr Gregory scored through her name before she'd spoken.

-Shifty eyes, I'd have to count the silver. Oh well, let's see what tomorrow brings.

Tomorrow brought Mrs Marshall. Mrs Marshall was probably in her mid thirties.

"How old are you?

"Thirty five, Sir"

Mr Gregory liked her, or he liked his guess being correct, a good sign.

She handed him a wedge of papers. She came recommended by a Mr Spacing; Mr Lewis considered her a 'great loss', and a certain Mr Smith would be only too pleased to have her return.

"These are all men!"

"Yes."

"Did these men ... had these men no wives?"

"All of them, Sir."

"But isn't it unusual for the men to write the recommendations, the references, and not the women of the house?"

"I don't know, I do know the men were pleased with me."

-*Mm.* "And the wives?"

"Well, they liked my work. It was later, by coincidence these three wives became jealous of the civility their husbands accorded me. Of course, I wouldn't stand to be so accused of dalliance. But such as it is, we poor women have to protect the little we have, our honour."

"Indeed. I see. Well, of course there isn't a wife in this household to concern herself, with any dalliance."

"Really, Sir?"

"No, my daughter took our servant with her. My daughter recently married, you see."

"Yes Sir. I do indeed see, I understand."

Mr Gregory put a tick by her name. "I do have someone else to see, but if you'd like to leave your address, I will contact you, shortly." And as she rose to leave, she turned to him and smiled.

The last woman was fat. Not plump, fat. She had several chins and her face was a full moon, including the craters. He crossed through her name. -*Eat me out of house and home.*

He wrote to Mrs Marshall, informing her he was pleased to offer her the position at 6/6 per

week, plus room and board. And so Mrs S Marshall installed herself in the kitchen, and put her feet firmly under the table.

***

The ferry left the pier. Susannah, Emily, and George waved goodbye to Agnes and Henry on the jetty, and made their way to the cafe. The ferry pitched, Emily who had never been at sea, said she'd go on deck, "Get some air."

George sat opposite Susannah at the table covered with a white linen cloth. A waiter arrived supporting a waxed moustache asked them, "May I take your order?"

"Two teas, and potted ham sandwiches, I think." George said without consulting his new wife.

Susannah glanced at George, before resting her eyes on the more interesting sea, and the foam covered waves. Susannah nibbled her sandwich daintily. George was bored. He'd finished his tea and sandwiches ten minutes ago, it was wearisome sitting here watching Susannah's trying attempts, to chew.

"Excuse me Susannah, I'll have to take some air," she nodded briefly, and he left the cafe for a stroll around the deck. Emily was standing at the rail looking forward to the Isle of Wight, watching, as it grew larger. George came beside her.

"Not having anything to eat?"

"No, I ... I'm not sure I'd keep it down."

"Not used to being all at sea, bobbing about on the water?"

"Oh, don't."

Emily stood with her hands on the rail; George placed his hand just next to hers, little finger, just touching little finger.

"You know I had no choice."

""Do I? You're talking about this, this marriage of yours?"

"Yes, it isn't what I want, I had no choice."

"Didn't you? You didn't have a choice when she jumped on you? Did she tie you up? But you! You still managed to stick it up her, didn't you? So you wanted her then, didn't you?"

"It wasn't like that, Emily."

"Tell me then, what was it like?"

George moved away, not far, his hand remained on the rail, but their fingers were no longer in contact. "You know how jealous she was ... she was hurt ... my affections, well, they weren't reciprocated ..." -*Is there no peace from these suffocating women?*

"Well yes."

"The day she came to my room ...well there was something else ... something I hadn't told you."

Emily's big eyes, grew bigger; alert to news, and flattered she should be taken into his confidence. She wasn't sure how she should react to this new piece of information, but as in the best stories, the heroine would sometimes be chilly.

Emily stared out to sea. "Well?" -*Go on, better be good.*

"She, Susannah did come to my room, as I said. But there is more. I was shocked to see her standing there. She was bundled up in a large coat. As you know women, females well, they're just not allowed in that building, apart from the cleaner. Well anyway, I couldn't believe she'd come, I couldn't believe she knocked at my door. Well, that was difficult enough ..."

"Yes!" -*Blimey*. "What happened then?"

"She dropped her coat."

"Dropped her coat? On the corridor's floor?"

Emily looked at George as if he'd gone 'round the bend'.

"She had nothing on!"

"Nothing on?"

"Nothing! Not a stitch"

"You mean, she was naked?"

"As the day she was born, you can imagine. Well she shouldn't have been there anyway, and bare, nude... I just didn't know which way to turn ... Then we heard the main door clang and footsteps. If she were discovered ... found like that ... Expelled, probably. I don't know what would have happened to Susannah, but it would have ended badly."

"Well, yes," agreed Emily, paying no attention to it not ending at all well anyway. "But you weren't seen with her? She wasn't exposed?" -*If that were possible.*

"As soon as I heard those footsteps, I pulled her into my room. It seemed the best course to take, at the time. ... But ... naked in my arms ... and she is beautiful."

Emily frowned.

"But she's so slow, so dull," he added, quickly.

Emily agreed with a nod, choosing to forget the young lady who a few months ago, was a vibrant happy girl.

"She kissed me, and I, well I was weak. I should have refused her but she was so ... ardent."

"Ardent?"

"So it was just the once and I regretted it almost immediately, such a mistake. Emily say you'll forgive me?"

-Blimey, forgive him?

"I know it's difficult, but there is something good to come from this."

-What bloody good? "Good?"

"I'll see you every day, you're Susannah's maid. Just think Emily, we can be together, and no one will suspect!"

Chapter 21

They'd taken the Isle of Wight Railway; The Invalid Express passed through Sandown and Shanklin. They arrived at a small hotel in Ventnor. Susannah retired to bed leaving George in the restaurant nursing a glass of port. He swore the young bellboy winked at him as he passed. And he realised, when he was in the bathroom looking in the mirror he saw confetti sticking to locks of his hair.

Susannah lay tucked up in bed, the covers to her nose, curled on her side and pretending to sleep. George tossed off his clothes leaving them scattered, like a trail, as he closed in to the bed. He pulled the blankets back. Susannah lay wrapped in a high necked, thick cotton nightdress. He lay down beside her.

He didn't turn down the light. He looked at her, her hair snagged tight back. He thought, -*She's deliberately making herself unattractive.* Which for some reason excited George. So he kissed her. She lay with her eyes and legs clamped tight shut. He leaned over and held her, kissing her on her mouth. Her eyes opened.

"What do you think you are doing?"

"I'm consummating my wedding, and so are you."

"I don't think that is necessary."

"It's my right and it's your duty. We have to do it to make our marriage legal."

"I'd have thought in my condition it would be obvious that it had been."

"Oh yes in your condition, but that was before our wedding, so it rather doesn't count."

"I have no idea what you mean. And what's more I don't care, and if it wasn't for ... for—"

"Your condition!" George said, helpfully.

"Yes, I would never have wed you. I don't want you near me." And she threw the blankets to the floor. "There, sleep there," she said, pointing at a space on the floor. "I'll not have you."

George leaned over her, and took her face in his hand and kissed her lips. Susannah tried to turn her face away. But he held her mouth to his face and he smiled and that little sharp crooked tooth glinted in the gaslight. He tugged open the bow that was tying back her hair and it tumbled over the pillow like a wave.

***

She pulled from him. George enjoying the tussle allowed her to do so. So he watched as she struggled and wriggled. And with dispassionate interest drew up the hem of her nightdress. Here she lay, the goddess Susannah, the pert nosed, goddess of Schoolboy devotion; her pubic hair thick, bouncy and blonde. He raised the nightdress higher, the hem, and snatch of material wrapped around her throat. Her breasts uncovered, were full and firm, the nipples large and red.

"My God, Susannah those are magnificent." - *Strange, I hadn't noticed before!* And he moved his mouth to her nipple and he sucked.

Susannah cried out, "You're hurting me."

"Don't be so silly; what do you think a child is going to do? It'll be sucking on your tits eight times a day. This one he sucked, and then that one, taking them in his mouth in turn. "I've seen women breast-feeding. They look to me, to enjoy it, they seem reposed, resplendent."

"You've no idea what you're talking about!"

"This is what I'm talking about," and he sucked her nipples in turn, again and again, harder this time, and the more she squirmed the harder he sucked. She pushed him from her. George smiled down at her. "And sometimes, when the babes have teeth, well they chew. I've heard of women having their nipples chewed right off." And he nibbled at her areola just to show her.

But in truth, he was all ready bored. And he mused how could a woman, so lovely, so exquisite, be such a bloody passion quashing, dullard?

Even his dick found her tiresome; it wasn't standing to attention. Rather it languished at half-mast like a boat entering port. He decided a little pokery might raise the sail. His finger stroked her thick, curly hair. His finger pushed at her and she clamped her legs, closer together. "Oh, for fuck's sake!" He slid his leg over hers and pressed his weight between her legs, which as he intended, separated her knees.

He considered whether he should go and find Emily, she'd get his dick to rise and be bloody grateful. Susannah cried out again and pushed his hand away, but her thighs thrust forwards as if in search of something. "Oh well if it's offered," and he went between her legs, took his weight on his elbows and with his hand on his dick guided it, well home, I suppose. This would be his comfort fanny, any port in the proverbial storm and a safe harbour. And he shoved his dick home, thrust a couple of times, erupted. Lay on her for several minutes more, then kissed her on the cheek.

"Night my sweet." And he turned out the light.

Susannah -*I'd stab you if had a knife.* Was remembering the circumstances of this wedding, how she'd arrived at such a point.

George was on top of her pushing and prodding. She knew that this was something that she couldn't bear, not now and not for the rest of her life. Either I die, or he does. George was doing something with her most sensitive parts. His sucking on her breasts bloody hurt. It hurt. They'd been sore for a couple of months, he was right though; infants did suck away at breasts, she knew also that no woman had ever had her nipples chewed off by a child.

-*So he was trying to frighten me for his own pleasure.* Susannah decided then, while his fingers pushed and pulled at her. That she would serve that dish of revenge, cold. And against her will, her body responded to George's pressing and pullings. Her toes curled and the strangest most delightful ripples rolled over her body, waves crashing one after the other. This feeling was not to do with George's fingers but satisfaction in her resolve. Her mind had cleared, the fog had gone. She would make George sorry for his actions. This fortitude galvanised her, no more flotsam floating on a sea of his actions. A lightness of spirit and a wonderful feeling flowed through her body, from the tips of her toes to the top of her head.

And the next morning she didn't feel that dark weight bearing own on her shoulders. And she smiled at herself in her reflection as she combed out her hair.

"Glad to see I've put a smile on your face."

And Susannah smiled up at him.-*Oh, you have George, yes indeed, you have.*

-*Women all the same, pretend they don't, when they do.*

***

Emily enjoyed her holiday. She'd been on a train, then a boat and then another train. She was staying in a hotel! But that was it! While she slept under the rafters, Susannah had a large suite of rooms on the first floor. It wasn't fair! -*That should be me in that big bed, in that beautiful room. That's my husband, would've been too, if not for you.*

Susannah was having a bath. Run for her by Emily who was now laying out her clothes for the morning on the bedpost. Emily knocked on the bathroom door.

"Yes?"

"Will that be all now, Miss Gregory?"

"Come in."

Susannah lay in warm scented water, up to her neck, her long hair hanging over the rim of the bath.

"I didn't hear you, what was it you wanted?"

"I just wondered if there was anything else you needed, or can I go off and fix the hamper?"

"Ah, I thought you said something else! I thought you called me Miss Gregory."

"I ..."-*Bitch.*

"No Emily, there's nothing else for you to do here, thank you."

George was sitting on the bed when Emily returned from the bathroom. He smiled at her and patted the space beside him. He placed his index finger to his lips and pursed, a be silent, "Shh." Emily looked from George to the bathroom door. Then returned her gaze to George and smiled.

-*Bloody teach her.*

And so Emily Babcock sat her self down with a little shuffle next to George, and cocked her head to one side. George laid her hand on his trousers and showed her what he was feeling about her. And Emily couldn't help herself, she giggled.

"Is anyone there?"

They both laughed together silently, like two naughty children caught scrumping.

George put his hand up Emily's skirt.

"Hello?"

"It's me, George I've just come to ... I left my watch." I'll be back in a short while. He rose, and opened and closed the hotel room's door. He pulled a face at Emily, leaning over her, he told her to be quiet.

"I will," she whispered, and giggled again.

George stuck his mouth over her lips, stifling the giggles in her throat. His hand slid up her skirts and his dick was urgent and hard; his balls throbbed, he wanted it hot and hard and now.

His hand reached her thigh. She wasn't wearing any drawers. Did she know, had she prepared the ground? His fingers felt for the slit between her legs. And she moved her arse and legs on to the bed. He pushed up her skirt. No drawers, but she wore a corset. -*Women.*

George removed himself from his trousers, he was hard and upright, not like last night; he was beginning to think Susannah was a bad influence on him. But now, here he was more than ready, and here she was, Emily, his maid, laid out on this bed with her brown worn boots, red stockings, and no knickers. He leaned over her, placing himself between her legs. He kissed her, tasting the tobacco on her breath. She smelt slightly of onions, or something. He held his dick in his hand and laying on her, he knocked its head against her and jammed it into her. Her boot heels were sticking in his back, which for one reason or another further added to George's pleasure. With every thrust, her arse rose to meet him. So George went headlong, deeper and deeper diving into this warm and soft flesh. Pounding and thrusting. George moaned.

"Are you still here, George?"

"I ... I can't find the bloody thing!"

"Have you looked under the bed, it may have fallen there last night."

And Emily couldn't help herself, she giggled throatily.

"Who's that?"

"Just me Susannah, I've just stubbed my bloody toe." He thrust further into Emily, her hips rose to meet him. It was as if she was trying to suck the life out of him. Entomb him within her body. One final thrust, and done, it was George who trembled. He shivered as Emily grasped his dick with the muscles of her cunt bearing down on him, and with one almighty thrust spewed him from her body. "Jesus Christ," gasped George, how the hell did you do that?"

"Shall I help you?"

"No Susannah, I've got it now, I'll go and see how Emily's doing with the hamper."

And they both rose from the tangled bed and arranged their clothing. A little damp patch on George's trousers, but nobody would notice.

They closed the door after them. Emily went upstairs to fetch her hat and George downstairs to a cigar and a coffee. The Bellboy winked at him! *-He bloody does know, no mistaking it this time.* And the Bellboy looked at George, raised an eyebrow and then looked down at George's crotch and that little patch of dampness and winked, again. George rolled his eyes and smiled. The bellboy, in that tight trousered uniform, smiled in return.

***

Joseph, now she'd agreed, saw no point in waiting. "I've waited a descent interval, and neither of us is getting any younger."

Dolly thought about it, and he was right. *–Just jump straight in.* "I think you're right." *–Why not?*

Joe leaned back in his chair.

"But we'll have to wait."

"But you said ..." And he leaned forward again. "We have no need to wait."

"Just 'till George is back; a fortnight is that too long Mr Bridger?"

Dolly had much to sort out there was her dress; she had no time to have one made. She'd have to have a white gown this was her first, and only wedding. May would help her, she'd know someone; she was a good sorter outer.

Joe leaned back in his chair. "Yes, but I'll put up with it."

Glad was walking up Charlotte Street, dragging Freddie along in her wake. *-He's here somewhere.* And she asked a few people.

"He was here a minute ago…"

Lil looked at the letter, why on earth would someone write to Mr Walter Rackett, c/o 31, Hope Street, Landport, here? The kettle on the stove boiled, she could steam it open. She'd read about that in 'The Girl's Annual'. Super sleuth, Abigail Crabshore, solved the mystery of the missing diamond tiara, by steaming open a letter. She wondered whether she had time. How long does it take to steam open a letter? And Wally could be walking up this street at this very moment; she peeped out of the window just to check. But no Walter! There was however; Gertrude, and she was heading in this direction.

Lil plonked the unopened letter on the table. – *Foiled! But Abigail would have found a way forward... She'd have ...*

"Hello Lil, oh good, kettle's on. . ." she said, as she lowered herself into a chair by the table. "Where's... What's this then?"

"It's a letter." And she poured hot water over the leaves."

"Mm, I see Abigail's having an effect, there's no hiding anything from you is there?"

"It's for Wally."

"Wally? Wally Racket? Who, for goodness sake, is writing to him here?" And she stood up, went to the cupboard, and brought out a loaf of bread, a board, and a knife. "Will the others be long?"

"Don't know, they've gone off to find him." And placed the pot and two cups on the table, as the door banged open.

"There's a letter for you Wally, there look," said Lil, hoping he'd hurry up and open it.

"Get another cup would you Lil; don't suppose you'll say no, eh?"

"Oh right, thank you Gert, don't mind if I do. Who's' it from?"

"We don't know."

"You could open it," Glad said.

Gertrude began sawing hunks of bread. "Glad, be a good girl, fetch us that pot out, would you?"

To the doorsteps of bread, she smeared dripping, giving each portion a good dollop of liquid with the brown bits underneath. Wally played with the envelope, but his eyes remained firmly on the bread and dripping held in various hands, but not his. Then she cut a big chunk, emptied the last great lardy dollop onto the bread, and handed it over. "'pect you're a bit peckish."

"Why ta, very much."

"Lil frowned."

***

"And what's wrong with your face young lady? You don't begrudge a guest a crust, surely?"

When Lil had finished chewing and swallowed. – *No talking with mouth full.* "He can't open his letter, now his hands are full."

Wally swallowed, and said, "You open it for me Lil, I can't read anyway." Lil's face took on a big smile. -*She alone had charge of this letter, the secrets contained within were hers, and hers alone t*—

"Well get on with it then," said Walter.

This was the first letter Lil had ever opened; she walked to the drawer holding the letter reverently before her, and rummaged around in the drawer for a knife. Wally wiped his chin, "Thank you Gert, that hit the spot. What about you mucky chops?" And he wiped dripping from Freddie's lip, cheek and that bit that had stuck to the back of his—

"Hu humm," said Lil. A cough, and a cue she was about to speak. Wally tapped his cup with a spoon. Quickly followed by Freddie who bashed the table with his fist. Lil waited for silence, and glaring at Fred might just make him, - *Shut up!*

"Come here Fred." And Walter hoisted the blighter onto his knee.

"We're ready for you now love," said Gert.

"Right, so I'll begin."

Gert wiped a way dripping from her lips, which hid her smile.

The letter opened with the knife, fingers still attached, Lil began, "This letter is addressed to Walter racket c/o 31 Hope Street, Landport."

"We know that! It was written on the envelope," Glad said.

Lil composed herself. *-Relations can be annoying sometimes, most times.* "In the top right hand corner... Fairview Hou—" And that was it, they were all of one voice, but saying different things. "That's May's address." "Mays' letter." "Why's May writing to me?" And finishing with Fred who yelled, "May."

"No mate she's not here," said Wally, as he bounced him up and down on his lap.

"May!" And Fred banged his hands on the table.

Lil rolled her eyes, "If I may have silence." *–This always works when Miss Quick says it in class.* But the word, May, set Fred off again. "May. May!"

Lil clapped her hands. Gert could no longer contain herself, and she burst into a great big grin; which she tried to restrain, but then Wally's shoulders started to shake, and Glad who thought he looked funny, giggled; and Fred laughed too, till he got hiccoughs. Lil surveyed the room with a scowl. Lil waited. The mob at the table slowly pulled themselves together. ...

"Right then, I'll—" Which set them off again. – *Right, I shall show you lot.* And she stood before them and read the letter, line by line, moving her lips without making a sound. They all looked at her.

"Well?" said Gert. Lil refused to speak; satisfied she had their undivided attention, she slowly folded the letter and inserted it back into its envelope.

Wally looked at Lil, at Gert and then Glad. "Well I never," he said. "Didn't have much to say, did she?"

"Come on Lil we'll be quiet now, we promise, don't we?" Glad nodded; Lil looked to Wally who nodded too. She ignored Fred, there was no controlling him.

"Dear Walter...

"Dear," did you hear that, she called me dear."

"A letter, that's how all letters are written." And Lil sighed.

"Dear Walter," Lil looked at this group sat around the table, testing to see who was going to interrupt her. 'I need a wedding dress—'

"She getting married?" Walter said.

"May getting married, well who'd have thought," echoed Gert. "Who to?" Walter frowned, he could go now; and placed Fred with Glad. Lil rolled her eyes. "If you would just let me finish."

"May!" said Fred.

"Shh," said Glad.

"Look, I won't read it—"

"Oh go on Lil, stop sulking," snapped Glad.

"I meant, I'll just tell you what it says, not read it."

"No, he wants it read, don't you Wally?" Wally was sure he didn't want to hear another word, and was certain he'd rather be somewhere else. *-Fancy May humiliating him like this; she could have told him, man to man - woman. Not in front of these people. Wasn't kind; not like May at all.*

***

"Oh, I might have something," said Gert. "Walter may be able to get the other. Won't you?"

Walter, who hadn't heard a word Lillian had said, had no idea what was asked of him; or rather, he did! And she was a cow wanting him to fetch and carry for her.

"Walter she doesn't have long, two week to three weeks," Wally was now in a major funk.

"I wonder if my old dress would be any good? No good to me now. Says here, it has to be big, and she's taller than me too."

Wally heard that, taller than Gert. May wasn't bigger than Gert. "Who wants the dress then?"

"Someone called Dolly; she cooks up at the house, says here."

Wally relaxed into his chair …"I'll try to get the stuff. What else does she want?"

"She wants a veil and some shoes. That's it. She says she'll make the bouquet, and she doesn't know where to get the cake."

"Bigger than you Gert eh? My god, the man's marrying an elephant."

"Oi Walter, that'll be the last dripping you get in this house. I'm going to look out my gown, see what it's like; we'll send it anyway, maybe she can use the fabric."

Wally rose.

"I don't have the shoes though, I died 'em black and wore them out. And the veil made good nets for me windows," said Gert. Lil nodded sagely.

Wally with a chance to redeem himself said, he'd try to get the veil and shoes, "What size are this monster's feet?"

"Size four," says here.

"Size four?" Wally had an image of this huge woman as an upside down triangle, tapering off to a point. "When's she coming to get this stuff?"

"Thursday say's here, and finishes with crosses. That's kisses, that is."

And Freddie landed a big wet noisy one on Glad's cheek. "Ere get off," she said, wiping away the slobber.

***

May dragged a cardboard box up the drive; she'd walked from The George... Joseph saw her and grabbed the package. "My God girl, you'll do yerself a mischief. You've not walked all the way from The George have you, not lugging that?"

"I'm here now."

"What yer got in there, then?"

"Just some stuff."

"Dolly, May's got some stuff here, in a bloomin' big box."

Dolly looked at the box now plonked on her scrub top. Joseph was pulling off his boots. Dolly and May were both at the stove.

"Is that what I think it is?" whispered Dolly.

"Depends what you think it is," answered Joseph.

"Eavesdropper. You leave those on," she said, pointing to his boots. "And take your tea with you to that shed of yours."

"Biscuits?"

Dolly by way of a bribe gave him a couple of the last shortbread.

"Ta very much." And he grabbed his tea and his Scottish biccies, and walked from the kitchen whistling.

Dolly watched him go, and witnessed the door of the potting shed open and close. "He's gone."

"Right let's see what we've got. He won't come back?"

"No, he'll have his tea, smoke his pipe, he won't reappear for a good half hour."

May took a knife from the drawer and cut the string. "Go on Dolly have a look, finger's crossed." Dolly took a deep breath; she hoped so much it was well, just right, but she knew that was unlikely, there were few women of her size and she knew it couldn't be new. A note on the top, addressed for May: 'Dear May, hope this is all right; it's my wedding dress, I won't need it again.' And then under that in another hand, Lil's: 'There's a veil and white shoes, no charge, that's what Walter said. Glad made that bag that's in there. And that blue thing, is a garter. I made that from one of Fred's old trousers. I embroidered it, I hope Dolly likes it. May smiled, and wiped a silly tear that'd brimmed in her eye.

"What's up May? You all right?"

"Yes Dolly, I just … Oh come on let's get this out, see what we've netted."

Chapter 22

"Satin, it's satin May, oh isn't it lovely?"

May thought the material ... wasn't sure it was the best for so ... so fulsome a shape... There was white lace net, about three yards, it looked new. "We'll have to sew this Doll; it's fabric not a veil, not yet."

"I'll do it in the evenings."

"We'll do it in the evenings, can you come up?"

"Oh yes, it's only me and Ferdinand, he'll howl but it's only for a while, he'll have to cope."

"And we grab a few hours when we're not on call, waiting for the bell to ring." May pulled out white silk covered slippers with a low heal and marquisette buckles. "Oh Dolly these are beautiful. Try them on."

Dolly sat on the chair by the table; and untied her boots. She wriggled her toes and May waited by her side while she prepared her feet for these wonderful shoes. Dolly drew in here breath, and she slid one on and then the other. She lifted her legs so she could see them. "Well, got them on."

"Come on then, stand."

Dolly slowly, and with deliberation, stood. "Oh May, they are .... They couldn't be more perfect."

"They're lovely Dolly, I'm so pleased. Are they comfy?"

"I don't care if they give me bunions, chafe and blister; but they don't squeeze at all, they're like wearing slippers."

May returned to the box. "These next two, are items Glad and Lil made," and she handed Dolly a drawstring bag made from white silk, lined with a gauze, the outside embroidered with forget-me-nots, and rosebuds.

Dolly was beside herself. "Just so kind, so...I'm so lucky." And she wiped away a tear.

"Hang on there Dolly; Lil's made you something, this could make anyone weep." May held out a blue garter, something old, something new, a garter made from Fred's trousers.

"It's lovely," choked Dolly, and burst out laughing and the tears flowed down both their cheeks.

***

Dolly was in May's room, she was trying on the dress. Dolly breathed in, and said, "Can't you give my corset laces a good tug."

"I will, but you'll want to breathe. We have to find six inches, if we can yank your laces in two inches, w—"

"Go on then yank."

May yanked and yanked. "Are you still breathing Dolly?"

"Yes," she gasped.

"Right, that's it, and no more. We'll do a gusset, like so, and with some lace ... we'll need to lengthen the skirt by four inches."

"Reckon it'll look all right?"

"We'll have to find some lace for the hem, and then sew the same on the bodice, so the whole matches. We'll let it out under the arm seams; I reckon it'll be wonderful. What we have to do though; is find some lace."

Dolly had an idea, she had a pair of curtains in her front parlour; it'd be worth the sacrifice. But no false idols need be sacrificed, Agnes just happened to have a bolt of lace. She'd had it for, "Oh for a long time." And could never decide what to with it. "Dolly you may have it, consider it your wedding present."

"Oh Agnes it's beautiful." And tears welled in her eyes; never had this woman cried so much, at such happiness.

***

The time drew nearer to Joseph and Dolly's marriage, a summer wedding, July. The small hamlet on the top of the hill was commissioned. The George Inn sequestered; bedecked and adorned, and all the friends and neighbours were invited, and none refused. George came holding a huge box with a large bow, a wedding gift.

"Oh, whatever can it be?"

"Dolly stop rattling it, you could break it, put it on the table with the other presents."

Joseph didn't understand why this woman who for years had bossed him, and scolded him, was doing as he said. And he puffed out his chest with manly pride, this woman of talent, and with the finest arse in the entire county, was soon to be his and would do his bidding. She was obeying him already. And he felt cocksure, and proud of his great bargain.

Since that day, George's wedding, he never touched her buttocks, not even looked. *-Well, had a peek sometimes.* It would be impossible not to see them, but he hadn't touched. No! Both he and she were saving themselves for their wedding night. And Joseph felt himself hardening at the very thought. He'd never asked her whether or what she thought, he wanted to honour her, and make this wedding day special for them both. And he was the man of the house. But which house? They hadn't discussed that either. They had one each. Both cottages had good points and both cottages bad; if they could roll them both together, why, they'd have the perfect abode.

Dolly had come down the aisle like a galleon in full sail, her white dress billowing out behind, her veil fluttered like an ensign on a mast. May had made a posy of pink and white roses Joe had grown. Never was a man so proud. Mr Spritely had offered to give her away, and he escorted her up the aisle in full naval regalia; even bothered to hang his ceremonial sword from his belt, such was the respect he afforded this great lady.

"I do," she said. Joseph couldn't believe it, after all these years. And a tear trickled from his eye as he kissed her.

And Dolly was stunned at how much she was loved, and following that kiss and that tear, she wept, for the sheer joy of it. And so they made their way from the church. So happy, both weeping. The party threw rose petals from Mr Spritely's garden but grown by Joseph. And a horse and cart awaited them; spoons and boots tied to the backboard to take them to the George Inn, and they vanished round a bend in the road.

***

May wiped her eyes. Agnes dabbed hers, hoping she hadn't black streaks under them. Susannah as fat as a whale had to sit down.

Mr Spritely nodded. He had a frog in his throat, that's what he said, when he asked people to make there way to the reception, but no words came out. George helped Susannah into the donkey cart. And they jogged at a leisurely pace towards the festivities. John held his arm out for May to take.

There was a stack of food, the village had contributed, and Dolly had helped prepare. May had decorated the hall. The cake stood three tiers high; a wedding gift from George. The broken icing faced the wall, "Told you shouldn't shake it." And after the feast, the toasts. But everyone knew Joseph was the luckiest man in the world, which was good because he was speechless. The fiddler started, and then the pipe and drum. Joseph stood up and escorted his woman, his wife to the centre of the floor. And there it was. Dolly raised her skirt and she jigged, and no one could believe how lightly she jigged and how fast her small feet flew. And Joseph stood back to watch her, clapping his hands in time to the music. Then came a reel. And everyone took to the floor. Cider flowed; there was rum of course, and a couple of bottles of champagne.

Everyone agreed it was the best wedding for along time. Susannah seated on the side, with her great belly before her couldn't dance, agreed it was, indeed, a lovely wedding. It was of course different from her own.

***

Henry handed Dolly an envelope, addressed to Dolly and Joseph. "Oh what can it be?"

"It's a card," said Joseph helpfully.

"Oh, Joe, you'll never guess."

"A card with a horse shoe on it."

"It is ... but it's our honeymoon."

"Honeymoon?"

"Southsea, Joseph; two nights, for us to stop in a hotel. Mr Spritely has paid."

Joe puffed on his pipe. "Southsea!"

"Friday and Saturday night. We just have to get there."

"Well we could take the tra—"

"Fancy him doing that. I've never been on a train."

"Ain't yer?" Puff.

"Nor for that matter, a tram."

"Ain't yer?" Puff.

"Or Southsea, never been to Southsea."

"Ain't yer?" Puff.

"What about you? When was the last time you were on a train?"

"Well, I never have, now you come to mention it, no." Puff.

"Have you been on a tram?"

"Well no, I never have." Puff.

"Southsea, I've never been there. Have you?"

"Dolly ...I never have, no." Puff. "I have an idea." Puff.

"You do?"

"I do." Puff. And he drew on his pipe.

Dolly hovered, and adjusted her cap, fiddled with the hem of her piny, rattled the spoon on the table. And then she asked, "Well?"

Puff. "Well." Puff. "We get the train out, and the tram back."

***

May was content. She had a pile of money, making her picture groan under the weight. She had amassed twenty-five pounds. She couldn't believe it. She managed from George's wedding to keep one of the five-pound notes. She spent £4/15/- on decorations and buttonholes. And five shillings went to Wally for finding her a contact who'd supply her with blooms for a knockdown, off the back of cart, price. She padded out the foliage and flowers with wild blossoms and leaves gathered from the countryside surrounding the house.

Dear John, had accompanied her; carrying her basket and helping her over stiles. He sometimes would stop and plant a kiss on her lips or cheek. He thought he was daring, May thought he was sweet.

***

Cecil wondered as he looked at this woman, how long it would be before, he could ... well ... make love? No! He didn't want to do that! He didn't love her. He wanted satisfaction; he needed to fuck her. And he needed her to accept that requirement. The rules, he hoped she'd understand. Of course, she did! *-If you think you're putting that thing of yours in me for the price of a daily, you are very much mistaken! There's a cost, everything has one; and I exchange my values for hard cash.*

Cecil, and his new daily, who he wanted to become his old nightly, wasn't living up to her references. She'd promised much and delivered little.

-Think you're getting me thrown in for the price of a chamois leather matey, think again!

There would have to be a coming together of some sort. But Cecil couldn't see how to achieve it; she was unrelenting. He tried this, and he tried that; and every time she swatted him away like a bluebottle over raw meat. Mrs Marshall was holding out for the piecework rate. *-I'd better nudge the stupid old git; if he doesn't* *cough up, he'll have clean windows, but no dirty basement.*

His frustration made him irritable, and he spluttered, "I'd like to …"

"Yes Sir," and she waited… And after a time she asked, "What would you like, Sir? I'll do anything you need. That's what I'm here for, after all!"

"Of course, you'll receive payment for all your duties."

"I understand that. But if you should fancy something on the side … extra, if you need something more than say, the washing and ironing, will I get paid extra for me extras?"

"I … I thought it would be all found; that's how it was with …"

"She's not here now, is she? I am, and of course, I haven't known you as long as she had. I'll do my duty; but if you need a bit more at night-time say, it'd be extra."

"I see." After a pause, he said, "How much? How much, extra'?"

"Depends, on the service you'd want," and she sniffed.

Cecil wondered what she'd do, how she'd react if he said, -*What if I want to thrust my dick down your throat? How much would that cost?* But he didn't ask that, he said, "I see. Well that's perfectly clear."

Mrs Marshall thought, -*It is?* So she took his bull by the horns, and said, "Ten bob for extras, that's it."

"Ten bob! Er … Shillings…"

"That's it, ten bob for extras. In the first instance, ten bob; but if you want more on top of extras well, we'll see how we go."

A couple of days later Cecil decided he'd test his ten-shilling's worth. So he pulled himself up to his full, five and a half feet, and he braced himself. After pulling the bell he leaned, in what he assumed was a nonchalant posture, against the mantelshelf.

Mrs Marshall tapped on the drawing room door, and after taking one look at him thought, -Bingo. "Yes Sir, can I help you?"

***

"Er, yes," said Cecil, emboldened by a glass and another of Teachers. He pulled a ten-shilling note from his pocket, and placed it on the table. Cecil cleared his throat and said, "Take off your clothes." -*Now, we'll see.* He turned to the hearth and poked about in the grate, sending sparks shooting up the chimney. When he turned to look at her again; his maid, his woman of all work, she stood before him in her drawers, stockings, and boots, the ten-bob note gone from the table.

She's done it! He'd been worrying… -*I'm too sensitive, that's my trouble!*

Cecil sat back in his chair, his feet resting on a pouffe. He sipped his whisky and added water from a glass jug. A woman wearing drawers, stockings and a pair of blue boots was standing before him in his drawing room. He didn't want to fuck her he could tell that; his dick confirmed his opinion. The warmth from fire, the glow from the whisky and this woman, delivered to him contentment. He liked sitting here, looking at her. Her breasts were full and she had large red nipples; her skin was the colour of cream and surprisingly smooth.

"Anything else Sir?" she asked. He wished she hadn't spoken; her voice had broken his reverie. He needed to assert his authority. Cecil croaked, "Unpin your hair." She did, and she shook it out. It wasn't long, it barely touched her shoulders; a disappointment. And it was dull; he shouldn't have bothered. I don't want to fuck you. He sipped again at his glass; and then gulped, downing its contents. He refilled it from the decanter at his side. He didn't think to offer a glass or even a sip to this person on the rug. Well after all, this was his ten bobs' worth; he wondered how far ten bob would allow him. "Now your ... those," he pointed, as he said, "Remove your drawers."

Cecil lit a cigar and puffed out a large plume of smoke; he held it in one hand and the crystal glass gripped in the other. She emerged from the cloud wearing just her boots and stockings. Ribbons threaded through the eyelets of her boots, ending in blue bows at her calves. A ribbon on one boot had a knot at the ankle, their frayed ends tied together. He sipped. He allowed his gaze to reach her ...private parts! Her hair was dark-brown. Some of those hairs had escaped the geometry of her triangle; and were sprouting along her plump inner thighs. "Lie there," and he pointed, "There! On this rug."

She lay now, before him, her breasts resting on her upper arms. Cecil said, "Legs akimbo."

-What the hell is akimbo?

"Do as I say," he croaked.

-I would if I knew what the bloody hell you're talking about! Mrs Marshall assumed various poses trying to find which one fitted the akimbo position. *-Oh right, this one.*

"Make yourself comfortable, give yourself satisfaction." How should he phrase it? "That!" he said, pointing at her. "I want to watch you." She took her finger... And he looked ... But that's not ... He stared. She was touching herself, somewhere... He unbuttoned his trousers. Mrs Marshall writhed. Cecil watched. She was enjoying herself. And he'd paid for it! Yes, a faint smile on her face. Quick deep breaths ... Her hips thrust upwards ... He dropped his glass and it bounced on the rug and rolled away... His cock stood proud. It was thin, perhaps; but his hand masked its girth.

-I've seen bigger crayons, she thought, but didn't say. And she lay back, and would have thought of England, but she dreamt of a new hat, that yellow felt ensemble with the mauve parrot's wings.

***

The Easter Fair sat on the slopes of Portsdown Hill, every year for three days.

By the swings, John Bridger with May on his arm met Mr and Mrs Susannah Spritely.

"Mrs Spritely," said John, responding to Susannah's nod.

"Won't you join us? We're going to the coconut shy," said George.

"Oh, do please come," said Susannah.

"Of course, delighted." May and John trailed after Mr and Mrs Spritely as they bestrode the Fair's turf. George was a popular figure with both the women and the men, that attended the fair. He received many smiles, nods and greetings. -*as was his due!* And acknowledged all! Susannah and May brought many an admiring glance from the men. And vicariously, both George and John were proud these women were theirs! And George was even more pleased, that both these women were his.

Susannah who was becoming large, asked May if she would mind if she leaned a little on her arm. And together, these women walked along the cabins, until they paused to watch men hurl balls at coconuts. One ball stuck the coconut hard, but it still didn't budge.

"Stuck in, that is," said May.

"Do you think so?"

"Wouldn't want to give away too many coconuts."

"Isn't that cheating?"

"Well, they have to make a living."

"I suppose, but they could do it honestly, couldn't they!"

May shrugged, and said, "One of them is loose. It's a question of knowing which one. If nobody is seen to win, no one would play."

George and John, with an idea to show off their manly skills, handed over their tuppences, and bagged three wooden balls apiece.

Dolly and Joseph met the party by the coconut shy. Dolly wore a great creation on her head. The wide brimmed hat she'd decorated with the flowers and foliage Joseph grew in his garden. A small spider spun a web between the brim and the crown, a delicate lace affair. Above this bonnet, small black flies circled. This miniature biosphere stayed in position by what at first appearance was a bandage tied under her chins, but on closer inspection, was a woven cotton tie Dolly had re-employed from her old drawers.

Dolly asked, "Emily not with you?"

"Er, no; I did mention to Susannah about bringing her with us, but …"

Dolly looked to Susannah for explanation. Susannah remained mute -*I do not explain myself to staff.*

"We, Er," said George, as if lost for words.

"Such a shame, she's no family round here, or friends…"

-*Not surprising!* And Susannah coughed.

"George, always so thoughtful."

Susannah thought -*And I'm not!*

Joseph stood by the shy smiling contentedly and puffing on his pipe. He'd been smiling since his marriage and before that, the Spritely's wedding. He was a man of contentment.

Mr Hawkins gave donkey rides; he'd decorated his cart with pussy willow and daffodils. Maisie wore a straw bonnet clamped to her bridle making her long ears stick out sideways, which gave her a woebegone expression. He walked from The George Inn to the fair for 6d per cartload. -*No more than four mind!*

Dolly said, "Daniel could fetch Emily, what d'ya think? Joseph, go and ask Dan."

"I—"

"Look, he's just dropping some people off at the gate."

Joseph gave Dan Hawkins his instruction, and a 6d pulled from his waistcoat pocket.

The shy man wanted these people to bugger off. He had their money, and other people were waiting, and they couldn't get anywhere near his booth for this barricade of bodies. "Come on ladies and gentlemen; let's see what you can do!"

***

Dolly decided she'd have a go. It was fortunate Joseph returned at that moment. Dolly was rummaging through her drawstring bag; the contents of which were strewn over the shy man's counter. He drummed his fingers "Come on, roll up, let's see the damage. Fighting shy?" A phrase he'd made up, its cleverness pleased him. And it always got the crowd smiling.

John threw his wooden ball, it hit the stump, and the coconut rocked. George threw his and hit the cup.

May whispered to John, "That's the one with the loose coconut."

John frowned and took aim. This time his ball went right of the nut, he'd missed. Now George employed his best under arm and bowled the ball, it dived, hit the ground, bounced, and ran towards the back canvas. John's turn, this time his aim struck the nut. It rattled, rolled, and then wobbled itself back securely and snugly into the cup. George wielded and hit the stump, which made a scar in the earth, and the stump was now at a jaunty angle.

The crowd, uttered, "Ooh."

Mr Shy handed three balls to Dolly, who handed two to Joseph. She aimed, and fired, shaking the stump; but the ball rushed passed, hit the back canvas, tore through the rent and landed at the feet of a stunned fair goer.

"Stump two," suggested May.

Dolly stopped, aimed, and released the ball, her dress straining under the force of the thrust. Her hat leapt from its mooring and hanging from the white thread ended at her shoulder blades. The spider clung to her hat on its web string, bouncing like a falling climber on a rope. The coconut trembled. The crowd breathed. And the nut sank back into the cup.

"Right," said Dolly, who'd brook no more nonsense from such a nut as that!

The final ball handed over, leaving Joe's hands free to light his pipe. She drew in her breath, stood on one leg. Leaned back, tested the throw. She eyed that nut. The crowd fell silent. Joseph drew on his pipe. Her arm shot backwards. She fired, he puffed smoke. The ball cannoned into the stump. The coconut jumped, rattled, rolled and teetered on the brink ... and finally ... fell.

The crowd sighed and applauded.

"See, ladies and gentleman, the lovely lady has won herself a prize!" the Shy man said, seeking to capitalise on his financial loss.

Dolly chose a china figurine. A husband and wife climbing into a four-poster bed, 'the last in bed to put out the light'. Which made Dolly laugh, 'cos it reminded her of Joseph and her dashing under the covers, but that wasn't for candle snuffing. Joseph offered this queen, this Amazon, his arm. And with head held high, escorted her from the applauding audience. The shy, where now many males crowded, certain of course, they'd out-do the coconut striking female.

From his position in the Crow's-Nest, Henry spied the donkey cart listing as Emily disembarked. Henry rotated his lens and looking further, focused the lens on Celia -*and that's her mother!* Henry carried on along, went past, then returned at what looked like a couple kissing under a bush. But they emerged, revealed as Joseph and Dolly. Slightly to the left May and—"

"Henry I've been waiting."

"I'm just enjoying the view."

"Well if you hurried up, you'd enjoy it more at close range, and with your own eyes." Henry capped the lens of his Grubb telescope. Offered his arm to his wife, and strolled along the burgeoning lane to the fair.

They converged on the beer tent. Coming in separately, but joining in one large party. Dolly showed off her new ornament, and wondered where she would position her prize? Indeed, in what house this china would live? They hadn't worked out the details. There were good things and bad things about each cottage. And so, as they couldn't decide, they moved between them. Joseph loved his garden, and the soil over years of loving nurture, had become dark and fertile; it would take another lifetime to make another ground as rich as his. But Dolly's cottage had a wonderful kitchen, with running water inside, and a large dining room facing south, overlooking the town of Portsmouth.

John of course lived in the garden house, which gave Dolly and Joseph hours of privacy to consummate their marriage, which they did on frequent and every available occasion.

Emily arrived she'd changed out of her black skirt into a light brown, cotton skirt with a cream high-necked blouse.

May said, "You look smart, are you here to meet a beaux?"

Dolly agreed, "But you should have decorated your hat, it's plain. Not like ours."

"No nothing could be like yours!" Emily responded. And she didn't even have the decency to blush. Dolly smiled, pleased Emily had noticed its originality and her handiwork.

Emily and Susannah; here were two women both discontented, one because she couldn't have George, and the other because she did. But both played their roles of obedient servant, and dutiful wife to virtuoso performance.

Dolly couldn't understand why they'd not invited Emily. But then sometimes the goings on of your betters was beyond the wit of the ordinary man and woman.

Emily trailed behind the little party. The group divided at the refreshment tent; the woman happy to sit outside on a bench, while their men went inside. Which left Emily out on a limb, from who and how was she going to get a drink? She had a thirst on her like a camel's arse.

John came from the tent, on his palm he carried a tray of drinks and a jug. Fortunately, he had included Emily in the glass count and she slurped her's down in one gulp.

Chapter 23

Susannah couldn't decide who she disliked the most, Emily or George? To be fair, she had made the decision, she hated them both equally, but for different reasons. George had granted Emily certain rights and the worst was Susannah was subject daily, to the haughty and overconfident air of Emily Babcock. He'd allowed this maid the right to assume she could affect airs! *-The impertinence of it!*

The fucking of her was one thing, but humiliation by a jumped up hussy was quite another. Where once Susannah felt a heavy weight bearing down on her, now anger inflamed her. This anger, like heat rose, and lightened her mood. She watched these two perform around her. They pretended blamelessness. They feigned innocence; not to protect her from the knowledge of their relationship but to revel in their dishonesty and stupidity of their role-playing. If she was going to suffer any more the smothered giggles and stifled chuckles, the haughty airs. Her requests to her maid, ignored. Then she, Susannah, would as best she could, avenge herself, or and hopefully, rid herself of both their company.

***

Susannah sat at the kitchen table, sipping lemonade. A flypaper hung from the gaslight; a brown tea-coloured ringlet of paper. Susannah watched as a bluebottle twisted on the sticky surface, struggling to free itself from its tacky grip.

***

It was good news; George informed her of his deployment to Dartmouth for officer training; he wouldn't return for two months. How would Emily survive without him? But this was something Emily hadn't reckoned with when she'd adopted her sullen attitude to Susannah. She believed she was safe, and protection would always be there. George would be on her side, no matter what. She had this wonderful man who loved her with a passion.

Emily had never been in control of anything. And now she was in control of this household and all who lived under its roof; which, did not unfortunately, include herself. She couldn't help herself; she loved to snub and rub Susannah's nose in it. *-That Susannah, so high and oh so, bloody mighty! She doesn't know about life or love. Just 'cos she's all right looking! But not as luscious as she'd like to think she is! The only girl around a school of boys, given her an overblown opinion of herself.* And she, Emily Babcock wasn't having any of that.

***

Dolly had prepared a basket of cakes, pies, and baked bread for the household of George and Susannah. May carried the basket through the lanes decorated with cow parsley; butterflies fluttered from the hedgerow, as she walked by.

The gate clanged behind May as she approached Downland; she caught sight of a movement in the front room and put her hand up to wave. But it wasn't an arm that waved in salutation; it was as May neared, a leg, a leg within a red stocking, and wearing scuffed, brown, unpolished boots. And behind those stockings, with a ladder, were white buttocks, thrusting. And if she wasn't very much mistaken, having been on the receiving end of that particular arse, it belonged to George. May drew closer, shielding her eyes with her hand, and there, laid out in full view, on the dining room table was, Emily.

-Fucking Emily. So that time in my room wasn't a one off. How long had it been going on? She watched as his arse, his muscles tense, pushed in and out. Stared as Emily thrust upwards to receive him, her legs wrapped tight around him, holding him in. So mesmerised was she, May hadn't heard the clank of the gate, or the carriage wheels on the gravel path.

It was when she removed her hand that shielded her eyes, did she see Susannah, reflected in the glass, watching her husband and her maid. May pulled Susannah and the perambulator away to the cover of the porch. They both stood, stock-still. And May said, "I'm so sorry."

"Why? Why should you be sorry? It's not you in there laying under that dog of a husband."

"No it isn't ... but."

"Did you know, did you know about this?"

Susannah opened the front door. May stood in the porch; took a deep breath, and followed.

A giggle came from the front room. *-I could bloody batter the stupid slut.* She took her cue from Susannah, who hadn't confronted them.

Pouring herself a glass of warm ale, Susannah said, "Here, have one." And she raised her glass. "How long? How long have you known?" Susannah wasn't shouting, which amazed May. She was calm. Susannah didn't show anger at her husband's betrayal, but would she at the disloyalty of her friend, and that friend, May?

"I didn't know. I didn't know it was still going on."

"Still?"

And May relayed what she'd seen at the night of the New Year's party. "I promise you, I didn't now it was still going on."

Susannah rested her glass down and picked up baby George who'd begun to cry. "He's hungry, like his father, no control over his appetites." And Susannah undid her blouse. And little George placed his pouting lips on her nipple and sucked. "Not going to chew them off then are you?"

"Only when he's got teeth!" said George, as he leaned on the doorframe. "What are you two witches brewing up?"

"We are having a private conversation. We couldn't find Emily, so we thought we'd help ourselves to a beer."

"She's around somewhere, saw her banging a carpet a while ago."

May rolled her eyes.

"Any beer going?"

"It's over there, in that cupboard."

"Where are the glasses?"

"We got ours from the drainer, perhaps you ought to have a look."

George was miffed, neither of those women had gotten off their ruddy arses to serve him beer in his own house. She shouldn't be surprised he sought comfort in the arms of another woman.

"I'm going to The George," he said. And with that, he was off.

There followed a silence. May nervously sipped her beer. She decided then to tell her everything; if she was to lose this friendship it wasn't going to be because she'd withheld something. She reasoned, tell the truth, and shame the devil.

"I ... I haven't told you everything!"

Susannah looked up and nodded.

May took this as her cue, "I... I don't know how or where to start."

"I can't help you with that as I don't know the story, but I usually find the beginning the best place."

And so the story unfolded and Susannah heard how May believed she was to marry, and then she saw the butterfly brooch.

"My brooch?"

"I chose it, he gave me the money to buy it, and then I saw you with it. Emily said, he had no interest in you, but you wouldn't leave him alone. That evening, I was returning to my room I heard something. I put my eye to the keyhole and there was Emily, with George on top of her."

"Where was I?"

"I think you may have been in your room, the Crow's-Nest."

"I see."

Here, May flexed the truth, she didn't want Susannah to know her as a common whore... Taking a coin in exchange for a cunt. "I knew then, George, never intended to marry me. I was just another maid, something to amuse himself with. I didn't feel hatred for him, just coldness. That night, Emily was sleeping in my room, I told her I knew she'd been with George."

So there it was, all out in the open, most of it. It was up to Susannah now. Emily entered; she seemed surprised to find these people in her kitchen.

"George, has gone to The George," offered Susannah.

"Is there anything I can help you with Miss ... Mrs—"

"No, not now."

***

May was looking at Susannah's clothes.

"Would you like this?"

"A corset, it no longer fits me, not since George's birth."

"Oh, you'll fit into again."

"It's about time you had one, you're not a girl any more. Look at those." Susannah nodded at May's breasts.

"I know, and I was going to get one, when I next went home. Susannah I can't wear that. It's a lace up the back type; I need one with hooks up the front, so I can dress myself."

Susannah went to the drawer under her wardrobe. "No sooner said! I've never worn this, never had to. Oh come on, try it."

May removed her skirt and blouse.

"Breathe in."

-*Blimey*. Who'd have thought? "No tighter, I need to breathe."

"I'll fetch my tape measure."

May looked at herself in the mirror. She wore a pink satin S-Shape corset, her breasts thrust upwards into a mono pillow.

"Nineteen inches. Look at mine, twenty-four."

"Susannah you've only just had a baby."

"Three months ago; here pull on these." And she pointed to the laces at her back.

"That's it, I'm not doing it any tighter, you'll suffocate."

Susannah took the measuring tape. "Oh well that's an inch off, it'll have to do. May, would you come on an outing with me?"

"An outing? ... If I can have the time off."

"Oh don't worry, I'll say to Henry I need you for a couple of days. What do you say?"

"What do I say?"-*Blimey!* "I'd love to, where?"

"We are going to Southsea. Strolling, shopping, and eating. Wearisome things like that."

"Little George?"

"We have Emily for that. Should we bring or leave her? Let's decide after tea. Here you wear this dressing gown, and I'll wear..." reaching into her wardrobe. "This." And brought forth a kimono.

"Oh that's gorgeous."

"Come on, let's eat." Susannah didn't have a bell to ring for the servant's attention. So while May made herself comfortable on the chaise, Susannah went to the kitchen and ordered tea.

They both sat back and sipped. The silence broken by a question.

"Will you miss George, when he's at Dartmouth?"

"Yes! I'll miss him. I'll miss him as one would miss anything. As a dog, misses a flea."

May giggled. "George, a mangy, flea bitten dog. You don't love him?"

"No, I never have."

"But ..."

"But I have his child?"

"Well, yes, but please, I didn't mean …"

"I did not have a choice! I've had no choice in the begetting, marriage, baby, or this house. I did however choose the furnishings!"

May wasn't sure whether to laugh, so decided to suppress the giggle. Susannah poured them both another glass of sherry.

"Are you laughing at me May Miller?"

"No, not AT you. I do think though, the bolster shows very good taste."

"When we go out, I don't want you dressed like that."

May frowned. "What's wrong with it?"

"Nothing, for a servant. But you'll be accompanying me, my companion. And so we will choose our outfits together. Come, let's choose what we'll wear."

May was finding it difficult to walk up the stairs. She could no longer see her feet, the corset thrusting her breasts so far out.

"You have to have faith. A belief the next step will be there."

"Mm."

Susannah tore open her wardrobe. And tossed out a pile of skirts, blouses, and dresses. "From this pile, we will choose. Shall we compliment or clash?"

May picked the blue silk skirt.

"Try it."

May stepped into it. It trailed a little at the back, like a mermaid's tail. May loved it.

"What about this?" Susannah held up a cotton, high-neck blouse, with fine lace coming to a tapering point just below her breasts. May blinked. "You'll need a belt." And she handed May a dark blue, embroidered with violets and pansies, belt with a silver buckle.

"Boots, here try these. I think they'll be too big. You'll have to get some though, you can't wear those."

And she pointed to the black, low healed boots, laying tired on the floor. "We'll buy some when we're there. That's an idea."

-It's an idea! May thought, *-But not a good one. New boots would cost over a pound. I won't, these boots will have to do.*

"I can stuff these."

"What?"

"Stuff paper down the toes they'll do. Do for a day anyway."

"We'll see."

"Now you choose for me."

May eyed the pile of silks, satins and cottons. She tugged out a pale green, satin skirt. A white silk blouse, with a square necked detail and high neck. The belt embroidered with pink and white rosebuds with a mother of pearl buckle.

"You in blue, and me in green, blue and green should never be seen."

"And we won't be forgotten."

"I'll wear my straw boater"

"And so will I. We'll decorate them the day before."

***

Susannah and May strolling Palmerston Road, both wore fresh flowers on their hats, as fresh as they were. Susannah's straw boater was decorated with gypsophila and white rosebuds; May's, similar but not identical boater, daisies tucked under the yellow ribbon.

And in their strolling, they met Agnes Spritely. Greetings, were of course, exchanged. Agnes introduced Susannah. "I'm sure you remember from our party, New Years Eve."

"Of course, delighted."

"Sir William Baker, May."

"Sir William."

"Ladies please, I should be the proudest man if you would grant me the opportunity to escort you to the Royal

Pier Hotel, where you shall be my guests."

Sir William sashayed along the road. To the right of him, the red headed beauty of Agnes, a rose in full bloom. To the left the buttery, blonde prettiness of Susannah, and linked through her arm the budding, black-haired handsomeness of May.

He paused, this caused for a celebratory cigar. And he puffed on his, rolled on a virgin's thigh, cigar. Accompanying these luscious lovelies, he met people of his acquaintance. He nodded and smiled. Sir William was a bit of a card, which of course increased his standing in the community further.

Sir William showed these females along, and acknowledged every greeting and nod. Agnes nodded, Susannah nodded, and what Susannah did, May who was the apprentice, copied. Every man turned his head. Every woman blinked and stared, as this train passed by. Of all the beautiful women in Hampshire, he, Henry, had herded all three together, a stag at rut. The steps of the hotel drew near. Ladies please, and he pointed to a saloon.

The manager of course had rooms for Sir Baker, and if the ladies would like to take tea, compliments of the establishment ... Susannah and May were asked if they would accept a room on the second floor as his guest.

***

May and Susannah turned the key in the lock. May threw her hat from her head onto the double bed. May opened the balcony door... The sea rolled and waved.

Susannah and May lay side by side. The sun setting on a sparkling blue sea.

"I love this place."

"This hotel?"

"Well, yes, but I meant this part of Portsmouth, Southsea. One day, when I have enough money I shall live here."

"You have some savings then?"

"I do, I have half of what I need, and I am going to have a shop. A flower shop."

Susannah looked out to sea, and saw not the lapping waves, but her future stretching out in front of her, as far and further than that horizon. A bleak, dull greyness, of happening to, a few grabbed proddings, and more unchosen children.

"You'll need a guarantor, you're unmarried. They'll expect you to have a man, to back you up." May stayed silent, she hadn't thought of the nuts and bolts, the practicalities. This was her dream, and no amount of bells ringing alarmingly, would waken her from that.

She didn't know how any of this worked. –*Hadn't even understood the meaning of annum.* May saw her future slipping away, she didn't want a man in her life. They were useful, a prod and then a coin, but sharing her life, her shop with one. No.

***

"No, I don't want to marry yet, perhaps never."

"I wasn't suggesting you married, I thought I would partner you."

–*Blimey.*

May watched the sails of a boat come from the horizon and grow bigger as they neared the shore.

"I have the education, class, and money. And I, with my contacts could offer us good clients. You May, have your talent, and intelligence, we would make a perfect team."

May was overawed. "What about George, will he let you?"

"I don't know, which is why I won't tell him. This will be our secret, and when finally I leave him he will have the comfort and the pleasure of Emily for succour."

Susannah took May's hand in hers, and gently squeezed, conveying the validity of her proposition. May looked at that hand, the manicured fingernails, smooth skin, and callous free palms. Then her own hands, broken nails, and dried split skin. "We're opposites, you, and me. Your hair blonde, mine black; brown eyes and blue, common and class, educated and ignorant, so contrary."

And Susannah said, "Married unmarried; useless, talented ..."

May raised Susannah's fingers to her lips and kissed them. The salt air and warm breeze blew the muslin curtains gently to and fro. Susannah kissed May's lips and touched her cheek with her lips. May looked into those deep brown eyes and their lips met. May tasted honey. Susannah sipped violets. May, kissed her, pushing her tongue between her lips, and tongue to tongue, they touched.

Susannah unhooked May's belt. They both giggled at this unstated desire forming as they took it in turns to remove each other's clothing.

They lay on this bed, both in their chemise and drawers. They lay facing each other; and both knowing now, they had agreed, out of curiosity, or lust, or comfort, to embark on this unknown journey.

They embraced, breast to breast, touching through cotton and through gauze. May took off her chemise, lifted it over her head. Susannah placed her fingers to those pert breasts, felt the hardening of the small, taut pinkness ... This seemed the naughtiest taboo, but then female love unlike men's was neither illegal, nor harmful! May slid her hand under the gauze chemise and touched her breast, so large and full. Each nipple hardened under May's caress.

Susannah removed her wispy gauze chemise, and it joined in confusion on the floor with those other jumbled, discarded garments. They drew close, nipple touching nipple, red to pink, lip to lips. Susannah's hand brushed along May's thigh, slid up pushing through the slit of the drawers, and touched the hair, dark and tangled.

Nude now, a light warm summer breeze blew, gently caressing their bodies. Her fingers pressed between her soft, white thighs. Warm and moist, she pressed her finger. And with her thumb, she stroked. She placed her lips to her and gently sucked, her lips so pert; smothering her with wet kisses. Susannah thrust her hips and May pushed forward with her fingers. She took from the bedside a small bottle of Brilliant, and with this oil anointed a candle and pressed forward into that warm honey flesh. Susannah grabbed at May to stay her hand, release her from this wondrous torture.

She moved to face May. Stroked her gently, caressing her softly with her tongue, sucking on the petite pinkness. Oh, and that darkness, such distinction to those white thighs. Susannah touched her, with her lips she sucked, and with her tongue she thrust. That bottle, plunged deep and May, May quivered, such delight. And now poised and moist, slotted fingers and in this way all caresses reached their crest and they rode these waves until the surf subsided and these two sighed with delight, abandoned to their joy.

They lay in each other's arms, sticky bodies entwined as one. Each had reached a plateau of understanding, and so they slept. Two people different and at once the same, but for May there was the softness, too soft, she needed something, harder.

Chapter 24

But now October had come and George Spritely was packing, he'd be gone tomorrow. Emily watched him as she packed his shirts. "I'll write," she said.

-Oh great! "I shall look forward to hearing all your news."

"You'll write to me?"

"I'll try, but I'll be busy and it would be awkward, don't you think? A letter written to my maid, delivered to Susannah?"

"But it'd be my letter."

"Which, she'd have every right to read, and in my handwriting!"

Emily had been looking forward to reading his letters; she'd have kept them safe. It would have been a confirmation of their relationship. And now he was going, she'd have nothing. "I'll think of you often; all the time."

"When it's nine-thirty in the evening, then I'll think of you, and you will, I hope, think of me. It will be our secret time, our shared time." Of course, George didn't give a hoot either way, she could think about him, or not, as the case maybe. "Do something for me Emily."

"Yes Sir."

"Raise your skirt."

And Emily did.

And when George said, "Higher!" She wrapped the fabric in a roll under her chin.

"No drawers!"

"It's hot, and they get in the way."

"They do, don't they?" George could see Susannah on the lawn a blanket spread out where baby George was lying, kicking his chubby legs in the air.

"Turn round."

And he pushed her over the table, her arse in the air.

He jammed himself in and thrust forwards.

Emily watched Susannah sitting on the grass, as George pressed home. And his hand brought her thighs banging against his legs. Emily's elbows rested on the table her hands supporting her chin. She stared at Susannah. Every thrust and push, was a slap around Susannah's chops.

"Just a little something to remember me by." And he kissed Emily on the nape of her neck, withdrew, and buttoned himself up. "Remember," he said, "at nine-thirty every evening, I'll be thinking of you, I hope you'll be thinking of me!"

"Oh yes, of course," she cooed.

***

Emily had gotten, as Emily's mother would say, 'above herself'. George was now gone. He'd been gone a whole week. And Emily's wages were due yesterday, Friday. Emily knocked on the living room door, and without awaiting a response walked into the room and found Susannah reclining on the chaise, The Lady placed on the floor by her side.

-*Lazy baggage!*

"Susannah! Mrs Spritely, I …"

Susannah didn't open her eyes but allowed this girl to carry on talking.

"Mrs Spritely, you've forgotten that it was my payday yesterday."

"Have I?"

"Yes."

"Have I forgotten your wage?"

"Well, yes."

"I don't agree."

"Mrs Spritely, I haven't received my wages. I'm sure it's an oversight."

"Hand me my bag, Emily." And Emily, for the first time, in along time, did exactly as Susannah bid.

"Here." And she handed Emily a sixpence.

-Are you stupid or just living with the fairies? "It's not 6d Mrs Spritely,"-*I'll jog her memory.* "It's six shillings."

"Six shillings? Why Emily that's rather a lot! Who gave you such a large amount?"

"I ... think it's the going rate."

"The 'going' rate? You're going then, are you Emily?"

"What? Pardon." -*What the bloomin'* hell is she talking about? But by now, it began to dawn on Emily there was something Susannah did have control of in this house, and that was the accounts. George never took an interest in money, never short of it, and besides, that was a wife's job.

Emily held her hand out and took the sixpence. "I'll expect the 5/6 tomorrow then."

"Yes you'll expect it tomorrow." -*But you won't receive it.* And Susannah, as Emily walked from the room said, "Would you fetch some ginger beer from the larder, I feel rather thirsty."

***

The next day and it was to be Emily's day off, she needed money to get the train to Winchester. But it was already ten-thirty, and still Susannah was not up. Of course, she complained that feeding George tired her, and she needed her rest. But what did she think other women did? What was so special about her?

At twenty-seven minutes past ten, Emily knocked on Susannah's door, and again not waiting for a reply, entered. Susannah wore a silk, chrysanthemum blossomed, embroidered kimono, she stared from her window onto the garden below.

"I don't recall having asked you to come in!"

Emily decided to ignore that quip. She owed her money, it was important, she was going to write to George about this, then we'd see! "I need my wages, I'm going home today, and it's nearly afternoon."

"Is it? And what time is it Emily?"

"Gone half past ten."

"That late?" And Susannah swept past Emily and into the nursery. Emily had no choice but to follow.

"I."

"Shh, not so loud. He's still sleeping, bless him. He's such a good baby. He knows his mother doesn't need to be disturbed, unnecessarily."

Emily lowered her voice, "If I could have my wages, I could get off."

"I suppose you could."

Emily decided Susannah had gone mad. *-Wait till George heard about this!*

"Mrs Spritely, may I have my wages?"

"You've forgotten something, I think."

"I haven't"

"Please is the word, and you've forgotten it"

Emily sighed. *-Bloody joking.* "PLEASE, May I have my wages."

"Fetch my bag."

-Please! One rule for her, one for me. Bitch.

Susannah picked up George, who'd started to grumble in his cot. She bounced him up and down on her shoulder. "Are you hungry little one?" And she lowered him to her breast. Emily returned with Mrs Spritely's bag. "Put it over there Emily. And Emily, I'll take tea."

"But …" But Emily in an attempt to get her money would, for now, obey. Stupid game Susannah was

playing, but she'd pay her back for this. *-You see if I don't.* It was now eleven o' clock, she handed Susannah her tea. Which Susannah didn't drink, but placed on the table under the window, the frame painted blue with winged pigs jumping over moons.

"Oh yes my bag." And Emily dashed over to pick it up.

"Now let me see, where did I put my purse?" she said, as she rummaged deeply into the bowels of the drawstring. "Ah, here it is." And she held it aloft and Emily sighed, -*At last, a day away from this snooty loony is exactly what I need.*

But Emily's hopes were dashed, after opening the brown leather purse, it revealed only a couple of coppers. "Oh dear, I don't seem to have any money. Here you are, you may have them." And Agnes held out the two copper coins.

"I need to buy a train ticket, it's not enough."

"Emily, I can't keep giving you money."

-You're not giving me money. I'm earning my wage. But she didn't say that. And if Susannah wouldn't pay her, in truth there was little Emily could do about it. Emily sat at the kitchen table, she had one silver sixpence and two coppers. She also held a pen; on the table was a piece of paper.

Dear George

I had to write to you, to let you know, that my wages have not been paid. So I could get the train. It was my day off and I only had eight pennies. Please write to Mrs Spritely and tell her my wages are six shillings payable every Friday,
I hope you are keeping well. And I remember you at nine thirty.
Yours truly
Emily -Babcock

-That'd show her. Emily walked to the post office, she'd invest some of her money sending this letter. A week passed, George hadn't written to her, he hadn't replied. Most peculiar. But that morning, the post delivered a letter to Susannah. She wondered whether it was from George. She pondered over what it said. Wondered when, most importantly, she'd get her money. She was owed twelve shillings, not including the eight

pence, that was a fee, for late payment, a commission.

Emily delivered the letter into Susannah's hands and hung about while she read it. "Will that be all?"

"Yes Emily, you may go."

Emily stood on tiptoes, trying to read over her shoulder at the writing. When that didn't work, tried to glean from her expression, the contents of the letter, and who it was from. But Susannah was impenetrable, as she placed the letter in her bag she said, "Thank you Emily, that will be all."

Emily wished it had been a post card. She should ask George to write on postcards! It would be like secret messages going back and forth, addressed to Susannah, but with a snippet for her. She'd write to him again and suggest it, and remind him too -*If she wasn't getting her wages, George, should and would, know about it.*

Monday morning no wages, Emily sent another letter, at this rate she thought - *I'll have spent all me money, just on stamps.* But of course, she wasn't paying for the paper or the envelopes. They belonged to Susannah and smelled of roses.

***

George wondered who would be writing to him on rose scented paper; an abysmal hand, with an inkblot on the envelope. He was embarrassed, and the other lads mocked him for his blotty friend.

It astonished George! The owner of this letter was his maid. Good grief! Was she so thick to think he would write to her? Or write to Susannah, on her behalf? What was he to say? Give the girl her wages, she's written to me with a complaint. Oh yes, that'd be good. And what were these postcards? Secret messages on the back of postcards! Addressed to Susannah but with a message for her, only she would understand. The girl's gone bonkers … But when the third letter arrived, he knew he could ignore her no longer. So he bought the first postcard he came across, something with a boat on, and sent it to Susannah.

Which simply said: I can't bear you writing me, ALL THESE LETTERS! He hoped Susannah would understand it as an ironic statement! She'd written nothing to him, and Emily would read as, stop writing to me.

But it had another effect. Susannah wrote to him. I haven't, she wrote, and don't intend to. This could concern the letters she hadn't written, or the wages she hadn't paid. And she'd signed it, your concerned wife Susannah. Emily sends her thoughts to you.

What the hell did that mean? It didn't mean anything to Susannah. She didn't know anything about the nine-thirty rendezvous. It was just a reminder, informing him she knew Emily. But it made George believe this woman knew more than he thought she did, although he'd kept his liaison secret from her. But Emily could be noisy! Yet Susannah had never burst in on them, and that, was that. George put it out of his mind; after all, there was little she could do. The next week and another letter; George screwed it into a ball and chucked it on the fire, without bothering to read it.

Emily had gone four weeks without wages, and had run out of money to buy stamps. Emily decided she'd not work, Susannah could make her own tea and dinner. But there was something she hadn't considered. She could, of course withdraw her labour but Susannah could withdraw her room and lodging. And if Emily didn't cook, she didn't eat either. So she resorted to what she knew best, she spat in Susannah's beef stew. George would be home in a fortnight, he could sort this out. But two weeks was or seemed such a long way away. And she had not a penny to her name, no money for tobacco, let alone stamps. What she needed was to find something; cash, tobacco or some saleable something, - *I dare you to tell George. Bitch.*

But Susannah had no intention of telling George anything, she'd allow Emily to state her case. To him, she wouldn't be answerable, or to her.

***

May was counting her money when there was a knock at her door. Without a reply or response, Emily stood in the doorway, her eyes big as saucers as she spotted the cache of coins.

"Where'd you get all that?"

"My wages, what'd you think?"- *Friggin' hell, just bugger off.* May was hoping she wouldn't sit on the bed because the rattling of the other coins would make Emily's eyes pop. Then she'd have something to enquire about. She'd managed to shove the bulk of it under the covers "Something you want?"

"Yes, it's Susannah, she hasn't paid me my wages."

"Why not?"

"'Cos she's a bloody stupid cow, and I can't even get home. I was wondering, too. I need some money. I'll pay you straight back, as soon as George gets here."

"George? What's George got to do with it?" - *Bugger off!*

"I wrote to him, I told him I need paying." May raised one eyebrow.

"What's that face for?"

"Just you! Writing to George. What did he say?"

"He hasn't written back yet, although he did write on the back of a postcard, a message."

May wondered, - *What the bloody hell are you talking about?* And pushed the one pound in coins into a heap. She wanted to shove it in her bag, but her drawstring was on the table, and she didn't want to leave her stash unguarded. There was nearly thirty pounds under this cover, and no way, on point of death, preferably Emily's, was she about to disclose it.

"Would you lend me some money?"

"I …"- *Great.* May pondered this. It's horrible, left without any money, and not able to go and see your family. On the other hand, she was a cheating rat bag, and she didn't blame Susannah, not one jot.

"I can't."

"You've loads there."

"I don't have loads. I have a pound, and this pound's my month's wages and my dad'll be needing it."

"Just ten bob, that's all. Just until I'm paid."

"That's two weeks away, I need this for when I get home."

"Just half, he'll take half and I'll have half." - *Mean bitch.*

"Emily, this is not my money, it's already promised, and I've shoes to buy, me dad's rent to pay." - *Blimey, why should my family go without because of your trouble?*

"Just tell your dad you didn't get all your wages, and you'll make it up next visit." Emily's eyes stared at the coins, so near and yet so far. She'd just to walk over there and snatch it. And she would too; but May, though small, was strong, a tough little thing. Emily knew, she knew how to look after herself.

"I'm not going to lie to my family. If I were to give you something I'd say what I'd done."

Emily saw hope in those words, a chink of light with the clink of coins.

"When is your next day off?"

"I'm owed two days, till now. Have worked all this bloody time and nothin' to show for it."

"Then you don't need the money, George'll be home before your next leave, won't he?"

Emily, foiled, "But I've no money."

"You're fed and housed, which is a lot better than some, and you know you'll get your money, sometime."

-Hard faced bitch.

- Stupid cow.

"Well, I would be able to get home if I had the money. Wouldn't I?"

"If, Mrs Spritely allows you to."

Emily hadn't thought of that. She'd assumed, if she'd the money and the train fare, she could go, as her time off was owed, but like her wage, it all depended on Susannah.

"I can give you …"

"Yes." Emily said hopefully.

"Some advice."

-*You're taking the piss now.*

"Get into Susannah's good books, and if you want to screw around with her husband don't let Susannah know."

Emily stood with her mouth open. "How dare you!"

"How dare I?"

-*That was mean. I don't even dislike this stupid cow, that much.* As if she were sorry for speaking so harshly, and in recompense, "Look I can give you sixpence, but that's all."

Emily looked at the other coins, and back at May. "Thank you." And she walked over to May and held out her hand for the silver sixpence. Emily, now thinking that they could be friends went to sit on her bed. More money could be forth coming …

"Don't."

Emily started back,

"I have things to do." May stood, but didn't move from her stash, like a bird protecting its nest.

"What have you done with your picture?"

May reddened "Picture?"

"Yes the one that used to be up there?" She said nodding at the empty nail.

"It fell off."

Emily's eyes narrowed. "I'll go then, thanks for the tanner."

May thought, -*I've got to find another hideaway.*

***

Emily was feeling bitter. -*Shouldn't be treated like this. It isn't simply, fair.* Her injustice spread to the library, and in she went and took Henry's pouch of tobacco. What had Henry to do with her gripe? That, no one would understand, or Emily explain! But she filched his tobacco and Emily enjoyed a puff on her pipe -*At last.* Plus, she had a sixpence. And it was a merrier Emily who returned to Downland than had left. Until she met Susannah …

***

Henry would, before dinner have a tot and a puff. Agnes had bought him a pouch of his favourite tobacco, Golden Ambrosia. But for the life of him he couldn't find it, he could've sworn he placed it in the desk drawer. He rang the bell.

"Yes Henry?"

"May, have you seen? Could've have sworn … my tobacco, it was here," he said nodding at the

desk.

"It's in your desk, saw it myself this morning." And she smiled at him and walked to the desk drawer. -*Silly old buffer; can't see for looking.* But as much as May peered and poked she couldn't find it, and where she could have sworn it was, it wasn't. "I can't understand it, saw it there myself, with these eyes."

"Would you fetch Dolly, perhaps she's shifted it." Dolly said she hadn't been in the library. And Henry who was tapping his pipe in anticipation and annoyance said, "Bloody odd, there's only us three here."

Which is when May looked at Dolly, and Dolly looked at May.

***

"Well, you don't think …"

"I don't know."

"She likes a puff."

"I …"

"I've seen her with her clay pipe."

"I—"

"What did Emily want with you this morning?"

"She—"

"She just said to me, is May here? And when I said you were in your room, she was off. Didn't even ask if was all right to go up or anything."

"Yes, she came straight in, didn't wait for me to ask her to come in."

"No! So, what she want then?"

"She wanted—"

"Looked well cross, if you ask me."

"She—"

"You upset her?" Dolly asked as she chopped the head off a pheasant.

"No." And May using Dolly's pause for breath said, "She wanted to borrow some money."

"Money? Why?"

"She reckons she hasn't been paid."

"Not paid? Why on earth wouldn't she be paid?"

May poked at the embers in the grate.

"Well?"

"I know she's not happy, about not being able to go home."

"Mm." And the bird was disembowelled.

Dolly couldn't make head nor tail of this information. She should inform Henry. It was all very odd.

***

Emily puffed on her pipe. She was sitting on a kissing gate.

"John." And she gave him her best smile.

"Hello Emily, you enjoying yourself?" And he tried to make out her features, hidden in a pall of smoke held under the brim of her hat, "Just taking a breather."

"That what you call it, is it?"

"Want a puff?"

John put down his wheelbarrow and walked over to May. "Smell's sweet, stuff my dad smokes, like he's smoking compost."

Emily held out her pipe to him.

"No thanks, Em." He leaned his elbows on the fence

Chapter 25

Now when your ship's in Pompey harbour,
And it's berthed on the Northern quay,
If the night is dark and stormy,
You take care of what you see.

Henry wanted his pipe, he needed a smoke. After ringing the bell, he asked Dolly to send May on an errand to fetch tobacco, even though it wouldn't be Golden Ambrosia. Henry gave May 6d, and told her to, "Keep the change." -*A ha'penny! Cor, ta!*

Now, as May made her way along Pigeon Coop Lane, she saw something that caught her eye, something red flashing in a sea of green. She stood to make out what this strange thing was. -*Bugger me!* THOSE red stockings! Those brown boots wrapped around the thrusting bare arse of someone she couldn't make out. So she went to the kissing gate and leaned closer.

And. -*The bitch!* It was John! - *Friggin' bitch!*

May noticed something else too; Emily's pipe leaning on the stoop. And beneath that, on the ground, a tatty drawstring bag, made from some grubby brown, velvet, curtain material.

May picked up the bag and peered in. Old Henry's tobacco! And in the side pocket, her silver sixpence. And then, a pair of white silk stockings, which looked much, like Agnes' stockings. Just then, the gruntings and groanings grew louder and John's tight butt, pumping faster. They were reaching their crescendo. So, no time to hang around, she grabbed the bag and -*Just because I can, the clay pipe.* And she ran all the way to Fairview.

"What on earth?"

"This!" As she plonked the bag onto Dolly's scrub top table. "Not just any bag, but Emily's bag."

"What you doin' with that then?"

"I'm returning it to its rightful owner."

Joseph scratched his head. -*Women!*

May upturned the bag, spewing its contents.

"Ere, that's Henry's tobacco!"

"I know."

Joseph tapped out his pipe.

"And these are silk stockings; and this is my silver sixpence."

"Which you lent her."

May said, "What's this?" As she continued rummaging.

Dolly rose, "That's my silver apple knife!"

And under the dirty blown hanky, two coppers.

Joseph stood up, went to the table, and filled his pipe with a pinch of Golden Ambrosia.

"Joseph Bridger."

"Dolly, 'tis a finder's fee."

"You didn't find it!"

And it was fortunate that Joe had his mouth full, because at that moment appeared his leather tobacco pouch. "Well, bloody cheeky baggage, I lent her a fill too!"

"That's probably when she nicked it."

"I did leave her … went to the … hmmph."

"I don't know who the tuppence belongs to, but she reckoned she didn't have a farthing to her name."

And Dolly walked over to the window ledge and lifted the upturned flowerpot. "The milk money's gone."

"Well, would you credit it?"

May shook the bag, turned upside down and another two pennies dropped out followed by dust. Dolly sighed and grabbed the washcloth.

John strolled back to Fairview pushing his barrow. He was trying to work out what had happened! Well, he knew of course. -*I'm a man, ain't I?*

But how it happened? He was, while the blood was still seconded to other less intelligent parts of his anatomy, remembering Emily bestriding the kissing gate.

He remembered the red stockings. Swinging her legs, to and fro.

-God it felt wonderful. He knew it would of course. He'd had his hand on his dick often enough, daring god to blind him, before or after growing hairy palms. But that! That was like being sucked into a great big bowl of trembling pink blancmange. Wobbly, wet and warm. He'd never experienced anything like it. He remembered being offered the pipe. Emily stood up, and was using John's shoulder to support herself, when she fell backwards. Her skirt flew up and … she wasn't wearing any drawers. He saw all she had, as she lay on the ground her legs spread. John was rapt.

"You could help me up! Standing there, gaping."

And John jumped over the gate, knelt over her, and she leaned up, and she kissed him. Least he thought she did, but anyway they kissed. And then they were in the bushes…

John pushed open the kitchen door, smiling still.

"You seen Emily?"

"I …"

"Only this is her bag, isn't it Joe? May found it. What I don't understand is why she'd leave her bag!"

"Answering a call of nature," said Joe

"What'd you think May?"

"I reckon that's it, a call of nature." And she looked up at John. Who blushed.

"Ee, 'ere look at him, soft beggar. Call of nature and he's blushing."

May pointed at the stash on the table, "She nicked all that. Emily stole it. She'll nick anything and everything, you know that don't you? Did she take anything from you?" May asked bitterly. And if it were possible, John reddened further.

***

May had to find a new hiding place. She worked on the theory that if Emily was a brazen hussy *-which she* *was,* she'd come looking for her stash, her sixpence along with the other 19/6. So she separated the pound from the rest, and replaced the quid in the back of the picture fame. But what to do with the rest of the haul? Emily would find what she expected to find and bugger off. But where to hide the bulk of the money?

May lay on her bed, it was then she noticed a short piece of planking in the corner, only six inches long. A builder needed a piece, an infill because he didn't have, and it wasn't worth it, just for the sake of a maid's room, to buy a full length. Just two nails secured this plank. May needed something to prise the board loose and that something would be found in the potting shed.

May took the hammer and clawed out the nails. Here the lathe and the plaster were strong enough to hold her treasure. She made the nail holes bigger and she could now secure the board with just stomping on the wood with her foot and lever it up with her fingers. May felt relieved, she wrapped her loot in a cloth and placed the bundle in between the joists. And jumped on the plank. Secure.

***

Emily festered, someone had filched her bag.

Dolly, May and Joseph had to decide what to do. This could be serious. And Henry would be curious about his tobacco, he would be expecting May any time … now. She had the Golden Ambrosia, but this type was not sold at the local shop.

Dolly said, "I'll say I found it."

"How did you find it?"

"I don't know, down the back of the drawer. In the hall. Maybe he'll think he dropped it!"

"Hmm."

"May you haven't spent the sixpence he gave you?"

"Of course not, I didn't get that far."

"Right, so I say I found the baccy. You give him back his sixpence. Henry will have his rum, and his smoke, plus his sixpence, sorted."

"I have an idea!"

They both looked at Joe incredulously.

"We give him my tobacco; I have a new pouch in the shed."

"Joe that's dishonest."

"Well, you'd be lying to him anyway, this way we make a profit, he gets his tobacco, we're all winners."

"'Cept Henry, who's lost his tobacco. Which no doubt you'll keep."

"I hadn't considered that," said Joe, with a wink.

"What do you think May?"

May thought, -*Tuppence is better than a farthing,* "It's a good idea! And Henry won't ask questions about who found the tobacco. Where I was for the duration? Why I didn't come back with the bought tobacco? It'd get complicated. Joe's idea is simple but effective."

"Sums him up." And Dolly smiled at the old git indulgently.

"I'll get me pouch." And as Joseph was leaving, "We have to sort out Emily though."

"We haven't dobbed her in, that's something, but it can't happen again. What do we do with her?"

"We'll think of something. But one thing's for certain we never leave her alone in this house again." Dolly agreed just as Joseph came back with his Old Fiery Shag.

***

Henry lit his pipe, and spluttered "Good god!" As a cloud of evil smelling fumes filled the air. He decided he would go to the shop and collect another brand of tobacco. Goodness knows what they'd sold May. It was a pleasant day if he wrapped up well, he would walk.

Henry tapped out his pipe and refilled it with Sweet Briar. He, Henry was not a happy man. He not only was not happy but he hurt. Betrayed, stolen from, and lied to!

And by May! I never would have thought. But there it was in black and white. May had never been to the shop, she'd never spent the sixpence. -*Thief!* He'd had foisted on him the most disgusting, sorry excuse for tobacco, he'd ever puffed.

Henry had had his dinner, Dolly had served him, and she was washing up the dishes before making her way home. At eight Henry rang the bell for May, he knew Dolly would be gone by now and he'd waited until this moment before confronting May. He was livid. And he'd run through many ideas in his mind but nothing stuck as much as, -*She's cheated me.*

May came into the library and smiled, "Yes Henry? How may I help?"

"Get my cat, May." -*Oh blimey, oh well, another sovereign.*

"Drawers May. Take off your drawers."

May did as ordered.

"Step over to the desk, bend over." May clutched the edge of the desk. Henry threw up her skirts they lay in a bunch across her back. She was wearing her pink and lilac striped stockings. Henry rubbed that smooth white arse, his finger pushed down into its crease. Then he stepped back, and whack. No warning. The cat came down across her arse. May flinched. That was hard, normally there'd be a slow building up, and then, somehow it wasn't painful. But this hurt. Tears sprung from her eyes.

"Sorry are you? Sorry now." And Henry whacked her again, raising his arm high and whizzing the cat down on her firm pink backside.

May gritted her teeth. -*It's worth it, it is. I'll be able to have my shop soon, but this is painful.* And she couldn't stand it, much longer. May never thought that lying was worth it. People may disbelieve you for the truth, or they could disbelieve you for the lie. The first was an anchor, the second, flotsam.

"Henry you're hurting me."

Henry didn't stop, nor did he respond but after a while, he said. "You enjoyed your farthings worth, then? Funny that, they don't remember you buying anything from the shop."

***

Henry dropped the cat and took up his dick. He jammed it right into May without tenderness or thought. But Henry was thinking, he was thinking of Lavinia, would she too have been a liar and a cheat? Just dreams, gone up like smoke from his pipe, 'til just the fragrance remains, then nothing.

What May couldn't see, as she lay bent over the desk, clinging to its edge, were Henry's tears. May was crying and Henry was crying. A sorry state. But circumstances were about to overcome Henry. Suddenly and violently it stopped. Henry cried out.

-Thank god for that. Now May would have her money, and she'd go and lick her wounds. She'd explain to Henry what had happened, but not include either Dolly or Joseph. But she wasn't going to take the wrap for that bloody scrubber. All would be well, she would make it up to Henry.

And then Henry shrivelled inside her and she took all his weight, she was pinned to the table. She tried to shrug him off, but he wouldn't budge. Her lungs compressed against the hard oak desk. But Henry would not move. He couldn't, he was a dead weight. The last moments on this earth he spent with his dick jammed into May, and his last action an involuntary spasm of pleasure mingled with the pain of believing May's deceit.

May struggled. "Henry you're crushing me." But Henry was deaf to her concerns. She managed to elbow him, nudge him aside, and she took a big gulp of air. Another wriggle and she was free, and Henry slid to the floor hitting it with a horrible, thud. He lay there, on his back. May looked down on him and the horror of her situation dawned. A tear ran from his eye.

"Oh, Henry. You silly old bugger. What have you done?"

And May knelt down beside him and took his hanky from his pocket and wiped away his tear, and the little fleck of spittle that had formed at the edge of his mouth. And then she took the hanky and wiped his dick clean and dry. And popped it back in his trousers. "No need to be found like this, is there old boy?" And May knelt by his side on the Turkish rug, and held his head on her lap, stroking his hair. She bent over and lightly kissed his forehead, "Forgive me Henry. I didn't lie to you, and I forgive you, 'cos you didn't know. Amen." Her hand reached over and closed old Henry's eyes. Then as she was about to go and seek help, although now there was no rush, she took the silver sixpence from her pocket and placed it in Henry's hand.

"I didn't nick it, see."

May stood in the hall, with her back to wall, listening to the ticking of the clock. Now she grasped how silent the house had become, and she was alone, and there was a dead person in the library, and it was dark. And she flew out the front door, running all the way, not stopping, until she reached Joe and Dolly's front door.

Joe and Dolly were woken from their slumber …

"Who's that?"

"I don't know."

"Going to have the hinges off in a minute."

Dolly shifted off the bed and peered out the window, "Can't see anything."

Joe was on his feet, and treading down the stairs, quickly followed by Dolly.

"Oh—Christ!"

"What? What!"

"Stubbed me bloody toe!"

"Where's the candle?"

"No! They'll see in and we won't to see out."

Dolly stood behind the door with a rolling pin, and Joseph had grabbed his rake. Thus, both suitably armed …

The knocking came again.
"Who is it?"
"It's me. It's May."
Joe turned to Dolly and said, "It's May."
And Dolly said, "What's she want?"
"I don't kn—"
She thrust back the bolt and opened the door. Joseph grabbed a lamp. It was one of those lamps lit by a candle. But although old, it was effective, it had a silvered metal circular reflecting plate that shone out a beam of light. And off they trudged, Joseph brought up the rear, lighting the way for May and Dolly. Dolly led, for if she were in the middle her giant behind would cast a shadow enough to eclipse the moon.

Chapter 26

George came home within hours of receiving the telegram. Dolly greeted him with a tear in her swollen eyes, and a soggy handkerchief screwed in her fist.

"Oh George."

"It's OK, Dolly." And then he cuddled her, or she'd clutched him to her, either way they hugged.

"I'll get you something to drink. Tea? Maybe something stronger?"

"I think I'll have a brandy, Dolly; where's mother?"

"She's in the library, least she was the last time I saw her." And she sniffed.

Agnes ran to George. "George, thank goodness you're here!"

And they held each other. They broke away when only when Dolly arrived with George's brandy.

"You're sure you won't have anything, Mrs Spritely?"

"No thank you Dolly. Would you prepare a lunch for us?"

"Of course." And she sniffed, again.

***

Henry's funeral and burial was at the church of St Peter and St Paul. It wouldn't suit her, but she made an emergency trip to Southsea to buy eighteen yards of black taffeta. And charged, by Madame Le Merchand, the exorbitant price of four guineas, "Eet was a rush job! I 'ave to cancel me other work." This was more than the cost of the fabric and the paper pattern, by a great margin.

Agnes had much to do. Invitations sent; how to choose which black card edge, scalloped or plain? The servants were to have new uniforms, fortunately black so they could use them later. Funeral parlour invoked, and solicitor instructed. Agnes went about her widow's duty calmly and with dignity. Dolly was in charge of supplies. And Agnes had decided on the new fangled idea of a buffet. Dolly didn't know what a buffet was, but once advised she more than rose to the challenge

Henry processed down Cow Lane, his coffin passing fellow officer, Francis Austen. Maisie drew up the rear of this procession, her cart draped with black gauze ribbon and bay leaves; interlaced with zinnia, rosemary, and statice. Black and navy ribbons plaited through her mane. Her harness decorated with two black rosettes and in a nod to the naval officer, the centre picked out with navy-blue ribbons and in the centre a brass naval button with an anchor. She drew the neighbours who couldn't walk the mile to the church, and she nodded solemnly at her duty.

***

The funeral went off well, no reason it wouldn't! The procession returned to Fairview. It saddened Dolly she wasn't able to attend the service, but she and May had important duties to perform, here in the house. The food arranged on the sideboard, May had made a centrepiece of towering foliage, and black grapes. A photograph of Henry overlooked the table, draped in black crepe, like curtains on a window. The library mantelshelf supported a garland of bay leaves and lilies; decanters and crystal glasses stood in orderly ranks on the library table. May and Dolly greeted the guests, and took their hats and coats

But they were mourners too, Dolly had been with Henry, since his marriage since, they'd bought this house. Agnes had chosen Dolly from five other women, and if she were honest with herself, she chose her because she was the plainest. Not that Agnes had cause to worry about her husband's errant ways. For now, he was smitten with his handsome wife. But anyway, best not to be sorry. And so she'd taken her mother's advice, and took on the plainest. And there was none plainer than Dolly.

And she never regretted her decision. Dolly was faithful, a great comfort, indeed, almost a friend! And it was Dolly who, after the gardener had dropped dead, suggested someone in the hamlet who could take over the responsibility of Fairview's lawns; Joseph Bridger.

Dolly greeted and took the coats of Susannah and George -*Oh blimey,* Emily, let's hide the family silver! Dolly raised an eyebrow in May's direction and May blew through her teeth.

"Emily, you stay here and help the others."

So here, the three stood in the hall. A noisy silence surrounded them, broken by Maisie's hooves on the gravel and the last of the mourners welcomed. May and Dolly were now off duty! Except they were on duty of another kind, keeping an eye on Emily; she was not to be left alone, not if they could help it, which they couldn't...

***

Emily hadn't time to talk with George, no sooner had he arrived home, then he left again, to visit his mother. Emily was not in a good mood at all, she hadn't had a smoke in weeks, her bag had been nicked. -*Wait till I get my hands on them.* She'd received no wages, hadn't been home, and now George snapped at her. Plus she'd taken on extra duties at Fairview for the funeral. It wasn't good enough.

-*AND when I arrived, no one talked to me. What have I done? Bitches, both.* Emily walked to the library and May appeared in the doorway. Emily hoped she would have been able to find some tobacco. -*But not with those beady blues, peering at me.* Dolly was loitering in the hallway, but when Emily turned to enter the kitchen, Dolly arrived.

"Would you like a cup of tea?" asked Dolly, not sure of what not to say; it was easier being silent when there were three of you dumb, but with just the two ... seemed a bit well, difficult. Impossible.

"Yes please, shall I put the kettle on?"

"No, it's ok. You sit there, I'll do it." Dolly filled the kettle. But then the kitchen door opened.

"Dolly would you help at the buffet, someone wants some of your towering jelly and blancmange but have concerns about imminent collapse?"

"Yes Mrs Spritely." And that was that. Emily was free from scrutiny. They needed Dolly, and she didn't give the baggage another thought.

May helped male guests to cigars, and served brandies. They were chatting about Henry, recalling anecdotes, and telling shared jokes. May liked that, he was, it reminded her, dear old Henry, such a generous old buffer. And she smiled as she returned the decanter to its place, and remembered Henry, there, lying just there, where Mr Burton's black brogues now stood.

At the end of the evening and the last of the mourners gone home, Emily escorted Baby George and Susannah back to Downland. George would stay this night in his old room and keep his mother company. Later they would have the reading of the will. And then each day after there would be the getting used to the reality of Henry no more, there were no ceremonies to distract from that bare fact.

***

Dolly and May were enjoying the fruits of the buffet, and finishing off the wine. Dolly had left Emily alone and May knew nothing about this, until Joe arrived looking for his tobacco, "I know I left it by the window, I know I did, I know."

"When was this, Joe?"

"'Bout an hour ago, I thought I'll just oil me rake and shears, close the doors and come in the potting shed for a smoke, end of the day sort of thing."

May looked at Dolly and said, "I was in the library, the last I saw her she was heading to the kitchen and you following."

"Who? What?" Joe scratched his head.

"Emily! Was she left alone?"

Dolly stirred her tea. "Agnes wanted me. I ... The baggage! Wait 'till I get my hands on her."

"Look we don't know anything yet before we go accusing …" said Joe.

"Well, let's have a look around, see if we can spot anything else missing," May said, as she left to check her room.

The picture was leaning at a jaunty angle and turning the picture around the backing was off and her money gone. "Bitch."

May jumped, but the floorboard hadn't moved. -*Thank goodness,* But it didn't stop her checking, she prised the board loose, the wrap was there and unfurling it her money too. May stomped the floorboard back down, and turned to check the rest of her room; her silk stockings, gone, and Henry's hanky with the blue anchor. *-Bitch, bitch, cow, baggage, bitch, scum.*

"Could you make a little more noise? Only I think my mother's just roused; she's not fully awake, and it would be a shame to let her sleep in peace."

May turned, and looked shamefully downward, he was right of course! *-The only thing my mind's been on is my money,* "Sorry George. I'm sorry, I didn't mean to. I …"

May waited, tense as a rabbit in front of the hounds, but George didn't jump on her; he withdrew, and she heard his footsteps go down the stairs and his bedroom door open and close. -Bloody hell.

***

May disclosed her inventory of missing *–filched, items.* Dolly's knife too was gone, again; Joe's tobacco. "But we don't know what else she's taken, not unless we can find her stash."

"Well, you were lucky last time finding it like you did, not likely she'll be that stupid—"

"Brazen," said May, not realising this was the first time she'd ever interrupted Dolly, and succeeded.

"—again," said Dolly.

"If you'll excuse me, I'm off to the George, I'm going to get a packet of baccy, and she's got me pouch. Me leather pouch, it's got my initials on it … cow." And Joseph stood on the kitchen threshold balancing on one leg while he pulled on his boot.

"We won't be seeing him for a while, fancy nicking his baccy! He'll be having a drink or two. Agnes put some money on a tab at the pub for anyone who wanted to toast Henry. Generous of her I think, don't you?" May agreed.

***

The solicitor arrived at Fairview late morning. Agnes, George, baby George and Susannah were seated in the library. The solicitor said, "I ask Mrs Dorothy Proudley, Mr Joseph Bridger, John Bridger and Miss May Miller attend."

And so the group assembled at the back of the library behind the chairs of the family members. "…This being the last will and testament of Mr Henry Horatio Beresford Spritely." George inherited Fairview House. With George's Mother, rights to remain and enjoy the property while she lived, and granted £1500 pounds a year. George received the house but would not move into it, he had his home, and he would not move in with his mother. He also received £800.

Baby George received the Grubb telescope, but received no money. Henry believing that if more children should come along, and there was no reason they shouldn't, they would feel unfavoured by their Grandfather. Joseph received £100. Henry reasoned if changes occurred at Fairview, Joseph would have at least nearly his yearly income to assist him until he found new employment. He'd also granted rights, until his death, to the use of the land, Joseph now enjoyed and butted on between Henry's house and Joseph's garden, hereforth called the vegetable pot. Joe stood, and nodded, his hat grasped to his chest, he couldn't believe it.

Dolly's bequest was £95 pounds, for the same reason as he'd left Joseph his year's salary. She also received the silver apple knife, which was generous of Henry, if only she knew where it was….

John was left £50. Miss May Miller received £25. Henry reasoned she hadn't been with them as long as his other employees, yet it would grant her security for at least six months.

And he hadn't forgotten his old shipmate either. The man who saved his life by jumping into freezing water and dragged him back by the scuff of his neck to the ship after he went overboard; he left Mr Ernest Arthur Miller £10.

Henry had pitched his legacy in just such a way, everyone felt please with their bequest. *-An unusual circumstance,* thought the solicitor. Usually after a reading, some or other person would have a reason to feel affronted. Of course, he'd written his will before he viewed May as a lying cheating baggage. He hadn't had the time to change it. But she hoped now; knew, now he was on the right hand side of God: Know I, May Miller, Miss, had not betrayed or stolen from Henry Spritely, Mr. And he was, like her, content and happy for his unaltered bequest.

The solicitor enjoyed a glass of sherry before the cart arrived to haul him back to the station and his Southsea practise. They, all of them in that library room raised their glasses, and George said, "To Henry." And they all repeated, "To Henry." And baby George gurgled.

***

May was on a mission; Dolly had given her the leftovers from Henry's funeral banquet. The hamper filled to bursting. Wine, ham hock, fruitcake, jelly, and crystallised fruits strained the basket and strained May's arms. During her walk she realised, she had enough money. She could afford her shop. It surprised her then, she suddenly felt a chill of fear. Yet it was something she had been trying to accomplish for a long time. And now it was here. She had to find the shop, and stock it. The stock wouldn't be expensive, she could buy cheap, from the market, and sell high. She would add her talent and she knew she would be a success. Lil would be leaving school in the summer and she wanted her to work for her, her father had ten pounds. Life for once was good. So why did she feel so scared?

***

May pulled the shawl close around her. The rain pushed against her. Drops fell from her hair onto her eyelashes. She sheltered in the porch waiting ... Emily opened the door. May stepped in and close, out of the rain. May raised her eyebrow, looked at Emily, up and down.

"I want my quid back."

"What quid? Haven't got any quid of yours." Emily smiled.

"The quid, my quid. But don't worry one way or another you'll pay, and you'll pay because I say you will. Whether it's now, or then, or maybe later, you owe me and you'll regret it."

It surprised Emily how intimidating May could be, she was smaller and slighter; but then it's the place she comes from. -*Hard as bloody nails, slum dweller.*

May walked on through to the kitchen and deposited the hamper on to the table. Emily had felt the force of May and she wanted to say something, anything. But what that something was she didn't know.

"Is that you May?" Susannah called. She was in the back room, in the conservatory; baby George was on a rocking chair looking out at the rain.

"I've brought provisions from Henry's... Well Doll... It would be a shame if it went to waste."

"Sit here, next to me." And Susannah patted a reclining chair.

"Would you like some refreshment?" asked Emily, scowling from the doorway.

"May, would you?"

"No, I don't think so, thank you." Not trusting Emily not to gob in it or add something equally unsavoury.

"We're fine Emily. You may go. Oh, and Emily the hamper in the kitchen please sort it and work out what meals we may have from it."

Susannah poured May a sherry.

"Are you going to pay her?"

"Do you care?"

May considered the question. "Yes."

"You do!"

"I'll say this, she may go home and if she doesn't return, I'll not be…I'll not miss her."

"Ah."

May was annoyed and said more than she intended and more than by her nature would normally say. "And neither would Dolly or Joseph." - *I think.*

Susannah remained silent. And May bit her lip. Then Susannah finally said, "Neither would I." And giggled. And May, from relief or just because she couldn't help herself, chuckled.

May didn't know where this was going and she felt she'd said enough. –*Blimey.* It was then that baby George saved the day by sending out a large belch, which shocked him so much he looked around him to see who, in his presence could make such a terrible noise. And he yelled his displeasure. -*Who was the culprit?* Which set Susannah and May into fits of giggles and from that unspoken loud expulsion they decided unspoken to become the firmest friends.

Chapter 27

A steady stream of visitors coming and going in a tidal stream kept Dolly at her stove. The busy, filled days lasted for two weeks following the funeral. Then it stopped. The business ended. George returned to Dartmouth, and Agnes stayed for increasing periods at Southsea. Fairview stood mostly empty. Dolly cooked only if she received instruction from Agnes she would be returning home on such and such a date. -*What did she do down in Southsea all the time,* Dolly wondered. Dolly and Joseph had only enough work to keep them occupied.

George spent as much time at Fairview as he did in Downland, much to Dolly's delight, and Emily's chagrin. This night he spent in his old room curled on his bed. He had no interest to return to his house, his marital home. He didn't find comfort or a haven there. His fault, he supposed, somehow! But now there was another reason about to break.

Emily cornered him in the dining room on one of Georges' rare visits to his Downlands home. He was holding the paper, a glass of port in his hand and a cigar burning askew in the ashtray. The crossword, although George held the pencil, was mostly complete, in that George had solved and filled in only two of the spaces.

"George!"

"Emily, perhaps it would be possible, you would knock … and then wait for a response?" George had run out of patience and interest in Emily. -*I'm just too nice…!* She moaned. She nagged. Even after … with his father … and before even … at the funeral. She complained to him. And about Susannah! Susannah had done this! Susannah hadn't done that. Who on earth did this baggage think she was?

"What is it Emily? I take it you're not here to ask me if you can serve me anything."

"Oh Sir, I'd serve you any time," she said playfully.

George groaned inwardly. He wondered why this stupid slut thought she could speak to him in such a way. "Agnes has paid you?"

"Yes, George." -*Well, get to the point then.*

"Susannah has taken baby George to Fairview; Dan and Joe are going to give him a ride on the donkey cart."

George looked at the crossword, aha. –*Asinine.* "He'll enjoy that." And he doodled a noose on the paper's margin.

Emily shifted her weight. "George, I have to speak to you."

"I noticed Emily. Well, you have. Thank you for the chat. Now if you don't mind."

"George I have to tell you… I'm in a condition."

George took a sip from his glass. -*Oh, do bugger off!* Emily was intruding, she was invading his time, -*Was there no place for peace!* And his solving of this crossword. "You are in a condition? What the hell is that supposed to mean?"

"It means, I am up the duff. Full to bursting. Expecting."

"Congratulations!"

Emily was stunned she'd run through many scenarios and this wasn't one of them. "Well it's yours you know"

"So you say!"

"What are you going to do about it?"

"Well if you hadn't noticed I'm married, arguably happily."

Emily shifted her weight again. -*Bloody could ask me to sit down.*

It was now that it finally dawned on Emily how vulnerable she was. It should have been a shot across her bows when Susannah controlled her life, by not paying her and thereby stopping her from returning home. But she believed George would help her, and he did, he gave her, her wages after confirming with Susannah they weren't paid. But strangely, he hadn't even suggested that she should take the lost days off. She thought it was because he'd wanted her with him, a comfort after his father's death. She felt generous in not pursuing that point …

***

It shocked Emily, all the power she believed she held was ebbing away. *-If George thinks he's getting away it, he can think again!*

George convinced himself that his actions toward Emily were understandable, more than that, noble. He couldn't, and he wouldn't have his wife treated in such a way. Respect is needed. That girl had gone too far above her station! *-Trouble is, I'm too soft. Well, no more!*

Emily bashed at the coals in the grate. *-Talk to me like that, the bastard!* She buttered the bread, added a slice of ham, a pinch of salt, a grind of pepper and a gob of spit. *-He's bloody loaded; he should do right by me.*

She'd seen herself as the lady of this house, conveniently forgetting that, that position was filled. At worst, the fifty pounds a year should be maintained. But what had George offered her? Twenty-five pounds in lieu of wages, and that was to be that! *-That was to be the end of it! I don't think so! -That'll be me, kid in tow, no money, and no help. No, I'm not having it.* So if George wouldn't help her, *-As he should!* Well she would have to help herself. The next morning she made baby George a boiled egg for his breakfast. And Susannah was serving him soldiers that flew in his mouth, a mother feeding her chick. *-And in a few months … My God!*

Susannah was waving a piece of bread dipped in runny yolk, in front of George's eyes. When Emily said, "I'd like a word, if I can?"

"Of course you may." And Susannah pulled a whooh, whoo, whoosh, surprised face as the soldier whizzed by George's face, missing his open mouth. George chuckled. And then the soldier marched back, about turned, and landed in his mouth.

Emily waited, watching the profile of Susannah as she played at feeding George. She hadn't even bothered to look up to her. And this thing she wanted to impart. Well, it was important. And in a moment, she'll ask me what it is. This would be the opening shot for her salvo; but Susannah, well it's like I'm not even here.

"Mrs Spritely?"

"Yes Emily?" And the bread dipped into the eggie, weggie.

And still Susannah didn't look at her.

"I'm in a condition."

"Ooh, open the hatch."

"I'm stuffed, up the duff."

"Watch out tummy."

"It's …."

"Here it comes." And the soldier dived for cover in George's foxhole.

"It's George's."

Then a pause. Georgie looked up at Emily.

"I said. It's George's."

"I heard you, there was always that possibility."

"Pardon?"

Susannah raised her eyebrow and fired her parting shot. "Well if you will lay with your arse in the air on my living room table. I doubt whether the table leg is responsible."

Emily was flabbergasted. She was cool, no, cold. No wonder George wanted me. But unfortunately, he didn't want Emily anymore.

Emily understood what a precarious position she'd found herself in. She saw the workhouse beckoning. Emily devised a plan; well, it was better than the workhouse. And he did have his own cottage and a job. Some said he was good looking; he was kind. -*Simple more like.* But still!

So he wasn't her type! But then neither was working the streets with a screaming brat in tow. Nor did the workhouse suit, it didn't suit at all. Yes, John would have to do. So having settled that, she went off to impart the good news to John Bridger.

***

She found him doing something with a pile of dirt, tossing it about. She leaned on the garden wall. "Hello John." John smiled; he remembered that day, and that warm shaky wobbly wonderfulness. And his dick rose in salutation.

"Emily."

"Can I come through?"

"Course, here."

And he stopped doing whatever he was doing, and held the gate open for her to walk through. Emily began her story, and for good measure managed to leak a tear; which slowly trickled down her cheek. It wasn't all together fake; if this didn't work then she knew she'd have something to cry about. John had no idea what she was talking about; but thought how he'd like to throw her on her back and shove her skirts up, followed quickly by his dick. But it's never a good time to talk with a bloke, not when the blood's rushed from his brain.

"Please say you will at least think about it?" As she reasoned, the best time to talk with a bloke was when his brain was drained of blood; the dick taking priority. And she tumbled into his arms. And she looked into those big blue eyes; which looked a bit too much like May's for her liking. And John wrapped her up in his warm embrace and hugged her. Kissing her hair. They walked together to the storage shed, where the mower and seed packets were kept.

It was as soon as they'd closed the door that John kissed her. -*Oh well, why not?* Cement our bond, Emily reasoned.

John rolled the canvas they used for covering the mower. He pulled Emily down on to it and she lay blinking up at him. He knelt to one side of her. His hand found the hem of her dress. He pushed it up. It made a big wodge around her waist.

"Just be gentle with me John, for the baby's sake."

John was his on his knees; he looked like he was at a prayer. He found the space between her legs; and he unbuttoned his fly. His dick leapt from his trousers and stood to attention, and when he bent over her, it pointed the way, urging John, the body to follow; and be quick about it.

Emily raised her skirts even higher. -*He could have his eyeful.* And there she touched herself, inserted her finger, made moist and ready for his thrusts. John led by his dick, climbed aboard, and rammed home his point. He thrust and she clung to him, her brown boots holding his arse close against her. -*No mistake now John boy, is there?* And while she lay under him, she noticed a small blue butterfly caught in a web; the spider running its ring of silk around and around the struggling shape. She glanced at her nails; she should have washed her hands. Oh well!

And then she felt John's movements change; he trembled. His thrusts became more urgent. Her feet gripped his arse, holding him firm; he could no longer move backwards or forwards. Retreat was impossible. John groaned and she released him, and allowed him to finish. And as he did, she clenched him, and with a sharp flex of her muscles, she spat him out. He rolled onto his back ... panting.

John reeled. -*My God.* He couldn't believe anything could feel that good. And while he was thinking those thoughts, he hardened again, and he wanted to climb aboard once more. But Emily pushed him away.

"No, we have to think of the baby."

And it dawned on John what Emily had been talking about all this time. Baby -Condition -Be careful -Shouldn't have! -What will befall me? -Marriage -Baby -Birth -Mother -Matrimony -Spring Wedding ... All those words, he'd heard them all; but only now did they register. Only now, was he making sense of them. But he reasoned he could do this everyday; two times a day, three times, if he wanted. Whenever or wherever he wanted it! And that was what marriage meant for John Bridger; at that moment anyway ...

***

Emily swaggered, she had a ring on her finger, and she enjoyed showing it off while she served at the table of Susannah.

"So, I take it you've become engaged? I couldn't help but notice you're wearing a ring?"

"Yes Mrs Spritely, I am betrothed to Mr Bridger, the younger." Just in case there was any confusion.

"Yes I'd heard that. You will of course want to leave us soon?"

"I was hoping to continue until it got awkward, like."

"My dear, it's always been awkward, wouldn't you say?"

"I don't know, but my wedding's not till March and everyone will be invited, an all."

"I think you should rest more."

"Really? I do get tired."

"George has given you twenty pounds I believe."

"He did."

"But you're still here?"

"Well, I thought I could get some money to put by."

"And what do I get?"

"Pardon?"

"What do I gain from this? You receive money to 'put by'. I pay for someone I dislike, to maintain in my company. Do you see?"

"I ..."

"I'd like you to leave."

"But ..."

"As you said, you're tired."

Emily went back to the cottage -*Nothing's going right, bloody nothing.* She pulled out the kitchen table drawer and withdrew the tin containing ten pounds and another couple of quid in silver and coppers.

***

Emily was as fat as a pea-pod. And John, he was disappointed in married life. It wasn't what he expected it to be. She promised, "After the baby is born." And she just got fatter and fatter. He hoped she'd just pop. He wanted a fuck. That's what marriage is for. So John waited. And it was like he'd never wed, except he knew what he was missing. And he slept against this woman's back and sometimes he'd wake and he wished she wasn't there. And then, he wanted to shove it into her and his hand would roam over her, she felt like a watermelon.

"Not now John, after."

And John would climb from the bed and he'd throw cold water over his head, and if that didn't work, well there was his hand. But now he knew what he was missing, and it didn't satisfy him, but only gave him relief.

John mentioned something to Joseph. And Joe said that something to Dolly.

And Dolly said, "Well of course she won't be wanting to, look at the size of her."

And Joe, said to John, "Course she won't want to now. That's the way of it."

And John sighed.

The baby finally came and they named her Elizabeth, after John's mother. But she didn't, funnily enough, look anything like either of them! Fair-haired she did have blue eyes at first, but then they, after a few weeks miraculously turned brown.

John tried to ram it into Emily.

But it was, "Too soon." And. "I'm breast-feeding."

Joe said, "It's just the way it is."

And John thought, *-If this is the way it is, then what's the bloody point?*

He'd shagged her twice. Had a child that looked nothing like him, and a woman who wouldn't bear for him to touch her.

"That's marriage for you," Joe said.

"You and Dolly, don't do it then?"

"Dolly and me … er … well, she's special. Not your ordinary woman. No. Your marriage is well, the way it is. …. Your mother and me, we were much the same as you and Em…"

John looked out to the horizon and shivered.

***

In their married state and with the frustration of pregnancy, dark clouds rolled in until the storm burst in a clap of thunder.

"You'd rather have married May, wouldn't you? Admit it."

-I would. But John didn't say a word

"Your precious May, fucking everything. No wonder she has so much money probably works the dock on her days off."

John frowned. *-Shut up, you.*

"Well she didn't snare you, did she?"

-No, you bloody did.

"Or George."

-George what's he got to do with it?

"Don't you sit there playing the innocent either?"

-Please, shut, UP.

"Yes, George and her in her room, in the library, everywhere …"

John was not saying anything, he was so quiet, so deep, sheltered within himself even his thoughts were silenced.

"She didn't tell you that, did she?"

-May and George, no it can't be ... He'd woken. It can't be true. But then he recalled those whispers, the encounters the sneaky glances. It would explain...

"No, she didn't tell you about George, when you were fucking her."

-What?

"You're precious little May, don't think I haven't seen those long lingering looks you give her. You wish you'd married her, don't you."

-Oh, yes. And John rose and at the door, he turned to her and said, "I've never lain with May." And he added, "Unfortunately."

John knew now, his wife was not only a bitter and twisted jealous baggage, but a liar to boot. He'd never touched May. Now he knew she made stuff up he didn't believe May and George either. He regretted even doubting May, for that one moment.

***

In an earthenware bowl decorated with red roses, Susannah poured boiling water. Into this steaming bowl, she dropped half a dozen unfurled flypapers, and stirred the brew with a wooden spoon. The water turned the colour of weak tea. She covered the concoction with a muslin cloth.

Susannah decanted a pint of flypaper juice into a used ginger beer bottle, pulled the metal lever firmly closed, and wiped the bottle dry. She rinsed the bowl once, and then another two times, *-just for safety's sake!* Dried the bowl and tossed the muslin cloth onto the fire, followed by the wooden spoon. The bottle stowed in the pantry; at the back of the bottom shelf, behind stoneware jars, glass jars, and storage tins. Her day's work done, she joined Georgie, who'd just woken with a gurgle from his afternoon nap.

***

George missed his father; he couldn't put it into words, he had this empty hole deep within him. He wanted his son to miss him, yet there was no reason why he should; George had hardly ever spoken to him, and had never picked up the little blighter.

He pledged he would change. I can have a relationship with him. It'll take time, but I can do it. But for George there wasn't plenty of time... -*It's not Georgie's fault.* The lies his parents ... At least he was beginning to blame himself, if only half way true, it was a start. And George celebrated with, not a port, no he'd have rum, like a man. -*Christ all mighty!* Even though it was, - *Bloody hell!* Awful... He'd practise, he'd get used to it, his tot, like he'd practise getting to know his son. "Cheers pa," he said, to the empty chair opposite him.

Georgie toddled in and George took him onto his lap and read to him: The Ugly Duckling. Georgie sucked his thumb and leaned against this big man. -*Blimey, that's not a flicker of a smile on Susannah's lips? She can be pretty, sometimes.*

And slowly, he made small steps in gaining his son's love. And if not love from Susannah, at least she didn't cut him; and would stay in the same room with him ... as long as Georgie was there.

***

Agnes worked out. Now she was on a tight budget. It would be cheaper to rent rather than stay in a hotel. With that intent she set to scanning The Evening News ... And she found it, an apartment overlooking the sea ... She took it on a lease, -*Oh well, same as renting.*

For this brand-new apartment, she bought everything new, just a couple of ornaments from Fairview, sentimental objects. George could have the rest, have it all. She had a large bay window with a balcony that looked over the Solent. She was, she supposed as she sat here staring out to the Isle of Wight, a mistress. No, if she were, she'd be a poor one; self-financing as she was. A lover, they were lovers, Sir William and her. And she was grateful for him; peculiar how you can love two people but in different ways. Silly old Henry, she missed him still. Not one complaint from him, even when she'd spent so much on new clothes and beautifying, and all for another man too.

She would until her dying day place flowers on his grave and after, she would join him and their two children. What if I'm ninety when I join him, twice his age? An old shrunken crone, "Hello Henry, I'm here…" - *Poor Henry, scare him to …* what a horrible thought. And she told herself to, "Stop it." -*Far too gloomy.* And she picked up The Lady's Realm, turned to the feature on dresses and styles from New York.

***

May was in a quandary. Her dream was so close and yet so far. Practicalities, she was a single woman and too young to hold a lease in her own name. She would need a guarantor? A husband or a partner or find another solution…! She'd fulfilled one part of the journey and now the other part would begin, but how? In hindsight, the first part seemed easy …

If she were to marry then all she owned and worked for would be given to her husband. At least the man got something; whereas, she'd make a gift of all her worldly goods and the rights to her body. -Bugger that.

So that left …? Nope. Joseph? Her father? A possibility, but again he could just sell everything and she'd be back to square one. Dolly? Nope. Agnes? Every time she wrote someone in, she ruled them out. There had to be a way. But what the heck was it? Susannah, a lovely, lovely woman but not to her taste and not in her class.

May had decided, she'd wait! She'd wait until she was twenty-one. What she'd do in the mean time, with a bit of help from Wally, was take a stall in the market, serve an apprenticeship. -*Well, I have to learn the ropes.*

And I don't know until I try, that what I will do, I can. I shall put in the years and see if I can turn a profit ...She would of course seek help from men. *-Of course, from men.* But she would not be owned by them. Or used!

***

"I'm leaving."

"Leaving? Leaving!"

"I'm giving in my notice."

"You think you're flush, don't you? No need to work. It won't last, money doesn't, it's sand. It'll run through your fingers quicker than you would believe."

"I know—"

"No, you don't. Henry's left you a few quid, it's a generous sum, but it won't last forever."

"Dad, they don't need me any more ..."

"They may not, but that's their decision, not yours. And you're getting paid."

"I am, but I want ... I want to do something, something else."

"You think I wanted to work in the yard?"

"No, but you wanted to marry mum. And you did, and working in the dockyard was the price you paid. It's the price you paid, like my grandmother paid."

"And where did that get her?"

"It got her the man she loved, she accepted the—"

"She accepted poverty for generations, that's what she accepted, impoverished her daughter."

"And dad, you'd have never met mum, and wed her; is that what you would have wanted?"

Ernie sighed, where had his little girl gone? There was a truth to what she said, he acknowledged that much, but she ... she was his daughter, he'd no idea who she was, except, he loved her, he loved...

"I'm going to take a stall," May said.

"You know who keeps the roll on the stalls?"

"Wally's negotiating on my behalf."

"Wally!"

"He's a good bloke."

Her father went and knocked out his pipe. He looked up at the photograph of Lavinia, was she smiling? Ernie shrugged, he was losing control. May she's been.... "You don't have a choice."

"I do, I do dad." She hoped he'd give her his blessing, if not acceptance. Ernie wasn't speechless; he just didn't know what to say! Her dad worried; he ran through every permutation: Of how she'd go broke, and the worst, sent to Portsea Island Workhouse.

"Not too far for you to visit me then!" May reminded him about Alfie, he did it, and so would she. Alfred Hostler sold sweets on The Hard before he had a stall; a shop, another shop and then a factory.

"It can be done," said May. May asked, "I wondered, would you put me up? I won't be here long."

Ernest frowned. "Put you up? No! Bloody put you up. This is your home! Such as it is."

They were both silent then. And then he said, "This is your home and don't you bloody forget it!"

"Thank you....I'd like Lil and Glad to come on board too, if they suit."

"Work with you? With what? You have nothing."

Chapter 28

She'd see Wally. She knew he was looking for something. He'd even toyed with joining the navy. But his heart wasn't in it, blimey he'd even been sick on the Gosport ferry. A deal, she'd strike a deal with him and for a deal to succeed there has to be something in it for everyone. Marrying for money was a no gainer, 'cos if you marry and the wife, you'd lose the blinkin' lot. Wally waited, leaning against the tearoom's wall, hat pushed back from his forehead eyeing up any young woman that would stray into his orbit. Then May … Wally stood and straightened his hat, stubbed out the cheroot and tucked it into his top jacket pocket.

"At your command," and he offered May his arm.

"My command Wally, is for you to shut your face. WE have business and a quid to make."

Wally raised an eyebrow, "As you wish."

"We need somewhere private."

"The Bakers Arms, no one, but no one goes in there!" And she took his outstretched arm.

***

"Wally, I need a stall. I want it right on the corner outside Samuel's jeweller's. If not there, opposite right on the Commercial Road." Wally sucked air between his teeth. "I don't think you'll get one there. There's a waiting list. And well … The only way you can get on that roll is Charlie Price!"

"Then we'd better arrange it."

Wally chewed on the inside of his cheek. "You coming home then?"

"Yep, don't know whether it'll be at me dad's though." And May flushed and finished her Port.

"Another Wally?"

"Don't mind if I do."

"I want to ask you something too." As May returned from the bar with a port and lemon, and a Brickwoods for him.

"You were right about this place …Where is everyone?"

"I heard it's haunted."

May rolled her eyes, "Oh yeah right, full of spirits!"

"Well, yeah, but no. The landlord done the barmaid in, you can still see the bloodstains on the floor."

"Oh piff."

Wally held up his arms, pulled the jacket over his head, and made an impression of a ghost.

"You Walter, are a twit."

"But you love me really."

"I have a proposition for you."

"I will."

"Wally!"

"I accept your proposal."

"You haven't heard it yet."

"I'm all ears." And to add interest he pressed his hands behind his ears and pushed his ears out.

"Now if you've finished. I'd like to offer you a job."

Wally frowned …but listened.

"I can offer you five bob a week and I'll not stop you doing whatever else you're doing either; as long as I get first call on you. What do you say?"

Wally had listened. But he was thinking. He was thinking, -*Blimey, with that much, I could afford rent on proper lodgings.* Be warm in winter. Bread, his wages, and scavenging, his butter … "I can do other stuff too?"

"I said so, didn't I? But if I need your help, I want you there for me, first and foremost."

Wally stuck out his hand, the one he'd just spat in, and they shook on it.

***

The Bakers Arms became their headquarters; strange, the more they frequented the pub, the busier it became. First, it was some old bloke, peered in, saw the young couple sitting there. *-Beer must be all right. Never go into a pub that's empty!* From that day on, the chair by the hearth was his place. Later he'd put a pewter tanker behind the bar. This is, *-Me local.*

The next time Wally and May visited, the old bloke was there before them seated by the fire. They were followed by a couple of men in suits, not good suits, but suits nonetheless. The landlord began to wear a clean apron, every other day. *-Things are looking up.* He vowed he'd never sue anyone for slander again; especially a man of the cloth!

"So Wally, how's that stall finding going?"

"We've got to see Charlie Price, you'll have to pay. And May, when we get there, let me do the talking." May sighed.

***

Charlie Price said, "I May have something for you. It's not a stall though. It's a lockup, on the corner of Pye Street. The front opens right up, could lay out a stall on the front and use the back for storing stuff."

"Sounds good."

May kicked him in the shin.

"But we were thinking, something on the corner, outside Samuel's on the Commercial Road."

"Ah yes, I remember now, the butterfly brooch."

Wally and May glanced at each other.

"I may be able to fit you in, at a squeeze. Course it'd upset the other stallholders they'd have to shove up a bit; have to grease a few palms. You understand?"

Wally nodded. *-God, it's hot in here.*

"What about the lockup, you'll need one to store your stuff?"

"We'll take just the stall for now, see how we go," said May. It was Wally's turn to kick May, who'd opened her gob.

"It'll be a five-pound. And ten bob a week thereafter. And don't even think of being late with the rent, I've heard every excuse, and I don't like any of them."

Wally looked at May who blinked slowly.

"We'll take it."

And Wally and Charlie shook on it

They'd both risen when Charlie said, "Another thing," and they stopped at the door.

"Open the drawer." Wally moved towards—

"Not you, her."

May pulled open the drawer, and there in the drawer, on top of a pile of trinkets was a blue butterfly; the butterfly brooch.

"Look familiar?"

May looked up, "One butterfly brooch looks much like another."

"And there was I thinking you were a connoisseur, just the way you were so fussy like. Picking over everything, pawned it did you?"

"I …"

Wally interrupted, "I took it. I sold it, needed the money."

"And where was this then?"

"Down The Hard, I think"

"Oh right, not Winchester?"

"Winchester?"

-*Bloody thieving cow.*

"I'd like you to buy it back."

Wally looked at his feet. "How much?"

"Five pounds, so that's ten pounds ten shillings all together and I want it next week … at the latest."

***

"Christ Wally, I don't want the brooch, I'd never be able to wear it."

"It's the price of the stall and you've got the best pitch."

"I know, but bloody hell, it's going to take forever to recoup that. I could've had the lockup too, for the price of that bloody brooch."

"Pawn it, sell it, give it away, either way it's the price of the pitch." Wally was irritated, he felt she was criticising him, it was the best he could do. Charlie Price would sell his own fingers if they turned a profit for him. Truth was, Charlie scared the shit out of him. May stopped by the ferry slope and took his hand in hers.

"I'm sorry Wally, and thank you."

Wally pushed his hat to the back of his head; puffed out his chest and stuck out his elbow and said, "Come m'dear. I shall be proud to escort you to our head office; 'sides, I could do with a bloody drink."

"Me too, he scares me."

"Don't worry; I'm here to protect you."

***

"He's right though, Wally, I do need somewhere to put stock."

"I have an idea."

"Oh, no."

"You may mock. But your stock will be secure, the guard is a bloody huge, mean looking bugger. Nothing, but nothing gets past him. Just you wait until you meet the very talented, Barnaby."

Barnaby glowered at them. His huge frame filled the doorway, blocking the entrance.

Wally pulled a carrot from his jacket pocket and Barnaby took it gently in his velvet-covered mouth.

"Talented?"

"Just wait."

Barnaby crunching his carrot sounded like the percussion section of an orchestra. And then … drum roll, Barnaby let go, a rip-roaring fart.

"The wind section, he is a one horse-band"

"That's some talent. Can we go in, now we've bribed the guard?"

"Wait for it ... wait for it."

Barnaby belched.

"Good grief!"

"See, not only is he the percussion and the wind section, he's the encore; the whole ruddy show. Ain't you, me beauty?"

"Pye Street stables, my official, unofficial residence. For the cost of one carrot, plus or minus an apple, he don't let just anyone in you know."

"So what is this then?"

"This May, is your new stockroom."

May looked at Barnaby, "What does he think?"

"He thinks an apple a day, and he'll let you pass." Wally waited, he hoped she liked it. Prayed she thought this a good idea.

May glanced around her, "Wally!"

Wally waited.

"It's genius. Absolutely perfect, even got my own horse guard; no one else's got that, 'cept the Queen, God bless her."

"Plus, he doubles up as a blanket if it gets too nippy."

***

So the next time Agnes was home May resigned giving two weeks notice. Agnes was, or so it appeared genuinely upset. May asked herself why she had stayed, when that time ago she wanted to leave, loathed being here. But now, George was otherwise occupied and she'd made good friends, Dolly, Joseph, Susannah ... even Agnes -*well not a friend, but more than an employer.* Then there's John, and John was the reason she had to leave....

"Agnes if you should need anything from me anything at all, I'm here." And she handed Agnes a card she'd had newly printed. It was the first card she'd handed out. May's Flowers and the Pye Street & Commercial Road, Landport addresses. "That one's my storage place," pointing at the Pye Street print. "I don't know where I'll be living, just yet."

"I don't know. Who'll … I rely on you. I trust your good taste, my makeup."

"I can still do it for you, but you've managed so well, and if you want something, well, just write to me, and I'll get it."

"Oh May, so many changes. I don't think I can bear it."

May put her hand over Agnes'. "It does get better, the pain goes eventually."

"I hope so …" And she wiped her eyes. "I do hope so. I haven't been … wasn't the best wife."

"We're none us as good as we could be, we always think … well, nothing is going to change, we have forever and the next day. And we never say the things we should've." May thought of her mother, arms up to elbows in scummy soapsuds.

Agnes agreed there wasn't much for her to do here. But in the evenings, May would go to the library and read. She read fiction and studied George's old English books. She copied from them and studied them. With her reading skills improved, not many words confounded her, and if they did, there was always that huge dictionary she would heave onto the table.

***

She packed her few belongings and walked along the lane with Dolly at her side. "I needed something from the shop."

"What?"

"I'll know when I get there." Dolly waited for the tram with May.

"Write to me." May boarded, stood with one foot on the step, turned, and hugged.

The tram conductor said, "Are you getting on or not? I've got a timetable to keep."

"Come and visit me when I'm settled," she said, as she put her head out the tram window. "I have an idea that may be good for all of us."

Dolly waved a white hanky then dabbed her eyes. "Bloody silly, not as if you're going to Australia." And they waved and waved, until neither could see the other. And Dolly, blew a honk from her nose.

***

"I'm going to do this dad. It's a chance and it's one I have to take." And she dropped her bag
on the floor."

Ernest didn't respond, and then he simply said, "It's nice to have you home."

May took off her hat and hung it on a bamboo rack behind the front door. May moved into her old home in Hope Street, but it wasn't right. She needed something else, somewhere else. It was different in Hope Street with Gertrude; it was one thing listening to your parents creaking bedsprings, but quite another … -*Ok, Gertie wasn't a stranger, but she wasn't family either.* May shoved the pillow over her head, but she could still hear the rhythmic creak, but muffled.

Lil giggled. May pinched what she thought was Lil's arm, but it was Glad's leg, and she woke up with a start.

"What?" What's goin' on?"

Dad said, "Nothing. Go back to sleep." And the bed vibrated with Lil's swallowed titters.

The next day a crate arrived at Hope street. The deliverymen managed, somehow, to wiggle it through the front door. All four surrounded the box, May, Lil, Glad and Freddie, now talking and talking. Oh, how wonderful it was when she'd first heard him say her name, "May." Now well, he never stopped. "May, what's this?"

"May?"

"May when? May why?" And sometimes just, "May?"

"What?"

"Nothing."

"May, what's in the big box?"

"You'll just have to wait and see." The two men set about the box with a crowbar. The room had grown dark, shaded by the many faces outside, pressed against their window. In that big box was a Singer sewing machine. One where you pushed your feet up and down, but had to pull the wheel at the same time. May couldn't get the hang of it; it was like patting your head and rubbing your belly at the same time.

But Glad took to it like a duck to water, and she'd sit at it all-day and every day. You could make loads of tiny stitches in the time it took to sneeze; it was brilliant. At The Landport Drapery Bazaar May bought eight yards of blue cotton material for a new dress. Different from a new to her dress; worn in by another, but mostly worn out. Lil cut it out from a pattern in one of Mrs Spritely's out of date magazines. Glad sewed it, and with the remnants, Fred had a new pair of trousers. She made this, and then that; for other people too, and they paid her for her sewing labours!

***

Ferdinand met May by the gate. He sat on the fence. May blinked at him and he politely closed his eyes in acknowledgement. He jumped from the post and led her up the garden path. His tail pointed left. Not as an indication of his intended direction, since he swept right! But his tail still bore the scars suffered at the teeth of maddened Max, the terrier.

Dolly opened the front door. "Come in, come on in; and you fur ball. Kettle's on; go through, we're in the kitchen."

"Oh, this is lovely." May said, not addressing anyone in particular.

With a little of Henry's money, -*Thank you Henry.* they'd had plumbing installed in the house! A tap with running water, and beneath that a big oblong white ceramic sink with a plughole, water drained from it into a tank outside. Above the sink in front of the window a red gingham curtain stood halfway, suspended on a wooden pole. And the interior, white washed. Ivy and winter jasmine, sat on the middle of the table in an earthenware pitcher.

Ferdinand jumped on to Joseph's lap. *-It was going begging and he wasn't doing anything with it.* Joe woke with a start. "Blimey! Pass me, me pipe Doll. I'm pinned down!"

"Here you are Joe," and May handed him his smoking accoutrements.

"Aye, hello May. Thank you. You've met this moving hearthrug?"

"He escorted me in. Didn't you, fur ball?" she said, as she rubbed Ferdinand's ears.

Joseph had his tobacco stowed in his leather pouch; a gift from Dolly. She'd had his initials stamped on it too. J.O.B. Joseph Oliver Bridger, she thought it a good reminder for him as he puffed on his pipe, tucked away in the potting shed! There's work to do and it's your JOB.

***

"So what do you think?" asked May.

"Well, I won't want you to pay me; you take all the flowers you want."

"No, that's not it, I don't want a few flowers I want many flowers; I want certain flowers and I'll need your advice. I won't be able to do that if you won't let me pay you. It's about the land that Henry left you, we would turn it over to flowers."

"Well I thought it was going to be vegetables."

"You'd still have your vegetable plot, the one in your garden. It's supplied you these years, would you need all that extra produce?"

"Well, I was thinking I might sell some of the veg, make a bob or two."

"See, that's my point. You already have a market, a place to sell your produce. You sell to me, but not veg; flowers and sometimes fruit."

"Seems like a good idea to me, Joe."

Joe scratched his head, he couldn't find fault with it, but that didn't mean there wasn't a flaw, just he couldn't see it. But if Dolly liked the idea and wanted to do it, and he was to get paid, just for growing a few flowers, well what could he say but …

"Okay, we'll see how we go. Put the tea off, this needs a drink to celebrate our new, er …"

"Business venture," May offered.

And they all … Ferdinand spread his claws on Joseph's knee, a warning. *-Just because those two are standing, no need for you to nick MY lap...* Two stood, one sat, and raised their glasses.

Chapter 29

The Queen died. It shocked people, even though she was a very old lady. No one could remember a time when she wasn't on the throne. It was a cold wet England. And as with all ill winds this one blew May a head start. Wreaths bought for display in shop windows sat alongside images of the Queen; Made by May, her stall thrived.

Everyone wanted a token no matter how small, regardless of how meagre. From the smallest hovel to the grandest mansion, the people marked their respect.

May channelled this collective need. She gathered as much fresh foliage as she could find at this time of year. But she'd need to travel to Joseph to find out what he could add. May used her creative skill to make silk out of January's pig ear. Calling on Dolly and Joseph she paid two pounds for their foraging and picking efforts. She'd decorate a few select wreaths with crystallised fruits, which were plentiful in this winter season. Although she stored the goods with Wally and the horse guard, they were not safe! Barnaby, he ate a whole bloody tray. He was more than a one-horse band; he was a friggin' orchestra plus the audience and the encore.

***

"We need to build a cordoned area, sealed off from the fruit thief."

May sighed, "Barnaby you're a beast," And the animal had the bloody cheek. *-Sure that was a grin.*

"You should have brought him an apple, you promised; he probably thought that was for him."

The cordoned area kept Barnaby from the goods. It narrowed Barnaby's living quarters, but it made up for it though, by being an excellent arse scratching device.

May recruited her family. Glad, Lil, little Freddie, but most surprisingly even Gertrude lent a hand. Glad sewed black crepe and trimmed black ribbons; tied to the few white roses available and augmented with white statice, bay, and laurel. They clipped, they cut, they poked and they pinked. They made garlands and wreaths and swags. Wally shifted the lot to the stall alongside a bust of Queen Victoria. Buttonholes and black armbands all did surprisingly well, cheap but honest, tasteful.

May doled out the money on this equal effort and after costs were paid, had equal shares. They all got five bob, Freddie too, Ernest put it a tin, Freddie's tin, for his education. Father Dolling though, came at close of day.

"And how are you doing May?"

"Very well, Father."

"I wondered, if you had anything leftover that could be put to good use decorating our church? Just leftovers mind!"

"Oh yes Father, I'm sure."

"And if you'd be able to come and help with the decoration, I'd appreciate it."

"I'd be honoured, Father Dolling."

"We're giving a special commemorative service for the Queen, you'll be there?"

"Of course."

"Good, good." And he turned just as Mrs Whittle, who'd spotted him, and ducked behind a crate of potatoes. "Mrs Whittle, Florence, I haven't seen young Thomas and—"

"Oh Father they ... I can't ...I shan't let my boys go to your school any longer, because kneeling wears out the knees of their trousers!"

Father Dolling - *God love him!* Knew how to get a deal, he ought to work the market, he'd make a fortune. And May smiled as his great cassocked backside threaded down Charlotte Street. All the people of the parish nodded and smiled as he weaved through the throng. A particular affluent would show fear, knowing that Father Dolling would always get what he wanted, like Charlie Price. But what one gained from love the other got by fear.

***

Mabel died a year after Henry's death. These were two lovers, free to marry if they wished. William did wish. He wasn't someone who enjoyed his own company. And he needed someone to take care of the house, keep the servants in line, take care of him.

So two weeks after the last sod thudded down on his wife's coffin lid. Sir William Baker proposed. He went down on one knee. Agnes recalled the night in that hotel room, but his intent his proposition was something else. He had a ring sheltered in a leather box; a diamond cut circular solitaire, a diamond forever. A circle, a never ending something. He liked that, the symbolism. And if she refused him, which he doubted, the jeweller promised to take the ring back. "We'll look on it as a short term loan."

"Of course ..." Sir William Baker said, after Agnes said, "Yes."

"...we'll have to wait a year. But there will be much to organise. Properties to sort, sell, decisions on where to live made. The wedding, honeymoon." It would take a year. For decencies sake. And Agnes wasn't good at decision making. Agnes felt overwhelmed. To be the wife of Sir William. – *Would I be a lady?* But it meant much work! But she knew someone, or two, who would help her.

William popped the cork on a bottle of Bollinger; it foamed and fizzed. "To us," he said.

**

Agnes would surrender her rights to live in Fairview, one decision made. -*Well I'm hardly there now. I can visit George whenever, as a guest.* Two decisions taken. "If that's what you wish, of course you're welcome to visit and use the house, at your convenience. So nothing has changed."

"But George if you wanted ... you may wish to sell."

The thought had never entered his head. But he supported it, it did give him flexibility. He went to his mother and he hugged her. "Thank you," he said.

***

Agnes wrote lists, a growing pile of paper by her chair sat in front of the large bay window overlooking The Solent. Should she sell her lease or rent this flat? At the moment rent. Would she move in with William, in his home? She pondered this as the ferry turned south heading for Ryde. No, she didn't want to do that. The ghost of a previous wife stalking the halls, no that wouldn't do. They'd have to move house.

So renting this flat maybe that would be a problem if they needed capital! Agnes pulled up a footstool, such hard work. It would indeed take a year or more of planning, she didn't recall it being so difficult when she married Henry. She'd have to discuss it with William.

She picked up The Lady's Realm, and looked at the summer brides. But where to honeymoon? So many decisions. If they went abroad, a different wardrobe would be necessary. William was right, a year wasn't a long time, so much to sort. She decided to call on Miss May Miller. She'd know what was what; although her engagement and their intended marriage was a secret… Well, May wouldn't say anything. May kept her counsel; it was like trying to crack lobster from its shell, trying to get anything from May.

She would write to Madame, Louisa Le Merchand, just regarding her honeymoon clothes. Madame knew people in her circle, the wedding dress would have to wait. Her diamond glinted in the light from the window. Exquisite. Agnes smiled.

May read the letter and wrote by return, and asked whether Sunday would suit? Agnes replied, 'we'll have tea. I'll expect you for four o clock.'

-I wonder what she wants? Thought May. "Bloody odd."

"You talking to me?" asked Wally, as he pushed open the door.

"If the cap fits!"

"Fresh tea's made, help yourself."

Wally set two cups down, handed her, her tea and pulled a brown bag of broken biccies from his pocket.

***

George thought, *—I could release capital from one or the other.* Downland or Fairview. He would sell Downland and move his family household to Fairview. Although the title deeds were his, they could have moved earlier, but until now it had seemed his parent's house. He informed Susannah of his decision.

Joseph and John would help with removing any belongings they wanted to take with them. Of course, Fairview was furnished. George supposed he'd sell the furniture at Downland. He'd allow Susannah to make those decisions. *—Well, she has to do something!*

"Coming to live in Fairview," Dolly said. "It'll have to be top and tailed, all the dust sheets have to come off."

"Will you be still woman?" Joseph said. "You've not had your instruction yet"

"Perhaps I ought to call on Susannah see what she wants me to do."

"She'll tell you soon enough."

"Perhaps I ought to make a start."

Joe tapped out his pipe.

"So when are you and John moving their effects?"

Ferdinand rolled on his back. The fire glowed life in the hearth.

"Don't know, only found out today. I'm content to wait. See this hearthrug, this ginger one. Take a leaf out of his book; he snoozes when he snoozes, he works when he needs to work."

"Humph, I don't want to leave it to the last minute. You know what this means though, don't you?"

"Yes, I'll have you going on and on until you've done something at the house."

Dolly decapitated a carrot. "It means we'll both have work. Our future's secure."

Joe thought they were secure anyway. Dolly rented her cottage to John, took half the rent she could have received for the cottage, but then John was Joe's son...

Ferdinand captured Joe's sock. "See that? He's relaxed, but then there's that moment, hunting, when he's alert and works his socks off, well mine. Took no time to snag it that's for sure."

***

It was one time, just one time! Maybe revenge, maybe lust. John was tending his plot. May watched. He was bigger now. He'd filled out from his gangly form. His shoulder muscles rippled, glistening in the heat. His braces hung loose over his slim hips, and his white cotton shirt clung to his body.

"Hello John, Dolly sent me, with this." And she raised her hamper.

John looked up and smiled, thrust his spade deep into the earth. He pointed to a wooden bench to the side of the plot underneath a spreading oak.

May opened her hamper, "My goodness got enough in here, even a tablecloth!"

"She looks after me, does Doll. My dad got lucky with her."

"What about you John?" May spread the gingham cloth on the bench between them.

"I'm fine," he said, as he looked out into the distance …May admired him, for that. He wasn't disloyal; not to his wife. *-Even if that wife was Emily. Or maybe I just imagined it, that flicker of sadness. I expected to … I wanted to see it.*

"Ooh, ham and egg pie." In the hamper were also, a jug of cider; bread and cheese and fruit cake.

"Help yourself May; I'll never eat it all. Normally take some back with me for an evening meal."

May noticed he didn't say home. *-Oh, stop it; May Miller.* May sipped her cider. Dolly had thoughtfully popped in two glasses. *-Just in case.* They sat in companionable silence munching on ham and egg pie. May watched the swallows dart.

"They nest along the lane, at Fort Widley."

"Come on John, let's take a walk." May said, as she rose.

John hesitated for just a second and then grabbed his cap. *-Why not!* It can't hurt, make the most of this day. The corn grew high, sprinkled with red poppies, blue cornflowers and ox eye daisies. "Beautiful."

And they climbed the fence and John held his hand out to her, so she wouldn't fall. *-And God forgive me, I wish she'd fall, let me see your petticoat. No, your drawers. No let me ...* John sighed.

"Something wrong, we can go back if you want? I know it's my day off. But it's not yours. I'm sorry."

"No I don't want to go back, I want to stop here. Lie with my back against this earth and watch the corn heads sway against this blue sky, forever."

May thought that was a beautiful idea; and so beautiful she wanted to do it. "What are we waiting for?" And she dashed off into the cornfield with John running after her. And when they reached, what they thought was the middle they threw themselves onto the ground and watched as the corn ears folded around them like a golden rocking cradle.

John picked cornflowers, and made a crown for May's head. "No not a patch, not a patch on the blue of your eyes."

"Mm, but similar to yours," and she held out a poppy, "bloodshot."

John laughed, and he kissed her because he could, and because she was here, and it was May in flaming July.

***

And she kissed him. And she planted her cider tasting tongue into his mouth. Tongue to tongue. John cradled her head and undid a button on her blouse. He kissed her neck and licked the sweat that trickled between her breasts. Unbuttoned her blouse and gripped her corset and tugged loose those too tight hooks.

"Your turn, your shirt." She reached up to him while he was leaning over her and undid his shirt buttons, slowly ... revealing the few black curling hairs on his chest. She tossed his shirt onto her blouse, his shirtsleeve embracing her blouse.

"Oh May!" May undid her skirt and raised her hips so she could slide out of it. But that was a step too far for John. He folded over her and his lips found her lips and they kissed. His hand slipped inside her chemise, searching. May grabbed his trouser fly and unfastened ... just a couple of buttons.

John moaned. She could feel his hardness. He was so ready. His lips sort hers and he kissed her. His hand slipped under her petticoat to her thighs. His hand tugged at the ribbon tie holding her drawers together. May wore, just a muslin chemise. Sheer. John could see the pale pink outline of her nipples and the dark triangle of the hair that adorned that space between her thighs.

He pushed up her chemise. His face was level with the top of her thighs, her black curly hair shone under the summer sky. He leaned his head against her thigh; and her hand caressed the crown of his head, stroking his dark hair. He put his mouth to her, and he kissed her, and tugged so gently on those curling hairs. He wanted to see her, to taste her. May lay, on that meadow bed. And John knelt between her legs, a man at prayer. Yet May didn't recoil, or turn her back to him. She lay here and welcomed him, opened her legs to him and for him. Wider now, He bent his head and kissed her. His tongue tracing the delicate contours of her lips.

"Oh May."

May pushed him away. He made to move, close to her.

"No..."

John frowned, -*She can't deny me... too.*

But she had no intention of denying him. She laid him down in that cornfield. The yellow ears against the blue sky ... His buttons ... May unfastened just three more ... She could see the outline of him, hard and firm. She pulled at his trouser's waistband ...and ...he poked out. Peeping from a sea of black curls.

May kissed him.

John groaned.

"Raise your hips," she said. And May knelt at his feet. And she pulled off, in a couple of yanks, his trousers. That coarse fabric, constrained him, so.

He lay there, watching swallows dart. Corn ears framing his view. She lowered her head over him, her loose tangled hair, tumbled forwards, shielding her face from John's gaze. Hiding him as she licked a tiny droplet, like morning dew on a rose petal. And she gripped and sucked, and took him far into her mouth. Holding him firm in her hand, and tasted the saltiness of him.

May said, "Look at me now."

And he did.

And he smiled, that gentle, tender smile. He showed his white, straight teeth. May came and stood over him, straddling his shoulders. Her chemise moving slowly in the summer breeze; she lowered herself. Lowered herself, until they kissed, lip to lip. His kiss ... his kiss as soft as a butterfly's flight.

John raised his hand. Stroked her lips, before ... he placed his thumb... and his fingers dipped into her ... soft, warm space.

He blew. He ran his tongue ...

Oh, and he sucked ...

And he, kissed ...

And he, licked ...

And May …she, groaned.

And her thigh muscles tensed.

And she raised herself up on high.

And she stood. *-I bloody love you. You stupid, handsome, fucker.*

She stepped back.

Straddled his thighs.

She raised her arms … to heaven, threw off her … chemise.

John made to move. May, placed her foot on his chest, steady him, she smiled down on him. Took him in her hand. Steering him, poised under her, holding him… tight in her hand, his dick, hard, firm tall …searching, wanting, and, oh … so, needy.

And she piloted him. She steered him towards her and he touched her shore. And she released him. Her hand…freed him.

But her body claimed him. She sank over him

Lower and lower she went, until she reached the bottom.

And she rose, and she bobbed.

He was drowning … drowning in her beauty. He could bear, no more.

So he rolled her … onto her side. But he rolled with her. And he caught her. And he grabbed her. Oh, so urgently. And he thrust. And he clutched, and he had saved her.

May brushed at his trousers trying to remove the cornhusks and freed some of the seed tangled in his hair. And he asked her to turn round, so he could check, she was free now, from old debris. And he picked squashed cornflowers from her hair. And he kissed the nape of her neck and he smelt her scent, violets and honey and the tang, of May.

- Oh May, just the smell of her, May. "John." She turned to face him, looking up into those deep blue eyes, "It's okay." He kissed her again. He wanted to keep her

here, forever. He took her hand in his and they walked arm in arm until the gate … And they walked in familiar silence. Side by side along Pigeon Coop Lane.

***

In the kitchen with Dolly, May said," I have something …"

"How was John, he enjoy his dinner?"

"We did."

"Thought he'd like to share, he doesn't get much in the way of company. Silly lad. Still, he made his bed."

May took the opportunity of Dolly's silence. "Look what I've got," and she drew from her bag the butterfly brooch.

"How on earth?"

"It's a long story."

"I've got time, kettle's on."

And May told all she knew.

"Winchester?"

"Mm."

"Emily comes from Winchester."

"I know. I wondered if you'd put it back for me, in Susannah's jewellery box."

"I won't."

"You won't?"

"No, I've no cause to go upstairs and rummage about. What I'll do, is drop it at the back of a drawer or the back of a chair. It'll just turn up. Doubt she's missed it though. Well at least, she never

said." May poured hot water over the tea leaves. "Susannah's got someone else now. A new maid." And she laughed. "And what's funny?" "Well, she's a clunking, great, plain thing; like me." "Ooh, you'd better watch out, you know what Joe's like."

Chapter 30

There was no mistaking it now. She'd never been regular, so it caused her no concern. *–It'll come when it comes.* But it didn't come; the linen pouch with cotton threads to tie to her waist remained unused in her wardrobe drawer, that month and the next. She may as well say it all. Get it all out. Although how the hell she was going to say to him she was pregnant? *-With child perhaps!*

"There's something, something I need to say to you. You may not think it's so nice to have me home when you know."

Ernest looked at her, his eldest child and thought. *-By Christ girl, you look and sound so much like her, Lavinia.* And he sat down and he waited. Whatever this news was! But he knew, knew just by the look of her... "Well?"

"I'm ... I'm having ... I'm with child." Well at least her father knew, so she wouldn't have to face him. He would, she suspected, keep it to himself. *-It would be up to May to explain the who, what, where and why.* Her father didn't say a word. Not one sound passed his lips. But what he did though; he went to her and for the first time he held her. Held her tight. Surrounded her in his big worn embrace.

No one else need know, not just yet; she had a few months grace before explanations were necessary.

***

Father Dolling *-Oh God!* How on earth to tell him, he'd be the next one to tell. He'll be so disappointed in me. She would visit St Agathas', If Father Dolling were there, she would confess, if he weren't, just a word with our Lady; a request for forgiveness and understanding, whispered in a prayer.

He wasn't. He was, "At the gymnasium," said a woman, shoving daisies into a pot, *-Thank you God.* May felt relieved. *-Bloody coward.* But a period of calm was welcome. Her father, she'd crossed that hurdle. But Father Dolling, he never told you off ...not much, but he'd look disappointed, hurt. He gave you a powerful, horrible feeling of guilt, with great generosity. Father Dolling who'd given up a decent position to slum it with us Portsea dwellers, so he may improve us, and we'd *–I'd failed him.*

***

Her father had news, "I'm going to be wed."

It shocked May. Her voice choked in her throat. "Congratulations."

"Say it like you mean it. Have another go."

May sighed. "I hope you'll both be very happy."

***

Joe was planting gladioli bulbs and rosebushes, the ones May had mentioned specifically. He was planting them in rows. *-Like bloomin' vegetables.* Not like a garden at all.

The garden plot graced with mature apple and plum trees. Emily bloomed, and she was content. What surprised even her, was Dolly would send a basket of food. "Well it is Joseph's grandchild after all, so she says! I've the feeling if she gets some of it, there's nothing can be done about that."

"You know May I was hoping, you and John."

"Emily got there first."

"I ... still, well I'm speaking out of turn, but I still don't like her. I do my best, but ... and she is John's wife."

"And the mother..."

"Mm, yes well, Lizzie she's a delight. I'd love her whoever the father ... either of them."

"You know don't you?"

"You haven't seen her, but she and Georgie they could be brother and sister, probably are, according to Susannah."

"Ah."

"It's John I feel sorry for, not having a child of his own."

May thought then, of her own swelling belly. "What's she like, the baby?"

"Lizzie? Oh she's the sweetest little thing, reminds me so much of …" and Dolly for once, was

lost for words.

***

"You're filling out," said Joe, as the door burst open and hit the wall behind, and in a second, in tow, came his shadow, Ferdinand. "Those two are inseparable," said Dolly. "Dick bloomin' Whittington and his cat."

As Joe stepped over the threshold.

"Boots."

"That's' him, the name of Dick's cat," said Joseph, grinning.

"Take `em off."

May took a stool to the kitchen door. "A rose in full bloom, that's what you are May," said Joe.

Dolly looked at May again. *–Mm.* Could just be me and my suspicious mind... She'd like to have some time alone with May, but that wasn't today…

***

Susannah took the ginger beer bottle from the shelf. It wasn't Susannah's purpose to kill George. She no more intended George to die, than she intended to dangle from the end of a rope. But just a little, now and then; when he was…bad.

George decided to move home, no consultation; just a teaspoonful of flypaper juice in his tea. What harm would it do? He sacked her maid; the teaspoonful overflowed … Oh well! He took a new maid…

George sometimes experienced the most wretched, griping stomach pains. And his gums did bleed. His tooth wobbled free from its gum. *-Rear molar, thank Goodness.*

He gave her brooch to that maid; intolerable behaviour. The brooch held many hateful memories. Still, it wasn't his to give. And another spoonful, dribbled over his favourite, Dundee cake. Almond halves decorated the top in three circular rows. George commented, "Roasted almonds, and so moist. Delicious."

***

Dolly had her suspicions confirmed. Dolly met May at the tram stop. May wasn't blooming, she was fat. And no amount of loose clothing on a little thing like her would hide that bump. Dolly suggested tea, "Just until it stops raining." *-And without Joseph confusing the conversation.*

They sat in Jones' teashop. *-May though, is annoying! She's not said a bloody word, nothing.* So with subtlety and tact she'd winkle it out of her. "Who's the father then?" May sighed. And looked out to Portsmouth spread out beneath her. Dolly frowned and stirred her tea.

"You don't take sugar."

"I know."

"So why are you stirring the tea into a storm?"

"Because you ...unless you've put on weight in just one place are carrying, expectant. If you don't want to talk about it, I'll shut up."

May bit into her crumpet, a little butter oozed down her chin she wiped it away with her napkin.

"So whose is it then?"

"Dolly, I can't tell you that."

Dolly sipped and thought, and then mulled ... she doesn't want me to know. Why doesn't she want me to know? "Why don't you want me to know?"

"It's not you Dolly. I haven't told anyone, and yes, I am having a child."

Dolly decided to take another tack, an indirect route. Wheedle it out of her. "When's it due?"

-Well it's a piece of information that can't be kept secret, not for long, so. "April."

And Dolly worked backwards counting out on her fingers. *–July.*

"So are you going to marry him?"

"No, I ..."

"What?"

"I'd tell you, I would if I could."

"It's not Joseph is it?"

"Dolly!"

"Well?"

"Dolly, of course it isn't."

All the customers who'd turned their gaze at the raised voices turned back to their teas. The waitress came and asked, "Is everything all right?"

"Very nice, tea. Thank you," snapped Dolly, at this unfortunate interruption. She looked at May again.

"Dolly, no it isn't Joseph I wouldn't go with ... I wouldn't go with another woman's husband."

–Joseph! But this is Dolly, and that is Joseph, and to each other they are the most desirable beings. So well suited, so in love they couldn't countenance everyone not feeling the same about their partner. But she had been with another woman's husband.

"Well that's something."

"I'm glad I've put your mind at rest."

But Dolly's mind wasn't at rest, it was fully exercised. "So if you can't marry him, is he married? Married already?"

May sighed, "Dolly I said I wouldn't marry him, he did ask." Which was true but also a lie, different times, and different dates. *–Now please, enough already.*

"Won't marry him, but if he's free? Give a name to the little b..."

"He or she'll will have a name; Miller."

Dolly now had a brilliant idea, this would tell her. "So what will you call it?"

"Alfred, if it's a boy."

Dolly was disappointed, again! She'd didn't know anyone called Alfred. "And if it's a girl?"

"Lavinia, after my mother, or Phoebe after my grandmother, or perhaps I'll name her after my nosey friend!"

Dolly grinned, she'd like that. *–I'll would knit something.*

***

May would visit Susannah who'd been in similar circumstances.

After, *–bloody ages. The door opened ...*

-Oh Christ!

"Well hello May, you're blooming."

"Hello George, I've come to see Susannah."

"Oh that's a shame, you've missed her; she's in Winchester visiting her sick father, so I'm told."

-Well, not everyone's a liar, like you.

"Come in, won't you?"

"No thank you. You'll let Susannah know I called." And just in case he didn't she added, "I'll write to her."

"George? Oh sorry..." said a flushed faced maid, fidgeting with her pinafore ties.

-Who the hell are you?

"This is Beryl, Beryl this is May."

"How'd you do?"

"Very well, thank you."

And then May turned to George and said, "Annie not here, then?"

"Oh well, she had to go, wasn't up to the job." And he smiled.

Beryl pushed a tendril behind her ear.

"I see. So when are you expecting Susannah to return?"

"That May, is a good question, rather depends on the nature of her father's illness."

"May I have her address?"

"You may, May. I'll write it for you."

May now feeling safer because of the presence of Beryl, crossed the threshold.

***

Susannah's father was a bit put out. Of course he enjoyed seeing and having his daughter and grandson stay. But it did rather quash his ten-shilling extra. Nor did it suit Mrs Marshall. She had her eye on a new coat, that new coat with the fox fur collar. And he wouldn't even sneak a quickie. A five bobber, no! He was as celibate as her purse was chaste. Susannah received a letter from May asking if she could call on her, or perhaps Susannah would visit her in Portsmouth.

It was with an anticipated sense of relief Cecil waved Susannah away at Winchester station. Cecil could now have his extra.

Susannah didn't want to move to Fairview she didn't want to move anywhere with George. Nothing had changed, he told her they were moving and that was that. He'd sacked their maid, and that was that... She was told, after.... But she could live in Downland, and he in Fairview.

***

His hair thinned. He was ageing fast. A sore on his pate, wouldn't heal; if he'd had a little more hair the pustule wouldn't have shown. His joints creaked. He wondered if he had syphilis and vowed to be more careful... His doctor prescribed Savarsan, a new drug. What his doctor omitted to tell George, Savarsan contained arsenic! But why should the good doctor, inform his patient of such detail? It was unfortunate George didn't understand, he'd such a bad wife.

***

The train crossed the sea channel at Hilsea. The earthworks. *-We'll join up one day. Downland sucked into Portsmouth.* Georgie banged on the window, with his podgy hands. "Moo cows, moo cows."

A man reading The Telegraph frowned as he peered over his glasses. Susannah smiled at him and pulled George to her lap.

"Portsmouth and Southsea," shouted the guard.

And the man opened the door and helped her from the carriage. He tipped his hat and strolled form the platform swinging his silver topped cane back and forth. And there, there was May. May wearing a big, baggy coat.

"Susannah. Oh, Georgie look at you, a big little man now."

"A man, a man."

"I see we have something to talk about," said Susannah as she nodded towards May's stomach.

"Before you ask, I won't tell you who the father is."

-We'll see thought Susannah, we'll see. "So nice to see you May. It's good to be away."

***

They went to the tearooms in Southsea, the Queen's Tearooms. "Please, follow me," said the maitre de. He wafted a white cloth around a just unoccupied table, disturbing the crumbs from the chairs and table. He snapped his fingers for the waiter to clear the dirty pots and cups. Another click and a waitress arrived with a new tablecloth. Within one minute, they were seated.

Susannah said, "My goodness that was impressive."

"Memorable, certainly."

A cake stand with three tiers, wheeled towards them. An oak stand with sandwiches on the top layer, followed by scones and cakes, finishing on the third with cream cakes and fancies; all sitting on little doilies bordered with lace.

May asked, "What are you going to do?"

"There is nothing much I can do. My father would of course take us in. But I'm married now, it would be awkward for him ... A man in his position. May I ..."

May placed her hand over hers.

315

"I hoped you and me …Silly isn't it," Susannah said.

May picked up her spoon and stirred slowly. "No not silly, what we did, how we were, I don't regret for one moment…"

"But?"

May looked down and just before she began to speak raised her head and looked into those deep brown eyes …" –*Christ this is difficult.*

"It's not what I want, who I am."

"We can't always have that." –*Oh well, who'd have thought! I wanted to be born in a mansion, attend a public school, wear diamonds and pearl—*

"Georgie." Susannah tugged George away from the cake stand. "Just one cake, and that doesn't mean tasting all of them until you find the one you want."

May smiled. –*I wonder if the cakes I bought were all dribbled on before I had them?*

Susannah reached into her pocket. "I have a gift for you, Susannah placed a tiny box, wrapped in gold paper, and tied with a blue velvet ribbon, onto the table.

"It's so beautiful; I don't want to open it." Georgie reached out, he obviously wanted to take that particular chore from her hands.

"No George, mustn't take what isn't yours."

May looked up, just about to say it's all right. But of course, it isn't.

"I'll open it and show you what it is."

"Have it?"

"No Georgie, but you may hold it for a moment." – *Sins of the father*.

"I called on you when I was visiting Dolly. She didn't know, or at least didn't say you were away."

"Ah, I see."

"So, it looks like we both have something to talk about."

"As if we ever needed a topic."

And they both smiled. May sipped hot chocolate and handed Georgie a biscuit. "He's a handsome boy."

"He is ...just like his father."

May raised an eyebrow.

"Although I hope it's all he's inherited. I'm doing my best to make him... consider others. But he receives so much attention, so many compliments."

"He is charming I can't imagine...."

"Mm, George is charming. Everyone thinks ... adores him, everyone loves him."

"So he says."

"Ah well ..."

May held in her a hand a butterfly, a butterfly with a pin on the back a sapphire blue … that brooch. "Susannah I couldn't."

"It's meant for you." –*It keeps turning up.*

"May I?" May nodded, and Susannah reached over and pinned the butterfly to her blouse. And that brooch pinned to her breast by George, Susannah quickly pushed that memory away. Georgie touched it with his small fingers.

"Butterfly."

"Yes Georgie, butterfly."

"Pretty."

"It's beautiful, Susannah, thank you."

"Don't thank me, my motive is purely selfish." May touched the brooch now pinned to her chest. "I found our maid wearing it. I stole to her room and reclaimed my lost property. …. Georgie, NO! … Consider it a bribe, who is it?"

"Susannah I can't tell you."

"Well it's not Joseph." May rolled her eyes. Susannah smiled.

"So it's George ... I don't think so. It can't of course be your friend, Walter…" And each time Susannah watched May's face. She'd run through each name, she'd sit here all day if necessary; and May would of course not tell her; not with her voice, not with a spoken denial.

"You can fish as you much as you want, I won't say."

"I always thought Mr Bridger handsome." May blushed.

-*So there we have it.* Susannah wondered what Emily would make of that. Emily, so keen to share her gossip about George with her. *–A piece of information I will keep to myself, for the moment.*

May took the bill. "My treat." May pulled from her purse the exact amount to the very last copper.

"Thank you Madame," said the maitre de. He assisted them from their seats; loitered, and lingered. May opened her bag. "A tip, for such service."

The maitre de held out his hand, nodding. -*Obsequious, pompous, prig. And anything else I can think of, alphabetically.* May, placed it in the man's hand, and folded his fingers over the coin.

"Oh Madame, thank you."

"It's nothing. Really!"

Susannah, Georgie and May left the premises. So they didn't see his expression when he opened his hand to reveal what he believed a silver sixpence, and there, a farthing, and a none too clean farthing. "Well!" -*Just goes to show, appearances, so deceptive.* And he sniffed.

***

And everyone said, "There's no mistaking whose baby that is ... it's May's! The spit of her, I wonder who the father is?" Wally got ribbed somethin' terrible. But he couldn't have been prouder. He didn't care who the father was. "Why should I Barnaby, eh?"

***

She was just a docker's daughter,
Her living was earned on The Hard.
But though mud larks are called filthy,
with that brush she'd not be tarred.

***

Printed in Great Britain
by Amazon.co.uk, Ltd.,
Marston Gate.